A CLIMATE OF
VIOLENCE

BY RUSSELL O'NEIL
Jonathan

A CLIMATE OF VIOLENCE

RUSSELL O'NEIL

New York APPLETON
CENTURY
CROFTS, Inc.

Copyright © 1961
by Russell O'Neil

All rights reserved. This book, or parts thereof, must not be reproduced in any form without permission of the publisher.

All names, characters, and events in this book are fictional, and any resemblance which may seem to exist to real persons is purely coincidental.

Library of Congress Catalogue Card Number: 61-13337

681-1

Printed in the United States of America

To Charles

A CLIMATE OF VIOLENCE

I.

As the old shabby Chevrolet convertible sped through the hot, moonless August night, it seemed to violate the still air. The leaf-heavy limbs of trees growing close to the highway waved violently in the car's wake like viewers at a parade, and then were still again. Rubber whined thinly against concrete as the road wound its way up the great verdant hill which walled the valley. The broken speedometer registered zero as if exhausted by its efforts at indicating the dangerous speed.

The girl in the middle of the front seat said, "You slow down, you crazy fool!"

"Aw, Ida, you ain't scared, are you?" the driver said smiling but keeping his eyes on the road.

"I don't know what you think you're doin' anyway, way out here in the middle of nowhere," she said. "I got to go home."

"We're just goin' for a little ride, Ida," the driver said.

"Yeah, Ida," the boy on the other side of the front seat said. "We're just goin' for a little ride."

"I told you," she answered, "I got to go home. You turn this car around, Armand."

"What about showin' us what a man and a woman do together?" the driver asked, his smile giving way to mock surprise. "You said you was goin' to show us."

"I said I could show you. I didn't say I was goin' to. Now you turn around."

"I'll just bet you could show us, Ida. I sure bet you could," the driver said, smiling again.

"You really know how to do it, don't you, Ida?" the boy on the right said.

"Sure I know."

"How many times you done it?" he asked.

"None of your business," she answered, without looking at him.

Armand leaned toward her, pushing Ida's hair aside with his face, and whispered into her ear. Ida threw her head back and laughed a high, shrill, artificial laugh.

"What the hell'd you say to her, Armand?" asked the boy in the back seat.

"Come on, Ida," the boy on the right said, "tell us what's so funny."

"Gimme that bottle, Johnny," Artie demanded of the boy on the right.

Handing him the bottle Johnny said, "What'd you say to her?"

"Hey! Don't spill that whiskey on my dress!"

"What have you got under your dress, Ida?" Johnny asked.

"That's for me to know and you to find out," she told him.

"I'd sure like to find out," he said.

She laughed again with a great display of enthusiasm.

"Hey, Ida," Johnny said, "did you hear the one about the farmer who kept a pet gorilla in his barn? This travelin' salesman comes along and . . ."

"I heard you like to do it standin' up," Armand said.

"Johnny's tellin' a joke," Ida said.

"How'd you like to do it with me standin' up?" Armand asked.

"Shut up, Armand," Ida said. "Johnny's tellin' a joke."

"Or we could do it layin' down in the back seat," Armand went on.

"Hey, you better turn this car around. I got to go home."

"It's not late, Ida," Johnny told her.

"Hey, Ida, when you goin' to show us like you said?" Artie asked.

"Don't you be so brazen," Ida answered.

"You don't mind when Johnny says it," Artie said, a bit petulantly.

"Johnny didn't say nothin' like that," Ida said.

"When are you goin' to show us, Ida?" Johnny asked.

"I might show you sometime," she said, turning to him.

"You got the hots for Johnny?" Armand asked. "I know a place you could do it, and me and Artie would just watch."

"Cut it out, Armand," Johnny said softly, not looking at anyone.

"Cut it out?" Armand said, leaning forward and casting a quick glance at Johnny. "She's practically invitin' you to give it to her."

"Lay off," Johnny said irritably.

"You're terrible, Armand," Ida said.

"What's the matter, Johnny?" Armand asked. "You scared?"

"Scared of what?" Johnny said, still looking straight ahead.

"I don't know, buddy," Armand answered. "Maybe of not knowin' what to do."

"I know," Johnny said quietly. "Give me the bottle, Artie."

"Sure he knows," Ida said.

"Why don't you let him prove it, Ida?" Armand asked.

"You're terrible, Armand," Ida repeated. "Come on, I got to go home."

Johnny brought the bottle down from his lips and was swallowing mouthfuls of air on top of the whiskey, when the car slowed and made a sharp turn onto a dirt road. In seconds it had nearly resumed its former speed.

"Hey! Where're you goin'?" Johnny said.

"This ain't the way home, Armand," Ida said. "You better take me home or I'm goin' to get mad."

"This is a short cut, Ida," Armand told her.

"Armand, this road doesn't—" Johnny began.

"Shut up," Armand snapped. "And besides, Ida, right here along this road would be a good place for you to show us."

"You stop talkin' like that," Ida said, quietly.

"You didn't mind talkin' like that back in town," Armand said. "You said you knew all about what a man and a woman do."

"Well, I could show you," Ida said. "I'll show you sometime when it ain't so late. I got to go home, Armand."

"Well, just tell us about it then, while we're drivin' back," Armand suggested.

"Yeah, Ida," Artie said, "why don't you tell us about it?"

"You stop it, Art," Ida said to him. "You're too young to be talkin' like that."

"I'm old as you," Artie said.

"You're only sixteen," Ida said.

"I'm seventeen, and so are you," Artie replied indignantly. "And I'm older than Johnny, too, by four months."

"Well, I'm nineteen, Ida," Armand said, "and I'm goin' to let you in on a little secret. I know all about what a man and a woman do together. You couldn't show me nothin'."

"All right, then, take me home."

"Hell, Armand, maybe we better take her home." Johnny said with an attempted air of boredom.

"What the hell is it with you, Johnny?" Armand said angrily. "You chicken or somethin'?"

"No, Armand," Johnny answered. "It's just that, you know, she keeps sayin' she—"

"I don't think Johnny knows very much about what a man and a woman do, Ida," Armand interrupted. "Why don't me and you put on a little demonstration for him? We don't want him to be ignorant."

Without warning Armand reduced the car's speed and brought it to a complete stop. The sudden cutting of the motor created a remarkable silence. Behind the car was a narrow, trailing cloud of dust that in the darkness looked like an alley of fog.

"Give me that bottle, Johnny," Armand said. "I need a little refreshment."

Johnny took a quick drink of whiskey and handed Armand the bottle. Armand wiped the top of the bottle inside his closed hand and raised it to his mouth.

"What are you stoppin' here for?" Ida asked. "I thought you was takin' me home."

"I'm stoppin' because this road don't go no further," Armand answered, shuddering a bit from the shock of the big swallow of whiskey. "That's the end of it right up there in front of us."

"I got to go home, Armand."

"It's a hell of a long walk," he answered. "Now, what was it you was goin' to show us?"

"Armand . . ." Ida began.

"It was somethin' about screwin', wasn't it?" Armand said. "You're so willing to do it with Johnny, why don't you do it with me?"

"I don't want to . . . with you or him," Ida said. "I got to go home."

"You got to go home about as much as I do," Armand said, and there was no longer even a trace of humor in his voice.

Armand lifted his arm to the back of the seat and put it around Ida's shoulders. She pulled away quickly and unintentionally pushed herself against Johnny. As her body pressed against his left hand, he could feel the narrowing of the side of her brassiere, and quite accidentally his right hand fell against her breast. She gave a quiet, frightened cry and pulled away toward Armand.

"Hey! Ain't no flies on you, Johnny!" Armand said in delight. "Guess you know more than I thought."

Artie's hands streaked over Ida's shoulders and down toward her breasts.

"Come on, Ida," he said, "let me have a little, too."

Ida wriggled free of Artie's grasp, and as she moved toward the dashboard to evade him, he said, "What's the matter? Ain't I good enough for you?"

Ida sat stiffly hunched forward on the middle of the seat. Armand stared at her, his thick, pale lips compressed to a thin line. He lifted the bottle to his mouth again and choked slightly as he brought it down, so that some of the whiskey escaped from the corners of his mouth.

"Here, Johnny," he said, "take this friggin' bottle out of my way, and we'll get this thing goin'."

Johnny took the bottle and drank from it. In his excitement he took more whiskey than he had intended, and he began to retch terribly. He closed his eyes and the car seemed to leave the ground and swirl crazily in the air. As he conquered the impulse to be sick he heard Armand saying, "Come on, Ida, let's me and you show the boys how to screw."

He reached out for her with both hands, and as she started to pull away, she felt Johnny's thigh against her own. She tried desperately to stand up in the car. Armand pulled her down by the arm, and she landed roughly against his heavy body.

"Don't do that, Ida," Artie pleaded breathlessly, leaning forward against the front seat. "Don't try to run away . . . please."

"Maybe we better take her home, Armand," Johnny said, "if she doesn't want to."

"What the hell do you mean, take her home?"

"Come on, Johnny," Artie said, "you ain't chicken."

"I mean if she doesn't want to. . . ."

"What do you want to do, take her home and pick up her old lady instead?" Armand asked, grinning. "*She* wouldn't give you no struggle, you can bet on that."

"You can damn well bet on that," Artie said, imitating Armand's grin.

"Don't you talk about my mother!" Ida said quietly, but sharply.

"We know we can't pick up your mother, Ida," Armand said. "She's probably busy with some salesman from the city."

"You shut up!" Ida cried.

"Okay, I don't want to talk, anyway," Armand said, and reached out, putting his hand on her belly.

Ida pushed wildly and futilely against Armand's arm, then suddenly she slapped him hard on the jaw.

"Goddamn you!" Armand shouted without taking his hand from her. Then he took her left arm and put it behind him. He leaned toward her, pinning her arm against the seat.

"Take her goddamn other arm, Johnny!"

"Armand, maybe we better . . ." Johnny started to say.

Artie tore the whiskey bottle from Johnny's hand and said, "Go on, grab her, Johnny!"

Ida had already begun to wave her arm frantically to elude Johnny, and he watched it flailing as if Ida had been stricken by a convulsion. It hit him across the face, painfully, and he reached out in automatic defense and subdued it. He sat holding it at arm's length before him with both hands as if it were a struggling snake, until Artie leaned forward and snatched the arm out of Johnny's grasp. He pulled it back against the seat and cried, "Lean back, Johnny!"

Johnny fell back against the seat and felt the ridge of Ida's arm against his side. She struggled wildly, her young body rising from the seat and falling back again in a kind of rhythmic, compulsive dance.

Armand's anger had subsided immediately. With his fat hand he rubbed Ida's breasts with a flat, circular motion, as he might have polished the hood of his car.

"Boy! Feel them titties, Artie!" Armand said without enthusiasm.

Artie's hand started over Ida's shoulder, but stopped in the air next to her head. He looked into Johnny's face.

"Why don't you feel her, Johnny?" he suggested, hesitantly.

Trying hard to focus on Artie's searching eyes, Johnny said, "You go on."

"Are you goin' to?" Artie asked.

"What the hell's the matter with you guys?" Armand shouted. "You queer or somethin'?"

Then, only inches before his eyes Johnny could see Artie's hand, pale against the dark print of Ida's dress, contract, depress the flesh of her body and ride back on its young resiliency. Then lightly, caressingly, it moved around, until again, convulsively, it tightened into a brimming claw. He tried with all his mind to imagine the sensation which existed in Artie's hand and could not.

He heard Armand say, "Come on, Johnny, reach over here and get a feel. There's room. I'm movin' someplace else." And Armand's hand slithered down Ida's body like a lizard.

"Come on, Johnny-boy," Artie said hoarsely and shifted his head and hand to Ida's left side.

Johnny looked at Ida's face. She had stopped struggling for a moment and stared at him. He could see the terror and the pleading in her eyes. He looked back at her breasts, rising and falling with her heavy breathing. He tried so hard to know the feel of her body with just his eyes that they opened to an astonished wideness, but he felt only an aching, ignorant emptiness. He placed his hand on her shoulder and let it slide along the rise of her breast. He closed his hand and knew that he could never have imagined what he felt. She began to struggle again, then, and made little whimpering sounds. As she writhed, Johnny felt her breasts moving independently of the rest of her body, and excitement seemed to expand inside him with an unbearable pressure. He fell forward until his lips were pressed against Ida's face, and as they moved she felt their moistness on her cheek.

"Don't . . . don't fight . . . Ida," he whispered haltingly. "It . . . it's all right . . . don't . . . Ida. . . ."

His hand moved in wider and wider groping until it reached across her breasts. He was startled by the bare flesh of Artie's hand. Then roughly he was pushed away.

"Armand . . . Armand . . ." Ida said, her voice trembling with her body.

"You like it, honey?" Armand asked quietly, digging into her.

"Armand . . . stop . . . don't . . ." She could hardly speak against the terror which constricted her throat.

Suddenly Ida's arm slipped from under Johnny's body and tore at his hair. Artie grasped it quickly and as Johnny fell back upon it again, he felt her tears fall on his hand.

Still she struggled and felt the hands darting across her body like bugs on the surface of a pond. The hands crept, walked, crawled, scrambled over her until one touched the bare flesh of her leg, and it seemed to her like the body of a great rat upon her. She screamed and her whole body stiffened with the power of the sound.

"You scream if you want, Ida," Armand said. "Nobody's goin' to hear you up here."

"Maybe we better take her home," Johnny said.

"What the hell's the matter with you?" Armand said angrily. "Don't let all this fussin' fool you; she done this a hundred times before."

"She seems scared," Johnny said.

"Scared? She's been screwed more times than a mother rabbit. Everybody in town knows that."

"Sure, Johnny," Artie said, "everybody knows it."

"Maybe not, though," Johnny said.

"What do you mean, maybe not? Look at her old lady. She was a whore before you was ever born," Armand said.

"Just because her mother does it, it doesn't mean . . ."

"Come on. Let's get her out of the car," Armand commanded.

As Johnny started to help Armand move Ida out of the car, Armand barked instructions as if they were moving a piece of furniture through a narrow doorway. As soon as Johnny put his feet on the ground, the earth seemed to tilt crazily, and he fell into the high, stiff weeds. He sprang to his feet quickly, fighting the giddy drunkenness. But by the time he had regained his balance, Artie had replaced him and the three had moved off into the darkness. He could see them ahead of him, awkwardly pushing through the waist-high foliage as if they were two boys and a girl playing in a swimming pool. He began to laugh foolishly, and as the giddiness again surged upward through him, fell against the side of the car and leaned on his outstretched arms. With a deep, trembling breath he straightened again. Then he thrashed through the weeds and caught up with the others. He heard Artie say, "Where're we takin' her?" Artie's physical struggle with Ida gave the question an unnatural inflection.

"Just past them trees there on that little rise," Armand said.

"Let me go, Armand!" Ida cried, gasping. "Don't do nothin' to me!"

"I ain't goin' to do nothin' to you that ain't been done before," he answered. "Now, quit that wigglin'!"

He took one of his hands from Ida's arm and grasped her neck. He squeezed until her sobs gave way to a low, quiet moan, and her shoulders hunched against his hand. All of her effort turned to enduring the knots of pain at Armand's fingertips, and she went on quietly.

Johnny stumbled and nearly fell. When he looked up, he saw the motionless upright silhouettes of the trees and the three dark figures moving against the still, straight lines.

"Artie!" he called and the last syllable was swallowed in the trembling of his body.

He saw the figures stop, and their stillness made them invisible against the trees. The movement began again and a dimly recognizable Artie emerged from the darkness, while behind him the two small, black figures reached the top of the little rise. They stayed there for a moment in a flurry of activity, like two birds at a crust of bread, then disappeared behind the mound of earth.

"What's the matter? You sick?" Artie asked impatiently. "No, just dizzy," Johnny answered. "What's Armand goin' to do to her?"

"He won't do nothin', I guess. We're just goin' to fool around with her. Come on."

"Do you think we ought to?"

"Christ, Johnny," Artie said, sounding suddenly frightened. "What do you mean?"

"I mean, do you think it's right?"

"But she's a whore, ain't she, like Armand says?"

"But what if she's not a whore?"

"She has to be, don't she, Johnny?" Artie pleaded. "The whole town says she is."

"But if she doesn't want to fool around, maybe we shouldn't make her."

"Come on, Johnny, don't talk like that," Artied whined. "I . . . I want to fool around with her. It won't do no harm. Come on."

"I don't know if we ought to."

"Johnny, are you . . . are you scared?"

"Not scared."

"What then?"

"I don't know."

They heard Armand's voice calling to them through the darkness. "Come on, Johnny. Armand needs us."

Johnny felt a vague, but growing familiarity as he neared the trees. He took hold of a tree to steady himself, then he vaulted up the incline and stood weaving at the top. At first he saw before him only the sky, which seemed a brighter blue now. Then he saw pale stars and the black horizon of the hill across the valley, the hill across whose side the town was strewn as if by some gentle giant. He saw the lights of the town, gleaming larger and brighter than the stars against the dark hillside, and he knew where he was.

"Hey, Johnny! Come on down here," Artie called urgently as he went on ahead.

Johnny looked toward the voice, and dimly he could see the three of them a short distance down the hill. Behind them the earth sloped steadily to the river far below them. There was not a house or a light or a sign of life between them and the floor of the narrow valley. He stumbled down the hill to join the others.

"Come on, Ida," Armand said. "Let's sit down."

She was quieter now and her body stiffened at Armand's suggestion so that he was not able to force her to the ground. Suddenly he stooped and hit her sharply behind each knee with the edge of his hand. Her legs buckled, and he pulled her to the earth beside him. His arm went across her middle and held her tightly. She kicked violently and hammered at his head with her fists.

"Grab her, goddamn it!" Armand shouted, ducking his head to avoid her blows. "Grab her arms, Artie, before she beats the shit out of me!"

Artie took her by the wrists and pinned her arms to the ground above her head, but her legs flailed wildly, her flat-heeled shoes flying about like angry, caged birds.

"Grab her feet, you dumb bastard!" Armand called to Johnny, who stood motionless just beyond the kicking legs.

For a moment Johnny looked dumbly at the legs, then fell upon them as if he had collapsed. He twisted Ida's right ankle badly as he landed on it, but her left foot caught him squarely on the jaw. As he reached to subdue that other opponent, he was conscious of the pain, but as if it existed separately of itself, outside his body.

Armand stood up and looked at the rigid, motionless girl beneath him.

"Look at her," he said, "layin' there waitin' for it."

He walked around Artie to the other side of Ida and looked down at her.

"Don't she look good, though?" he said. "About to be took and nothin' to stop it!"

He stepped across her with his left leg so that she lay between his feet and placed his hands low on his hips. He issued a long, low, breathy moan.

"Hey, Armand! You ain't goin' to do it to her?" Artie said.

"I ain't? You think we been goin' through all this just to feel her up or somethin'?"

"But you ain't really goin' to do it to her. . . . I mean all the way?"

"I don't want to disappoint her," Armand said.

"Geez, Armand . . ."

"And I got news for you, buddy, you're goin' to do it, too."

"Screw her?" Artie said, and the very uttering of the words made his excitement mount.

"And Johnny, too," Armand said.

"But she doesn't want to," Johnny said thickly.

"Goddamn, Johnny," Armand said, looking over his shoulder. "Don't you know nothin'? Her not wantin' to is half the fun. That's why she's pretending not to want to. That's the way it's supposed to be."

Ida's voice was almost surprising to them, so thoroughly had they forgotten her humanity. "I never done it."

"Hah! That's a laugh," Armand said.

"I never done it at all," she said flatly, unable in her terror to express any emotion.

"Horseshit, Ida," Armand said. "I know guys that done it to you."

"Maybe she's tellin' the truth when she says she never done it," Johnny said, with urgency squeezing through the thickness of his speech.

"Well, if she is," Armand said slowly, seriously, "she'll never be able to say it again."

As Armand bent toward the helpless girl beneath him his body throbbed, not with excitement, but with strength. For the Armand that he knew existed had at that moment emerged from within the tortured imposter who had stolen his identity. An Armand—assured, unafraid, powerful—had risen to conquer the lonely, frightened, unloved pretender. The resurrection of that long-lost self was Armand's joy, and for him the act which accomplished it had no further meaning.

The slope of the hill added to Johnny's sense of imbalance as he lay across Ida's feet. He could feel them desperately trying to kick against his chest, and from somewhere far up the hill toward the trees he could hear her voice muttering in a kind of toneless song, ". . . never done . . . it . . . I didn't . . . Mama . . . never . . . I never . . . never . . . done it . . . I . . ." and the kicking would stop and the muttering swell into a high, thin, delirious wail, opening into the hollow roundness of a sob. Then the kicking would begin faintly and the "Mama . . . never . . . I never . . . done . . . it. . . ." Then there was a silence through which came the heavy hissing of partially impaired breathing. With an arresting suddenness all movement stopped. He heard Armand's choked, frightened voice saying, "Goddamn guys! She must've been tellin' the truth! Goddamn!" There was movement again, then, but the kicking had stopped. Johnny rose and stumbled into a patch of high weeds, where he fell to the ground and was violently sick.

When he heard his name called in a croaking whisper, he realized that he did not know how long he had been lying alone in the weeds. He had not been asleep, but his faculty for measuring time was somehow impaired. Great hunks of time seemed to break off from the whole and drift into oblivion.

"Johnny!" the croaking sounded again. "Where are you?"

"Over here," he answered.

Artie stood over him then, saying in the same husky tone of emergency, "Come on. Armand's finished." He waited for Johnny to move.

"Are you . . . are you goin' to do it?" Johnny asked.

"I don't . . . I don't know," Artie answered. "Aren't you?"

"I don't know."

"I . . . I guess we got to, now that Armand done it."

"I don't know if we ought to," Johnny said.

"I don't know either, but I keep thinkin' about . . ." Artie was silent then.

"About what?" Johnny asked.

"Well, about them guys at school. How we could show 'em. Man, how I'd like to tell that Kenny Rimbaud I screwed her! Him always spoutin' off about screwing his stepmother's sister up on their farm and all that jazz." Artie seemed not to be talking to Johnny any more. He seemed simply to be talking into the darkness.

"Are you goin' to do it, Artie?"

"I will if you do."

"Do you think it'll hurt her?"

"Christ, I don't know, Johnny!"

"I don't think we . . ."

"Come on, Johnny. I'll do it if you will. Come on."

"Well . . . you got to go first."

"First? Me?"

"Yeah."

"Aw, Johnny, I . . . okay. I'll do it. Come on."

Artie moved away then and Johnny could see only the white of his shirt as he followed. He heard Armand saying irritably to Artie, "You find him?"

"Yeah."

"Where the hell is he?"

"He's comin'," Artie said, looking past Armand at Ida lying on the ground.

"Go on," Armand said, "Do it."

"Yeah," Artie answered, "I'm . . . I'm goin' to."

Artie had often imagined his first sexual experience, but now as he moved toward Ida Praul to make reality of those vague, inaccurate imaginings, his anticipation was dulled by his gnawing eagerness to have it done, which, he did not realize, was greater than his need to do it.

The glow of Armand's cigarette guided Johnny across the hillside. Armand was sitting only a short distance from Artie and Ida, and Johnny could see them plainly as he approached. As he stopped before Armand he could not speak for his great awe and deep embarrassment. He found it difficult to believe that what he saw was in fact taking place. He wanted to turn his back, to move away, for he felt certain that he—that no one—should be witness to this event, but instead, he stared steadily at the incredible spectacle.

He realized then that Armand turned his head occasionally and stared at Artie and Ida. He would turn back and puff on his cigarette, blow out the smoke hissingly, then turn again to watch. Suddenly, Johnny wanted to hit Armand, for Armand's greedy watching made his own watching seem more shameful. It shouldn't be like this, he told himself, with people watching and waiting. It should be . . . private, secret even. Just two people alone with nobody else to know. Yes, it should be secret. Didn't Artie know that? he wondered drunkenly, and illogically turned back to them as if he might see the answer. He saw only the climactic, convulsive tremors of Artie's body.

With each step that Artie took toward him, Johnny's apprehension rose—and with it his desire.

"It's your turn," Armand said without looking up.

"Yeah. Go ahead, Johnny," Artie said and his voice shook with the trembling of his body.

Artie was taking cigarettes from his shirt pocket. He did not see Johnny searching his face for some word of encouragement, for some bit of instruction, for a hint of what to expect. Johnny turned toward Ida, wishing that they were alone, but as he moved toward her, the others receded into a distance far greater than the physical span between them and him. He stood looking down at her, his vision blurred by the whiskey. He could not tell if she was conscious or not, but he wanted desperately for her to be.

He bent to her and whispered, "Ida. Ida."

She turned her head and made an unintelligible, inscrutable sound.

He touched her then, but she did not move. The eager readiness of his body ended his uncertainty. He did not care now where they were or how it should be or if Ida was awake. His just-born desire for Ida and his ancient desire to know conquered all difficulties as with a strange sadness he saw the black trees rise out of his range of vision. The warm wetness of the thing beneath him was the only evidence of its life, until, close to his ear he heard a prolonged sound of pain. And he felt pain, too, and thought that they felt it together, shared it. Then it was gone, as were the hill and the earth and the grass and the night into a total existence of inexplicable sensation.

"Let's get out of here," Armand said, starting for the trees.

"Wait till I wake her up," Johnny said and bent weavingly toward Ida.

Armand took him by the shoulder and pulled him up savagely.

"What the hell do you mean, wake her up?"

"What are you goin' to do, Armand, leave her here?" Artie asked with growing terror.

"You can't leave her here," Johnny mumbled.

"What do you want to do, take her home to Mama . . . like that?" Armand asked.

"We got to take her back into town," Johnny said.

"It's just about a mile down the hill to the river. She can walk down there and into town herself. You want to carry her down there and into town? You just ask yourself first what the hell you're goin' to do with her when you get her there."

"Christ Almighty!" Artie whined, impatient and frightened. "What are we goin' to do, Johnny?"

"We got to take her home," Johnny said thickly.

"You stupid son of a bitch, we can't take her home like that!" Artie shouted.

"I'm getting out of here," Armand said and started again toward the trees.

"Come on, Johnny," Artie said and turned to follow Armand.

"We got to take her home," Johnny repeated with slow overemphasis, explaining what seemed to him in his drunkenness to be a simple truth.

"There ain't no choice, Johnny," Artie said. "We got to leave her."

"No," Johnny began, "we got to—"

"Come on for Christ' sake!" Artie said, grabbing Johnny's arm.

He dragged him up the hill, and over Johnny's thickly mumbled protests, was saying, "Shut up, for Christ' sake! Shut up!" as they disappeared over the little rise.

Ida lay alone on the hill with her pain. As Armand had predicted, she did not again during the dark remaining hours of that night protest that she had never done it. Now and again she did call out to her mother, uselessly, as even Ida's dull mind fully understood. She did not move during the night, though many tiny things swarmed and crawled over her. Only when the hot morning sun had risen and fixed the scene of outrage in its pure, golden light, did Ida get up and hobble grotesquely down the hill, across the bridge and into town.

II.

MORNING WAS SO MUCH IN THE ROOM THAT ITS PRESENCE SEEMED almost an intrusion. It was almost surprising that the room's contents had not taken on the sharp, yellow color of the sun. Instead everything had become more itself: the refrigerator and sink and stove gleamed whiter; the marbleized linoleum, busy with a hundred dull reflections, seemed more like real marble; the spotless apple green walls and cabinets appeared to have been painted the day before.

Although she was not aware of it, Mary Taylor was as brightly delineated as everything else in the room. As she prepared breakfast for her family, she quietly hummed a tune which had been popular nineteen years before, when she had been single and dating the man who was now her husband.

Her many movements as she went about her work were not quick, but had about them—like everything she did—a certain firmness, an intensity. She did not ever open the refrigerator door and stand, one hand on the still open door and the other lifted to her face as she tried to remember what she was looking for. When Mary Taylor opened a door, she usually knew what was on the other side, and she either accepted it or rejected it and closed the door. Although she had prepared thousands of such breakfasts, there was about her neither the relaxed sluggishness of boredom nor the quick ease of familiarity. There was merely a determination to accomplish what she had set out to accomplish—the breaking of an egg, the greasing of a frying pan, the tilting of a salt shaker. This resulted in simple, unhurried, economic activity.

Once again Mary had got up far ahead of her family. With innate modesty, and quite unnecessarily, she would hold closed her already securely tied housecoat as she picked up the morning newspaper from the front steps. Back inside the many-windowed sunporch she would pause to inspect the neighborhood with one sweeping, comprehensive glance which would tell her that Mr. Sweeney probably had a hangover, since he had stopped in the middle of clipping the privet hedge; that Frances McGovern was over her attack of asthma, for the newspaper and the milk were gone from the step at the regular hour for the first time since her husband and children had taken over the household chores; that poor old Mrs. Chambers, prevented by arthritis from tending her own garden, could not afford the handyman again this week, and the weeds were gaining advantage. This information was of little interest and less use to Mary, for she did not gossip and she did not presume further upon it. The morning's local intelligence would be relegated to the status of lore by the time Mary reached the kitchen. Soon the coffee would be steaming and the table set, and Mary would have reached a point at which she could do no more until the rest of the family caught up with her.

Mary had already started for the stairs when the sound of her daughter's footsteps made the summons unnecessary. Mary had frequently said that Lois could do with half as many stairs as there actually were, since she went both up and down them two at a time.

"Good morning, Mother," she said, streaking past Mary and into the kitchen.

"Good morning, Lois," Mary said, turning to watch her daughter and experiencing one of the countless, sudden moments of withdrawn observation intrinsic in parenthood. From her quiet vantage point Mary wondered if Lois knew how pretty she was.

As Lois sped into the kitchen, the sun struck her pink and white cotton blouse and her immaculate pink slacks with a stunning suddenness.

"Gracious! I'm starving!" she said, hunching her shoulders and shaking her head in the agony of her hunger so that her short, softly waved, blond hair jiggled comically. As a result of her meticulous grooming and her natural exuberance, Lois usually looked either like a small adult behaving childishly or a large child performing a remarkably accurate imitation of an adult.

"You needn't stand there suffering, dear," her mother told her. "If you'll sit down like a normal human being, I'll give you something to eat."

Lois pulled back a chair and hurled herself into it with such force that Mary was genuinely afraid that she had hurt herself.

"Lois! Be careful!" she said.

"Oh, don't worry, Mother," Lois soothed. "I won't knock anything over."

"You've got to learn to sit in a chair instead of bouncing into it."

"Oh," Lois said, thoughtfully. "Can I have tomato juice instead of orange?"

"*May* I have tomato juice," Mary amended.

"*May* I have tomato juice?"

"Yes."

"Gee, Mother, we'd get a lot more said if you didn't correct me."

"The object of talking isn't necessarily to get as much said as possible," Mary told her, pouring a glass of milk.

Lois stopped serving cereal to herself and, with the tilted box still aloft, looked intensely troubled.

Mary had started toward the refrigerator, but seeing her daughter's expression, she too stopped, a dish towel hanging limply in her hand, creating for an instant a sunny tableau.

"Lois, what is it?"

"I think I thought it was," she said, pouring cereal again. "To get as much said as possible, I mean."

"Well, in a way I guess it is," Mary said. "But you ought to try to say it correctly, too."

"But as long as people understand what you mean . . ."

"If you say what you mean—absolutely—then there's no danger of people not understanding."

"Mother, I'm not trying to be a smart-aleck, really, but I don't see what that has to do with 'can I' or 'may I.'"

Mary closed the refrigerator door and with two eggs cradled in her hand turned to Lois and said, "'Can I' means 'am I able.' 'May I' means 'am I allowed to,' so you ought to have said 'may I.'"

Lois looked at her mother for a moment, then plunging a spoon into the cereal said, "You're absolutely right, of course. . . ."

"But you don't think it's important."

"I know that it must be if you say it is. I'll try to remember, honestly. 'May I have some tomato juice,' but 'Can I do long division,'" she said, balancing one against the other by waving the milk-wet spoon from side to side.

"Lois, please don't point with your spoon—or with anything else."

"I'm sorry, Mother," Lois said quite calmly, "but you'll have to overlook some of my faults while I'm working on the others."

"I suppose that's only fair, but would you mind if waving the dinnerware is one of the faults I didn't overlook and you worked on?"

"All right," she said, and buried the offending instrument in the cereal. "Mother," Lois said after a moment.

"What, Lois?"

"If you had to say what the object of talking is what would you say it was?"

"Why . . . why, to communicate, I suppose."

"Wouldn't it be an awfully quiet world if people only talked when they wanted to communicate?"

"Blissfully."

"I know I don't only talk when I want to communicate," Lois declared with great honesty. "Gracious! I can talk for hours without wanting to communicate once!"

"I know."

"Sometimes I even talk to myself, and I certainly don't want to communicate with me."

"Lois, eat your cereal."

"Yes, Mother."

For a moment Lois ate her cereal. She tasted it and looked at it and smelled it and felt it, but for only a moment.

"Sometimes I talk so I don't have to communicate," she said, staring at the refrigerator and nearly matching its expression.

"What?" her mother asked, turning full around from the sizzling eggs.

"Sometimes, when I have to say something that I don't want to say, I just talk and talk and talk. And the next thing you know it's time to go and I've got away without saying it."

"What on earth are you talking about right now?"

"Well, like last year when I didn't invite Mary Ella Frost to my birthday party."

Her mother waited.

"The next day in school she came up to me and said 'Hello Lois,' and I think I should have said something to her. But I just talked and talked about school and all without saying anything. And then the bell rang . . . and I got away. Have you ever done that, Mother?"

"No," Mary said, turning back to the eggs.

"Do you think I should have done that?"

"It must have been very embarrassing."

There was a moment of loudly-frying grease and quietly-munched cereal.

"Mother."

"Yes, Lois."

"May I have the tomato juice?"

"Oh, Lois, I'm sorry," Mary said, crossing to the refrigerator.

"It's all right. Nobody's perfect," she said.

"Lois, that wasn't a very nice thing to say."

"I'm sorry. I didn't mean it to be—not nice."

Mary looked at her daughter questioningly for a moment, then poured the tomato juice and put it on the table before her.

"Thank you," Lois said.

"You're welcome. Your eggs will be ready in a minute."

"Oh, good! I'm starving!"

"Ah, it's my poor, underfed daughter," John Taylor said, entering the kitchen.

Lois twisted around in her chair. "Good morning, Daddy!"

"Good morning, Lo," he said. "Morning, Mary."

"Good morning, John," Mary said. "I'd better hurry with your breakfast. You're late this morning."

"Yes, indeed," he said. "Can't be late on Saturday. That's the day when all the wage-earners spend the wages they've spent the week earning."

"What are wage-earners, Daddy?" Lois asked.

"People who earn wages," he said, stooping to her and whispering loudly.

"John, the child deserves a sensible answer," Mary said.

"He's just being funny, Mother," Lois said.

"I know that Lois, but . . ."

"Wage-earners are people who work for money," John said.

"Are there people who work for something else?" Lois asked.

"I'm not sure, daughter, but I don't think so," he told her.

"Wage-earner is just an expression for people who have jobs, Lois," her mother said.

"Gracious, almost everybody's a wage-earner, then." Lois observed.

"Just about," John said.

"I'm not, though," Lois said.

"Not yet," John agreed. "Where's the paper, Mary?"

"On the breadbox where it always is," Mary said.

"If it had been a snake, you know what," he said. He took the newspaper from the breadbox and laid it next to his place at the table. Then he started toward the refrigerator.

"Now John," Mary said, "it's much simpler if I'm the only person on his feet in the kitchen. Just sit down, and I'll get your tomato juice."

"Can I have orange instead?" he asked.

A fit of laughter seized Lois. Her mother glowered and her father's face reflected deep concern, but no power on earth could have dammed the flood of her amusement.

"Oh, Daddy! What you said!" Lois was finally able to utter.

"*What* did I say?"

"You have just washed right out of your daughter's mind a lesson on the difference between 'can' and 'may,'" Mary told him.

"Oh no, Mother," Lois said. "I'll never forget it now!"

"All right. All right, *may* I have orange juice?"

"And *can* you get to work on time?" Lois said.

"And *can* you mind your own business?" her father asked.

"I wish I had business to mind," Lois said. "I mean a business like yours."

"Pretty little girls of thirteen don't, as a rule, own used-car lots," her father said as he sat down.

"I bet I'd sell cars like mad if I did own one," Lois predicted.

"Yes, I'll bet you would," he answered, opening the newspaper to the sports page.

"Are girls ever used-car salesmen, Daddy?" Lois asked.

"Let your father read his paper, Lois," her mother said.

"It's all right, Mary. I can read the paper later." He turned to his daughter and chucked her under the chin. "But I can't talk to monkey-face once I leave here."

"You could if you'd take me with you," Lois said.

"Lois, dear, a used-car lot is really no place for a little girl," Mary said.

"But Mother," Lois protested, "I might just decide to be a mechanic when I grow up. And if that's the case, I can't start too young, can I?"

"How can you be so pretty and feminine-looking and be such a tomboy?" Mary said, looking over Lois' head as she always did to indicate that she was being rhetorical.

"I didn't say I was definitely going to be a mechanic," Lois said. "I might be a manicurist or something glamorous and girly like that. Or a lady doctor. May I go, Daddy?" she asked with a glance toward her mother.

"Your mother's probably right, Lo," he said. "You'd just be bored hanging around there."

"Oh, heck!" Lois exclaimed and sulked into her cereal.

"Lois," Mary said.

"It's just slang, Mother," Lois explained firmly.

Lois cast an accusing glance at her father and returned to her food. John Taylor looked smiling at a picture of Casey Stengel, realized that it was Casey Stengel and found himself thinking of Lois. He silently reaffirmed his thought that she would probably be bored down at the lot. Lois is never bored, another thought said insistently. If things become too quiet for her she may do something undesirable to amuse herself, but she is never bored. But Mary was right, he thought; it's no place for a little girl. It would be busy today and full of grown men who—he smiled again, as if to fill the pause—who would just love Lois. No, men did not come in to admire his beautiful little daughter; they came to look at automobiles, and getting them to buy would occupy all his time. Lois would be in the way. It would not surprise him if there were some truth in her boast that she would sell cars like mad. No. No, Mary had already said that she couldn't go, and she'd be very upset if he reversed the decision. Maybe some other Saturday. He would talk to Mary about it.

The footsteps which Mary now heard on the stairs were heavier than Lois'. They were the footsteps of her son, Johnny. He was nearly six feet tall and lithely built. His hair was not so light as Mary's nor so dark as John's and was cropped short so that it lay flat across his head. His face, which was good looking in an unspectacular way, gave the impression of being unusually expressive, which was curious, for he seemed always to hold it deliberately in an attitude of expressionlessness as if he were afraid that it might reveal some carefully guarded secret if he were to abandon his control of it. Only his bright blue eyes seemed to rebel against this control. They laughed when his mouth did not; they clouded when his unlined brow failed to wrinkle in distress; they narrowed when his full lips stayed soft and relaxed in spite of his anger. Because of this facial immobility, some people felt that Johnny Taylor was not so bright as he might be. Those who saw the paradox wondered at such reserve in a boy of seventeen.

"Morning, Mother, Dad," Johnny said, moving toward the table.

"Johnny!" his father said. "I didn't think you'd make it."

"You might speak to me," Lois said. "I'm small, but I'm here."

"Hi ya, Lo," Johnny said.

"Good morning, Johnny," his mother said, stopping her work to look at him, smiling.

"You've made quite a recovery," Mr. Taylor said. "When I saw you fifteen minutes ago, you were bleary-eyed and half naked."

"John!" Mary said.

"What?"

"What kind of a thing is that to say in front of the children?"

"Mary, he was walking toward the bathroom half asleep with just his pajama pants on. What—"

"We certainly don't need a physical description of the scene," she said, turning back to the stove.

"I didn't start out to give you one," John said. "But I would like to know what's wrong with what I said."

"It just needn't have been said," his wife answered without looking at him.

"That doesn't answer my question," he said. "Nothing *has* to be said. The word naked is a—"

"John," his wife said, turning now, "can't you see you're embarrassing Lois?"

"Lois, who has seen Johnny in just his pajama pants every morning of her life since she's been old enough to see Johnny at all?"

"Not because I've had my way," Mary said.

"What do you want him to do, come to breakfast in a dressing gown and an ascot like . . . like George Sanders?"

Lois smothered her uncontrollable giggles with a notable lack of success. Her high-pitched gurgling made her father aware of his own random humor and he smiled broadly. With a glance at his son he superimposed upon the image a full-sleeved, quilted robe with wide, satin lapels, their V-shaped gap stuffed generously with a monogrammed silk scarf. Johnny's innocent, unsuspecting face floating above these imaginary garments gave John's portrait an irresistable clownishness and he joined Lois with only slightly better controlled giggling. Although the thought of her son in an elegant dressing gown was more appealing than ludicrous to Mary Taylor, a picture remarkably like her husband's fancied one flashed across her mind. She at least controlled her laughter. But as she looked at Johnny all unaware and saw the broadly comic element in his utter vulnerability, control became more difficult. She looked away and quite unintentionally looked directly into Lois' face. The pale blue eyes were shining wet with tears; the soft, clear skin flushed rose pink; the delicate, small-lady hands partly covered the full, guiltily laughing lips. She looked for all Mary Taylor's world like a hysterical angel. When Mary threw back her head and laughed her husband and daughter abandoned their last attempts at discipline and laughter rose above the table like a song.

"What's so funny?" Johnny asked, and had he made a funny face and stuck out his tongue, he could not have contributed as fully to their amusement.

For a moment he was annoyed by their physical inability to explain to him. But as he watched these beloved people—free for a moment of every human care and ill, fleetingly but wholly dedicated to their laughter—his own concerns were driven from his mind. He smiled, tittered and then laughed. And at that moment they were united, as if they had joined hands and sat, laughing, in an unbroken circle of humanness.

They could not all stop laughing simultaneously, so that as the mirth of one subsided, the hilarity of the others would draw it back again. Out of sheer physical distress Lois and her mother quieted their laughter at nearly the same time.

"I've got to sit down for a moment!" Mary said.

Broken bits of laughter still ran through the conversation.

"I . . . I wouldn't mind," Johnny said, his voice trembling, "If I knew what we were laughing at."

That unfortunate admission recalled the original image to the others and the happy chaos was born again. And born again with it through the mysterious phenomenon of laughter, was the rare oneness which no deliberate effort, no unifying crisis seemed able to achieve. In magnificent accident a family sat howling happily as one being, mindless of its past, heedless of its future; old wounds, old kindnesses, all memories forgotten; fears of what would be, baseless premonitions, all anxieties gone.

"I'm afraid you're just not the dressing gown type, Johnny," his father said.

"Is that what you were laughing at?" Johnny asked in both surprise and annoyance.

"I think so," his father said. "I don't know what *they* were laughing at."

"Don't pay any attention to him," Mrs. Taylor said, returning to her work. "I think you'd look very nice in a dressing gown."

Lois chortled and, casting her a fierce glance, Johnny said, "I'm glad you think so, but I'm not giving you a chance to find out. Lois'll just have to go on looking at me half na—"

He stopped abruptly and began to eat his cereal.

"I'm glad you had the good taste to stop," his mother said, putting a plate of bacon and eggs before her husband. "John, you'd better hurry now. It's eight-thirty. Johnny, do you want two eggs or one?"

"I just want coffee, Mother."

"Now, you can't go to that terrible grocery store and carry orders around all day on an empty stomach."

"Mother, I'm not hungry. Anyway, I don't want to be late."

"What's so terrible about the grocery store?" John Taylor asked.

"We won't go into that," his wife said. "Johnny I'm glad to see you have a sense of responsibility, but at the same time, you have to eat."

"Mother, I'm not hungry."

The door chimes rang and their soft sound was startling at this early hour. Looking across the darker living room, which lay like an island between the sunlit kitchen and the bright sunporch, Mary said, "Now, who on earth can that be?"

"I'll get it, Mary," John Taylor said, rising.

He was quite surprised to see Ben Summerfield, in his blue, brass-buttoned police chief's uniform, standing at the front door. With his surprise he felt a vague amusement as one might at an unexpected event in a play. He stepped down the one step to the stone floor of the sunporch and opened the door. The huge, dark-clad figure seemed to fill the doorway and block out the light. Ben's kind, roughened, heavily folded face was a bright patch in the blueness.

"Why, hello, Ben," John said.

"Good morning, John," the big man answered.

"This is a social call or an official one?" John laughed self-consciously, quickly dismissing the concern which whispered across his mind. "Well, come on in, Ben. Don't stand out there in the wind."

As he stepped past John, Ben saw Mary leaning into the kitchen doorway, her face trying to twist its puzzled expression into one of hospitality. He saw Lois still sitting at the table, but hugging the back of her chair as she turned toward him. He saw the sunlight on Johnny's face.

"Morning, Mary," he said.

"Why, Ben Summerfield, how are you?" she called. "How are Sarah and the kids?"

"All fine," he answered.

"Mary, put out another cup," John said, reaching for Ben's shoulder. "Come on and have some coffee."

"No thanks, John. I've got to be getting back to the station."

"Oh," John said quietly. "Sure."

The two men faced each other in a curious silence. Ben looked as if he thought that John might say something that would give the chief of police some reason for being in his house at eight-thirty on a Saturday morning. Seeing the expression and having nothing to say, John began to look puzzled.

"Like to talk to you for a minute, John," Ben said finally, looking at the stone floor.

"Sure, Ben. Come on in the living room," John said, confident, innocent, searching his mind for a forgotten traffic ticket—or perhaps a U-turn he had thought unobserved.

"Uh . . . no, John," Ben said quietly, his face suddenly wrinkling into a mask of creases. "Uh . . . mind if I close this?" he asked, pointing to the glass-paneled door between the porch and the living room.

John looked at Ben for a moment, then without speaking, turned and closed the door. When he turned back, his face was frankly troubled, although it did not reflect the faint hostility which had been born in that moment of mysterious activity.

"I don't know how to say this, John," Ben told him.

"Well, for God's sake, Ben, what is it?"

He looked over John's shoulder to assure himself of privacy and saw the interior of the house, shattered by the many-paned door. Then he looked directly into John's eyes, and for the first time his own showed how deeply he was troubled.

"It's Johnny," he said.

"Ben, what the hell do you mean, 'It's Johnny'?"

"I'm goin' to have to take him in, John."

For an instant John Taylor felt only a noise inside him which was so loud that nothing else seemed to exist. Then it stopped, and in the ensuing silence of reality, he could hear even Ben Summerfield's breathing.

"You're going to take Johnny to the police station?" he asked very slowly and very clearly.

"I don't have any choice, John," Ben told him.

"What'd he do, ring some doorbells last night?" John asked, as his mind, scrambling vainly back over the minutes to reach that so lately safe time of levity, rejected this man and what he said.

"It's serious," Ben said.

"I think we better sit down and talk about this," John said, crossing toward the gaily patterned porch furniture.

"This isn't between you and me," Ben told him. "It's not something we can settle."

John stopped. Nothing he did seemed right. No thought, no word, no movement seemed to halt the black force which was pressing toward him. He turned back to Ben. "But you are going to let me in on it," he said sarcastically. He saw Ben swallow and shift his heavy body awkwardly. It made John regret his sarcasm.

"John, I've known you for a long time. There ain't a man in this town I like or respect more than you. If you know that, you can't think I ain't told you what this is all about just to make myself important. It's a goddamned hard thing to tell a man, and I don't know how to do it."

"Okay, Ben," John said, all hostility gone now. "Just say it, straight out."

"Last night three boys raped little Ida Praul. She's named Johnny as one of them."

John looked at him, his expression unchanged except for a slow, slight hardening of the eyes.

"I guess I really shouldn't think you're such a son of a bitch for saying that. I guess . . . I guess you can't know Johnny like I do. And if she named him, she named him. That must seem pretty simple to you."

"John, listen . . ."

"Yeah, very simple. I don't know how . . . I don't know what did happen, but this Ida Praul is wrong, that's all."

"John, will you listen . . ."

"No. You listen, Ben. Take Johnny in, huh? She's so wrong that I'm not even going to let you suggest this filth to Johnny! I'll straighten this thing out myself. You, coming in here and telling me my son's a . . ."

"Will you calm down, John?" Ben said, extending his upturned palms toward him supplicatingly.

It was only the realization that he was, indeed, excited that quieted him.

"Because I know you," Ben said earnestly, "and because I know Johnny, I picked up the other two boys first and took 'em in. They both named Johnny before they even knew that Ida had named him."

After a moment of silent retreat, John renewed the attack.

"I don't care if Christ Almighty named him, he couldn't have done it!"

"All right, but I'll have to take him with me."

Striding toward the door, John said, "I'll settle this thing right now. I'll bring him out here and ask him. He won't lie to me. You can stand there and hear him tell the truth."

"John," Ben said.

John turned to him, his hand already on the knob of the door.

"If you want to ask him, go ahead. But you better do it in there."

"What are you talking about?"

"Johnny is under arrest. Anything he says in front of me can be used against him."

John nearly laughed at the sound of the old legal cliché. Yet, slightly distorted, worked into a sentence uttered by a man incapable of a pose, this trite phrase, for him a symbol of make-believe, of literary fantasy, was the instrument which crystallized the vaporous minutes which had passed since Ben had entered his home.

"They're waitin' for me, John. I can't put it off much longer."

"Yes. Yes," he said, not looking at Ben. "I'll have to talk to him first."

"Sure," Ben said. "Go ahead."

But John did not go. He merely turned toward the door and stood, wondering what he would say to Johnny.

"Do you think he did it, Ben?" he said without turning.

"I don't know. It sure looks like it, John, but I . . . I don't know."

When he pushed open the door and saw Johnny still sitting at the kitchen table, he was sure that he had known from the beginning that it was true. It was not true of his son, who had lived each day of his life in their house; who had been afraid of turtles; who had wet the bed; who had played with a brown velours bear under the Christmas tree; who had covered his body with the clothes he had bought him and survived on his food. But it was true of the boy who sat at the kitchen table, who was somehow also his son.

He walked into the kitchen where the sunlight now seemed thinner, less yellow, and where an unnatural silence hung in the place of rising laughter.

Mary looked into his face and could not remember a time in twenty years when he had looked quite that way.

"John, what is it?" she said, almost in a whisper.

"There's been a mixup of some kind down at . . ."

"John, what is it?" she said, raising her voice.

"There's been a mix . . ."

His voice trembled, and he turned to Mary and took her by the shoulders with both hands as he had never before done. Lois slipped from her chair and stood with her back pressed against the wall. Mary's body became rigid under this unaccustomed grasp.

John spoke slowly, carefully, as if trying to remember the lines of a poem of long ago.

"Mary . . . just for a little while . . . maybe only a few minutes, I don't know . . . but for a while . . . you mustn't . . . ask me anything. There are things I have to do . . . that I don't know how to do . . . and that you wouldn't either. But I'm going to do them . . . from minute to minute . . . the best I know how. And the only way for you to help me . . . and I need help . . . is to be quiet and do what I ask."

He released her and Mary crossed the room and put both her hands on Lois' head and stood very close to her.

"I'm going to talk to Johnny alone," John went on. "I want you to go on up to my bedroom, Johnny. You're not to go and talk to Ben while I'm gone, Mary. Just . . . stay here with Lois."

He started from the room behind Johnny, who had quietly left the table. At the doorway John turned back to them.

"I'm sorry, Mary," he said.

When he got to the bedroom, Johnny was standing just a few feet inside so that there was barely room for John to enter and close the door. He nearly brushed against him, but the boy did not move. He looked into his son's face and saw that tears had begun to run down the now bloodless cheeks.

"Johnny, you know why Ben Summerfield is here," John said.

Johnny nodded almost imperceptibly.

"I don't want you to think about what you're going to tell anybody else—your mother or Ben Summerfield or the neighbors or anybody else—just me. I only want to have to ask you this question once in your whole life and you've got to tell me the truth, because everything I do from now on maybe for the rest of both our lives is going to be based on what you tell me. Did you rape Ida Praul last night?"

"Yes," Johnny said, and there seemed to be no voice, but only breath under the word.

"Oh, my God," John said quietly, closing his eyes. "Oh, my God. Oh, my God."

He opened his eyes and held out both his arms to embrace his son, but Johnny had turned his back.

III.

IDA PRAUL LAY FOR A LONG TIME, STARING UP INTO THE PALE BLUE sky as the sunlight spread over her like a golden liquid. Even in the brilliance of that sunlight, her thoughts were black with the memory of the night. Her confusion lessened with the coming of the day, and for the first time her memories were ordered. She remembered having lain in the dark, listening to the fading voices with what was to her their futile urgency, for urgencies had been beyond her then. Yet each utterance had worn its owner's identity like a suit of clothes. She had heard the flat, colorless voice issuing its curt and angry commands, like the barking of a small, irritable dog, first nearby, then farther away, then not at all. She had heard the frightened, impatient whining, answered by the dull and heavy legato of drunkenness. It had become a receding duet as if its performers were moving off in search of the irritable dog. She had lain with her eyes closed, thinking of nothing—that is, thinking of so many things simultaneously that no one thought had ever become a realization—for a long time which she did not attempt to measure. Then she had become aware of the pain.

When she had opened her eyes and had seen the stars blinking merrily against the blue velvet sky, she had known that the pain had been there for some time, mounting until its intensity had conquered her unwillingness to admit its existence, for it would be a symbol of what had happened.

Though they were gone then, she had remembered the voices and had wondered how long they had left her. Her mind had gone back further, and she had found that her then burgeoning terror had blurred her memory and unbalanced the importance of events. She had remembered bits of sentences, not as parts of a conversation, but isolated, disconnected from any whole. She had remembered without sequence the weeds scratching at her legs, falling to the ground, stumbling up the small mound of earth. Dozens of images had whirled about through her memory, until with bitter certainty she had relived those moments of suffocating helplessness when she had lain pinned to the earth.

She had closed her eyes again, hoping to blot out the image of that grim face descending toward her own. But in the blacker dark of sightlessness the image had been brighter, and she had felt again the heavy power of him, commanding, inexorable. She had moaned under the unbearable pressure of the recollection, then the image had faded as had the barking of the irritable dog.

When she had felt on her cheeks the warm, narrow course of her tears, she could no longer resist the final act of surrender, and she cried openly. The dreadful thing that she had wanted never to happen at all had happened as she had feared it must. She was spared the guilt which willing participation would have brought, but she had been filled with an unspeakable loathing of herself.

When she had opened her eyes again, the sky had turned a soft gray, and one pale star gleamed above the horizon. She called out feebly, "Mama. Mama," hoping that her call might somehow draw her mother to the hill. If Peg Praul had come upon her daughter in this pitiable attitude of defilement, she might have taken her in her arms, comforted her, lulled her with some soft song of sleep. She might not have accused her, made her in her defense live again those hideous, unclean moments. But her mother had not come, and Ida had been afraid to go home to her.

Finally the sun shot yellow streaks through the trees at the top of the hill, and insects buzzed about Ida as if she were a large, dew-soaked plant which had sprung up in the night. Birds sang and fluttered busily about their own affairs as if nothing had happened to Ida. And, hearing their oblivious chatter, she knew that it was time to go.

When she first stirred, the pain was so great that she fell back upon the ground. Moving slowly and carefully, she got to a sitting position, but when she tried to stand, she found that her right ankle was swollen and discolored and hurt badly under her weight. Looking down at her ankle she discovered the red-brown stains of dried blood on her dress. It shocked and frightened and repelled her all at once, and she swatted at the stains with her hands as she might have if she had found a great, brown spider there. She leaned heavily on her injured ankle, and pain shot upward through her leg. Her pain and her fear and her horror of herself converged upon her and produced a compelling panic. Crying and calling out in monosyllables of terror, she fled, limping, hobbling, stumbling down the hill.

Far below her was the white concrete road which came off the bridge, turned, and made its way across the lower part of the hill just above the river. In the leveling of the roadbed a steep bank had been cut out of the earth. When Ida reached it, she sat on its edge and dropped herself down the short, steep incline to the shoulder of the road. She lay there for a moment, sobbing and gasping in her exhaustion. Perspiration made mud of the dirt on her face and arms. Her hair was matted and disheveled, with bits of brown grass clinging to it. Her legs were scratched and covered with trails of clotted blood. She rose and made her way along the road to the quarter-mile-long bridge. She started across the oatmeal-colored span of concrete; and the nearer she came to town, the more fantastic a figure she presented.

She reached the end of the bridge and made her way up the gentle slope of Main Street past now sleeping neon signs which would soon again blink palely against the daylight; past the Bridge Tavern and Rumson's Shoe Store and the Sally Lee Dress Shop and the Economy Drug Store; past opaquely reflecting shop windows which fleetingly bore her image; past the blind, many-bulbed marquee of the Bijou movie theater, still and unspectacular now without its electric ripples of colored light. There was a strange stillness and silence among these instruments of churning and flashing and glowing. As Ida moved haltingly through this silent landscape, it took on an atmosphere of otherworldliness, and Ida herself the quality of a tragic Alice-in-Wonderland.

When she turned at the corner of Main and Third, where St. Clement's Roman Catholic Church held its spired head high above the earth, she began to hurry, drawn by the terrible inevitability of seeing her mother from her more terrible aloneness. When she reached her mother's place (she always thought of it in those words), she did not enter by the front door. In her mother's childhood the room into which the front door opened had been the parlor, crammed full of horsehair-covered furniture. It had been used only on the most formal occasions: the rare visits from distant relatives, more frequently for funeral viewings, and once for someone's golden wedding anniversary. No one had ever entered the room otherwise, except to clean it. It had not been a parlor for thirty years now, but for thirty years Ida's mother entered and left the house by the kitchen door. The punishment-inflicted habit overcame even Ida's panic, and she went through the cool, dark, narrow passageway between the two houses to the back door of her own. She stood in a moment of final hesitation, looking up at the back porch. Then eagerly she wiped away the tears with her grimy hands as if to improve her appearance and went into the house.

This truly was her mother's place, for Margaret Praul owned the house, had inherited it when her own mother had died. Just after Ida had been born, Peg, as everyone called her, had quite arbitrarily added the "Mrs." to her name. She could not remember ever having been questioned about it, even by her closest relatives and friends. It was then, too, that Peg had converted the house into apartments.

The two apartments on the upper floors were quite small, but livable. Peg had spent nearly all of the little money her mother had left to make them adequate. With what was left she made a place to live for herself and her daughter on the first floor. There was the former parlor with furniture Peg's mother had bought before Peg had been born. The big, ugly sofa had been discarded, and in its place was a Hollywood bed. The room served more as Peg's bedroom than for its original purpose. In the kitchen there was a large, wooden, oblong table, covered with a tablecloth of flowered plastic. In one corner was a booth of inexpensive construction board which housed the bathroom equipment, including a stall shower lined with galvanized metal. The water made a sound like rain falling on a tool shed. The narrow back porch provided both storage space for the several treasures which Peg had long ago removed from upstairs, and a bedroom for Ida. There, every night of her life with the exception of the most recent one, Ida had slept among a clutter of ignored and dusty oddments—an empty gilt picture frame, a peach-colored silk lampshade with black fringe, a walnut coat tree with one broken limb. There was an electric heater—a cone of asbestos and metal filaments which glowed against a round metal reflector—to warm her on winter mornings. The kitchen was the center of Ida's life. There she performed most of the functions of her limited existence. There she ate, played, did her homework, bathed and, sometimes on winter Sundays when it was too cold in spite of the heater to sit on the porch, daydreamed.

When Ida went into the kitchen she found it in a not unusual state of disarray. It was quite dark in the room, for the blinds were drawn, and she was aware of the strong odor of stale tobacco smoke. This was no more unusual than the disarray, but it always sickened her. The large glass ashtray on the table was piled high with the debris of smoking, and empty beer cans stood about it. Ida rarely went into her mother's bedroom, which was separated from the kitchen by a faded print curtain. She walked across the kitchen and stood so close to the curtain that her nose almost touched it. When she tried to speak she found that her throat was clogged and constricted. Even after she cleared it her voice was hoarse.

"Mama," she called quietly.

She heard her mother groan and stir heavily.

"Mama," she said again.

"What? Huh?" her mother said, and she seemed to pronounce the sounds without consonants.

"Mama, should I come in?" Ida asked. "Is it all right?"

"Huh? Yeah, come on in if you want to."

Ida succeeded more completely than usual in ignoring what she saw. In this rare state of self-concern she barely noticed that her mother wore only a slip and lay across the bed, on which the covers had not been turned down. Peg Praul did not see her daughter enter the room, for her face was turned to the wall, and she had not yet opened her eyes. Her face was a homely one, but it did not strike the viewer with horror or pity and was repellent only in a relatively subtle way. Her eyes were too pale and never clear. Her nose was large and broad. Her skin was not blemished, but it was a coarse and somehow imperceptibly yellow skin, so that it never looked clean, even when Peg had just washed her face. She had a good mouth, which in her plain face seemed too full, too curvaceous. It was only when one had perceived this total effect, after a moment or two, that one realized Peg Praul's grossness.

Ida stood now just inside the room, as close to this side of the curtain as she had stood to the other before her mother had sluggishly granted her permission to enter.

"Mama," Ida said again.

"Uh," her mother grunted without moving.

"Mama, look at me," Ida pleaded.

Her mother squirmed on the bed, then turned to Ida and slowly, laboriously opened her eyes as if she were opening the great, wooden doors of a cathedral. Her eyes, red as sores, stared stupidly, unseeingly at the girl before her. Gradually, an expression of incredulity spread across her heavy, callow face. She sprang to a sitting position, then to her feet, and stood blinking and staring at her daughter.

"Ida!" was all she was able to say for a moment. "Ida! For the great love of Jesus, Ida! Ida, what the hell happened to you?"

Grateful for the absence of rebuke, for this tentative indication of concern, and released, if only for a moment, from the doleful monotony of self-loathing, Ida began to cry, loudly, freely with an infantile lack of inhibition.

Her mother did not move, but stood looking at her across the darkness of the room, saying with a slowly increasing shrillness, "Don't cry, baby. Ida, don't cry, baby. Don't cry, baby."

"Mama!" Ida said in protest to her mother's immobility.

"Ida, for Christ' sake, tell me! What was it? You been in a car accident? Somebody beat you up?"

She took one step toward Ida and stopped. "Ida . . . you didn't . . .?"

Ida wanted to scream at her mother, but the old chains of fear and worship and mystery held her even now, while her mind raged against the automatic accusation. Ida stared at her mother, wondering why she did not at once assume Ida's innocence, curse her tormentors, dress her wounds, caress and comfort her.

"Mama. They did it to me. All three of them!"

"Oh, you poor kid," Peg Praul said quietly, and Ida's heart rejoiced. "Come on in the kitchen, Ida."

Almost smiling, Ida followed her mother past the curtain and into the kitchen, happy that she was to be cared for after all. Tenderly her mother would wash the blood and dirt from her body. How gentle would be the examination of her tender flesh. Her mother might even comb and stroke her matted hair. For this moment, Ida knew she would have submitted again to all of last night's injuries. Last night no longer mattered.

"Sit down at the table while I clean you up," Peg said, going to the sink. "Are you hurt bad?"

"No, Mama," Ida said sweetly, "I don't think so."

As she ran hot water into a white enamel basin, Peg said "Now you tell me all about it, honey, while I'm washin' you." She brought the basin to the table, then crossed to a window and raised the shade. "Good Christ!" she said when she turned and saw Ida in the sunlight. "What they done to you!"

"I . . . I can't tell you about it, Mama," Ida said, avoiding her mother's eyes in her embarrassment.

"I know it's awful, honey, but you got to tell me how it happened," her mother said.

"Oh, Mama, I can't tell you what they did to me!" Ida said, turning her head away from Peg.

"Well, can't you tell me where it happened, where they jumped out at you? Didn't you see what they looked like?"

"Yes, Mama," Ida said. "I know who they were."

"You know who they were?" Peg asked, holding a dripping washcloth over the basin.

"Yes, all three of them."

"Ida, you better tell me all about this now."

"I . . . I can't."

Peg turned Ida's face toward her with her hand and said, "Listen, you, if three guys took you out and laid you . . . well, that *is* what you're talkin' about, ain't it?" she asked, as Ida winced.

"Yes," Ida said.

"Well then stop lookin' so innocent, as if you didn't know what I meant." She threw the washcloth into the basin and went on, "If that's what they did and against your will, I want to know about it and quick. But if you had any part in it, if you egged 'em on or wanted it and then changed your mind, you better say so right now."

"Mama . . ."

"Ida, do you understand me? If you was forced into this, then it's rape. But if you was just all . . . if you wanted to, or if you egged 'em on, you'd never stand a chance in court."

"In court?"

Peg thrust a stubby index finger at Ida and said, "Listen to me. I'm goin' to ask you questions, and I don't want no more cryin' from you or turnin' away. I want answers. Where'd all this happen?"

"On . . . on the hill across the river."

"Jesus, Ida! There's hills for twenty miles along the other side of the river. Don't you know exactly where?"

"Yes . . . I . . . I know."

"How did you get there, in a car?"

Ida nodded.

"Did you go with 'em willingly?"

Ida nodded again.

"Oh, that's just great!"

"But I didn't do it, Mama!"

"You just said they . . . they did it to you!"

"But I didn't want 'em to, Mama!" Ida shouted, bursting into tears again. "They dragged me out of the car and held me down, and they . . . they . . . I tried to get away. I couldn't."

"That's all I wanted to know," Peg said.

Her mother strode across the room, swept the curtain aside and went into her bedroom. Ida did not turn her head to watch her mother go. Gradually she stopped crying, but the sweetness and joy and warmth had ended too. When those things had replaced her horror, she had understood. Now they were gone; and although it seemed strange to her, her horror did not return. She did not care a bit about last night, but felt only a dull disgust for herself and her mother and the three boys and for everything she had ever known.

"Who were they, honey?" her mother asked, ducking through the curtain and zipping her dress.

Ida watched her mother combing her hair and applying her makeup at the mirror over the kitchen sink.

"Armand Rapp, Artie Schlier and Johnny Taylor," Ida said so calmly and clearly that her mother turned for a second look at her.

Putting the comb on the drainboard, Peg said, "You were limpin' before. Can you walk to the police station on that foot?"

"Yes, Mama," Ida said. "Do I have to go like this?"

"Just like that, baby. Come on."

As Peg reached the door to the back porch, she stopped and turned to Ida. "No," she said, "let's go out the front way, honey."

She crossed the kitchen and pushed back the curtain to wait for Ida, who had struggled to her feet and stood by the table.

"Mama," Ida said.

"What?"

"Am I . . . am I a whore now?"

"Are you . . . well, Jesus Christ, Ida! What an idea! No, baby, you're not."

IV.

IN AN ANCIENT, BITTER PATTERN JOHN TAYLOR HAD TURNED AWAY from his son's turning away. At the top of the stairs he had muttered, "Come on down, Johnny." He had himself got halfway down the stairs when a very real dizziness made him clutch the banister and hope desperately for his sense of balance to return. He closed his eyes and nausea swelled up in the darkness. For a moment the panic was increased by the images of Mary and Lois and Ben Summerfield, waiting with equal ruthlessness, which whirled about in his mind. He saw them all frozen eternally in their various attitudes of anxiety, never to be released into the next unknown, more horrible and conclusive moment. Then he opened his eyes.

As familiar sights returned to him, he knew that above everything else he must put down his panic. Gradually, the elements of his vertigo seemed to slow their swirling and separate themselves into units of thought. There remained only to arrange the units in some order (even the wrong order now seemed better than none at all) and to execute them in that order as if he had a plan. First, there was Lois: he would send her to her room immediately. Eventually she would have to be taken aside and given some carefully prepared explanation, but there was no time for that now. Next, there was Mary, who might in this matter be only a little less a child than Lois. She would have to be told something, certainly not the truth, not like this, not with Ben Summerfield waiting in the house. She would know that Johnny was involved in a crime. It was the nature of the crime which he must hide. Then he would have to call Jim Beyers. Jim had always told him that lawyers were like doctors: the earlier you called them in, the more good they were likely to be able to do. He wouldn't have to explain the details on the telephone; Jim would understand. That was all. It seemed so simple, but he was trembling as he started down the stairs with Johnny just behind him.

He thought that perhaps Ben Summerfield would have gone out to the car to wait, and as he saw him still standing on the porch, his hands clasped behind his back, he seemed to John to be unnecessarily watchful, suspicious, on guard. He looked at him with a sudden hatred so obvious that it embarrassed Ben. And seeing the embarrassment, John wanted to apologize, but merely softened his expression. He heard Johnny's footsteps stop behind him at the bottom of the stairs.

He turned to his son and said slowly and quietly, "Johnny, stay right here." He walked the few steps to the sunporch door and said, "You'll have to wait a few more minutes, Ben."

Ben looked at him for a moment, then sighed and said, "All right, John."

He walked through the living room and into the kitchen. Mary and Lois were standing just where he had left them.

"Lois, I want you to go up to your room," he said softly.

He had expected her to protest, but he had underestimated her terror. She looked at him with the eyes of a small and frightened animal and sped past him up the stairs to her room.

"Mary, I'm afraid Johnny's in some trouble," John said. "It looks like he might've got himself involved—with some other boys—in a . . . in a robbery."

"Oh, God, John!"

"Now, we don't know anything yet, so don't go getting yourself all upset. Ben doesn't know too much about it himself. We're just going to go down to the station and find out what's what."

"But Johnny wouldn't steal!"

"Mary, just let me go along and find out about it. There's no use talking about something we don't know anything about."

"All right, John, all right. But I know Johnny wouldn't steal."

He looked at her for a moment and, deciding that he had done better than he had expected, turned to go into the living room. Johnny remained the only threat to his plan, and he must get him out of the house. Mary followed him and before he could speak, she said: "Johnny, don't you worry. Your father and I will stand by you. We know you wouldn't steal."

"Mother . . ." Johnny began.

"Mary, would you go upstairs and get me the jacket to this suit? I have a phone call to make."

"All right," she said, eager to do her share in her son's behalf. "And don't you worry, Johnny."

"Go with Ben, Johnny," John said when she had gone.

"Dad, you didn't tell her . . . I was a thief?"

John stood for a moment in awe of this selfish naïveté.

"What did you want me to tell her?" he asked. And in the silence he added, "Go with Ben, Johnny."

The boy turned and went out of the house with the sad, but vigilant, policeman close by his side.

Mary came down the stairs as the front door closed. She stood clutching John's jacket as her eyes followed her son and the policeman along the narrow strip of cement that cut like a miniature airfield runway through the front lawn. John went to the telephone and dialed Jim Beyers' home number. He looked across the room. Mary had not moved, but stood looking at the small black sedan which imprisoned her son.

"Hello, Jim?" John said. "Jim, we've got some trouble. Could you meet me. . . . What do you mean, you know?" He glanced at Mary quickly, but she had not heard. "Christ! Not already! . . . Jim, will you ask her to keep it to herself?" He rubbed his eyes with his right hand and said, "I'll be there in ten minutes. . . . No, he's out front in the car with Ben Summerfield." He looked through the window in the living room wall—which the enclosing of the porch had rendered incongruous, yet somehow convenient—across the porch and lawn to the car, as if to check the accuracy of his statement. "No, I won't let him say a word till you get there. Ten minutes. Thanks, Jim."

He picked up his hat from the table by the door and took his jacket from Mary.

"Mary," he said.

For the first time since she had come downstairs her eyes moved, and she seemed to have difficulty focusing them on him.

"Mary, I want you to stay in the house until I come home. And try not to let anybody in. It's just that . . . well, it's just that in a case like this the less said the better. All we want is the truth, and a lot of gossip and stray talk just makes it harder to get at. So just wait for me to come home. I'll be as quick as I can. Will you do that, Mary?"

John walked out to the curb, around to the far side of the car and got into the front seat next to Johnny. As the car vibrated to the turning of the motor, he looked back at the house. Mary stood in the front doorway with a handkerchief pressed to her mouth. She was still standing there, motionless, when the car turned south on Elm Street and out of her view. John felt a pressing need to say something, but could think of nothing to say. He knew that Ben, too, felt the awkward silence, and a thick embarrassment surrounded them. Somehow the tension in the car made him uncomfortably sensitive. He had automatically put his arm across the back of the seat, and beneath his hand he felt the warm smooth plastic of the seat covers. His knees were pressed against the dashboard, and when he tried to move them, he discovered that his legs, which seemed too long, were cramped, and that there was no comfortable place for his feet, which now seemed huge. Almost suddenly he felt Johnny's leg against his, and his arm, stretched across the back of the seat, seemed to him to lie around Johnny's shoulders protectively. He took his arm from the back of the seat and folded his hands in his lap, where they felt heavy and awkward.

From Elm Street the car turned into Fourth Avenue and from there into lower Main Street. The stillness which had surrounded Ida was gone now. Shopkeepers turned their keys, and fluorescent lights blinked bluely into action. As the wide green shade rose in the window of the Economy Drug Store, the sunlight plunged into the jewel-colored liquids in the big apothecary jars, and their blue and green and red—seemingly lit from within—became too vivid, too beautiful to bear for more than a moment. John looked at his watch. It was five minutes past nine, and he knew that whatever he felt, his day was still young and likely to be very long. He thought suddenly of Johnny. And as he turned carefully to glance at him, rigid and staring straight ahead, he was sickened at the nature of the private terrible day his son was now beginning. No, he thought, bitterly; last night was the beginning, when he had touched that girl. Or perhaps when she had foolishly touched him, or first glanced at him knowingly one day at school. Or perhaps even earlier, when she had let him tell her a joke, or had just been too free with him. Or perhaps it had little to do with her, the beginning, and was even earlier, on a day when the boys had been fooling around, trying to outdo each other. Or perhaps, he thought with a vague dread, it had been even earlier than that—much, much earlier.

The car slowed and came to a stop before the tiny, dirty-faced building known as the Borough Hall. Without looking at either of them, Ben got out of the car and slammed the door. He stood waiting for them on the sidewalk.

"Johnny," John said, while they were still in the car, "they probably won't ask you much. But if Jim Beyers isn't there don't say anything except your name and address and that your lawyer'll be there in a few minutes." John wondered if he was dramatizing.

"Okay," Johnny said weakly.

Ben pushed open the door of the building and stood aside. John and Johnny went by him and into the dark, narrow hall.

"Right here, John," Ben said, indicating a partially open door on the right. John went in first, and Johnny and Ben followed. The room was small and had a strong, dry identifiable odor. The walls, which needed painting, were dark brown to about eye level and a paler, drabber brown from there to the ceiling. Varnishes and stains had been applied to the woodwork apparently at highly varying whims in regard to color, and had turned the once pale and unresisting wood an ugly, artificial brown.

John had taken only a few steps inside the room when he stood before a large desk, behind which sat Willard Ziegler in his blue and brass uniform. John had gone to high school with him and considered him an old friend. Even before they could exchange greetings, John became aware that the room was crowded and that two distinct sounds were evident. One was a quiet sobbing, and the other was a woman's voice talking continuously. Suddenly the voice was louder and intelligible for the first time since John entered the room.

"There," it said. "That's him! That's the other one! Johnny Taylor! I know him!"

John turned toward the voice, which had been behind him. On a high-backed bench to the left of the door a man with steel-rimmed spectacles and a bushy, graying mustache sat with his arm around the sobbing woman, whose face John could not quite see. Next to them, staring at the floor, was a slim, light-haired boy whom he recognized as Artie Schlier. And next to him sat the woman who had spoken, one arm around a young and disheveled girl, the other extended full length with pointing index finger, stabbing at Johnny.

John was angered by the voice and by the unnecessary melodrama of the pointing finger. Yet beneath his anger he recognized and remembered Peg Praul. He had not seen her for years, and he thought how strange it was that in a town of this size he had not seen her, passing his place of business or leaving a drugstore as he stopped in for cigarettes or shopping at the supermarket as he waited in the car for Mary. The homely little child beside her must be her daughter—Ida, that was the name. Christ! They might at least have picked somebody pretty . . . and the shock at his own thought stopped him.

"What the hell kind of kids are they, I want to know," Ida's mother was saying. "The three of them, holdin' down my little baby and rapin' her out there on that hill. . . ."

The woman in the arms of the bespectacled man sobbed louder, and over the sobbing John heard Jim Beyers' voice saying, "Mrs. Praul, for the moment that's only an allegation. It's one that we're all fully aware of, so you needn't keep repeating it."

John turned back toward the desk and saw Jim Beyers coming toward him.

"An allegation, is it?" Peg Praul shouted with such force that Jim stopped, and with this everyone else in the room looked toward her. She had jumped to her feet and now pulled Ida up from the bench to exhibit her. "Look at her! What does it look like to you, she just came from the movies?"

"I can think of about fifty ways she could have got to look like that," Jim Beyers answered, "and none of them has anything to do with rape. We all understand how you feel, Mrs. Praul, but it's enough that you've formally pressed the charge of rape. Standing there shouting isn't going to convince anybody."

"You get a doctor in here right now," Peg demanded without altering the tone of her voice. "He'll tell you she's been raped."

"He can tell perhaps if she's had sexual intercourse," Jim said, "which does not necessarily indicate rape."

"We called a doctor ten minutes ago just for that purpose, Mrs. Praul," Magistrate Harris Loomis said from behind the desk which he now shared with Willard Ziegler. "If you'll just sit down and wait quietly, we can get on with this thing."

Harry Loomis looked at her over the top of his rimless bifocals, quite obviously waiting for her to resume her seat. When she had sat down, ungently pulling Ida to the bench beside her, he sighed heavily and looked up at John.

"We'll have to book the boy, John," he said quietly.

"Harry, isn't there something we can do about this?" John asked.

Again surmounting the obstacle of his glasses to look at Mrs. Praul, he said, "I'm afraid not." Then turning back to John, "We'll have to book him."

Jim Beyers had come to John's side. He looked toward the door and said, "Up here, Johnny."

Johnny came and stood at the desk between the two men. In response to the magistrate's questions, Johnny gave his name, address and date of birth so quietly that Willard Ziegler would have had to ask him again had he not already known the approximate answers.

"Why don't you go and sit down over there, Johnny," Jim Beyers said.

John's eyes followed his son to the bench at the right of the door, and for the first time he saw the room's other two occupants. The older one he knew to be George Rapp, and the younger was so accurate a smaller version of him that he could only have been George's son. George Rapp was a huge man whose great bulk made him look shorter than his six-foot-three-inch height. He wore a white shirt without jacket or tie and khaki trousers drawn up against the under side of the enormous orb of his stomach. His fingers, the first two of his right hand heavily stained from constant smoking, were long and fat and his palms were wide and thick like small steaks. There was no delineation between his jaw and the short stump of his neck, so that his head seemed to grow directly out of his broad shoulders. His hair had not been cut recently and lay in great brown waves over his squarish head. He had a nose like a monstrous infant's, formless and seemingly without cartilage. Only his eyes were small; they were close together and peered narrowly from a superabundance of flesh. Sitting sullenly by him, Armand seemed to promise complete fulfillment of his father's image.

Jim Beyers beckoned to George, and ponderously he rose to join him and John in a corner of the room. Jim also tried to attract the attention of the man with the mustache, who was still so involved in comforting the sobbing woman that he did not notice.

"Mr. Schlier," Jim called across the room.

"What?" the man cried, startled, as his eyes roamed about the room almost frantically.

"Would you come over here for a minute, Mr. Schlier?" Jim said.

The woman looked up then, her eyes red-rimmed and her cheeks shining pinkly with the wetness of her tears. For a moment they sat huddled together like two frightened squirrels. Then he spoke to her quietly in German, patted her shoulder and got up to cross the room.

"Have you gentlemen talked to an attorney?" Jim Beyers asked confidentially, looking from Mr. Schlier to George Rapp.

Mr. Schlier shook his head slowly, and George Rapp said, "I didn't know if I'd need one."

Jim looked at him somberly for a moment and said, "You need one."

Still shaking his head and looking toward the ceiling, Mr. Schlier said, "What have they done? What have they done?" In his thick German accent he pronounced the w's as v's and the th's as d's.

"We don't know yet if they've done anything," Jim said shortly, but with a firmness clearly meant to instruct.

"They done it, all right," George Rapp said. "Armand knew what he would've got if he didn't tell the truth. And he told me."

"Look, I'm not a criminal lawyer, but my advice is to forget right now that Armand told you that—for a while anyway."

"I'd just as soon have you handle it, Jim," John said, "Johnny's side of it, anyway."

"That's okay by me, too," George said.

"It's out of the question, whether it's okay by you or not," Jim said.

"Well, I don't want some shyster from in the city handlin' it," George Rapp insisted.

"I don't think you . . ." Jim started.

"Jim," John interrupted, "I'd rather have someone I know and can trust."

"Have you lost your mind, John?" Jim said. "Don't you realize . . . no. Good God, no, I don't think you do!" He stared for a moment at all three of them. Then he turned back to John and said, "If this case comes to trial—and I don't see how that can be avoided now—and these boys are convicted, your seventeen-year-old son might well come out of prison damn near forty!"

For a moment John felt tears well in his eyes, and as he tried not to cry he saw the years, Johnny's best years, wither. He saw the life he had given his son, not taken by some unfathomable yet acceptable act of God, but transformed by a grotesque foolishness into an agony of imprisonment, empty of meaning, empty of purpose, spent in futile retribution. He saw his own life and Mary's—if she were to have one after this—swallowed in the monstrous void of Johnny's punishment. He would have cried had Jim Beyers not spoken again.

"That's the worst that could happen, of course," he said, "but don't forget for one minute that it could happen. So you don't want me. You want the best goddamn criminal lawyer you can get, and you want him fast. There's a man in the city, fellow I went to school with. He's got as good a reputation as any man in the East. I've already put in a call to his office, but he's not expected till about eleven. I'll get to him then."

"Whatever you say, Jim," John said.

"Yeah," George Rapp agreed, "whatever you say."

"How could my boy—how could any of these boys do such a terrible thing?" Mr. Schlier said in his heavy accent, looking at them as if he expected someone to answer and tell him how they could have done it.

"Mr. Schlier," Jim Beyers said, "you don't actually know that they did such a terrible thing."

"But that poor little girl," he said. "Look at her!"

"All right," Jim said sharply. "They were all out together in Armand Rapp's car, and the boys got fresh with her. She panicked and jumped out of the moving car. They were scared and didn't go back to see if she was hurt. That's one explanation for her looking like that, since you seem to expect one. It's a crime, too—but it isn't rape. So you don't know that your son raped that girl."

Mr. Schlier looked at Artie, then back at Jim Beyers.

"No," he said, "but I'm afraid that he did."

Very suddenly the door opened, and a red-faced man of about sixty-five strode into the room and up to the desk.

"Hello, Harry, Ziggy," he said. "Got here as soon as I could. Left two patients sitting in my waiting room. Why, hello, John, Jim. And George Rapp."

He stopped talking and turned in a full circle, looking around the room. There was not a face in the room which he did not recognize. Some of those faces he had lovingly coaxed into the world. He had probed and peered intimately, skillfully into the bodies of most of them. Through this intimacy he had come to regard these people—in fact, all people—as his wards, to be not only healed, but protected, guided, scolded. And curiously for most of these people—regardless of their ages—the attitude was a reciprocal one.

"Over here, Dr. McKenna," Peg Praul said. "It's my little girl."

"You mean Ida?" he asked, starting toward them. "By God!" he said as Peg assisted the girl to rise from the bench again. "Bring her across the hall."

He took Ida's arm, and the three of them left the room.

When John turned toward the door to watch them leave, he saw Johnny, sitting on the end of the bench, staring at the floor. Quickly he looked at Armand and Artie and he shuddered, for all three, as if in a concert of guilt, stared fixedly downward, their faces identically empty of expression. Yet despite their mutual preoccupation, there was a loneliness about them which isolated them as much from each other as from everyone else. He crossed the room and sat beside Johnny.

"It's all right, son," John said. "We'll stick by you."

"What . . . what can they do to us, Dad?" Johnny said without looking up.

"Don't worry about that," John answered, feeling suddenly guilty for his sympathy with this rapist, yet unable to do anything but indulge his sympathy. "We'll have one of the best lawyers in the East. Don't you worry." And with an insistent disgust he thought, *Guilty or not, don't you worry.*

"But . . . what can they do to us?"

"Johnny, I said don't worry about it," John answered almost harshly.

"I'll find out eventually. I'd rather know right now, Dad."
"You can't think about that. Maybe there won't even be a trial."
"But if there is?"
"If there is, we'll win it."
"Dad," he said, looking up at him now, "if there is a trial and we don't win it, then what?"
"Johnny..."
"Dad, tell me."
"Well... prison."
"How long?"
"Nobody can know that. And it's not going to happen, so..."
"Don't make me ask you over and over, please. How long at the most?"
"At the very worst—and it won't come to that—at the worst..."
"What?"
"Maybe... twenty years. But it won't come to that, Johnny."
"What would Mother do?" he said, staring at the floor again.

John had no chance to answer this unanswerable question.

Just as suddenly as it had before, the door burst open and Dr. McKenna came in, followed by Peg Praul.

"Would you please tell me, Harry Loomis, why in the name of God that injured girl has been in this police station since six-thirty this morning without anyone calling a doctor?" He picked up the telephone on the desk and dialed a number, talking as he did so. "That it didn't occur to this ignorant, selfish woman who hasn't the instinct of a sow with a baby pig, I can with great disgust understand! But that you could sit here— This is Dr. McKenna. I want an ambulance at the Borough Hall immediately.... Yes.... All right—but that you could sit here in the same room with that bleeding child and not call a doctor is enough to put you out of office and in a prison cell yourself!" He slammed the telephone into the cradle and looked around the room, his greenish eyes staring in outrage. "A blind man could have seen that that girl was hurt. Are you all so deeply concerned with the plight of the men who raped her—and somebody sure as hell did—that you have no regard for the victim?"

"Is she hurt bad, Doctor?" Peg Praul asked.

"If I weren't compelled by the courtesies of my profession to inform you, you'd be the last person in the world I'd tell! I was called in here only to determine whether or not the girl had been sexually attacked. You all—including you, Mrs. Praul—seem far more interested in proving or disproving rape than you are in Ida's physical well-being, or you'd have called me a damn sight sooner! I don't know how badly she's hurt—but she's been assaulted, and she's in deep shock! She should have been in a hospital hours ago, and would have been, with any normal mother, or normal law enforcement officers either!"

He slammed the door in the face of the abjectly pursuing Peg Praul and left in the room a stunned silence. The sound of the telephone was like a tinkling cannon.

"Magistrate Loomis speaking," Harry Loomis said, trying to recover some measure of his shattered officialness. "Yes, I called him. . . . No. . . . No, he couldn't get back in time anyway. . . . Yes, would you do that? He has my number. . . . Yes, thank you very much." He sat back in his chair and with his arms extended placed both his palms flat on the desk. His head was tilted slightly forward and his eyes were focused on nothing, his lower lip protruding thoughtfully. After a moment he turned his head toward the men in the corner. "Jim," he said.

Jim Beyers went to the desk and bent close to Harry Loomis' ear.

"I hope you understand that I'm in no position to fix bail in this case," he said quietly. "Unfortunately, there is no county judge sitting until Monday. I . . . I don't like to do this, but I'm afraid I'll have to hold the boys until then."

"Couldn't you release them in the custody of their parents?" Jim asked.

"You're asking me to release three accused rapists?" he asked. "You've been in civil law too long, Jim."

"But, Harry, two of them are just high-school kids. You can't lock them up in those lousy cells back there for two days."

"They might get locked up for a lot longer than that."

"Release them in *my* custody, then. I'll take full respon—"

"The responsibility is mine, not yours."

"Give them a break."

"Would you release them if you were me?"

After a moment, Jim said, "I don't know."

"I'm going to hold 'em."

"All right, Harry," Jim Beyers said. "I'll tell them."

He went back to the others, calling John to the corner again. "I'm afraid your boys are going to have to stay here over the weekend," he said.

"Jim, can't we . . . post bail or something?" John asked.

"No," Jim answered. "John, if the girl were Lois, would you want the boys who might have raped her running around loose for the weekend?" There was no answer, and he said, "It doesn't mean anything in the long run. It's just . . . unpleasant. But that's how it is."

"You folks can . . . visit as much as you like," Harry Loomis said, standing up behind the desk. No one answered and he picked up his briefcase and left the room.

Ben Summerfield had received his instructions from the magistrate and he moved to obey them. Then there occurred a series of events which seemed entirely appropriate to the onlookers, yet extraordinary to the participants. With a resounding Teutonic moan, Mrs. Schlier lurched across the bench to embrace her son. George Rapp shuffled with inarticulate embarrassment toward Armand. John and Johnny Taylor stared at each other with more mutual concern for Mary Taylor than they felt for each other or for themselves. In a few seconds Artie had wrenched free of his still sobbing mother, Armand had turned silently from his outsized father and Johnny, without a word, stood up to join Ben Summerfield at the door. In a moment the boys were gone, and their parents stood together in the small room, each avoiding the eyes of the others, for their curious want of something to say. Then slowly they filed past Peg Praul and out into the street, where the siren of the ambulance could already be heard.

V.

Lois' bedroom was at the front of the house, and she had crouched at the window looking like a mischievous elf, but with brimming eyes wetting the sill as she watched the ominous black sedan in the street below. She had seen that man (once Mr. Summerfield, but now a Russian secret policeman) take Johnny out to the car. She had waited, paralyzed with dread, for the car to drive away, when she was sure her heart would stop beating and she would die of her brother's aloneness. When her father had appeared beyond the edge of the sunporch roof, she had nearly cried out through the open window, "Daddy! Daddy, bring him back!" but she hadn't, only hoped that he would and cried harder, though still silently. She had watched him get into the car, seen it pull away from the curb and turn into Elm Street, and the thought that Johnny was no longer so completely alone did little to comfort her. Like a swimmer starting a backstroke, she pushed herself away from the window and, with a wail that served as proxy for all her silent weeping, started for the stairs.

Still standing in the doorway, Mary heard the thumping of Lois' feet on the stairs. It was different from the sound of her ordinary descent only in that it was accompanied by her shrill weeping. Mary turned and saw her standing in the sunporch doorway, her face soaked with tears and her eyes wide and questioning. She turned away from her daughter's look and closed the front door, for she realized that she had no answers to give. She could not tell her what little she knew of the truth; ingenious as she had always been at manufacturing stories for Lois, her own emotional state and Johnny's enigmatic arrest created a challenge she could not meet. Again Mary turned toward her daughter only to find her waiting with unusual patience.

"Let's clean . . . up the dishes, Lois," Mary said, starting for the kitchen.

She had not known what she expected Lois to do then, but she felt no surprise at being halted by the barrier of Lois' little body, fixed in the doorway.

"Mother!" Lois said, prolonging the syllables, so that the word rang with her incredulity.

"What, Lois?" Mary said, and she was angered because she felt ashamed without knowing why.

Lois frowned and, shaking her head slightly as if she could not believe that she had to ask, said, "Why did they take Johnny away?"

"I . . . I don't know, Lois," Mary said.

"You let them take Johnny away and you don't even know why?"

"I mean I don't know for sure," Mary said, her confusion mounting. "And besides, they didn't 'take Johnny away.'"

"Yes, they did!" Lois cried. "I saw them!"

"Johnny and your father went to answer some questions. They'll be back in a little while."

"That's not true, Mother. I know it isn't."

"Lois!"

"Then tell me what they have to answer questions about! And why did Johnny have to go?"

"Lois, I'm your mother. Don't pester me like that."

"Then tell me, Mother."

"I don't know for sure. Your father knows. We'll just have to wait."

"I don't believe you!"

"Lois . . . Lois, go into the living room at once."

Lois turned, ran across the room and threw herself onto the sofa, sobbing loudly. Mary stood by the porch door for a moment, her hand raised to her forehead, trying desperately to think of some word which would not only calm Lois, but would allay her own steadily heightening confusion. Then, pulling her housecoat more snugly about her and tightening the half bow of its belt, she followed her into the room.

"Lois, you mustn't behave like this," Mary said. "You're not old enough. You're a little girl, and little girls just can't expect to know and discuss all the things that adults do."

Lois looked up at her mother, her crying quite suddenly suspended. Her eyes looked now like wet wounds.

"Then you do know why they took him!" she said.

"I told you, I don't know for sure."

"And you wouldn't tell me if you did!" she cried, and Mary was startled by the malice on Lois' little girl face.

"Lois, you'll understand when—"

"He must have done something horrible!" Lois said.

"Lois!"

"If you can't tell me it must be something horrible!"

Mary was stunned into silence by this irrefutable logic, and in the silence she began to apply that logic to herself. She remembered John's expression after he had talked to Ben Summerfield, his extraordinary conference upstairs with Johnny, his strange, halting speech and numbed manner, his instructions about visitors, his vagueness about the alleged offense. As nearly unthinkable as Johnny's being a thief was to her, it seemed now insufficient motive for any of John's behavior. Her suspicion awakened terror in her own mind, and her terror more certain suspicion. If *she* couldn't be told, it must indeed be something horrible.

Lois was standing now and crying again as she stared at her mother.

"You . . . mustn't say . . . that," Mary said, and her image of Lois blurred through her own tears. She thrust her handkerchief to her mouth to gag the sound of her crying, but it did little good. They stood facing each other, their mutual weeping in mutal fear the only evidence of their sharing, until Lois moved suddenly and Mary, half extending her arms, for a few terrible seconds was both afraid that her daughter would come to her and afraid that she would not. Then she realized that Lois had passed her and run up the stairs to her room.

Mary was not one to cry, even when she thought it might help her. Resolutely, she pushed her handkerchief into the pocket of her housecoat and went into the kitchen. As she cleared the table of the breakfast dishes and, again as she ran the steaming dishwater, she consciously had to pull her mind out of an undercurrent of thought. This disturbed her deeply, for her old trick of busying herself into thoughtlessness had always been one of the major comforts of her life. She found herself wondering if perhaps she ought to have told Lois something, even the truth. But was it true that Johnny had stolen? It couldn't be, so there was no point in distressing Lois with something that would turn out to be only an accusation. Then why had Ben Summerfield taken him away like that? What if it was true?

"It couldn't be. It couldn't be," she kept repeating half aloud, and beneath the utterance she was thinking: if I can't accept it myself, how could I expect a thirteen-year-old girl to accept it?

When she had finished the dishes and scoured the sink, she dried her hand with paper towels and leaned backward against the stove to inspect the kitchen. There was no more to be done. She threw the crumpled paper towels into the wastebasket and went upstairs to change into a dress.

The door to Lois' room was closed, and Mary decided not to look in on her. She went to her own room and closed the door behind her. She took her underclothing from a bureau drawer and opened the double doors of her clothes closet. The underclothing she put on a shelf in the closet. Then she took off her housecoat and nightgown. Deftly, almost hurriedly, she put on her brassiere, panties and slip, so that she was not naked for more than a few seconds. Mary was uncomfortable when she was naked, even while bathing.

She slipped into a cotton housedress with tiny, pale printed flowers, crossed to her dressing table and sat on the bench before it. Mary used her mirror only to see what she was doing. She rarely simply looked at her image. If she had, she would have seen that she was no longer pretty as she had once been. Had she been in the least vain, she could have been an attractive woman. Her figure was still good, her features were almost monotonously regular and her hair was a not unpleasant shade of brown. But the most Mary ever achieved at her dressing table was an appearance of extreme and agreeable neatness. If her hair had been prematurely gray, she might have been striking, for her skin was smooth and clear. But Mary did not hope for this; she was not even aware that it might eventually happen.

She had brushed her hair and put on lipstick and was standing in the upstairs hall trying to decide whether or not she should go in to see Lois when the doorbell rang. She started nervously and felt a flush upon her skin. It was an unusual reaction for her, and it reminded her of the cause of her nervousness. She went downstairs and saw that her neighbor, Frances McGovern, had rung the bell and stood peering anxiously through the panes of the front door. As she stepped into the sunporch, she remembered John's asking her not to let anyone in, but now, with this woman standing at the door, it seemed silly. Anyway, it certainly couldn't apply to Frances McGovern. And even if it did, there was absolutely no way Mary could refuse her entrance to the house.

Frances McGovern's maiden name was Frances Moriarty. Her mother's maiden name was Kelly, and her father's mother's maiden name was McCall. Among her great-great-grandparents' names were O'Brien and McCarthy and Shaughnessy and Riordan. Whether as a matter of principle or merely by accident no one seemed to know, but the enchanted Gaelic line had never been broken. Social progress had been forced upon succeeding generations only by irresistible economic pressures, and Frances, leaning as she did towards the ways of her earlier forbears, regressed wherever possible. Had Mary met her later in life, she would probably have loathed her, but they had gone to school together (Frances only for nine years) and had been friends for most of their lives. Mary did not approve of most aspects of Frances' life and person, most conspicuously of her speech. But over the years Frances had been Mary's most reliable friend and neighbor and that reliability was a quality which Mary valued.

Mary opened the front door and said, "Hello, Fran."

"I came as soon as I heard. Jesus!" Frances McGovern said, coming into the house and going straight to the kitchen, which was her natural habitat.

"What do you mean?" Mary said, following her guest.

Frances turned abruptly in the kitchen doorway. "About Johnny," she said.

"How . . . could you hear about Johnny?" Mary asked, amazed.

"Mare, is there anything I can do?" (Wherever feasible, Fran reduced given names to their first syllable.)

"How could you hear about Johnny, Frances?"

"Kay Beyers called me," she answered. With obvious effort she lowered her short, round body into a chair. "That wasn't what she called me about, of course, but she told me."

"Oh," Mary said quietly. "John called Jim."

" 'Course I was already on my way over when the phone rang. I seen Ben Summerfield's car out front. And when John and Johnny drove off with him, I said to myself, 'You better get your ass over there and see Mare. She's goin' to need somebody.' "

"Well, I don't, Fran," Mary said. "I appreciate it though. Want some coffee? There's some from breakfast. We didn't have a chance . . . we didn't drink it all."

"No, but I'd sell my soul for a glass of beer. I'm spittin' feathers."

Her large, dark-rimmed blue eyes followed Mary to the refrigerator and stared at her frankly as she poured the beer. Frances did not always analyze situations fact against fact, but she knew many things intuitively and trusted her intuition implicitly. She was aware of and admired Mary's powers of restraint, but she also knew Mary's weaknesses and that this situation would strike at the heart of them. Mary was too calm. Something was wrong.

Mary put the glass of beer and the open bottle on the table before Frances. Frances picked up the large glass and drank three-quarters of its contents without a pause. Through the line of foam on her upper lip she said, "Jesus, Mare, is there anything as good as a glass of beer in the morning?" She wiped away the foam with the back of her hand. Mary was standing at the stove, waiting for the coffee to reheat. Looking directly at her back, Frances said, "I bet you haven't even cried yet, have you?"

Without turning Mary said, "No, why should I cry?"

She poured the coffee and sat down at the table while Frances watched her steadily, both genuine concern and irrepressible curiosity driving her on.

As Mary stared at her coffee without speaking, Frances said, "I never knew anybody like you. If it was me, I'd be up to my ass in tears by now. And if the truth was known, I bet you'd feel a hell of a lot better for a good cry yourself."

"There's no reason to cry. Johnny didn't do it."

"Oh," Frances said, lifting her eyebrows. "Then that's that."

She drank the rest of the beer in the glass and began pouring from the bottle. She stopped suddenly, and looking wide-eyed at Mary, said, "Holy Christ, Mare! Where's Lo!"

"Upstairs in her room."

"You didn't tell her?"

"No, I just couldn't. I don't know what to tell her, Fran."

"Jesus, Mary and Joseph!" Frances said, her hand covering her eyes. "I never even thought of it till now. What can you tell her?"

"I'm hoping it'll all be over so quickly that she won't have to know much about it."

"But even if it blows over, it'll be in the papers."

"Maybe John could call Bill Phipps down at the *Clarion* and keep it out."

"Not if I know Peg Praul," Frances said, pouring the rest of the beer. "And I'm sorry to say I do."

"Oh, Fran!" Mary said, her face tightened into a frown. "It wasn't Peg Praul they robbed?"

"Robbed? Mare, what do you—oh. . . . Oh, no. Kay Beyers just men—"

She could go no further. She sat staring at Mary, her teeth clenched and her own forehead wrinkled now. Mary stared back, her face holding on to its frown. Both their minds seethed with unwanted, eagerly pursued thoughts. Frances knew at once what was wrong and, as she thought of John's futile efforts to protect Mary, she cursed herself. Her brain darted vainly in all directions after some way to undo the damage and the result was only remorse and confusion. Mary realized that somehow, without knowing it, out of her own suspicion she had led Frances on. And now at only a hint of what must be this unbearable truth, she wished that she had not, that she could lead Frances back, back to that less cruel ignorance that had been hers but a few minutes ago. But as surely as Frances had been unable to go further, Mary was unable not to.

"Tell me, Fran," Mary said.

"There's nothin' to tell, Mare," Frances answered. "Kay Beyers told me about it and said somethin' about Peg Praul bein' mixed up in it. That's all."

"All right," Mary said, getting up from the table. "If you won't tell me, I'm going down there to the police station and find out for myself."

"Don't do that, Mare."

"I've had enough of being lied to. I'm not a child like Lois. Nobody has a right to keep the truth about my own son from me!"

"John was only tryin' to help. He knows he can't keep it from you."

"What is it, Frances?" Mary said, leaning on the table. "For God's sake, tell me. Johnny didn't get mixed up with Peg Praul?"

"No. No, Mare, it's not that."

"Then what is it?"

"I could cut my goddamn tongue out!"

"You said yourself John knows he can't keep it from me. He'll have to tell me when he comes home. So you tell me . . . please, Frances!"

"All right. Sit down," Frances said. As Mary sat down again, Frances tilted the beer glass toward herself and looked into it. "Peg Praul's little daughter, Ida, says that Johnny and two other boys . . . raped her . . . last night."

Mary was so fully aware of a number of reactions that she felt almost conscious of having to make a choice among them. For the first time in many years she thought of Johnny's body, and she saw it in her mind as she had last seen it in reality: as it had been when he was eight years old. She had opened the door without knocking and gone into his bedroom as he was preparing for bed. He had turned at the sound of the door and stood for a few seconds naked, holding his pajama pants in one hand. She had seen the pale, flawless skin stretched thinly over the evident ribs; seen the now flattening midriff, the regrettably obsolete navel. She had seen the dear, hairless abdomen, the precious lack of development between the long, hidden muscles of the thighs. Then, swiftly, he had pulled the pajama pants across him and killed her joy. "Excuse me," she had said and left the room, closing the door behind her. She had put out of her mind her incompleted thoughts, but the image had remained always. Now again it flashed across her mind, and in its wake came an image of Johnny as she had last seen him: handsome, adolescent, nearly six feet tall. Then this image, too, was naked, and she was sickened by the sight of it. Yet her revulsion did not disperse it, but she saw it at its man's work on the vague and misty body of a female child. There rose in her a hot, senseless anger toward Frances McGovern, and she put it down with her hatred of Peg Praul, who deserved just such justice. She was filled with a surge of abysmal pity for Peg Praul's daughter, who she remembered was in Johnny's class at school. Again she thought of Johnny with a pain and dread which caused a low, prolonged sound to issue from her throat. Her mind began to fill with speculative pictures of the time and place and manner of the alleged act, until it brimmed so, that there was no longer any thought. There remained only an almost physical struggle against even the possibility that it could be true.

"I don't believe it!" Mary said. "I *won't* believe it!"

"I know it don't seem possible," Frances said.

"You know Johnny, Fran. Why, he couldn't even . . . have relations with a girl who'd let him, let alone . . . rape somebody."

"Sure, Mare."

"Well, he couldn't! You know he couldn't!"

"Johnny's one of the best kids I ever knew," Frances answered. "And I'll be goddamned if I can imagine him rapin' Ida Praul or . . ."

"Is that her name?" Mary asked quietly.

"Yeah, Ida. Or anybody else. But Johnny's seventeen years old, Mare. Hell, the first boy I ever slept with was fourteen."

"I don't want you telling me that you think he . . ."

"I said I couldn't imagine Johnny doin' it. But you always think of Johnny as a baby. That ain't a good idea. Why, I bet you if he wanted to, Johnny could do it to a girl as good as . . . well, as my old man could. Not that that's sayin' so much. Mare, I'm one for speakin' the truth. When I want to tell a lie for a good reason, I tell one, but there's a time for the truth. And the truth is I don't think Johnny did it, but Jesus Christ, Mare, I'd almost rather think he did do it than to think he couldn't. . . . Not the rape, the rest of it, I mean."

"Who are the others?" Mary asked.

"George Rapp's son, Armand. And some kid named Artie somethin'-or-other. German. I don't know him. Now, that Armand Rapp, that big, fat slob—hah! Look who's talkin'—he could rape the blessed Saint Theresa without a wink."

"Fran . . ." Mary said faintly.

"Oh, Christ, Mare, I'm sorry! You got any whiskey? Why don't you have yourself a good shot?"

"Fran, is it . . . all over town?"

"Well, if it ain't, it's a wonder. That Peg Praul should've been put away years ago for her own good. At six-thirty this mornin' with people already on their way to work, walkin' and ridin' the buses, she dragged that little girl through the streets all the way from her place down to the Borough Hall! If that ain't the work of a woman without all her buttons, I don't know what is!"

"I don't think even Peg Praul would've done that unless . . . unless she had some real reason."

"That doesn't mean that Johnny had anything to do with it."

Looking toward the ceiling, Mary said, "Even if he didn't, what are we going to tell Lois?"

"Mother of Jesus, Mare, I don't know! I just don't know!"

They did not know that there was no longer any reason to invent a story. Lois had heard the doorbell and had come half way down the stairs and crouched there throughout their conversation, forming a quite new, quite distorted image of her mother and Frances McGovern.

VI.

As John and the others came into the street, the ambulance stopped before the Borough Hall, its whining siren dropping in pitch to a low growl and then into silence. On the way its piping had lured the curious, the idle, the adventurous in its wake, and they began to arrive, some hurrying joyfully, some pretending to have happened by, some frowning in excited expectation of the dire. As they formed a group outside the building they began to question each other.

The driver of the ambulance and a white-suited interne appeared supporting Ida between them, her arms across their shoulders. Behind them came Dr. McKenna and, immediately behind him, Peg Praul, hurrying as if to catch up with the others, but reluctant to pass Dr. McKenna.

"There's Peg Praul!" a voice said.

"Hey! That's Peg's daughter there! The hurt one!"

"Name's Ida," the boy said.

"You don't suppose somebody shot Ida Praul?"

"Ain't you heard? She got raped last night!"

"What's it all about?" someone asked John Taylor, who had come out of the Borough Hall with the others.

"I don't know," he said, without looking at his questioner.

John and the others who had been inside had been absorbed by the crowd so that they were in no way outstanding. Ida was helped into the ambulance and Dr. McKenna climbed in behind her. Peg Praul stood in the street looking through the open door of the ambulance at Dr. McKenna. He extended a hand toward her, and she took it, pulled herself inside and sat next to her daughter. The siren started again and at so short a distance its sound was personal and frightening, and it demanded the crowd's attention. The ambulance pulled away from the curb, and every face was turned toward it. The silence it left was soon filled with the anti-climactic exchanges of the spontaneous little gathering, which had already begun to disperse. In a few minutes there remained, standing strangely apart, only the five people who had come from inside the Borough Hall.

"There's nothing more to do right now," Jim Beyers said. "You might as well go on home. I'll be in touch with you."

"Okay, Jim," George Rapp said. He looked at the others, then turned and walked away.

"You'll hear from me, Mr. Schlier," Jim said in the silence.

"Thank you. Thank you, Mr. Beyers. Goodbye, Mr. Taylor," Otto Schlier said. He took his wife's arm gently and, talking to her quietly in German, went through the street toward their home.

"Did you drive down, John?" Jim asked.

"No, I came down with Ben and the boy."

"Come on. I'll drop you at the house."

"I think I'd rather walk, Jim."

"Oh. Sure. I'll call you as soon as I hear from the city. Where will you be, at home or at the lot?"

"I think I'll be home. I've got to tell Mary sometime. It might as well be now."

"I don't envy you that."

"I don't know just how to do it."

"She's a grown woman, John. Just tell her."

"Yeah. I guess that's it. I'll be waiting to hear from you."

John watched Jim Beyers get into his car and drive away. Jim hurried a bit, for he felt that John was waiting for him to go, although he did not know exactly why. The car stopped for a traffic light at the corner, then turned north on Main Street.

John waited for a moment longer and started in the opposite direction from the one Jim had taken. He felt suddenly impatient with himself. He took the last cigarette from his package, crumpled the empty package fiercely and threw it as far out into the street as he could. He tried twice to light the cigarette while walking, and each time the match went out before he succeeded. He stopped walking and took a deep breath to help put down his rising anger. Then he struck another match, cupped it too closely and burned his hand. Having now a recognizable excuse for his anger, he muttered, "Son of a bitch!" and threw the burnt match to the ground. Quickly, self-consciously, he looked up at the frame houses on both sides of him, sitting pompously above the sidewalks on their high, green banks. On the porch of the one nearest him sat an old man, working his rocking chair with deliberate enthusiasm. His eyes were so large and so unnaturally bright that even from the sidewalk John could see their faint, vitreous blue shining with that same vacant intensity with which he rocked. All at once the eyes seemed to John to be focused on him, mocking his burnt finger and his cold cigarette. He looked away from the old man, struck another match and rushed it to his cigarette so that the first puff of smoke was filled with the hot, sour, yellow taste of burning sulphur. He walked up the hill through the tunnel of green-perched houses until he realized that he was hunched and hurrying as if he were running a gamut of curious spectators. He stopped suddenly, startled, pulling back his shoulders and found himself standing in the shade of a large and ancient maple tree at the corner of Fourth Avenue and Spencer Street. He had not stood on this corner for many years, for he had had no reason to be there. Nor had he one now, and he did not like being there without knowing why.

He looked for a beginning of what he now admitted was his strange behavior, and his mind went back to an image of Jim Beyers getting into his car. Why had he waited until Jim was out of sight before starting home this long way? Jim certainly understood his need to be alone, to have time to think. Jim was a good friend, a little stubborn sometimes and with a lot of opinions, but a good friend. He had known Jim almost all his life, and he . . . why had he waited until Jim was out of sight? But he'd already answered that; there was no use going over and over it. Jim had always been a good friend. When Mary was in the hospital and he'd lost his job, it was Jim . . . but why had he waited? There wasn't time to go back over every thought. A question comes up, the answer pops into your mind and you go on. You don't have to remember the answer. You know you answered it at the time, and that's enough. What was he thinking about? Jim Beyers. He remembered when Jim had graduated from high school and gone to college. It must be nice to come from a family with enough money just to send you to college when the time comes. His own family . . . but why? The question struck at him again. All right. It was something about Jim understanding his need to be alone. . . . No, that didn't make sense. Well, it wasn't important. There were other things to be thought about. There was Johnny in jail. And there was Mary waiting to be told. That was what he had to think about. What was the best way to tell Mary that . . . why had he waited? The question would not be dismissed.

He was still in the shade of the big tree, and he looked up at the intricate black and green pattern above him. He was here in this quiet, untrafficked part of town because he was ashamed to be seen. He had waited until Jim Beyers was out of sight before coming this way because he did not want Jim Beyers to see his shame.

He stood for a moment dazzled by the mystery, by the sweet relief of self-understanding. He frowned up at the leaves, remembering how hard he had tried to avoid that truth, how skillfully he had dodged the question, how cleverly he had tried to convince himself that he had already answered it. His mind darkened like the shade around him as he thought how many questions he had succeeded in escaping, how many senseless answers he had accepted of himself in more than half a lifetime.

He moved out of the shade, across Fourth Avenue and up the continuing slope of Spencer Street. It wasn't enough, he told himself, just to be ashamed. He had to know *why* he was ashamed. He was startled now, for he had expected the answer to be there. He had thought somehow that merely to ask was to know. And so he was shocked to find no reason for his shame.

Why *am* I ashamed? he asked. He looked about him at these other houses, come down now off their green banks as the hill become gentler. Why am I skulking through the back streets of town like a—yes, like a criminal. I am, after all, not a criminal. Here in this lonely place of truth he could say it, perhaps nowhere else, perhaps never again, but now he could say it. There was a criminal, and he was in jail. The criminal's name was John Taylor. And he was the flesh of his flesh, the fruit of his seed, his son.

As he climbed that gentle slope John Taylor made a decision, for truth appeared suddenly, remarkably: if he was to be ashamed, he must find a reason for his shame; if he could find no reason, he would not be ashamed.

He searched as ruthlessly as he was able for the reason. What had he, as a part of his son's life, done or not done that would afford him some measure of responsibility for this criminal act? Could some unknown act of his have served as example for this crime? Was it possible to have failed so completely as a father without knowing of the failure?

What kind of life had John Taylor, Jr., had? Or, more importantly, what kind of life had he given John Taylor, Jr.? The only financial difficulties his family had ever experienced had been too early in his life for him even to have been aware of them. Things had been fairly good after that. He had always had an allowance, large enough for his limited needs, yet small enough to teach him the value of a dollar. He had known summer trips to local lakes and amusement parks and yearly excursions to the seashore. He had been given a church and enrolled in and faithfully sent to its Sunday School. Perhaps John could have been a little more active in the church, could have urged Johnny to take more interest in it himself, but Holy God, a boy doesn't commit rape because his father doesn't go to church every Sunday!

Certainly he had never seen or heard anything dirty in his own home. Oh, no: Mary, with her modesty, could never be accused of letting anything... smutty... happen or be said in front of the children. Nor had they ever fought in front of the children, however things may have been going between them. In the last year, even over Mary's objections, he had tried to be a little freer with his talk when Johnny was around, and rightly so. Seventeen wasn't too early to start including the boy in such things. No doubt he was finding out a lot more than they guessed, anyway, as boys always do. It was a healthy thing to start including him. When had he started doing that? It had been very deliberate, he remembered. It was last winter. Lois had gone off to a Girl Scout meeting, and Johnny had just finished his homework and come into the living room to watch television. Some big-busted blonde in a low-cut dress was on the screen, singing a sultry song. "Oh, turn that off. She's disgusting," Mary had said. "She's not disgusting, Mary," he had answered. "I think she has a certain... appeal." "John," Mary had said, bristling. "Of course, she doesn't appeal to a woman," he had said to his wife, "but she does have a certain appeal for a man. Right, Johnny?" "Yeah, but we're missin' the Nelsons, Dad. It sounded pretty funny in *TV Guide,*" Johnny had said.

That had been the first time any reference to sex had been made in front... no, there had been something else, something earlier. It had been a long time ago. Then the whole unpleasant atmosphere began drifting back, to surround him like a crawling, summer fog.

It had been an unpleasant day; not a customer had come near the lot. He had come home—to their old house, the rented one—tired from the tension and inactivity. He had not taken off his overcoat when Mary had come hurrying through the living room.

"John, I have to talk to you about something," she said.

"What's wrong?" he asked recognizing the anxiety in her voice.

"It's Johnny."

"Mary, what do you mean, 'It's Johnny'?" he asked irritably. "What's wrong with him?"

"You don't have to bite my head off," she answered. "It's not my fault."

"I've had a long day, Mary," he said wearily. "A long day without customers. If this is something serious you want to talk to me about, all right. If it isn't, I don't want to be bothered."

"If it wasn't something serious, I wouldn't bring it up at all."

He took off his coat and put it into the closet while Mary stood waiting obviously for the end of these necessary, irritating mechanics. He went by her and sat in his chair by the radio under the bridge lamp. She stood for a moment facing the closet as if he had left the room, then she turned toward him and said, "Johnny had some trouble at school. An awful kind."

"What other kind of trouble is there, Mary?"

"This is something even you have to take seriously—as hard as that may be for you."

"All right. Just tell me."

"I know you've noticed; I've seen you looking. I guess we should've talked about it before, but we didn't. Johnny just won't keep his hands out of his pockets."

"Oh, Mary, for Christ's sake."

"You know what I mean. I've seen you looking."

"So it's winter. His hands are cold and he puts them in his pockets," John said, deliberately baiting her. He picked up the evening newspaper and began to read.

"John," Mary said.

"Mary, you're a grown-up woman and a mother. If you mean your son plays with himself and you want to say so, I'll talk to you about it. If that's what you mean and you can't say so, I don't think it'd do much good to talk to you."

"The fact that you're vulgar and I'm not isn't the point."

"What is the point?"

"Now, you listen to me, John Taylor. His teacher, Miss Benson, has told him several times in the last few weeks to take his hands out of his pockets. Well, this morning at school she pinned his pants pockets closed with safety pins."

"She what?"

"You heard me," Mary said, looking away. "I can't think what must be in her mind about us."

"About us?"

"Don't you think she's asked herself what kind of people have a nine-year-old son who . . ."

"I don't give a good goddamn what she thinks about us," John said. "But you know what I think about her? There must be something wrong with her mind."

"Be that as it may, Johnny has to be made to stop doing this."

"He'll stop. He'll get over it."

"John, can't you get it through your head that it's got so bad that even his teacher noticed it?"

"Oh, yes. I've got that through my head, but I find it hard to believe that she did what she did. You mean that Johnny had to go through the whole day in front of all the other kids with safety pins on his pockets?"

"Yes, and I'm afraid it didn't do a bit of good."

"What good could it do?"

"Maybe none, but it's more than we've done about it. I want you to do something right now."

"Like what?"

"I want you to go upstairs and talk to Johnny. He's in his room waiting."

"And what am I going to say to him?"

"For God's sake, John, he's your son, and it's a man's job to talk to him about such things."

"Mary, can't you understand: I just don't know what the hell to say to the boy."

"Well, somebody's got to say something. And you're the somebody. We can't just ignore it any more."

John looked up at the ceiling as if he could see his son through it. "All right," he said. Getting out of the chair was a great effort. "I'll try."

As he went up the stairs, John was conscious of the expenditure of energy necessary to lift each foot to the next step. It was as if he were walking through cold, heavy mud. He realized as he reached the top of the stairs that he was embarrassed, embarrassed to talk about such things with his son. He pulled back his shoulders and thought, "That's goddamned foolish." But his face was flushed as he opened the bedroom door and went in.

Johnny was standing at the far end of the room, looking out of the window. When he turned around at the sound of the opening door, John could not see his deep terror. He could not see the fully incredible tensility of the young nerves, for the unmarked face which he encountered was yet incapable of so terrible an expression. He saw only, without seeing the condition, that even in this abject state Johnny's hands were in his pockets.

"Hi ya, Johnny," John said, closing the door.

"Hello," Johnny said in his little child's voice.

"I hear you had some trouble at school today."

"Yes." And the hands appeared like two frightened pink birds.

"I want you to know that I don't think what Miss Benson did was very . . . smart."

"She pinned my pockets closed," Johnny said, and the first faint droppings from his eyes nearly sent John from the room.

"Yeah, I know," John said. He had been taught to approach children vernacularly. "I don't think she should have done that."

"It was awful, Dad," he said, wet-faced now, and without the sophistication to turn away to hide his crying.

"But then I guess you shouldn't have done what you were doing," John suggested.

"No," Johnny answered.

"Why do you do that?" John asked with a low tremble of laughter trying to soften the question, as much for himself as for Johnny.

"I don't know," the boy said. "Sometimes I don't even know I *am* doing it." One hand now held the other to keep it from its terrible preoccupation.

"It doesn't look very nice, Johnny," and in the back of his mind a lewd, mocking, necessarily insane voice said in Johnny's thin soprano, *Yeah, but it feels nice.* The boldly interrogative expression of his face frightened his son, and he sensed it. But he had to make certain that this burlesque-house event had truly taken place within his mind and had, indeed, nothing to do with his son.

"I don't know why I do it," his son said and ended the brief travesty.

"It would be a lot better if you didn't do it."

"I won't do it any more," Johnny said, and the crying was in his voice now.

"I'd like you to promise me that you won't."

"I promise," and the pink birds fluttered toward John supplicatingly.

"Well, I guess that settles it," John said. "Wash up and come on down to supper."

John had already turned to the door, had his mind on the knob when he heard his son's voice, wet with tears. "I won't do it any more, Dad. I promise!"

He turned around again and said, "I believe you, Johnny." Then he left the room.

He was surprised to see before him the glinting windows of the sunporch of his house. The quiet, thoughtful trip through recently alien streets was over, and he regretted that he had not got much thinking done. He felt, in fact, utterly unprepared to penetrate that glass and painted wood façade to tell his wife that their son was in jail for having raped the daughter of the town whore.

VII.

JIM BEYERS EASED HIS CAR IN BETWEEN THE TWO DIAGONAL WHITE parking lines just in front of 103 Main Street, the Murray Building, where his law office was. He took his car keys, but did not bother to lock the car, not on Main Street in mid-morning.

He climbed the stairs to the second floor and opened the metal and frosted glass door marked James C. Beyers, Attorney at Law. With three strides he crossed the waiting area, then went through the wooden gate past the empty desks of his receptionist and his secretary, noticing only the stillness of the room. He went into his own office, threw his hat on the old, gently billowing leather sofa and sat at his desk. He picked up the telephone and dialed his home. When he heard the busy signal, he hung up and sat back in his swivel chair. He looked around the room and reaffirmed a decision he had made more than a hundred times: even though he could afford it, there was no point in moving to larger or more luxurious offices; the clients he might want to impress were more impressed by frugality than by quite legitimate signs of success.

He smiled to himself and looked across the room at his legal warriors. He went to the book shelves and took down a volume of the State Penal Code. He leafed through it for a moment, then took it to his desk, reading as he returned. After a few minutes he tried his home phone again and found it still busy. He went back to his book and had read for nearly an hour, getting up now and then to check a case citation across the room, when the telephone rang.

"Mr. James C. Beyers, please," an economical female voice said.

"Speaking," Jim answered.

"Just one moment, please. Mr. Stephen Hertzog calling."

Jim heard the click of the "hold" button, a short silence, then: "Jim Beyers! How the hell are you?"

"I'm getting along, Stephen. How are you?"

"Couldn't be better. Do you know it's eighteen years since we've seen each other?"

"I don't think I realized it was quite that long."

"Since our tearful parting at law school. Twenty years ago this summer."

"Eighteen years."

"It's good to hear from you, Jim. What are you up to?"

"Oh, I'm practicing, of course. Have a wife and two kids. Nothing terribly exciting. You've become quite a name in the profession."

"Oh, I'm doing all right. A little work and a lot of luck. What's on your mind, Jim?"

"I have a case that I think may interest you. I'm not sure it's a very desirable case."

"What are you doing, civil?"

"Yes."

"And this is criminal, of course."

"Yes."

"What's the charge?"

"Rape."

"That's always fun. How old's the girl?"

"Seventeen."

"Well, at least it's a girl. How about the man?"

"Men."

"All fifteen years old, I hope."

"Seventeen, seventeen and, I think, nineteen. Take your pick."

"Be a sport. Can't I have all three?"

"Sure, but I'll only guarantee the fee for one."

"We can talk about fees later. Which one's yours?"

"One of the seventeens. Son of a high-school friend of mine. And a hell of a nice boy."

"Apparently. When did he do this nice thing?"

"Last night."

"Where are they now?"

"In the local jail."

"Get them out. Unless, of course, there's evidence to support the complainant's accusation. Is there?"

"There's the outraged indignation of a local physician who seems all too willing to attest to the crime."

70

"That'll do. Did they do it, Jim?"
"My guess is—"
"I didn't ask for your guess. Did they do it?"
"Somebody did or they—"
"Where were you last night?"
"All right, all right. I don't know if they did it."
"Can you find out?"
"I think so."
"Then do."
"What do you think, Stephen? Do you want to take this?"
"I don't know. When can I see the boys?"
"When do you want to?"
"Hold on a minute. I'll check. . . . Tomorrow afternoon. Two o'clock."
"I'll arrange it."
"I'll be driving. Where do I go when I get into town?"
"Okay. You'll probably come over the bridge. Just keep going up Main Street about six blocks. Turn left on Willow Avenue. It's on the left, about a block in."
"I'll see you there at two o'clock."
"Thanks, Stephen."
"And, Jim—"
"What?"
"It was nice to talk to you. See you tomorrow."
"So long."

Jim hung up and stared at the phone. He had not been surprised by Stephen's efficient manner. The minimum of empty, time-wasting amenities was somehow refreshing.

During the first two or three months of school, Jim had felt sorry for Stephen, who seemed to him to be lonely, and he decided to befriend him. Well into their second year, he came to realize that, instead, he had been selected by Stephen to be his friend. He remembered now how it had come about. He hadn't thought of it for years, but now he remembered effortlessly every word of Stephen's explanation. He had been urging Stephen to come into town with the "gang" for an evening of beer drinking, and when Stephen had declined gently, Jim had told him that he mustn't think the other fellows didn't like him.

Stephen had laughed quietly and said, "To me that is of no consequence whatever. Jimmy-boy, cultivating people takes time—something we all have too little of—and most of them aren't worth it. Whenever I get into a new situation, I pick out one or two people I think will be worth it and make friends with them. That's as many as I have time for with all the other things I plan to do. If you try to get to know a hundred people the law of averages almost guarantees you a couple of good experiences. But I don't do anything by the trial-and-error method I can do a more practical way. If I went with you into town, I'd just make your buddies uncomfortable, because they don't know me—and they don't know why they don't. No, you go ahead, Jim. I'll be happy in my scholarly solitude."

Jim remembered, too, that it was a short two months later that he had stood at a school dance with a dozen friends and watched, speechless, Stephen Hertzog's dazzling display of social adroitness. Jim had watched Stephen with a pretty, quiet girl, coming toward that circle of young men and women, with whom Stephen had lived for a year and a half in deliberate self-exile. Jim prepared to lead the group in a show of casual warmth toward this alien. With barely a word to Jim, Stephen had begun an irresistibly witty monologue centered about the most current campus gossip, touching now on some little-known victory of Jack Elliott's, now on a nearly forgotten flash of classroom brilliance by Chick Beardsley, now on a secret vanity of Bobby West's, drawing them each, one by one, into his jocular discourse until those who had not yet been included strained almost visibly in anxious anticipation. Before the evening was over Jack Elliott had danced three times with the pretty, quiet girl whom Stephen had brought. And Stephen had danced three times with Jack's date, Mary Ellen Rafferty, and had arranged to call on her in the city during summer vacation. Jim had not known then that Mary Ellen Rafferty was the daughter of Kevin Rafferty, the boss of the city's ancient but robust political machine.

That was the fundamental ingredient in the formula of success, Jim thought—oh, not the ingenuity or the resourcefulness, but the single-mindedness, the oneness of purpose; the rest would follow if one had that. It was a way of life. Dressing because men of the world of law dress; eating because one had to stay alive to practice the law; sleeping because it refreshed one for the next day's study of the law; smoking or not smoking, loving or not loving, singing or not singing; they were matters of indifference, for they bore no importance in relation to the law. This was the prerequisite for success, not the quiet substantial success which he enjoyed, but for the brilliant, pyrotechnical achievement which Stephen Hertzog knew. Jim did not envy him, for he knew that that way of life must exclude much of living. But for himself . . .

He picked up the phone and dialed his home again, and again the line was busy. He kept the receiver to his ear and heavily pushed down the button to break the connection. Then he dialed John Taylor's number.

"Hello, John? It's Jim Beyers. . . . I just had a call from Stephen Hertzog. He's the attorney I told you about. . . . He's coming up to see us tomorrow. In the afternoon, two o'clock. . . . No, he's going straight to Borough Hall. . . . Well, you'll be there tomorrow at two? You understand that he hasn't definitely taken the case. I imagine we'll know tomorrow. . . . All right. I'll see you then!"

He hung up and leaned back in his chair and sighed a deep sigh of sympathy for John Taylor. Of all people for this to happen to, John Taylor seemed to Jim about the least likely. And Mary—by modern standards Mary was strict with her kids. Hell, she was practically Victorian. How could this happen in such a family? There just wasn't any way of knowing what kids were going to do, no matter how carefully you brought them up. Some outside influence that you couldn't possibly know about. . . . Of course, it had to be that in John's case, just as it would have to have been in his own. His own kids. No, not happy, oblivious little Seth, right smack in the throes of puberty without even knowing it. And David—well, David was just too bright, even at seventeen, to get himself into this kind of trouble. Not that Johnny Taylor wasn't a bright boy and a damned nice one, too. What could have happened? What ever could have made him do such a thing? Poor John. Just about the only man in town he knew well and unequivocally liked. Too bad John wasn't able to get to college. He would have made a hell of a . . . a hell of a what? Pretty much anything he wanted to be with a little guidance and a decent education. Probably would have made a better marriage, somebody with some spirit, some real warmth. Oh, Mary was a good wife. Nobody with a pair of eyes could deny that, but . . . he was never entirely comfortable with Mary. He sometimes wondered if John was. They'd have to have the Taylors over to dinner in the next few days. Only a gesture, but a decent one. Yes, they'd do that—regardless of Kay's inevitable objections. He'd simply insist. What the hell was she doing on that telephone?

He tried his own number again and finding it busy, hung up and dialed it again and again and again with increasing intensity until finally there was the pause for the miracle mechanics to take place and he knew the phone was going to ring.

"Hello," his wife's voice said innocently, unaware of his impatience.

"I've been trying to get you for over an hour. What have you been doing on that telephone?"

"Why, I only talked to a couple of people. You must have called at just the wrong times."

"Kay, I have called intermittently for . . . oh, never mind. Who were you talking to?"

"Who?" She waited as if trying to remember. "What a strange question. Just a couple of the girls."

"What about?"

"What on earth is wrong with you, Jim?"

"Nothing is wrong with me. I asked you a simple question. What were you talking about?"

"Well, let me see: a recipe for angel food cake, the thunderstorm on Tuesday, the PTA meeting next Thursday . . ." She paused.

"What else?"

"Jim, don't deliberately make me angry."

"You weren't by any chance discussing Johnny Taylor during either of those 'two' phone calls?"

"The subject came up."

"And I don't suppose you made any calls specifically to discuss Johnny Taylor?"

"I did not."

"Kay, I'm not going to go into the age-old discussion with you about the ethics of my profession, and I'm not going to try again to convince you that you are bound by those ethics not to discuss any part of my business affairs with anybody, even if you happen to have come upon such information inadvertently. I simply and firmly forbid you to discuss with anyone Johnny Taylor or any aspect of his case."

"Jim, if somebody calls me and asks if I know where Johnny Taylor lives, I can't say, 'No, I don't,' just because he's a client of yours."

"He is not a client of mine. But can't you understand that anything you may say can be construed as having come from me in a breach of ethics? And can't you understand that you are in a position in which you may have access to information which other people have not, and therefore all information coming from you sounds authentic? And that any information you receive automatically is considered to have been received by me as well? And that you have no goddamn moral right as a human being to gossip about Johnny Taylor, but as my wife you have no right even to mention his name? You'd better take this seriously, Kay: not one word to anybody about this whole business. And I mean not one word."

"All right, Jim, all right. If anybody calls me and asks me if I've heard about it, I'll say, 'No,' and 'Isn't that awful, but the roast is burning and I've simply got to run.' Will that make you happy?"

"At least it won't contribute to my unhappiness."

"Well, I wouldn't want to do that. What time will you be home?"

"I won't be much longer. And, Kay, please remember what I asked you."

"You didn't ask me, Jim; you forbid me. How could I forget?"

Kay Beyers put down the telephone and uncrossed and recrossed her legs. She sat by the telephone table in an early American ladder-back chair. On the table before her were a nearly overflowing ash tray, her Parliament cigarettes and her dainty, silver monogrammed cigarette lighter. She took a cigarette and tapped the end of it on the table in a clinging habit from her days of prefilter smoking. Then she lit it and as she exhaled a thick cloud of smoke, picked up the telephone and dialed.

"Hello. Is Mrs. Allen at home? . . . Thank you. . . . Hello, Betty? . . . I suppose you've heard. . . . You *haven't?* Well, I suggest you sit down. I have a bit of news for you. . . ."

VIII.

AT THE SOUND OF THE FRONT DOOR FRANCES MCGOVERN TURNED IN her chair and Mary got up and retreated to the kitchen doorway. She did not greet her husband, but stood with both hands on the door frame as if she were hiding behind it. John looked at Frances' face, which reflected a mixture of curiosity and knowledge, and he knew that already the news had begun to spread.

"Hello, Frances," he said.

"Hello, John. Just havin' my mornin' refreshment," she said, holding up the half-empty glass of beer and smiling innocently.

"I think I'll join you," John said. He went into the dining room and returned carrying a bottle of whiskey. "Is there any ice out, Mary?"

"No. I'll get some," she answered.

"Where's Lois?" he asked.

"In her room," Mary said.

She went to the refrigerator where she stopped and looked back across the kitchen at her husband. Then she turned and took an ice-cube tray from the freezer compartment. Then she, too, sat at the table and stared straight at him, as if it were now time for him to begin.

John looked into Mary's eyes for a moment, then got up and went to the sink to put water with the whiskey he had poured for himself. When he returned to his chair, Frances said, "John, I'm afraid I spilled the beans. I could cut my tongue out, but I'm afraid I spilled the beans."

"What do you mean, Frances?" John asked.

"About Johnny," she said. "I thought Mary knew."

"Are you sure you knew?" he asked her.

"Kay Beyers called me after you talked to Jim," Frances said.

"That was nice of her," John said and took some of his drink.

"I know what you mean," Frances said. "She's a bitch if ever there was one. She called more to pump me than to tell me anything. Anyway I thought Mary might need me, and I came over here shootin' off my big Irish mouth, not realizin' that we weren't talkin' about the same thing until it was too late. I wouldn't have told Mare for the world, John, if I thought for one minute she didn't know."

"I know you wouldn't, Frances," John said, "but just what did you tell her?"

"Why, about Johnny . . . and those other boys and . . . Ida Praul," Frances said.

"Is it true, John?" Mary asked quietly.

John looked at Mary for a long moment without speaking. There was an intense silence which was broken when Frances finally withdrew her attention suddenly as if waking from a hypnotic trance. She pushed back her chair and got to her feet with all the agility her nearly spherical body would allow, and said, "I'll be leavin,' Mare. If there's anything at all I can do, don't hesitate."

"Oh, it isn't necessary for you to go, Frances," Mary said, taking her eyes from her husband only for a second.

Frances stood waiting uncertainly for a more authoritative decree.

"I'm afraid you'd better, Frances," John said.

"John!" Mary said, not critically, but rather in astonishment. "Frances is . . . well, practically family."

"John's right, Mare."

"Yes, I am," he said.

"Now you call me if there's anything at all," she said, and she had nearly reached the front door.

"Thanks, Frances," John said as Frances left the house.

"John, where is he?" Mary asked and released all the anxiety into her voice.

"Mary, before I tell you anything else, I've got to make you understand that this is a very serious thing."

"Of course it is, but . . ."

"Mary, listen to me. Every word that's said on this subject could be important . . . could be . . . could be bad for Johnny if it's said to the wrong person. You can't talk about it to anybody but me, and we can't talk about it in front of anybody else. Now, you've got to promise me, Mary. With no exceptions."

"All right, John, but where is he?"

"He's in jail, Mary."

Mary said nothing, but pressed her crumpled handkerchief to her mouth and stared at John through her welling tears.

"A county judge has to fix bail, and there's no judge sitting until Monday."

John waited for a moment for her to answer; then, realizing that she was not going to speak, he went on. But while he had waited, he had come to another realization: that, not only could he no longer keep the truth from her, but that it would be pointless even to soften it for her benefit. He could no more keep it from her than he could deceive her about the color of grass. Grass was green and Johnny was a rapist. If Mary went outside she would see the grass; if she continued to live in reality she would know—would see, hear, read about her son. So he went on to tell her the truth as simply as he could.

"Mary, Johnny did rape that girl last night. I don't know just how or where and I certainly don't know why. But he did; he told me so himself. You asked me in front of Frances if it was true—just that he did it, I mean. All we have to do is say it's true in front of enough people and we could lose our son for twenty years. Not only that, but you put me on a spot, made me decide whether it was best to lie and deny that he did it, or tell the truth and admit his guilt. Mary, before this is over I may have to lie . . . and cheat and God knows what else to save Johnny from prison, but I don't want to be forced into it by my own wife without having a chance to think . . . to decide what I ought to do."

He, too, was silent then, for he had not thought before of this new aspect of the future, and his mind worked eagerly now with new images. Suddenly he saw Frances McGovern on the witness stand hesitating embarrassedly when asked if she had heard John Taylor, Sr., tell his wife that their son had confessed to him. Of course, she had not heard, but had he made one tiny, momentary error in judgment, she would have. Is that what it was to be like from now on? he wondered. Was he to be on guard at every moment, remembering where he had lied and where told the truth, constantly in terror of the threat of self-contradiction? What if there were witnesses who saw the three boys drive off with her? What if someone had witnessed the actual crime but had not yet come forward to say so?

Mary's voice brought him back to actuality. "What's going to happen John?" she asked.

He had nearly forgotten she was there. When he looked at her, he saw that she sat erect, her eyes shining with the residue of her tears, for she was no longer crying. He felt a faint echo of an old tenderness.

"I don't know, Mary, I don't know."

She looked away from him, patting her hair into place in the back, and said, "Do you know . . . how it happened? I mean, any details?"

"No. Nothing," he said and drank the last of his highball.

"Do you suppose he . . ."

"What?"

"Oh . . . never mind. I guess I'm just looking for something to say." Her voice seemed higher now than usual; it had an almost gay, frivolous quality. "It . . . it seems so strange. When someone doesn't come home for dinner without calling, or is in an accident or . . . or dies, you know what to do. You call the office or the grocery store; someone puts on his coat and hat and goes somewhere, somewhere definite—the hospital or a doctor's office—or you call the neighbors and offer sympathy, or they call you, whichever is appropriate." John seemed to hear a faint tremble of laughter in her voice. "And you bring yourself to face the fact that someone you once loved is now a body, and . . . and arrangements must be made to take care of it. So you call the funeral home. And you let your relatives know and the minister visits . . . and you know what to do and what to say. But this . . . there don't seem to be any rules, do there, John?"

"There are rules, Mary. We just don't know them."

"I mean, I don't even know what to ask you, John. Oh, I know I can't call anyone or talk to anyone who calls me. I know that now, John, believe me. But I don't even know what to say to you."

"I can understand that."

"Can . . . can we visit him?"

"Yes."

"You must be surprised I don't run upstairs and put on my coat and rush down to the police station. But I don't know what to say to him either. Oh, what a terrible thing! Just not to know what to say to your own son when he's in trouble! But that's what I was saying: there are some kinds of trouble I know how to deal with, but not this. What do we say to him?"

"I don't think we can see him till tomorrow. We'll work it out by then, Mary."

"Oh, I know now! We're supposed to send him clean shirts and underwear and socks! That's what they do. I must have seen that in a movie years ago, or read it. But that's what we're supposed to do. I'll go upstairs and get some things together."

She had not reached the doorway when John said, "Can't we take them tomorrow with us?"

She stopped and turned toward him. "Yes. Of course we can. I guess I was just looking so hard for something to do." She sat down again at the kitchen table.

"Mary, what did you tell Lois?" John asked, hoping to rouse Mary from the daze she had fallen into.

"What . . . what could I tell her? I said that Johnny had gone with you and Ben Summerfield to answer some questions, and that you'd both be right back. She knew something was wrong. She was very upset."

"Well, you'll have to talk to her now."

"John, she's thirteen years old. How can I talk to her about . . . about this?"

"*Somebody* has to talk to her about it. I think you ought to do it, not me, Mary. You're her mother."

"I don't know what to say."

"Haven't you ever talked to her? I mean, about sex?"

"No."

"Well, you . . . let's not tell her anything for now. We'll just say that we think Johnny may have done something wrong . . . made a mistake. Ask her to trust you for a little while, you're her mother. She's a good little girl. I think she'll go along with that."

"I'll try."

The telephone rang, startling them both.

"Why don't you go and talk to her now. Get it over with. I'll get the phone."

Mary went upstairs as John picked up the telephone. It was Jim Beyers telling him about Stephen Hertzog's call. Jim noticed the weariness in John's voice. When the conversation with Jim was over, John dialed the number of his used-car lot.

"Hello, Clint? . . . John. How's it going? . . . Fine. Think you can handle it without me today? Al's there, isn't he? And Tom? . . . Yeah. There's been some trouble. . . . What kind of trouble? . . . I thought you'd know by now. No, nothing like that. I'll tell you about it later. . . . No, no. Thanks, anyway. Clint, will you call Joe Sylvestrini about that blue Olds? . . . He was in on Thursday. I think we can sell him if you keep after him . . . Yeah. Now, are you sure you'll be all right? I'd rather not come in at all today. . . . Or maybe I'll drop in later for a while. I don't know. . . . Anyway, I'll check with you."

"John!" Mary said.

"Yeah, Clint. . . . Yeah. . . . All right. I'll call you later. So long."

He turned and saw Mary standing at the bottom of the stairs. Her face was pale and one hand, clutching her wadded handkerchief, was still raised to the newel post.

"Lois isn't in the house!"

"Oh, Christ!"

"Where could she have gone?" Mary asked, looking back up the stairs in real bewilderment.

"I don't know, but I can't think of anyplace that would be good."

"Maybe she just went over to that Allen girl's house. They've been very friendly lately. Do you think I should call the Allens?"

"I don't know. I hate to stir things up."

"But we've got to find her. Oh, why would she run off like this?"

"Can't you guess?" John asked.

"What do you mean?"

"I think she'd gone to find out what we wouldn't tell her."

"Oh, John! Suppose she does find out?"

"Maybe . . . you'd better call the Allens."

Mary crossed the room without a word. She put her hand on the telephone and said, "If she finds out some dirty thing about her brother, it'll be my fault."

"Don't start blaming yourself, Mary. It couldn't be helped."

"I could have told her something."

"You did," John said.

"I mean, something she could have believed."

"Good God, Mary!" John shouted, whirling around to face her. "If Lois finds out something dirty about Johnny, it'll be because Johnny did something dirty! *Johnny* raped that poor little girl last night! You didn't do it and neither did I!"

"You're right, John. We didn't," Mary said quietly. "I'll just call the Allens."

IX.

BETTY ALLEN HAD SAT DOWN AS SHE HAD BEEN TOLD TO BY KAY Beyers. She received her informant's intelligence as a one-celled organism closes around its microscopic meal. Her first statement of reaction had been, "Oh, Kay! How awful! Wait till I get a cigarette." She had scurried across the room to a reproduction Duncan Phyfe coffee table, took a cigarette from the box and found in her anxiety that she was carrying the table lighter with her as she returned to the telephone.

"I'm back," she said. "Go on."

Kay Beyers had gone on, telling her what she had known at the beginning and embellishing her tale with the information she had gleaned from her many telephone calls. Her choicest, most intimate knowledge had come from her second call to Frances McGovern, though she had had to cajole and plead for it, had had to pose, move quickly with elaborate cunning and pose again, as a hummingbird woos a flower. Betty averred her surprise, protested that this part couldn't be true and reaverred her surprise. She gasped equally strangulatingly at the fates of victim and perpetrator alike; interjected expectedly incomplete sentences which allowed the narrator to continue, as actors interrupt each other in a play. She said, "Oh, poor Mary!" and "Oh, poor John!" quite frequently enough to demonstrate her sympathy; she expounded suitably briefly on the unpredictability of life, eagerly allowing herself to be swept back into the tide of the news, until there was no more to tell. Then the drama was unexpectedly interrupted.

"Kay," Betty said.
"What?"

"Kay, unless my eyes deceive me, Lois Taylor is coming up our front walk at this very minute!"

"You're kidding!"

"I swear by all that's . . . good heavens, she's about to ring the bell! I'll call you back! . . . Of course, I will. Goodbye, dear."

Betty was already crossing the room when the doorbell rang. She opened the door and said, "Why, Lois. Good morning."

"Good morning, Mrs. Allen. Is Nancy home?"

"Yes. Come in."

Betty Allen had not seen Lois very often, but she knew that Lois' normal appearance was so crisp and fresh that even to her unfamiliar eye the disarray was striking. Lois' blouse was wrinkled and her hair mussed. Her face was flushed and her eyes were red-rimmed and swollen.

"Sit down, Lois. Is anything the matter?"

"No, Mrs. Allen," Lois said, sliding into a spacious wing-back armchair, in which she seemed to disappear. "May I see Nancy?"

"Of course, dear. She's upstairs. I'll call her. How are your mother and father?"

"Fine, thank you."

"Oh, and Johnny. How is Johnny?"

"He's . . . fine, thank you."

"Oh. That's good."

Betty started for the stairs, her mind working furiously, for a way both to satisfy her own curiosity and to avoid the stultifying anticlimax of calling Kay back with no new information. She stopped and turned back to the visitor.

"Oh, by the way, Lois, I heard there was a police car parked in front of your house this morning. Is that true?"

"Yes." Lois said very quietly.

"Isn't that a funny thing to have happen?"

"Yes."

She crossed to the Duncan Phyfe table for a cigarette, saying: "Why in the world was the police car there, Lois?"

"I don't . . . know."

Betty was bent over the coffee table, reaching for the cigarette. She looked up suddenly, surprised, and asked earnestly, "You don't?"

The suddenness, the directness of the question frightened Lois. "I mean . . . they wouldn't tell me, but I lis—"

"Yes? You what, Lois? Listened to whom?"

Nancy Allen, humming loudly in the rhythm of her descent, came down the stairs and into the room and the silence. She did not see Lois until she realized from her mother's waiting posture that there was someone else present.

"Lois! Mommy, why didn't you tell me Lois was here?"

"I was about to, dear. Lois and I were having a little chat. I have to make a phone call. Excuse me, children."

Betty Allen went through the dining room into the kitchen, closing the door behind her.

Betty had no trouble reaching Kay Beyers from the kitchen extension, for Kay still sat by the telephone, smoking anxiously. The first ring was not even completed before she answered.

"Betty?"

"Yes."

"What happened?"

"Nothing, really."

"Did she say anything? Tell you anything?"

"No," Betty said.

"Well, she must know about it," Kay Beyers said.

"Oh, she knows something, all right. She's terribly upset. I don't suppose I should have questioned her, really. She looked so . . . so kind of pathetic."

"Well, I hope you didn't just come right out and ask her."

"Of course, I didn't, but . . . I just feel I probably shouldn't have questioned her at all. I feel a bit guilty about it."

"But what did she say when you questioned her?"

"She said they hadn't *told* her anything."

"That's easy to believe," Kay said. "What in the world *could* they tell her?"

"But then she started to say something else. I think she started to say that she had listened . . . listened to something."

"Then what happened?"

"Well, Nancy came in then, and I certainly didn't want to go on in front of her."

"Where is she now?"

"In the living room. With Nancy."

"Alone?"

"Oh, good Lord!"

Lois had heard the kitchen door close. She peeked through the dining room to be sure of their privacy, then she ran to Nancy with tears streaming down her face.

"Lois! What's the matter?"

"Oh, Nancy, it's Johnny! He's done something terrible!"

"What, Lois? What did he do?"

"I don't know for sure! It's something about sex!"

"Oh, Lois!" Nancy said, darkly. "Shhhh." She put her forefinger to her lip and looked toward the kitchen.

"He did some awful thing with a girl last night, and they put him in jail! They put him in jail, Nancy!"

"In jail! Oh, Lois!" Lois' panic was infectious, and Nancy began to cry. "What did he do to her?"

"I don't know, but he must have hurt her bad . . . bad! Oh, but he wouldn't! Johnny wouldn't hurt a girl!"

"Lois! Lois!" Nancy wailed. "She couldn't die from it, could she?"

Lois gasped and held her cheeks with both hands as this new and dizzying idea struck through her brain.

"Could she?" Nancy repeated.

"I don't know! Johnny couldn't do anything to make her die! He couldn't! He couldn't!"

"Maybe she's having a baby! Maybe he did that to her! Maybe they have to keep him in jail because he's not married."

"Oh!" Lois cried. "I don't think Johnny *could* give her a baby! Could he, Nancy?"

"I don't know!" Nancy said, sobbing as violently now as Lois was. "I don't know how old you have to be!"

"Oh, Nancy, maybe that's it! Maybe he didn't hurt her! He couldn't hurt her, giving her a baby, could he?" Her eyes pleaded with Nancy for agreement.

"I don't think so! Oh, I don't know, Lois!"

Suddenly Lois' face wrinkled hideously so that she looked like a tiny hag.

"But they said he raped her!" Lois cried.

"Raped her?" Nancy echoed both the words and their terror.

"Oh, why didn't they tell me what Johnny did? Why didn't they tell me what Johnny did? Why doesn't somebody . . ."

At this moment Betty Allen came through the kitchen door saying, "Lois, I think you'd better . . ."

She stopped by the dining room table, truly shocked by what she saw and heard. She rushed into the living room, not meaning to be cruel.

"Lois! What have you been saying to Nancy? What have you told her?"

"Oh, Mommy," Nancy said in a long, sustained cry.

"Nancy, go upstairs!"

Nancy merely stood, her little hands clenched before her, and cried again, "Oh, Mommy!"

Betty was shaken and confused by the unceasing, painful sobbing. She tried to stop it with the sheer force of her voice.

"Lois! Lois Taylor, what have you told Nancy?"

"About . . . about Johnny . . ." Lois stammered, gasping for breath. The words were like stones in her raw, constricted throat.

"But what?" What did you tell her?" Betty shouted.

"He raped her! He raped her!" Lois screamed. "It's something dirty and awful, but they won't tell me what it is! Why doesn't somebody tell me? Why doesn't somebody tell me? Why doesn't somebody tell me?"

As Lois stood screaming the question at her, a word of recognition sprang into Betty's mind: hysteria. The word frightened her, and from deep within her there rose the dual urge to punish and to heal. And with it, from some vague place of memory, rose the remedy. She stepped forward and slapped Lois across her pink, wet face as hard as she could. Then she stepped back, crumbling inside, to await the effect of her medicine.

Its effect was instantaneous, stinging silence, which was soon interrupted, for Lois was quickly, thoroughly, horribly sick. Then she ran from the house, crying, gagging, retching all at once.

"Oh, Mommy!" Nancy said and ran upstairs to her room.

Betty began to follow her to attempt some explanation, but the ringing of the telephone stopped her.

"Hello," she said, distracted, but her attention leaped back to the telephone at the sound of Mary Taylor's voice.

"Betty, I'm sorry to bother you, but I was wondering if Lois could have gone over to your house. To see Nancy, I mean."

"She was here, Mary. She just left."

"Oh, do you know where—"

"Mary, there was some trouble."

"Trouble?"

"I went into the kitchen to make a phone call, and when I came back into the living room, Lois was hysterical . . . and Nancy was very nearly the same."

"Oh, my God!"

"They were talking about . . . about Johnny, of course. Lois was upset when she got here."

"I know, I know. But where did she go?"

"I don't know, Mary. I . . . I'm afraid I . . . I slapped her."

"You slapped her?"

"Mary, I had to. She was screaming and crying. It was the only way I could stop her. Then she ran out of the house!"

"Oh, my God! What have we done to that poor child?"

Mary hung up then, not in anger, but absently as she turned to her husband and to the immediate necessity.

"John, Betty Allen says that Lois ran out of their house, hysterical."

"I'll see if I can find her," he said and was already on his way through the sunporch.

He drove to the Allen house and around the block, then around two blocks, then three, in a widening pattern of search. But he did not find Lois, for Lois had kept on running when she left the Allens' for as long as she was physically able. When she stopped running, she was gasping, and at the bottom of each deep gasp was a terrible pain. Her mouth was dry and her tongue seemed to be sticking to the inside of it. Each compulsive breath made her mouth drier and she sucked vainly for saliva. Her throat ached badly from her crying and being sick, and the smell of vomit would not leave her. But even in her intense discomfort, she knew now where she was going.

She pushed open the big double doors of Borough Hall and strode into the building—and practically into the arms of Ben Summerfield, who was just leaving.

She took a deep breath to help control her urge to cry, and said, "I want to see my brother, Mr. Summerfield."

"What in the world's happened to you, Lois?" Ben Summerfield said, holding her at arm's length. "Come on in here and let's have a look at you."

He took her into the room where John had been that morning.

"Glory be!" Ben said, scratching the stubble on his chin and looking at Lois.

"I . . . I have to see Johnny, Mr. Summerfield!"

"I don't think that can be arranged, Lois. Will," he said, turning to Will Ziegler, "get John Taylor on the phone. Tell him I'm bringin' his daughter home."

"No!" Lois protested. "I won't go till I've seen Johnny!"

"Now, Lois," Ben said as Will Ziegler dialed the Taylors' number, "even if I could arrange for you to see him, you wouldn't want him to see you lookin' like that, would you?"

"I don't care," she said, weakly, for her young strength was rapidly draining out of her. "I have to see him."

"Come on. I'll take you home, and you can ask your mother and daddy if you can come later on and visit Johnny. Then you can get all prettied up, the way he'd like to see you, and you can come back."

Will Ziegler finished his quiet conversation, hung up and said, "They're waitin' for you."

"Let's go now, Lois," Ben Summerfield said, extending a hand toward her.

Lois looked up at him, her eyes half closed, her face drawn into a gentle frown. She was too tired now for anything but yielding to this irresistible kindness. She took Ben's hand and they left the building. When they got into the car, Lois sat silent and rigid in the front seat. But by the time they had turned north toward home, she had closed her eyes and slumped into what appeared to be a kind of sleep. It was not necessary for Ben to speak to her when they reached the Taylor home. Lois merely opened her eyes, and, like a cat uncurling from a nap, stretched gently into wakefulness, opened the door and slid off the seat. Without looking at him, she said quietly, "Thank you for bringing me home, Mr. Summerfield." Then she closed the door and started for the house.

Ben waited for a moment after she had gone inside. John Taylor appeared in the doorway, and Ben waved to him. John waved back and Ben drove away.

Dr. McKenna, who had just arrived, was waiting inside for Lois. She registered no emotion at seeing him or her parents. She waited for the doctor to speak to her.

Her mother looked at her and without moving said, "Oh, Lois!"

Then Dr. McKenna said, "Let's go upstairs, Lois, and have a look at you."

Immediately, Lois turned and went slowly up the stairs with the doctor following. John and Mary waited in silence, and in a few minutes Dr. McKenna returned.

"She'll be all right now," he said. "I've given her a sedative. She'll sleep straight through till morning, I should think. That's all she needs: sleep. Give me a call when she wakes up. I don't think you'll need me again, but let me know how she seems tomorrow. I suppose they kept Johnny and the other boys down at the Borough Hall," he added, his paternal attitude seeming to give him license to speak as frankly as he wished.

"Yes," John answered.

"I'm glad to see you understand that I was merely doing my duty there this morning," the doctor said.

"What do you mean?" John asked.

"Why, you wouldn't have called me if you bore any malice over that."

"To tell you the truth, I didn't even think about it," John said. "We've called you for so many years when we needed a doctor, that it's second nature."

The doctor's irritation raised the pitch of his voice. "Well, I *was* just doing my duty whether you realize it or not. That poor girl was savagely assaulted. I don't know if Johnny was involved or not. Doesn't seem to me he could have been, but somebody did it, and we've got to find out who." The doctor's pale eyes sparkled. Both the sparkle and his hair, which was the color of overcooked carrots, belied his sixty-seven years of age.

"It seems to me," John said, "that my job is to protect Johnny."

"Protect him if he's innocent," Dr. McKenna answered without hesitation, "punish him if he's guilty. That's what's wrong with children today: overprotected. Of course, in the eyes of the law he's innocent until proven guilty. That's the way thinking people will look at it."

"Yes, there're so many of them around," John said bitterly.

"Maybe more than you think," the doctor said. Suddenly he looked at Mary. "This is all terrible for you, Mary. Maybe I should give you a little something to calm you?"

"No, I'm all right, Dr. McKenna," Mary answered.

"It's a terrible thing for everybody: the boys, the town . . ."

"How much do I owe you, Doctor?" John asked abruptly.

"What?" the doctor snapped. "You trying to get rid of me, John Taylor?"

"No, I'm trying to pay you," John answered flatly.

"Well, I'll send you a bill," Dr. McKenna said hotly. "I gave advice to your father when you were a baby, and I'll stand here as long as I want and give advice to you. And if you have any sense, you'll take it, too."

"I usually do," John said, more wearily than agreeably.

"All right. You call me tomorrow about Lois. And let me know about Johnny," he added, going to the door.

"I imagine you'll hear without our telling you," John said.

"I don't listen to gossip. I hear it, yes. Can't help it in my position, but I don't listen to it. Call me tomorrow. Goodbye."

"Nosey old bastard!" John said as he watched the doctor walk out to his car.

"John!" Mary said.

"Well, what the hell does he mean, coming in here like a meddlesome old woman, telling me what to do and what not to do?"

"John! Dr. McKenna's one of the best friends anybody in this town..."

"What's so friendly about him? All he ever does aside from pill-pushing is meddle. He's always got his nose in everybody's affairs. And I resent it in this case."

"Nonetheless, he's a reliable old friend. And I won't have you making an enemy of him."

John turned to watch the doctor's car pull from the curb, and without looking back at Mary he said, "I wonder if he's the only enemy we'll be making."

Mary did not answer. She looked at her husband for a moment, then went upstairs and found Lois in bed.

"Do you feel all right, Lois?" Mary asked.

"Yes," Lois said, opening her eyes narrowly. "Just awful sleepy."

Mary sat on the edge of the bed and said, "Just go to sleep, Lois. Everything will be all right. Just go to sleep."

"Yes, Mother," Lois said, barely moving her lips. Her breathing was slow and deep now.

"Just go to sleep," Mary said again and reached out to stroke Lois' hair. Then she left the room and went downstairs.

"She's asleep already," Mary said.

"That's good," John answered. "I guess I may as well go down to the lot. No point in just sitting around here."

"Yes, I think that's best," Mary said.

"You be all right?" John asked, picking up his hat.

"Oh, yes," Mary said, reassuringly. "I have lots of things to do."

"Okay, I won't be long," John said and left the house.

Outside the house John paused for a moment to note what a physically beautiful day it was. He looked up at the sky and saw the cloudless blue broken by the fine, black lines of telephone wires, which he did not know, or even imagine at that moment, were carrying along their tensile length the ammunition of his new enemies and the armor of his old friends.

"I didn't mean to hit her," Betty Allen was saying into the telephone. "There just didn't seem to be anything else to do."

"Well, of course, you had to hit her," Kay Beyers answered. "She just would have got more hysterical if you hadn't. What did she tell Nancy?"

"I don't know," Betty Allen said. "When I tried to find out, Nancy locked herself in her room. She's really very upset, Kay."

"Of course she's upset. With Lois Taylor telling her such filthy things."

"How much do you suppose she said?" Mrs. Allen asked, glancing up toward her daughter's room with her brow wrinkled in dismay.

"They certainly weren't talking about ice cream and cake. You never know what goes on in other people's homes. Imagine Mary Taylor, prude that she is, having a rapist for a son and a . . . well, God knows what Lois is, talking that way to poor little Nancy. Have you talked to Grace Harkins?"

"With all that's been going on here I haven't had a chance to call anybody."

"Well, don't bother," Kay told her. "I'll give her a buzz right now. And let me know if anything happens."

"Of course. Goodbye, Kay."

" 'Bye dear." Kay Beyers hung up, lit a cigarette and began to dial. Suddenly she hung up and sat, thoughtfully, for a moment with her hand still on the telephone. Then she reached under the telephone table and took out the directory. A little apprehensively she dialed the number of a woman whose house was in the same block as her own and to whom she had said no more than hello in the five years since the family had moved into the neighborhood.

"Mrs. Sylvestrini?"

"Yes," a rather low, harsh voice answered.

"This is Kay Beyers."

"Oh. Hello."

"I know it must seem rather strange to you to have me calling you, but I was talking to an old friend of yours this morning—Frances McGovern. You know, Frances Moriarty."

"Yes, of course." There was a silence now. The coolness which Kay Beyers had heard in the voice merely whetted her appetite for battle.

"Do you know I didn't realize," Kay went on, "that you were Jean Meredith. Why, I went to school with your brother."

"The 'Sylvestrini' must have put you off," the deep voice said.

"Well, of course, I don't know your husband. Is his family from town?"

"He and your husband played basketball together in high school," the voice said expressionlessly.

"Isn't that a coincidence? And Jim never has mentioned it. Well, when Frances told me that you were Jean Meredith, I just made up my mind to call you. Poor Frances is very upset. She's a neighbor of the Taylors', you know."

"The Taylors?"

"Yes. Oh, my dear, you haven't heard! I'm sorry. I really shouldn't have said anything. I was hoping . . . I mean I thought you might have talked to Frances. It's nothing. Just forget that I mentioned it."

"Forget you mentioned what, Mrs. Beyers?"

"Oh . . . well, I suppose you'll hear it anyway. Do you happen to know Peg Praul?"

"I know the name."

"Well, she has a daughter named Ida . . ."

It was a very few minutes later when Frances McGovern picked her up her telephone. "Hello," she said.

"I never thought I'd see the day," Frances heard a familiar voice saying with no identifying preface, "when you'd turn into a backbiter like Kay Beyers."

"Now just a minute, Jean," Frances said, "don't go off half-cocked with me and start insultin' me or I'll come over there and kick your ass all the way up Twelfth Avenue. You don't—"

"She just called me, Frances, to tell me all about Johnny Taylor. Said she'd found out most of it from you."

"From me?" Frances fairly screamed into the telephone. "Why, that lyin' bitch! I never spoke as much as twenty words to her in my life. She called me this mornin' to pump me about it. I didn't—and still don't —know anything about what happened—except what *she* told me. I saw the police car out in front of Mare's place and was on the way over when the phone rang. It was her highness tryin' to get details from me. When she came to the point and told me what she was after, I practically cut her off and hung up. 'Course, that didn't stop her from callin' back later on."

"She's disgusting," Jean Sylvestrini said. "Somebody ought to go over there and tear her telephone out of the wall and ram it down her throat."

"Well, nobody's goin' to. The least we can do is not help her out by spreadin' the word ourselves."

"You don't have to tell me that, Frances," Jean Sylvestrini said. "The only person I told was Joe. He's working half days on Saturdays now. He called me to remind me about getting another case of beer for the weekend, and I told him about it. That certainly doesn't make any difference. You know Joe. Why, he's going to buy a car from John Taylor. It's a blue Olds...."

John knew as he walked across the flat cement expanse of the lot through the aisles of used automobiles that the news had reached his place of business. One of his three salesmen was with a customer. Another was busy with an inventory chart and waved hello from across the lot. The third was visible through the windows of the tiny cubicle of an office at the end of the aisle through which John walked. As he approached the office, John wondered how he knew. Was Tom Sauers' preoccupation with the customer a little too intense? Was Al Henderson's wave a bit too casual? Was the glance which Clint Staley cast through the window sort of furtive? Perhaps he was imagining it. He didn't really know, but he *did* know that they had heard about Johnny.

"Hi ya, John," Clint Staley said.

"Hello, Clint," John answered. "Looks pretty slow. Anybody been in this morning?"

"Oh, a couple of people," Clint said. "I think we're finally going to get rid of that green Ford. Chester Reeves is thinking about giving it to his kid for his twenty-first birthday."

"I was beginning to think we'd never see that thing go," John said, smiling faintly. "What about Joe Sylvestrini?"

"Uh . . . he . . . uh changed his mind."

"Changed his mind?" John said, looking across the two desks, which faced each other. "He was just about dead set on that Olds. What happened?"

"Well, I called him like you asked me to, and he . . . he just changed his mind."

"Did he give any reason?"

Clint stared at the desk top for a moment, then, still without answering, he looked up into John's eyes.

"You've heard about Johnny, haven't you?" John asked.

"Yeah."

"Did . . . did that have anything to do with Joe Sylvestrini changing his mind?"

"I'm afraid it did, John."

"What'd he say?"

"John, it doesn't make any difference what he said. He's just . . ."

"What'd he say, Clint?"

"Well, at first he just said he changed his mind. That seemed kind of funny, so I pumped him a little. I didn't know anything about what happened till he told me. I asked him what the hell that had to do with the Olds. And he said . . ."

"What, Clint?"

"He said, 'Maybe nothing.' But he said he couldn't help wondering what kind of a family a boy would have to come from to do a thing like that."

"That's great," John said. "I wonder how much of that there's going to be."

"Look, John, I know Joe Sylvestrini, and he's a nut. First of all, he's a fanatical Catholic. He's always looking for something to hang on non-Catholics, and I'd like to bet you that's what he's doing now. He's just using this as an excuse for taking out his prejudice."

"It doesn't seem to me to make much difference why he's doing it, Clint. He's doing it."

"It's just one guy, one isolated case. Don't worry about it."

"Did he say that—I mean, anything about religion?"

"No, I just know that's the way it is."

"Well, what did he say?"

"I told you, John. And he . . . he started talking about his daughter. She's in Johnny's class at school, and . . . well, I guess Johnny's taken her out a couple of times or something. He was rambling on about that, but that doesn't make any sense, either. So Johnny took her out. It wasn't Liz Sylvestrini he . . ."

"Everybody seems pretty well decided about what Johnny did or didn't do."

"I'm sorry, John. I didn't mean . . ."

"Forget it. I know you didn't, Clint."

"You know, some people always like to believe the worst. They're not worth worrying about, John."

"What about Tom and Al? Do they know about it?"

"I didn't tell them anything, but Tom's wife phoned him. She was ranting and raving. He told her to go to hell and hung up on her."

"I wish to God people would just mind their own business."

"That's a laugh! Do they ever?"

"I guess not." The phone rang then, and John picked it up. "Sure, Helen, he's right here." He handed the phone to Clint.

"Hello. . . .Yeah, I did. . . . Helen. . . . Don't you have any sense at all? For Christ' sake, Helen, I'll talk to you when I get home!"

He banged the receiver into its cradle and looked back across the desks from which he had turned away. But John had got up and gone out into the lot.

Mary had not stopped to plan; she had simply begun cleaning the living room. When she had finished she had moved without a thought into the dining room, where she had dusted and vacuumed and waxed the furniture. Then she had put away her equipment and begun preparing dinner. When John came back at five-thirty, dinner was ready.

They ate lightly and almost without speaking. Then John read the paper while Mary washed and dried the dishes. There was nothing in the paper about Johnny.

Mary came into the living room and turned on the television set. They talked occasionally in short, quiet sentences about the programs they watched. John had two glasses of beer.

At nine o'clock Mary said, "Think I'll go up to bed, John."

"All right, Mary," he said. "I'll be up in a few minutes."

John watched a local fifteen-minute newscast, then turned off the television set and went into the kitchen. He washed his beer glass and put it on the drainboard. He came into the living room and turned the latch of the door leading to the sunporch. He was about to turn off the last lamp when he straightened and stood, thinking for a short time. He went to the sunporch door, unlocked it and went out onto the porch. He stopped and lifted the welcome mat and picked up the key they always left for the last one home. He looked at it in his hand for a long moment and put it in his pocket. He went to bed then, but neither he nor Mary slept to any extent through that long night.

X.

THE TWO SIXTY-WATT BULBS WHICH LIT THE NARROW HALL OUTSIDE the cells seemed more to emphasize the darkness than to eliminate it. It had been just so in the morning when the three boys had been brought in and remained so now as if the back of the tiny jail were enduring a long, unchanging Arctic night.

Will Ziegler had brought three plates of beef stew to the prisoners from the Willow Luncheonette across the street. When the night man had come on Will had taken the plates—still laden with the rich, brown food—back to the restaurant and gone home. Now, at nine o'clock, the face of the night officer appeared dimly and suddenly at the end of the corridor, unseen by the occupants of the cells. "Can I get anything for you kids?" There was no answer. The heavy wooden, metal-coated door slammed shut, and the internal mechanics of its lock sounded into silence.

The prisoners had spoken little during the day. They had also moved about as little as possible. They had even tried to think as little as they could, but this was difficult. All activity seemed now to have a dual purpose: the accomplishment of its original, intended objective and the painful underscoring of the circumstances in which it was performed. One talked to a listener, unseen, hidden by the imprisoning walls, and dark thoughts of the hillside and of Ida returned. One went to the tiny sink in the corner of the cell and the three steps taken to reach it seemed somehow inadequate; yet the tepid water trickled down the throat and urged a fuller consciousness of this place. One rose from the iron cot with its musty-smelling mattress and with each fourth step the necessary reversal of direction stabbed deeper into the awareness, until one might turn to break the pattern and, facing the hard, accusing bars, return to the foul bed, to sit or lie motionless as if the victim of horrible burns which made movement agonizing.

This was punitive isolation from all that was known and dear and wanted. Here all was strange and unfamiliar, yet oppressive, adventureless. No decor, no ornament disguised the function of the four identical cells. The iron cots and their lumped and dented mattresses were cheap and old. The sinks and toilets had been installed when the ancient building had been built, and the woman hired to clean them once every two weeks was an old, careless and unreliable drunk. Actually, she had not been to Borough Hall for three weeks, and the ubiquitous soot from the factories along the river had found its way, settling and seeping, even into this remote place until it lay like a heavy layer of coarse gunpowder on the chipped and rust-stained porcelain, on the hard cement floor, on the harsh bed clothing. Now in the semi-darkness, as the bars cast their weak, gray interlacing shadows the soot became lost. One could not see it; one could only feel it, gritty and smudging at every touch.

"Johnny," Artie's voice said from the farthest of the three occupied cells. It sounded weak and uncertain.

"What?" Johnny answered.

"What . . . what do you think's goin' to happen to us?"

"I told you before, Artie: I don't know."

"Nothin's goin' to happen," Armand called from the cell on the other side of Johnny.

"But they say we raped her," Artie said.

"What do you mean, 'They say'? Wasn't you there?" Armand asked him.

"But I didn't know what we were doing!"

"You did pretty good for somebody who didn't know what he was doin'," Armand said.

"What can they do to us, Armand?" Artie asked.

"They can do a lot to us, but they ain't goin' to."

"What do you mean, Armand?" Johnny asked, leaning up on his cot.

"Who the hell's Ida Praul?" Armand answered. "She ain't nobody."

"What's that got to do with it?" Johnny asked him.

"You don't go to jail for screwin' the daughter of a whore."

"But we forced her to do it," Johnny argued.

"All right, so we forced her. You just wait an' see."

"Maybe he's right, Johnny," Artie said eagerly. "Maybe nothin's going to happen." He had come up to the front of his cell and, in his eagerness, had grasped the bars and tried to look along the corridor toward Armand. Suddenly he was aware of the cold steel cylinders in his hands, and it was as if that consciousness made them exist more fully. Quickly, he drew his hands away.

"I'll show you how right I am. I'm not even worried. I'm goin' to get some sleep."

Armand rolled over on his cot and felt, without particular consciousness the rough, dirty army surplus blanket against his face. Armand made good his boast, for soon sleep began to come. He rolled over again. Now on his stomach, he was dimly aware that he seemed to be lowering himself into unconsciousness. Fragments of his last waking thoughts floated about among the oncoming, uncontrolled images of sleep. With his ebbing conscious strength he tried to recall, to hold onto his precious version of himself. *Why should he be in jail? What did he do anyway? Ida Praul! She was nobody . . . nobody at all compared to the Armand Rapp who had taken her. The Armand Rapp who was filled with so much strength and power that the strength and power themselves became goodness.* He felt himself tilted, lying again on the slope of the hill, but he felt, too, the dirty blanket, and knew that he could not be on the hill. Neither could he be on the blanket, for both places had become unreal. Yet the hill tilted more steeply and through the unreality he felt again the deep, plunging sensation, so vividly that he was aware of his physical response to it. And his strength and power swelled. He knew suddenly that he was not alone in this nonexistent place. There was the girl beneath him, and two tall, faceless men stood watching him and pointing. A man with scissors and a comb and wearing a white, starched coat walked by, staring eagerly, disapprovingly. Mr. Leonard, the barber who had frightened him long ago, frightened him now. Frightened *him?* The powerful Armand Rapp cocked his arm to strike the flimsy barber, but his fist seemed to drag through invisible mud toward the retreating target. He feared the barber would be gone before the blow could be delivered. But suddenly the barber turned toward him. His right hand, holding the scissors, pointed toward Armand, while his left beckoned with the long, thin comb into the darkness behind him. The short, fat woman behind the barber wore a hat with a veil and a fur-trimmed cloth coat. Oh, he knew each felt fold of that hat, each octagon of its spiderweb veil! He turned it upside down and there were the beige label and the dark green ribbon around the seam, and the deep crown, like a great, friendly-smelling bowl where he could curl up kitten-like and sleep softly.

But the hat was not upside down. It floated above the fur collar of the coat until behind the veil he saw the woman's face. Why had she brought him to the barber with this girl beneath him? The barber didn't understand; that's why he pointed. Now she pointed, too, and puckered her tiny mouth and cried. He wanted to stop, she sobbed so violently, so bitterly, but he could not. The two faceless men, still pointing, were joined by another man, a huge man. It was his father and he did not point, but stood looking indifferently. Suddenly he laughed. Why was he laughing? Why? Then Armand felt the blanket against his face and knew about the jail. That's why his father laughed: because his father would not have been caught, but Armand had been. And what would happen to him now? Who would help him? The images, all except his mother and the girl, disappeared. His mother remained, pointing and weeping, and Armand knew that she was a dream. He was glad then that she had died so many years ago and could not really see him like this, with this girl who clung to his groin as if she had grown there. Why was the barber cutting his mother's hair? Oh, no, it wasn't her hair! Mr. Leonard was hacking delicately at the dear hat! Was his mother crying for the loss? No. No, she cried for him because he had begun again lowering himself to the girl. He was ringed around by the pointing, faceless men and his laughing father and his crying mother and the terrifying barber. But he had made good his boast: he had his sleep, and the other boys, hearing his garbled sleep noises, envied him.

"Can you sleep, Johnny?" Artie asked in a whisper.

After a moment the answer came. "No."

"Me neither. Boy, that Armand! He must be pretty sure we're all right if he can sleep like that."

"Yeah."

"Do you think he's right about it, Johnny?"

"I don't know."

"He must be if he can sleep like that, huh? . . . Did you hear me, Johnny?"

"I'll never be able to sleep if we don't stop talking."

"All right, all right. I was just wondering about it, that's all. I don't see how you can help but wonder. I bet you were wondering, too. What else can you think about but what's going to happen to us? What the hell else is there to think about? I sure didn't know what we were doing, honest. We must of been crazy! Taking her out there and . . ."

Artie's whispering, unanswered and growing fainter with each sentence, gave way to his silent thinking. He had risen and gone to the front of his cell to talk to Johnny. Now he turned and went back to his cot. How could he have known what they were doing? It seemed like such a good idea at the time. Of course, it was Armand's idea. He couldn't honestly say that Armand made him do it, but it was Armand's idea in the first place. Hell, he didn't even know they were going to do it—all the way—till they had her laying there on the . . . He lifted the top of the blanket and, without untucking the bottom, ineptly shook the loose soot from it. Still holding one end of the blanket, he turned his head, held his breath and squinted to avoid what he imagined to be a great cloud of dust. He let the blanket fall back to the bed and smoothed it out inadequately. He wished now that he'd never seen her lying there on the ground beneath him. It wasn't worth it for this. Why, he could hardly remember what it was like, with all the other things that were going on. He put a hand on each side of the bed and reluctantly lowered himself to it, as if preparing to perform an exercise. What else had been going on? he asked himself. Well, hell, there was Armand and Johnny right over there, and . . . well, it was the whole feeling of the thing, her not wanting to and . . . and it being dark and far away from everything. Sure, that's what it was. And then, too, there was the kids from school. Of course, they weren't there, but he was thinking about them, about what they'd say and how they'd envy him. It was all those other things, Armand and Johnny and all. What would Kenny Rimbaud say now? Maybe—he felt a quick flush of excitement—maybe he'd still envy him anyway. Maybe even more. Like as if he had robbed a bank or been picked up in gambling raid! Maybe it would seem exciting and glamorous to anybody else. The three tough and hardened criminals, looked at in their dark world of mystery by everybody else with fear and awe! Suddenly he saw, behind his closed eyes, his mother hidden in his father's arms out there in that room. He heard her quiet sobbing. His eyes opened as if of their own volition, and he saw the bars and the pale, artificially amber light and the shadows; smelled the stale, acrid odors; felt the hard, uneven mattress. No, there was no excitement, no glamour. There was only being alone, even more alone with those bars and those concrete walls there. It was like that first day in school. He could even remember his mother washing his face that morning. He had pulled and tugged at her all the way to school, trying to get her to hurry. What did he think he was hurrying to, he wondered now. "Artie Schlier," he had said, and he heard again the deep, guttural, saliva-filled "S-c-h-" of his name. He could still feel the flush, hear the laughter, see all those faces turned up at him, laughing, mocking. At lunch time they crowded around him, asking him questions. He thought they must be interested in him, and he answered quick and eager. He could still feel his smile. At first they tried not to laugh at his answers. They just giggled behind their hands, and he went on talking through his smile.

He didn't understand why some of them laughed, so he joined them and laughed, too. He didn't realize until all of them laughed at once that they they weren't interested in his answers. But why did they keep on asking questions, then? But it was the same after school. And when his mother met him at the schoolyard gate, he hurried her off, afraid that if they heard her speak, they'd laugh at her, too. That was when he knew why they laughed. That was the first day he refused to speak German at home. He was afraid for a while that he hated his mama and papa. Maybe it was the kids who teased him that he should've hated instead. But he didn't; he still didn't. He had nearly lost his accent by Christmastime that year, even though he didn't talk very much to anyone. But they always managed to trap him, sometimes even without trying. He tried to fake the words to the Christmas carols, which he knew only in German, but they caught him. It was just about then that he realized that he was trying, and he didn't stop trying once in all those years after that, even when he watched them starting clubs and gangs, saw two guys here and two there pair off as best friends, saw cliques start, parties given, all without him. Till this day he didn't know why they left him out. He thought he'd made himself acceptable by then. Maybe he'd just been too easy to get. But all of a sudden he knew he was used to being lonely, like you get used to a broken arm even though it still hurts. All the time he was trying to make himself what they wanted, he had to be alone. Then, when they were ready, it was too late. It had been too long.

There was that time when he met Johnny Taylor by the big tree just outside school and Johnny stood up for him against those other guys. He never really knew why Johnny did that, but they went to the movies that night and the next evening was the first one he spent in the Taylor home. He thought he'd settle for Johnny Taylor, thought that was enough, but it wasn't. At first he had hoped that Johnny would get him into things. What a laugh! Instead, Johnny started to have less and less to do with them—or them with him. None of it ever worked. It was still the same as that first day: he still tried to do what he thought they wanted, and he always found that they had trapped him again into playing the fool. And this last thing was the worst of all. All he'd got from it was their hating him. Maybe it was better than their laughing, he thought . . . and he began to cry quietly into the rough wool of the blanket.

"Don't cry, Artie," Johnny whispered. "Go . . . go to sleep."

Johnny listened for a moment, but the crying had stopped abruptly at the sound of his voice and did not start again. Was this what it was to cost? he wondered. Not everyone had to pay this, why did he? He was sure Ida would have done it with him willingly, so why did he have to pay? He hadn't dragged her out of the car and through the grass to the hill. He hadn't . . . but he had helped hold her down. And later, when she was helpless and couldn't resist—even if she had wanted to—he had done it. He was as much to blame as anyone else. He went to his cot and pulled off the blanket. He shook it out and put it back on the bed wrong-side-up. He looked down at the ready bed, and his mind saw Ida lying there, still and formless in the dark. Oh, why had he done it? Why? The image disappeared, and he dropped to the cot on his side and covered his face with his hands. In the deeper darkness behind his closed eyelids and his hands he was filled with shame and remorse. What was his mother thinking at this very moment, knowing he had done this dirty thing? How could he ever face her again with the knowledge between them of this dirty act of sex?

Then there returned the rare, but familiar, shocking image. Picture by picture it came, yet so swiftly that he could not avoid the ultimate scene. Although he had never actually seen it, it would come to him in sickening, startling detail. First, the pale pink wallpaper with the tiny silver bows. Then, the plainly molded mahogany bed with its spotless white chenille cover. Suddenly the cover would be gone, and there on the soft white sheets, he would see his mother's naked body, her legs drawn up a bit and spread wide apart. Again suddenly, his father would be there, hunched over between those long, straight legs, bending and straightening convulsively like an animal. He could see only his father's back, but as his body rose he glimpsed his mother's face, now wrinkled in pain; gone; now grinning in glee as he had never, never seen it.

He opened his eyes and rolled quickly over on his back. Is it like that? he asked almost aloud. Could they do it like that, his own mother and father? Well, of course they did it, he told himself, taking a cigarette from his shirt pocket. Sure they did, like everybody else. But the image was gone now. He struck a match, and in the complete darkness and silence it sounded to him loud enough to wake the others—if they were sleeping. He lit the cigarette, looked around for a moment for a place to put the match, then casually, yet sadly threw it on the floor. Why had they never told him about doing it, he wondered, if there was nothing wrong with it, if everybody did it? Maybe they were afraid he'd just do it along some lane, out in a car. . . . Yeah, maybe they were. Maybe that's why they never told him. But if they didn't want him to do it, then it must be wrong, and then how could they do it? They were married, that was the difference. He'd known that for a long time: it was all right if you were married. No. Goddamn it, no! He'd never understood that, not all those times he told it to himself, and he didn't understand it now. Marriage couldn't make clean something that was dirty. It just couldn't. If it was a dirty thing, and he felt it was, then maybe everybody was dirty. Maybe his mother and father were just as dirty as everybody else. Then why had he wanted to do it so much? Why did everybody—except maybe Catholic priests—and even them if you believed the stories—want to do it? Was it just a dirty, sinful impulse that God put in people? Why would God do that? Because of Adam and Eve? Why would his mother have to lie grinning under his father's pumping body because of Adam and Eve? Why would he force himself down on top of a poor, helpless little girl because of Adam and Eve? Oh, Christ, he didn't know! He wondered if anybody did.

"There!" His lips formed the word, his voice almost said it, for his own hand, unbidden, had come upon the physical excitement of his own body, rigid, complete, roused by these natural thoughts, by his earnest and inevitable seeking.

"There!" his lips said again. His hand closed painfully. Was this the cross he had to bear? Who gave it to him, made it ready before he even knew it, then called him dirty? Not God, he decided. Here he was, away from everything he was used to, alone, afraid, unable to eat or drink or sleep, yet capable of this. Who would put this power in him and call it dirty? No, not God. God wouldn't do that. And last night, sure he'd been scared and he'd known he was doing something wrong when he started toward Ida. But while he was there with her, it was as if he was looking for something. His body, electrified with excitement, found part of it. But he knew there was more. He kept hoping that she'd wake up; because he was sure that if she did, she'd tell him or show him or give him something that would make it complete. If she had, he might even know now the answers to all these questions. When he heard her make that one sound, he thought for a minute that it was going to happen, but it didn't. He didn't really know any more now than he had before. He guessed that Ida didn't either, and he was sorry for her. He hadn't a chance to think about it until now, but what he was afraid of—even last night when he was drunk—had happened: he had come away from Ida unchanged. It had all been a waste.

XI.

BREAKFAST AT THE TAYLORS' THAT SUNDAY MORNING WAS EARLY AND uncomfortable. The disinterested sun continued to shine as if nothing had happened, and each member of the family resented it, though to different degrees and in different ways and without being aware of the resentment. Hearing her bedroom door close quietly, Lois awoke to a gray, uncertain sluggishness alien to most children. She did not realize that the feeling was an aftereffect of sedation. When her confusion had gradually cleared and she remembered yesterday, she thought that her physical distress was part of the memory. As she went into the bathroom, she could hear the unusually muffled voices of her mother and father in the kitchen, and their doleful rumbling reminded her of the plight of her brother, which she was sure only she shared fully with him.

Her ablution did nothing to refresh her: cold water had lost its sharpness; soap wafted a sickening perfume; toothpaste seemed a viscous candy. She wondered if Johnny had these luxuries. Carelessly she selected the clothes which she would wear. She tried not to think of Frances McGovern or the words that had passed between Frances and her mother, but the effort made them echo in her ears. The memory of her brother's misfortune and all it meant to her followed her everywhere with the relentlessness of pain which has become so acute that at each new moment one is astonished that it does not cease.

John sat at the kitchen reading the thick sports section of the Sunday newspaper and sipping his third cup of coffee. The sleepless night had left him in that raw state of expectancy in which harsh sounds which would startle and annoy seem about to occur at every moment, until the very anticipation becomes distressing. He had thought all night about Johnny. He had decided well before midnight that his continued thinking was of no use to himself or his son, but the thoughts, degenerating into worry, had repeated and repeated themselves in his mind. He had gone over the day's events and felt that what he had done was well done. He could do no more until he had spoken with the lawyer from the city. But he did not sleep. Finally, the sunlight came, and he lay staring at it, wanting either to hold it back forever or hurry it on to some undetermined future time. Then Mary had got out of bed without looking at him. "Did you sleep?" he had asked. She had answered, "No. You?" "No," he had said.

Now, suddenly, he put down the newspaper and went to the windows over the sink. He pulled down the shades and said, "I don't know why, but I wish it had rained today." Then he went back to the table and his newspaper.

Mary did not answer him, partly because she understood and felt that his statement required no answer, and partly because she was deep in her efforts to busy herself. She returned her own cup and saucer to the china closet in the dining room. (She always used the good china for Sunday breakfast.) As she started back to the kitchen, she saw in the yellow diagonals of the sun, the dust on the backs of the dining room chairs, which she had cleaned and waxed so thoroughly only yesterday. She scowled at the exposing sun and hastily drew the blinds shut to close it out.

Mary was startled more by the sudden knowledge of Lois' quiet descent from upstairs than by her unheralded appearance in the kitchen. John, sensing a silence, looked up from his paper and was startled by his wife's expression of astonishment. He turned in his chair and said, "Hey! Good morning, Lo."

She looked at him for a moment during which John was genuinely afraid that she might slap him. Then she said, "Morning, Daddy." And after a not short time of searching the room, "Mother."

"Good morning, Lois dear," Mary Taylor said with an unaccustomed and awkward effort at sweetness which made her daughter look at her again after having looked away.

As Lois sat down, her mother said, "Better hurry, Lois. You'll be late for Sunday School."

Lois, her hands still under the seat of her chair pulling it close to the table, stared at her mother unbelievingly, at the same time hearing the chimes of the Methodist Church singing in her ears the notes and in her mind the words of "Jesus, thou art all compassion," which meant nothing to her in these circumstances or any others.

"Mary!" John said.

"Yes, John?" Mary said, blandly, trying to convince herself and them that she did not know what he meant.

"I . . . I thought," he began, looking at Mary with a sudden and quite uncontrollable distaste, "I thought I'd take Lois for a ride up around Watson's Ford this morning. She always likes to see the old Tracy mansion up there."

"And interrupt that string of 'Marksmanship Medals'? Isn't that what John . . . Johnny calls your Sunday School attendance medals, Lo? They look so much like the ones they give the soldiers. Oh, you'd better ask your daughter about that. She does love those medals."

"What about it, Lo? Do you mind missing one Sunday?" her father asked.

"No," she said, but with so little expression that her father went on, "Rather go for a drive?"

"Yes," Lois answered.

"I guess that settles it," John said.

"Lois," Mary said, "you're certainly getting old enough to at least try to make your own decisions, but don't you think that after six years of perfect attendance you might regret one Sunday of fun that would spoil it all?"

"Fun?" John said. "Mary, I . . . I don't think it's a good idea for her to go, to be perfectly frank."

"Why?" Mary asked, turning quite deliberately away from Lois to face John.

"Because I think it's a better idea for her to go with me," John said, matching Mary's deliberateness.

"In the first place," Mary said in a patient, gentle tone, "that doesn't answer my question. And in the second place, I don't think Lois' religious education should be interrupted by anything."

"Don't you think . . . it makes a difference?"

"I think everything should be normal. I think everything should be the way it always is."

"But everything isn't the way it always is," John told her.

"There's no need to make that perfectly obvious to everybody else," Mary said.

"It's already obvious, Mary."

"We've got to . . . Lois, dear, wherever you're going to go, it's Sunday. I don't want you to go dressed like that. Run upstairs and put on your pretty yellow dress while I fix your eggs." Mary started for the refrigerator.

Lois slipped from her chair and crossed the room. At the doorway she turned back to them and said, "When I'm grown up and married and have children of my own, I'm never, *ever* going to say anything I can't say in front of them. Then I'll never have to ask them to leave the room."

Her mother's exclamatory calling of her name shot past Lois as she walked toward the stairs. She did not turn back or answer, but merely went on up the stairs to put on her pretty yellow dress like a good little girl.

"John, what's happened to that child?"

"Well, she's been ignored and lied to and insulted and slapped and knocked out by medicine. About the only other thing that can happen to her is for her to be told the truth."

A sickening hysteria stirred inside Mary like an awakening snake. "I suppose you think that would have been better."

"Probably. Yes, Mary. It probably would have been better."

"You can't tell a thirteen-year-old girl that her brother is accused of rape."

"Not accused of, Mary. Guilty."

"Don't say that!"

"What's the matter, can't you be told the truth, either?"

"John, I . . . I'm having a very difficult time . . . controlling myself. If you . . ."

"I'm sorry, Mary. I shouldn't have said that. We're talking about Lois, anyway. I just can't understand why you want to send her to Sunday School if you don't want her to find out the truth about Johnny. If she goes, she can't help finding out the truth—or worse."

"Hardly at Sunday School, John."

"She doesn't get there in an armored truck. She's bound to meet other kids along the way . . . or, even worse, some prying grownup."

"What grownup would do a thing like that?"

"I know a lot of them. But why take the chance, Mary?"

"We've got to keep up appearances."

"Oh, Christ! To hell with appearances!"

"If Lois doesn't show up at Sunday School it'll be like . . . like we're admitting we know Johnny did it. But if she goes, it'll show people we have nothing to be ashamed of, nothing to worry about."

"But don't we have plenty of both?"

"You said yourself that we can't let people know that Johnny—"

"Yes, but I'm not going to sacrifice Lois to convince anybody."

"Even if it's best for Johnny?"

"Even if it's best for Johnny. Lois is going to suffer enough for what

Johnny did without sending her all over town to create an impression. For Christ' sake, Mary, how can you even think of such a thing?"

"I'm just trying to do what's best," she said, turning away from him.

"Mary, I know you are. We both are. But we can't let Lois go—"

"She's got to go out sometime, John. We can't lock her up to protect her."

"I know that. But we've got to . . . to prepare her."

"It's a little late for that."

"Yes, Mary," John said, almost angrily, "maybe too late by years. But we have to try."

"I suppose you're blaming me now for never having . . . having a talk with Lois."

"It would have been better if you did."

Mary stood facing him, leaning slightly forward. "And maybe if you'd had a talk with Johnny . . . it . . . it would have been better, too."

John looked into Mary's eyes for a long moment. "If you're trying to make me feel guilty . . . responsible for what Johnny did, you can just forget it. My father never told me about the birds and the bees, but I never committed rape."

Mary started from the room hurriedly, but John stood up in her path to stop her.

"Mary, we can't do this. We can't fight with each other when we should be . . . should be standing together to help Johnny and Lois." She did not answer him but turned her head away from him and looked down at the floor. "I'm not very good at talking like this, but I guess there are times when it's better to be able to talk. I guess I'm just learning that. Come on, now. Sit down."

"All right, John," Mary said without looking directly at him. "I'm sorry. I'm just so upset."

"You wouldn't be human if you weren't. This whole thing is . . . is so . . ."

"I know, John. Tell me what you want me to do, and I'll do it."

"I just want you to rest for now. We have to go to see Johnny this afternoon, and you don't want to be upset then."

"I . . . I'll be all right with Johnny. You know that I'm not usually like this."

"I know. You'll be fine. But I want to take Lois for that ride. I want to try to tell her . . . something . . . about Johnny, something she can believe."

"How will that prepare her to hear the truth?"

"I guess . . . I guess it won't," John said with a deep sigh. "Maybe that's what I have to tell her, one way or another, the truth."

"Oh, John, you can't. Not little Lois."

"Maybe little Lois can't be little Lois much longer. I don't know, Mary. I'm just going to have to start and . . . and see what happens."

"Be careful with her, John. She's so . . . so young."

"I will, Mary, I will."

He went to the bottom of the stairs and called, "Lois." Immediately her bedroom door opened and she appeared.

"I can come down now?" she asked.

"Sure you can," John answered. As she came down, quietly, even sedately, he said. "We're going for our ride now. We'll stop and get you some breakfast on the way. Your mother didn't sleep well last night, and she's very tired. Okay?"

"Yes," Lois said. She turned toward the kitchen and said in a tone just loud enough for her mother to hear, "I hope you feel better, Mother. Goodbye."

As they got into the car and started their ride, John made such obvious small talk that Lois was aware of being handled. In a few minutes they were outside the borough limits, where the earth leveled at the top of the valley and where Main Street became Wilkes Pike. John remembered when along the stretch of pike between the end of town and the Grangeville intersection there had been only a dozen houses—large, sturdy frame houses with backyards which did not simply end, but seemed rather to extend into successive areas of higher and higher grass until the grass became weeds and the weeds underbrush and finally the trees of a small wood. And each house had a huge side yard shaded by elm or maple trees.

Now most of the houses were gone, and the ones that remained seemed to do so only to mark a division between Valley Green Village and the Hawthorne Arms development, or between Hawthorne Arms and Fairfield Manor. The growth of new needs, new standards, was reflected in these small, less individual homes. Television aerials steepled the houses without exception. A power lawnmower stood ready in the breezeway between the house and the garage. Glowing, blond young women in Bermuda shorts, sneakers and man-tailored shirts glass-waxed the windows with the speed of machines.

John felt as he looked at this contrast that he belonged to neither of these two extremes of development, but rather to a transitional generation between them. It was a generation formed by a great depression and a great war; a generation which at one minute looked back leisurely on the large, frame houses of its grandparents and at the next found itself looking at the split-level dwellings of its children, hardly knowing what had happened to the years in between.

They had passed the Grangeville intersection now, where the pike crossed the highway to the city. Beyond that were occasional dairy farms with gently rolling fields of deep, incredible green, where utterly phlegmatic cows stood chewing heavily. Weather-blackened rail fences dipped and tilted and leaned along the outlines of the farms.

"It's beautiful here, isn't it?" John said.

"Yes," Lois answered.

"You're not your usual talkative self today, daughter."

"No, I don't feel much like talking."

"Oh, that's too bad. I wanted to talk to you about something."

"If it's about Johnny, I'd like to."

"Well, yes. Yes, it is about Johnny."

"Are you going to tell me what he did, Daddy? Or are you going to lie to me?"

"Have I ever lied to you?"

"I don't know. Have you?"

The truth, the truth, John heard in his mind.

"Yes, I guess I have," John said.

"Oh," Lois said quietly. "I didn't really think you had."

John gripped the steering wheel more tightly, for as his first strategy seemed to fail, he felt a mild panic. No, he must go on.

"It depends on what you mean by lying, Lo," he said.

"Lying is not telling the truth," Lois explained.

"Things aren't always that simple. Lo, do you remember a long time ago, when I asked you if you knew whether your brother had started smoking?"

"Yes, I remember."

"You said you didn't know, but it turned out a little later that you knew all along," he said. "You lied to me, didn't you?"

"Yes, I guess I did."

"Why?"

"Well . . . because I didn't want to squeal on Johnny."

"Do you think you should have lied?"

"No," she said. "But I don't think I should have squealed on Johnny, either."

"There. That's exactly what I mean. You were in a position when you had to choose between two things you didn't want to do. You had to decide which one was right. And according to what you just said, you still aren't sure which one was right."

"Which one was, Daddy?"

"Lois, I don't know. You see, I don't always know what's right. Nobody does. But until you're grown up, it's best to depend a little on older people to help you decide."

"Sometimes you can't. Like about Johnny smoking. I couldn't ask you what to do without squealing on him."

"I know. That's the way it is sometimes. You just have to stand alone."

"But I can ask you now. Which one was right, Daddy?"

"Maybe . . ." John paused, for he was thinking hard now, not trying to instruct, but thinking through a problem with his daughter. "Maybe I shouldn't have put you in the position of having to make such a decision. Maybe I was wrong."

"But I still had to either lie or squeal on Johnny. Which should I do?"

"Well, I look at it this way, Lo. I'm your father and you have a . . . a responsibility to tell me the truth."

"Honor thy father and mother, huh?"

"That's it exactly. So if I ask you a question like the one about Johnny smoking, you should tell me the truth even if you think it's going to make Johnny mad. Because your first . . . well, duty is to tell your parents the truth."

"I guess I shouldn't have lied, then."

"No, I guess not."

"There isn't any, 'Honor thy son and daughter,' is there, Daddy?"

"Well, no, not just that way. But there's . . . uh . . . what is it? Oh. 'Thou shalt not bear false witness against thy neighbor.'"

"Does that make it wrong for parents to lie to their children?"

"It's like I said in the beginning, Lo. It depends on what you call lying. Sometimes people tell lies to keep from hurting other people, and that can be a good lie. And sometimes we have to tell lies because the other person wouldn't understand the truth."

"I don't know what you mean."

"Well, here's an example. You know now from school that the earth is round, and everything stays on it by gravity. If you had a little brother who was four or five, who hadn't even started school yet, do you think you could explain gravity to him?"

"I don't know."

"Try to remember how you felt when you were five, before you even started school."

Lois wrinkled her brow with the effort, and soon she was remembering the summer when she was five-and-a-half years old, just before she went into the first grade. She remembered driving along a road much like this one. She had seen a great brown and white cow and had cried, "Oh, Mommy! There's a cow!" She had been truly excited, for she had found out not too long ago that cows were where milk came from, and she had formed an exciting image which this lovely, live cow cemented in her mind. She saw a long line of farm boys standing in front of the cow. Each boy carried an empty milk carton, and the first boy held his carton just under the cow's mouth. At the other end of this benevolent animal stood a gray-haired farmer in a tattered straw hat who pumped the cow by its long tail, and the creature contentedly spewed forth a narrow, steady stream of delicious milk into each carton.

Soon after this Lois had listened seriously as she was told about milking cows. But as she sat staring through the windshield of the car, she knew that no one could have convinced her when she was five that hosts of gray-bearded farmers did not gently pump their cows each morning to give little girls their breakfast milk.

"I remember, Daddy," Lois said. "I don't think I would have understood gravity then."

"You're not just saying that for convenience' sake?"

"Oh, no," Lois said, smiling to herself. "I wouldn't have understood. I'm sure."

"Well, then, if you had a little brother like that, you might tell him that . . . oh, that all the people in China walk around on their heads or something like that. Because you couldn't possibly make him understand the truth."

"I see."

"There are some things about . . . about what Johnny did—or might have done—that you aren't old enough to understand."

"And that's why mother lied to me?"

"Did she lie to you, Lois?"

"She said she didn't know what Johnny had done."

"At that time she didn't know."

"She didn't?"

"No. I hadn't told her yet. Frances told her. I just didn't tell her the truth. I wanted to be able to sit down and tell her in my own way, so she wouldn't be any more upset than she had to be. So she didn't lie to you."

"I guess I wasn't very nice to her."

"No, I'm afraid you weren't."

"I'll tell her I'm sorry."

"That's a good idea."

"Daddy," Lois said after a moment. "What *did* Johnny do?"

Rather a short period of time elapsed between Lois' question and John's answer, but quite suddenly, John had his most graphic picture yet of his son's act. He saw the pathetic little girl of the police station held, like a frail gray-brown mouse in a trap, by three surprisingly, alarmingly mature young men, while one of them—yes, it was Johnny—pounded her with his body. He felt his own muscles tighten in response to the thought of the force that those boys—that Johnny—had exerted. For the first time he felt the violence of her struggle, saw flesh tear, blood run. That's what Johnny did, he thought in answer to his daughter's question.

But had he any more right than Lois to "squeal" on Johnny? Could she see such a picture of her brother and not feel her worship turn to hatred and bitter disillusion? And what rule of life said that it was to be John Taylor, her father, who destroyed her idol? Yet perhaps her love for her brother was strong enough to withstand even this. After all, Mary's was; his own was.

But in the end John did not speak, for he could not bear the thought of shattering Lois' innocence with the picture of that struggle. Would not telling her just as surely be a kind of rape? He could think of no interpretation, no version of that image, fit for Lois to hear. There occurred to him no other-side-of-the-story which would not shock and horrify and confuse her.

Somehow, he would have to find the words to tell her that part of growing up was being filled with a longing to love, a longing to be closer to the one you love than you'd ever been to anyone. And that God had given us a way to do this. A way for two people to be so close that they were almost one. But sometimes people misunderstood the longing. Sometimes it went wrong. It was used for anger, for hate, for lust, for revenge, for habit, until you couldn't remember what it was really for or even what it was really like. Could he remember any more? Could he remember that big, empty house he and Mary had taken so that they could fill it with children? Could he remember Mary in his arms, in his thighs, in his mouth, when they felt and smelled and tasted to each other all of the sweet innocence of summer grass? Or could he remember only the later plank of her beneath him, either unwilling or with nothing to give, unless, roused into her own desire by the accidental aphrodisiac of alcohol, she performed her independent task, and they were like two hyenas drinking simultaneously from the same stream?

At the end of a long curve the sudden panorama of Colonial Inn, sitting at the end of a wide lawn, was spread across the windshield, and seeing it, John gave Lois her answer: "There's the Inn, Lo. How about that breakfast?"

"Daddy?" Lois said without taking her eyes from him.

"What?"

"I . . . I'm not hungry," Lois said.

"Oh. Well, we'd better be getting back, then," he said, looking at his watch. "Your mother'll be getting worried."

"Yes, Daddy," Lois said.

John drove into the driveway of the Colonial Inn, backed out again and started for home. When they had gone half a mile, he said, "Lo, I'll tell you later . . . about Johnny."

"Yes, Daddy," Lois said, not looking at him.

XII.

THE TAYLORS' PREPARATIONS IMMEDIATELY PRECEDING THE VISIT TO Johnny were distinctly funereal. Lois accepted her father's decision that she was not to go along with such seemingly silent indifference that he felt it necessary to explain: Johnny would probably be coming home sometime Monday, and it would be foolish for her to go through the unpleasantness of seeing him at the Borough Hall. Once this one uncertain issue was settled, the mechanics of preparation went on with the slow precision of a well-oiled, heavy-pendulumed grandfather's clock. Mary walked in and out of the upstairs rooms deliberately, but without haste, as she packed a small bag for Johnny. There was no discussion of what to wear or what was to be taken to Johnny or what ought or ought not to be said to him. For at this moment each person relied on his own instincts as a decent human being to show him his duty, just as in the time of death, someone lists the donors of flowers and sends thank you notes; someone else arranges the delicate matter of the order in which the relatives are to be called to the automobiles; someone offers bed and board to relatives from distant places.

Neither John nor Mary spoke as they drove to Borough Hall. When they reached Willow Avenue, John saw Jim Beyers' car and parked behind it. Then they got out of the car and went inside.

They went into the room where John had seen Johnny before. In a corner of the room to their left Mr. and Mrs. Schlier sat on the bench with Artie. They were much as they had been on the day before. Mrs. Schlier cried a bit less, but her eyes were red from previous weeping. Artie sat on the end of the bench, nearly hidden by his mother, his hands clasped in his lap, staring at the floor. They appeared to have said whatever they had to say to each other, and their silence frightened Mary.

She wondered what time Mr. and Mrs. Schlier had arrived and if she and John ought not to have come earlier.

"Hello, John, Mary," Jim Beyers said.

Mary turned from the Schliers and said, "Hello, Jim."

"I went back to see the boys when I got here," Jim said. "Johnny's fine."

"Thanks, Jim," John said.

"Hello, John, Mary," Ben Summerfield said, coming toward them. Over his shoulder he said, "Will, get Johnny, will you?"

"Hello, Ben," John and Mary said together.

"Sure thing," Will Ziegler said. He opened the top desk drawer and took out a key ring which held several very large keys. At the sight and sound of their jingling, Mary shuddered so noticeably that John took hold of her arm.

"Take him across the way, Will," Ben said as Will passed him.

"Oh," Will said, pausing for a moment. "Okay."

"You can see Johnny across the hall," Ben said to them.

"Thank you, Ben," Mary said and started for the door.

"Uh . . . Mary," Ben said, and she stopped and turned toward him. "The bag. Would you mind . . . leavin' it here, I mean. I'll have to go through it."

"What?" Mary said. "Oh, of course. I'll just put it here." She dropped it gently on the bench and went into the hall.

They found the other room the architectural twin of the one they had left, but against the far wall between the windows there was a couch of tufted black leather, one end of which sloped to a pillow-like rise. Placed about the room were four dusty tables each with a dusty chair at all four of its sides. The room looked as if some card club had simply deserted it long ago. Mary and John sat down at one of the tables, and soon the door opened and Will Ziegler appeared in the doorway.

"In here," he said over his shoulder, and Johnny came into the room.

He took a few steps toward them and stopped, staring at his mother. Then he turned his head away and looked at the floor, biting his lower lip.

"I . . . I'm sorry, Mother," he said, not looking at her.

"Come . . . come over and sit down, Johnny," she said. The sentence had begun uncertainly, but strength had come to it even in those few words. "How are you?" she asked.

He was seated now, next to Mary and across from John. "I'm all right." He stared at the table top now.

"It wasn't too bad, was it?" John asked. "Last night?"

"The jail?" Johnny said, looking up at him. He shook his head and looked back at the table.

"Johnny," Mary said. "Johnny, look at me. I know what you did, and . . . and I guess I hate it, but I don't hate you, so you can look at me. Everything's still the—"

"Don't, Mom," he said, reverting to his earlier name for her.

"What, Johnny?"

"Mom . . . I'm . . . I'm sorry," he said again.

"We don't want to talk about it, Johnny," John said. But your life's not over, and your mother's here because . . . because she loves you and . . ."

Johnny said miserably, "I just don't know what to do or say or . . ."

"None of us do, dear," Mary told him.

There was a great and heavy pause, which made John wonder how many more such pauses they would live through.

"How's Lo?" Johnny asked quietly.

"Oh, she's fine, Johnny," Mary said.

"I mean . . . how . . ."

"She doesn't know," Mary said.

He closed his eyes and swallowed and sighed heavily. "What . . . what'd you tell her?" Johnny asked with great effort.

"Well, nothing . . . really," Mary said.

Johnny looked up at her. "What are you going to tell her?"

"She'll have to know the truth eventually," John said. "We'll have to figure out some way of telling her."

"I wish she didn't have to know," Johnny said, not really to them, but simply aloud. "Do you think they'll let us out, Dad?" he asked after a moment.

"Oh, sure, Johnny. Well, I think so. We'll have to ask the lawyer about that."

There was a knock at the door, and John said, "Yes. Come in."

Jim Beyers opened the door and said, "Excuse me. May I see you for a moment, John?"

"Sure, Jim. I'll be right back," he said to his wife and son and went out into the hall.

"Out here," Jim said and went out into the street.

"What is it, Jim?" John asked when he had followed him.

"You understand that anything you tell an attorney is in the strictest confidence. I mean, you can tell him the absolute truth without hurting your case."

"Of course, Jim. I understand."

"Steve Hertzog asked me to find out if the boys were actually guilty. Has Johnny said anything to you?"

"Well . . ."

"That's what I mean, John. You mustn't be reluctant to tell either Stephen or me the absolute truth about that. You're perfectly right, of course, not to want to talk about it, generally, and I don't want you to. But the man who's going to defend them has to know."

"I asked Johnny when Ben Summerfield came for him," John answered. "He said yes, he did it."

"What did you ask him, specifically?"

"If he had raped Ida Praul."

"And he said, 'Yes'?"

"That's what he said."

"Well, so much for that. Of course, we've got to find out exactly what happened. Who knows what a seventeen-year-old boy thinks is rape?"

"Jim, you don't think there's a chance . . ."

"Who knows? If it was the first time for all of them and she was uncertain about it, but did it anyway, then felt tremendous remorse . . . well, she might have screamed and carried on so much afterwards that they thought it really was rape. I doubt it, but it could have happened that way."

"I'd give just about anything—"

"Don't even think about it, John. It's pretty slim."

When he returned to the room, John found Mary and Johnny sitting in silence.

"What did Jim want, John?" Mary asked.

"Nothing important."

"Dad, why isn't Mr. Beyers going to . . . to handle the case?" Johnny had difficulty with the words.

"He's not a criminal lawyer, Johnny. He just handles business matters."

There was another pause, which Johnny ended by asking, "What are people saying?"

"What?" his mother asked, but he merely looked at her, unwilling to say it again. "Why, I don't know that they're saying anything, Johnny."

"Naturally, nobody's going to pat you on the back for this, but you mustn't feel as if . . . as if you're marked. People forget very fast," John said.

"I don't think they'll forget this," Johnny said, thoughtfully.

"Johnny," his father began, but a knock at the door interrupted. The door opened immediately this time, and Jim Beyers came in with a man John and Mary had never seen before. He was neither handsome nor unattractive. He had graying black hair which was slightly wavy and a strong, dark face. John was accustomed to men who, on being introduced to a stranger, smiled, extended a hand eagerly, nodded rather self-effacingly. But when Jim Beyers said, "This is Stephen Hertzog," the man kept his distance and merely said, "How do you do?" After that he stood there, his large, hard brown eyes falling for a moment on John, then on Mary, finally coming to rest on Johnny at whom he stared without curiosity. His expression seemed to John to soften almost imperceptibly. Even then John sensed an aloofness in this man—a certainty, a self-confidence which was so overwhelming that it was nearly offensive.

"Glad to meet you, Mr. Hertzog," John said.

"This is Johnny Taylor," Jim said.

"Hello, Johnny," Stephen Hertzog said, rather softly.

"How do you do, Mr. Hertzog," Johnny said, standing up.

"May I talk to Johnny alone for a few minutes?" he said.

"We'll be nearby if you need us," John told him.

"I don't think I will. I'll talk to you when I'm finished. Thank you."

The others left and Stephen threw his hat onto the table. He smiled as he watched the swirl of dust in the air.

"Sit down, Johnny," he said. Johnny did so, but Hertzog remained standing. "Johnny, you and I, as you know, are perfect strangers. But we're going to have to trust each other as you have probably never trusted anyone but your mother and father . . . maybe even more than that. And we're going to have to do it right off the bat. There are lots of attorneys, Johnny, who would come in here and start to talk to you about school and baseball and your hobbies, but I'm not one of them. Because I haven't time to earn your trust. You're just going to have to look at me and decide whether you trust me or you don't. Okay?"

"Okay," Johnny said.

"Did you rape that girl Friday night?" Stephen asked. "I don't mean you boys—I mean *you*. Did you, Johnny?"

"Yes . . . I did."

"That's the only time I'm ever going to try to trap you, Johnny. I knew the answer to that question when I asked it. If you'd lied to me, I probably wouldn't have taken the case. Now I probably will."

"I won't lie to you, Mr. Hertzog."

"Good. And I won't lie to you. Now, Johnny, this whole thing could get very complicated, and the only way I can rely on you—and I'll have to—is for you to understand it. Don't ever let me go on, thinking I've made things clear when I haven't."

"Okay."

"The first thing we have to find out is whether or not you know what rape is. Your saying that you committed rape doesn't make it so. For there to be a rape, the girl must in some way and at some time be made powerless to resist. If the girl just didn't want to, and you started having intercourse with her and she just gave in of her own free will, there was no rape, no matter how strenuously she may have objected afterwards. Do you understand that, Johnny?"

"Yes, sir."

"All right. Did you force her to have sexual intercourse with you?"

"Not exactly. I think she . . . well, she wasn't awake."

"She was unconscious?"

"I think so."

"Johnny, this is terribly important. If you had walked into a room and found this girl unconscious and then had sexual intercourse with her while she was unconscious, that would be rape. Even if you had nothing to do with making her unconscious. Now, do you just think she was unconscious or do you *know* she was unconscious?"

"I'm pretty sure, Mr. Hertzog. She . . . made a . . . a sound . . . well, during it, but I don't think she really knew what was happening."

"What kind of sound?"

"A . . . a kind of groan."

"Did she at any time move, put her arms around you, cooperate in any way?"

"She didn't move or put her arms around me. I don't think she . . . cooperated, either."

"Johnny, I consider you to all intents and purposes a grown man. We're going to be doing a great deal of talking about sex, and I don't want you to be embarrassed by it. Just say in your own words whatever you have to say. You're not really sure about the cooperation part, are you?"

"No, sir."

"This was the first time for you?"

"Yes."

"You couldn't really know whether or not she cooperated, could you, because you have nothing to compare it to?"

"I guess that's right."

"Okay, Johnny. If the girl—what's her name?"

"Ida. Ida Praul."

"If Ida was unconscious, what made her unconscious?"

"I guess she just kind of . . . passed out."

"From what?"

"Well, from . . . you see . . . I was the last one."

"Who was first?"

"Armand."

"Ida wasn't unconscious then?"

"No, sir."

"How did you get her to do it?"

"We . . ."

"Go on, Johnny."

Johnny looked into Stephen Hertzog's eyes for a moment. Then he looked down at the table and said, "Artie and I held her down while Armand did it to her."

Stephen leaned on the table, sighed deeply and said, "*That* is rape."

"Well, I guess . . . I guess that's it, then," Johnny said.

"What?"

"I said, 'I guess that's it.' "

"But I don't understand what you mean," Stephen said.

"Well, I . . ." Johnny began uncertainly, ". . . if what we did was rape . . . then, we're guilty . . . and that's that."

Stephen Hertzog looked at the boy quizzically for a moment. "Johnny . . ." he seemed to consider further. "Johnny, if you mean that therefore, we go into court and plead guilty and you take your medicine . . . well, no, that is not the way it is." Johnny stared into the lawyer's eyes intently. "Don't ever think that again. There are degrees of guilt, Johnny, and the law affords us the opportunity to examine and explain all of them—at least all of them that are relevant. You've got to remember that."

"But . . . we *are* guilty, Mr. Hertzog."

"A man who steals a loaf of bread for his family is guilty of theft, but no jury I've ever seen would convict him, for instance. We can be reasonably sure that the district attorney will presume that you are flatly guilty of rape in the first degree. But even if that is true, we have the opportunity to reduce the degree from first to . . . I mean that the law allows us to try to prove that the circumstances under which you performed the act change the nature of the act to make it a less serious crime. Do you understand that, Johnny?"

"I . . . think I understand what you mean, but I don't see how it applies to us—to me."

"I don't either—yet. When I was in my first law office, I sat in on a case in which a man of thirty-five had waited in the bushes in a park from midnight until three in the morning for a woman—any woman—

to come along the walk. When one did, he pulled her into the bushes, knocked her out and raped her. No attorney on earth could make of that anything but first-degree rape. Do you think that what you did was like that?"

"No . . . no, it wasn't like that."

"That's how the allowances of the law apply to you. I think that what you did was truly different from what that man did. And I am going to find out specifically what the difference is, because in the eyes of the law—and even more important, in the eyes of a jury—that difference might just be great enough to win you an acquittal."

"You mean that . . . even if we did it, we could get an . . . an acquittal?"

"Johnny, the district attorney is going to assume from the start that you are guilty of rape in the first degree, that you have committed the most serious form of this crime. If you are going to have a fair trial, we have to counterbalance that assumption by going in the opposite direction and assuming that you have committed the least serious form of the crime—or, perhaps, no crime at all. And that may well be true. You may know what you did, but you don't know enough about the law to know how the law considers what you did. That's where I come in, and you must leave that—you must leave the whole matter of your guilt or innocence to me."

"I think I understand."

"Now, I want you to tell me exactly what happened from the time, say, an hour before you met the girl—Ida—until the police picked you up."

"Well . . . before we . . . it seems hard to remember what happened before. Oh, I went to the movies with Artie. Artie Schlier, he's . . ."

"I know."

"When we got out of the movies, we went to Fordyce's. That's a kind of soda fountain and candy store where we hang out. Armand, I guess you know him, too, well, Armand was there. He was sitting in one of the booths, in the back, with some guys his own age. Armand's about nineteen, I guess. Do you want me to tell you things like that?"

"I want you to tell me anything that comes into your head—as long as it's the truth."

"It'll be the truth, Mr. Hertzog," Johnny said, and Stephen heard the hurt resentment in his voice. "Well, the other guys wanted to drive up to Balligo Mills. There's a club they all go to up there, but Armand didn't want to go. So the other guys left. I guess I was talking to Old Man . . . to Mr. Fordyce, when Armand called Artie back to the booth.

Then in a couple of minutes, Artie called me back. Armand had a bottle, and he was mixing it with Coke. Well, he offered us some, and we started drinking them too."

"Do you often do that, Johnny? I mean, drink whiskey?"

"No. I mean, I . . . well, I've done it before, but I don't do it all the time." He waited for a moment for a judgment which did not come, then went on. "Well, we talked for a while, then we got up and went outside . . . you know, just like you do. You get tired of sitting. There's a railing made of pipes along the door to Fordyce's cellar, and we always sit on that. We weren't out there long when Ida came along with Virginia Lukens—she's another girl—and Armand said something to Ida. Then she . . ."

"What did Armand say to Ida?"

"Oh. You know, just some remark."

"No, I don't know. I'd like you to tell me what he said."

"Well, let's see . . . he said . . . oh, yeah. He said . . . 'Hey, Ida. Where'd you get the sweater with the bumps on it?' You know, a smart remark like that. Well, Ida sort of giggled, but Virginia pretended not to hear him. They both kept on walking. Then Armand called Ida over, but she didn't come right away. I guess she wanted to, because she made Virginia stop. I couldn't hear what they were saying, but Armand kept saying, 'Come on, Ida. I want to tell you something,' and things like that. I can remember Virginia's voice getting louder. She said, 'No, Ida. You can if you want to, but I wouldn't be seen talking to that Armand Rapp.' Well, I guess Virginia went on up the street then, and Ida came over and talked to us."

"What did she say?"

"She wanted to know what Armand wanted to tell her. Of course, he didn't want to tell her anything in particular. After she asked him a couple of times what he wanted, he told her a joke. It was a dirty joke. I don't remember it—I really don't remember it, Mr. Hertzog. But Ida laughed and hit Armand on the arm as if she was mad at him for telling her. Then she said, 'Ain't he awful, Johnny?' And I said, 'That's not so bad, Ida.' 'No, not really, I guess. I know lots worse,' she said, and Armand said, 'Come on. Tell 'em to us, Ida.' "

"Armand said something else then, too. I can't remember how he came to say it. Let's see . . ."

As Johnny fidgeted nervously, Stephen looked away.

"Oh, yeah. I remember now," Johnny went on. "Ida said, 'Little pictures . . .' " A short laugh issued from him. "She said *pictures* instead of *pitchers*. 'Little pictures have big ears,' she said, and Armand said . . . he said, 'That ain't what you got big ones of.' I guess you want to hear stuff like this, don't you, Mr. Hertzog?"

"I certainly do, Johnny. What did Ida say to that?"

"She said, 'I bet you ain't got nothing big.' Then she hit Armand on the arm again and we all laughed. All but Armand. He said, 'I got plenty for you.' And Ida said . . ."

And so Johnny went on, and Stephen was less surprised than Johnny at the detail in which he remembered the conversation. Johnny did not realize how many times since Friday night every word of that conversation had echoed in his mind. His remorse seemed to act like a tape recorder, capturing each inflection, each nuance in every voice. He did not know how grateful Stephen Hertzog was for that remorse.

"I don't remember the ride home very clear," Johnny said to Stephen Hertzog. "I remember feeling as if there was something I had to do. I guess it was about taking Ida home. I must have kept saying it to Armand and Artie. Of course, we didn't—take her home, I mean. I guess I should've done it myself. But I didn't." He waited again as if for judgment, and this time was puzzled when it didn't come. "That would've been the right thing, I guess, huh?"

"Johnny, you know it would have been the right thing to do," Stephen said. "But it isn't my job to scold you or punish you. I'm not going to express approval or disapproval of your acts. We may even see them differently, morally. My job is to look at them legally and to defend you in court, so don't worry about my opinion as to what you should or should not have done. What happened next?"

"I guess they dropped me off first. I remember trying not to make any noise going upstairs. I got sick again in the bathroom and I was worried about waking Mother and Dad. But I guess they didn't hear me. I went to bed and I was thinking about Ida—still thinking about going back to get her and take her home. But the next thing I knew it was morning, and I got up and went downstairs to have breakfast."

"That's when the police chief came to take you in?"

"Yes. I . . . I don't know what I intended to do . . . call Armand or Artie . . . or try to find out about Ida, but I couldn't do anything till I got out of the house."

"Did you say anything to the chief of police?"

"Nothing," Johnny answered. "My father told me not to."

"And you weren't questioned when you got here—or since you got here?"

"No, sir."

"All right, Johnny," Stephen said, getting up. "I'll be in touch with your family. You'll be seeing me rather soon."

"Is that . . . is that all you want to know?"

"For now, yes," Stephen said. He was about to turn when he saw the utter wretchedness of Johnny's expression. "I don't know yet, Johnny, just what I can do for you. It's much too early even to guess. But I'll be doing my best; you can count on that. Oh, and I think we can get you out of here tomorrow. That's not a promise, but I don't see any reason why we can't."

He went to the door then and, seeing no one in the hall, crossed it and went into the other room. Johnny could see him through the two open doors, standing just inside the far doorway. He stood there for just a moment, then he returned followed by Jim Beyers.

"Johnny, would you come over here now with your mother and father?" Jim Beyers said.

Johnny said, "Thank you, Mr. Hertzog. Goodbye."

"Goodbye, Johnny," Stephen said. When Johnny had gone, he said to Jim, "You were right. He is a nice boy."

"The Taylors are nice people," Jim told him.

"I'm not sure I'd go that far," Stephen said.

"Don't be too rough on John and Mary," Jim said. "They've had their problems."

"Who hasn't?"

Jim thought quite consciously of saying, *You, for instance,* but heard his voice say, "There's nothing in their home that would lead to anything like this."

"From Johnny's ignorance of and attitude toward sex I got the impression that there was nothing in their home that would *lead* to much of anything. I can't deny that Johnny wasn't led into this by his parents, but he certainly wasn't led away from it either—except, perhaps, by a passive and unidentified example. It's rather like saying, 'Now, why did little two-year-old Johnny stick his hand into the fire? He's never seen me do it.'"

"That's called accident," Jim reminded him.

"How would you like to go into court with a 'rape-by-accident' line of defense?"

"I frankly wouldn't like to go into court with this case at all," Jim said.

"I suppose I've had worse ones, but I don't find them springing to mind by the dozens."

"I told the officer to bring Armand Rapp in next," Jim said. "Is that all right?"

"Makes no difference. I'm fairly certain Johnny's story was complete and true. I just want to see the others and make sure that Johnny didn't inadvertently miss anything important."

"Here he is," Will Ziegler said from the doorway as Armand Rapp preceded him into the room.

"This is Mr. Hertzog," Jim said to Armand, who looked expressionlessly at both men.

"I'll be over with the Taylors," Jim said and went out of the room.

"I'd like to have a little talk with you, Armand," Stephen said. "Let's sit down."

Armand watched as Stephen sat at the table where he had been before. After a short moment of waiting, Stephen looked up at Armand, and in response to the look Armand shuffled across the room and sat in the chair opposite Stephen. He sat without adjusting the position of the chair and without any attempt to make himself comfortable. He simply deposited his burgeoning bulk in the chair and looked blankly at Stephen.

"Armand," Stephen began, "you're nineteen years old, aren't you?"

"Yeah," Armand said, not looking at Stephen.

"What kind of work do you do?"

"I work in the steel plant where my old man works," Armand answered.

"Well, you must make fairly good money," Stephen said casually.

"I do all right," Armand said.

"Are you a close friend of Johnny Taylor and Artie Schlier?"

"What do you mean?" Armand said quickly with undisguised suspicion.

"I merely wondered if you see a great deal of them or if you just happened to be with them on Friday night."

"They was with me. Why?"

"There is a certain difference in your ages, Armand," Stephen said patiently. "It seems a little unusual that you were together the other evening. I just wondered what it was you have in common."

"We ain't got nothin' in common," Armand said sullenly. "They just happened to be in Fordyce's when I was."

"I understand you were with some other fellows earlier, fellows your own age. Are they your regular friends?"

"I don't hang out with nobody regular."

"A lone wolf, huh?"

"Yeah. I guess that's it."

"Why didn't you go with the others to the club at Balligo Mills?"

"You been doin' a lot of sneakin' around, ain't you?"

"I haven't been sneaking around, Armand," Stephen said. "It's my job to find out everything I can that may pertain to the case. You see, Armand, the law is very complicated. Frequently non-lawyers don't know what's important and what isn't. So I find out everything I can and then choose for myself what applies. Do you understand?"

"Yeah, I understand."

"Then why didn't you go to the club?"

"Why is that important?"

"Armand, if I have to stop and explain every question I ask, we're not going to get anywhere at all."

"I didn't feel like goin'."

"What do you do at the club?"

"What difference does that make? We drink, play cards . . . dance with the broads sometimes."

"Oh. There are girls there?"

"Yeah. What of it?"

"I'm not trying to make something of everything you say, Armand. You don't have to be suspicious of me."

"Who's suspicious?"

"Forget it," Stephen said. "Is there any special girl you see at the club?"

"What? One of them lousy broads that hang out at the club? Are you kiddin'?"

"Not good enough, huh? What kind of girls are they?"

"Aw, just girls. Wops mostly. Good for a lay once in a while, that's all."

"Oh? Do you and the other guys lay them?"

"What?"

"Do you and the other guys lay them?"

"Well . . . yeah, sometimes. The other guys mostly. I don't go for that easy stuff. They're just cheap tramps. Anybody can get 'em."

"I take it there's some other, more desirable girl that you sleep with," Stephen said quietly.

"You mean . . . you mean a steady?"

"No, not necessarily. You say that your friends are satisfied with whatever happens to be available, whereas you aren't. I just assume that you find your sexual satisfaction elsewhere."

"Yeah, that's it."

"Where?"

"None of your business."

"I'm afraid it is my business, Armand. Everything you tell me is in the strictest confidence. Where do you find your sexual satisfaction?"

"I . . . I ain't going to tell you."

"When was the last time? Aside from Friday night, I mean."

"I . . . I don't remember."

"Come on now, Armand," Stephen said in a friendly tone. "You seem fairly selective about sex. Surely you don't have it so often that you forget."

"I don't know when it was. Not . . . not so long ago."

"But when?"

"I don't remember, I told you," Armand said loudly.

"Armand, if it is a fact that you never had sexual intercourse before Friday night, it will be very helpful in your defense."

"What? How?" Armand's eyes narrowed. "You son of a bitch!" he said.

"It would have been simpler for both of us if you'd told me the truth in the beginning. I can defend you properly only if you tell me the absolute truth every time I ask you anything. If I go into court with a defense based on lies that I don't know are lies, we'll both get caught. The difference is that I'll merely lose the case; you'll go to prison."

"Not because of Ida Praul, I won't."

"No? Did you rape Ida Praul?"

"You can't rape a whore."

"Why not?"

"Why . . . why, because she's had it before."

"A woman needn't be a virgin to be the victim of rape," Stephen explained.

"I think she does," Armand said.

"In any case, I understand that the doctor who was called in to examine Ida is prepared to testify that she was a virgin at the time of this . . . incident. So wouldn't that make it rape even from your point of view?"

"There's a lot more to it than that. Just because I got her cherry, it don't mean . . ." Armand stared at Stephen in a fury at the second unintended admission.

"Then you knew during the act that she had been a virgin?" Stephen asked.

"It don't make no difference whether she was cherry."

"But you knew?"

Armand looked down at his meaty hands lying in a loose grip on his thighs. His eyes and his head tilted upward suddenly, and he said, "Yeah. All right, yeah. I knew, not before, but while I was doin' it, she was cherry. So what?"

"You seem to be under the impression," Stephen said with ultimate calm, "that rape is more difficult to prove when the woman involved is of loose reputation. I would be the last to contradict you. You're quite right."

"I told them other guys, but they wouldn't believe me."

"But since the woman you raped was a virgin, how are we to prove she had a loose reputation? That's not much of a case, Armand."

"You're a stranger here. You don't know. Ida Praul's mother's the biggest whore in town. She—"

"You didn't rape Ida Praul's mother. As a matter of fact, you haven't told me yet whether or not you raped Ida Praul."

"I don't think I did."

"It can hardly be a matter of opinion, Armand."

"I think she was just actin'. I think she wanted it all the time, but she didn't want us to know it, so she put up a fuss. Tryin' to make herself feel like she was better than she is. She's just a little whore like her mother. . . ."

"She was a virgin."

"That's what she says."

"That's what the doctor says, and that's what you said a few minutes ago. Armand, you can't go into court and contradict yourself every few minutes and expect anything but a conviction for first-degree rape."

Armand looked at his hands again. He turned them over and stared into the deep, fat palms. "You want me to level with you, Hertzog?"

Stephen stared at Armand, feeling a kind of wonder at the boy's repulsiveness. "Yes, level with me."

"You ain't from around here. You don't know," Armand began, his head cocked to one side. "Ida Praul and her mother don't matter. Nobody gives a damn about 'em. You want a little advice, you just keep harpin' on Peg Praul an' what she is, 'cause nobody cares if she or her kid get raped. No jury ain't goin' to do nothin' to you for screwin' Ida Praul—she just ain't worth all the fuss."

Stephen got up and walked a few feet away from the table. He had known for a long time that to yield to genuine anger was foolhardy, often dangerous to one's own welfare. So long had he acted on this maxim that he had begun to distrust anger and seldom felt its full force. But he recognized it now in spite of himself, swelling inside him like a balloon inflated uncontrollably.

"All right, fat boy. Now I'm going to level with you. On the night of August twenty-third of this year, you assaulted a seventeen-year-old female human being. While two cronies pinned her helpless body to the ground, you completed the sexual act with this virgin child apparently without regard for either the consequences or the intrinsic immorality of the act. You have only to go into court with that cold fact exposed to a jury—any jury—and you will spend the next twenty years in prison. That's the way it stands as of this moment. The only person between you and that twenty years in jail is me, and I'm not at all sure I wouldn't rather be prosecuting you than defending you. So you'd better just knuckle down, fat boy, and start convincing me that you don't deserve that twenty years, because if I'm not convinced, nobody's going to be."

"Well . . . I can just get . . ."

"Shut up! As much as you'd like to be in the position of having merely had sexual intercourse with a panting slut, you are not. You have in fact raped a seventeen-year-old virgin, and a great many people are going to give considerably more than a damn about it—enough more to cut a twenty-year hunk out of your miserable life, and you'll be a broken, hopeless old man when it's past. I'm not sure you'd be a hell of a lot better without the twenty years in jail, but there's still a chance. If you want even a chance at that chance, you'd better say so right now, and you'd better say you want it on my terms, because that's the only way you're likely to get it. There are other lawyers and you're welcome to them—and *vice versa*. But if it's going to be me, it's going to be right now, and it's going to be my way—all the way. Just yes or no, Rapp."

He stared at the now moist, sweat-beaded flesh of Armand's face. The small eyes had narrowed to fear-filled slits. The hands made visible dents where they clenched the excessive meat of the thighs. The flesh of the face opened and the voice croaked, "Okay," and the vernacular was the only remaining pretense of self-control.

"All right," Stephen said quietly. He went to the door and opened it. Will Ziegler appeared in the hall from the other room. "I'm finished with him," Stephen told him. "May I see the other one?"

"Sure," Will Ziegler said. "Come on, Armand."

Armand rose and crossed the room silently. At the door he turned and looked into Stephen's eyes blankly again as he had when he had entered. He found Stephen's face set in the same finality he had heard in the totally controlled voice. Then he turned and went into the hall.

Will Ziegler ducked quickly into the other room and said, not unofficiously, "Artie Schlier? Over here."

Stephen heard a faint wail from the other room and saw on Artie's face, when he appeared in the doorway, the fading vestige of his wincing.

"Hello, Artie," Stephen said.

"Hello," Artie said.

"Do you want to come over and sit down?"

Artie crossed the room and sat across from Stephen as if he had been directed to. Quietly, respectfully, Will Ziegler closed the door behind him.

"Artie, I guess you know that my name is Stephen Hertzog. I'm probably going to be your attorney." Artie merely stared at Stephen, looking rather frightened. "Was that your mother I heard crying in the other room?"

Artie looked even more frightened and said, "Yes."

"She sounds very upset, but—"

"She's pretty old," Artie said.

"Old?" This was not where Stephen had intended to lead the conversation, but the statement seemed to him to be odd.

"Yeah. She's . . . she's pretty old," Artie said again.

"How old is your mother, Artie?"

"She's about fifty-nine."

"And your father?"

"He's about sixty, I think."

"What does your father do?" Stephen asked, following an instinct which he did not stop to question.

"He . . . he's in business."

"Oh," Stephen said pleasantly. "What business is he in?"

"He's in the jewelry business."

"That sounds profitable," Stephen said, mentally checking Artie's statement against Jim Beyers' information that Otto Schlier was an expert, though not very successful, watch repairman.

"Yeah," Artie said, looking away from Stephen.

"Are you a close friend of Johnny Taylor's?"

"Yeah, he's my best friend, I guess."

"You go to his house, know his family?"

"Yeah, sure." In spite of his nervousness Artie's curiosity was piqued.

"And he comes to your house, knows your parents?" Stephen went on, still unhesitatingly following the same instinctive line.

"Yeah, sometimes."

"How about your other friends? Do they visit you at your home?"

"Other . . ." Artie began. "Well . . . Johnny and me, we sort of pal around together alone."

"Oh, I see. You don't have other close friends?"

"Oh, I know other kids at school, sure."

"But you don't ask them to your house?"

"Well . . . no."

"Does Johnny?"

"Does he what?"

"Have other friends to his house."

"Yeah . . . I . . . I guess so."

"How long have and Johnny been friends?" Stephen asked after a moment.

"About four years, I guess."

"How about before that, did you have friends at your house much?"

Artie hesitated for a moment between a lie, which he felt somehow would soon be found out, and the truth, which was difficult for him to tell. "No . . . I guess I didn't."

"Why was that?"

"Oh . . . there . . . there's not too much to do at my house. There's the store there in front," he said without realizing the contradiction, "and we . . . there just isn't much to do."

"What do you do when you're all at other people's houses? At Johnny's house?"

"Oh, we dance," Artie began brightly, "or play . . . games . . . or just sit around and talk." The brightness in his voice dulled markedly as the sentence went on until the sound dwindled into silence, for Artie gradually realized the revelation.

"You couldn't dance or play games at your house?" Stephen asked softly.

"Well . . . we . . . like I said, Mama's pretty old. She . . ." Artie didn't finish.

"You haven't had many friends since you lived here, have you?"

"No, I guess . . . I . . . no."

"Artie, I don't mean to infer that you haven't been telling me the truth. I think that for the most part you have. But I want you to realize how important it is that you do tell me the truth—always, no matter what I ask you. Even if you think it has nothing to do with your defense, even if it seems to you more to your advantage for you to lie, you must tell me the absolute truth. Everything you tell me is in strict confidence. Not even your mother and father will know."

"All . . . right," Artie said hesitantly.

"Artie, I want you to tell me what happened on Friday night."

"I didn't mean to do anything wrong," Artie said, leaning forward in his chair. "I didn't think it would do no harm to go out with her."

"It wouldn't have done any harm just to go out with her. That's what I want to know about: what you did in addition to going out with Ida."

"I thought it was like Armand said, she was just making a fuss because . . . well, that's the way they're supposed to."

"Look, Artie," Stephen said, his voice hardening noticeably, "anything you did out there on that hill you did of your own free will. Nobody forced you to do anything. If you feel it's important for you to tell me what Armand said, then by all means tell me, but don't use it as an excuse for your own behavior. Now, go ahead and tell me what happened."

"Well, we got out of the car and went down the hill a little way. And then . . . then Armand did it and . . ."

Stephen sighed heavily. "Artie, what were you doing while Armand 'did it'?"

"I . . . I went to find Johnny. He went off somewhere."

Stephen's expression of skepticism was so unsubtle that even Artie read it quite clearly. "All four of you were standing up on the hillside just after you'd come from the car. What happened then—in detail?"

"Well . . . Armand and Ida . . . got down on the ground, and . . ."

"Artie, ever since you came into this room," Stephen interrupted unceremoniously, "you've seemed frightened. Are you frightened of going to prison?"

If Artie had wanted to lie, it would have been useless. His face was full of his terror. "Yes," he gulped faintly.

"You have good reason to be," Stephen said flatly. "And if you continue to lie to me, I'll give you a personal guarantee that that's just where you're going to go—and for quite a long time. Now, are you going to tell me what happened?"

"It was Armand, Mr. Hertzog," Artie pleaded. "Johnny and me wouldn't have done it if it wasn't for Armand. He—"

"I don't doubt that for a minute, Artie," Stephen said. "But what good do you think it's going to do you to say that now? You did do it, and you know that you did. You're seventeen years old, Artie. In the eyes of the law you are fully responsible for your own actions. No jury in the world is going to say, 'That terrible Armand Rapp made poor little Artie Schlier rape that girl. So we'll just send Armand off to jail and let Artie go free.' That isn't going to happen. My whole interest at the moment is your defense, and you don't even arouse any sympathy in me with that story. For some reason that I don't understand, you raped Ida Praul. I want you to tell me about it so that I might find out that reason."

"I don't know why I did it," Artie said miserably.

"I didn't ask you to tell me why. I asked you to tell me how. Now, tell me—the truth."

"When we . . . got to the hill . . ."

"How did you get Ida to the hill?"

"We . . . kind of pushed her . . . forced her."

"All right, go on."

"When we got to the place on the hill."

"What place on the hill?" Stephen asked, his eyes wide with alarm.

"The place where it happened."

"You don't in any way mean a preappointed place?"

"No . . . no."

"You didn't know, you didn't even suspect when you got into that car with Ida and the other two that what happened was going to happen?"

"No. Honest to God, I didn't."

"All right."

"When we got there, Armand made Ida lay down . . . forced her down, I guess. Then . . . Johnny and me . . . we fell on top of her legs and arms and held her while Armand did it. Johnny did go off someplace. He got sick, I guess. I went to look for him when Armand was . . . finished."

"Yes. Go on."

"Well, Johnny and me talked for a little."

"You talked?"

"Yeah. I told him Armand was finished and we talked about whether we ought to do it or not. We decided to go ahead and do it and . . ."

"Say that again," Stephen said harshly.

"Say it . . . ?"

"Say it again!" Stephen said. "What you just said!"

"I . . . I told him . . . Armand was finished . . . and we talked about whether we ought to do it or not. We decided . . . to go ahead and do it. . . ."

"That's fine. I don't ever want to hear you say that again, not to me or to Johnny or to your parents or to anybody in court, before the trial, after the trial—not ever. You are never to say, 'We talked about whether we ought to do it or not. We decided to go ahead and do it.' Do you understand?"

"Yes," Artie answered.

"Armand didn't hear you say that. Ida didn't hear you say it. Right?"

"That's right."

"So nobody's ever going to quote you, ask you if you said it. Right?"

"Yes."

"And you are never, under any circumstances, going to volunteer the information. Now, forget that you said it at all. Go on."

"I went over to where Ida was, and I . . . I did it to her."

"And then Johnny did it, and you all three went back to the car and drove home, leaving her there. Is that correct?"

"Yes."

"All right, Artie. Oh, I started to say before that you oughtn't to let your mother's distress frighten you any more than you're already frightened. I'm going to do everything I can for you. That's all for now, Artie."

Stephen got up and crossed to the door. He looked back and saw that Artie still sat in the chair, staring at him.

"Do you want to go back with your family now?" Stephen asked, opening the door.

Artie got up without speaking and went across the hall to the other room.

Jim Beyers saw Artie come out and at once went to talk to Stephen, who was waiting for him.

"Well, what do you think?" Jim asked.

"It's a tough one," Stephen said, lighting a cigarette. "And that Rapp boy isn't going to make it any easier unless he can be kept in hand."

"The whole Rapp clan is pretty much of one piece—and it's a very unpleasant piece."

"How about his parents?"

"His mother's dead. I'm afraid his father is about the worst of the lot, as is evidenced by the fact that he hasn't yet bothered to come to see his son."

"Armand seems to think that the reputation of this girl's mother gives him license to rape her."

"He didn't rape her mother—couldn't have raped her if I know Peg Praul," Jim said.

"My words exactly—without the comment, of course. It would

have been an entirely legitimate approach if the girl hadn't been a virgin."

"Yes."

Jim watched as Stephen drew deeply on his cigarette. He was looking at the ceiling, his eyes narrowed in thought.

"Have you decided about the case, Stephen?" Jim asked.

"What?" Stephen said, looking at Jim through the thick curls of smoke which wafted upward from his partially open mouth. "Oh, I'm sorry. I've been acting on that decision for the last hour, so that it just didn't occur to me that I hadn't told you. Yes. Yes, I'll take the case. I'll certainly reduce the fee as much as possible, Jim, but you understand that my whole financial setup is pretty stringent. I can't do it for nothing—or even next to nothing," he added with a little catch of laughter in his voice. "It'll cost seventy-five hundred dollars, and that, only if you'll agree to handle as much of the routine up here as possible."

"I don't know anything definite about the financial status of the others—aside from John Taylor, I mean—but . . . well, we'll manage it."

"I guess I'd better see them now," Stephen said. "Do you want me to talk to them about the money?"

"I'll take care of it," Jim answered. "I'll get them."

They came into the room and took seats silently, all reflecting the gravity of the situation they were about to face, yet with each personality finding its unmistakably individual means of expression.

As Jim Beyers was about to close the door, he saw George Rapp enter the building. He signaled to him, and George came into the room. Seeing the others seated, he joined them, sitting a little apart from them. Stephen was sitting so that he faced the group. He began to speak without looking at them, and the act of beginning seemed so abrupt that the listeners were startled.

"Many lawyers take great pains to develop what is called a bedside manner. I don't have one. It only serves to make the client and his relatives feel better, and in many cases—as in this one—that isn't a very good idea. It isn't a good idea because your sons are in serious trouble, and the sooner you and they realize it, the sooner we can get down to the business of doing something about it."

Stephen spoke very distinctly, and now and again his eyes darted about the room like the eyes of a bird. He was testing these people and watching for their reactions as a bullfighter watches, studying the effect of each pass to determine the speed and direction of the bull's charge.

"I don't know or care how you feel morally about what your sons have done, but you are entitled to know the legal nature of the trouble they're in, what their chances are of getting out of it, and roughly how I intend to go about getting them out of it in the event that you retain me. They're the things I want to tell you now. I'll try to do it in non-legal terms that you'll fully understand. First, the kind of trouble they're in."

As Stephen paused now, he felt that he had gained control. He looked up at them suddenly from the table top and went on.

"Although most people consider murder the most serious crime, they don't feel about murder the same revulsion that they feel about rape. In the law there is such a thing as justifiable homicide: self-defense or, in some extreme cases, incidents in which the victim has committed so monstrous an act that he deserves to be murdered. I've known cases, incidentally, when the rape of a man's wife was considered by the court a justifiable motive for murder. In any event, there is no justifiable rape. Perhaps it seems curious, but a woman may deserve to be murdered, yet she doesn't deserve to be raped. So in that sense we're dealing with a crime more serious than murder. To be more specific, I've discovered by talking to your sons that they did force Ida Praul to have sexual intercourse with them. That's first-degree rape, for which the maximum sentence in this state is twenty years. If we went into court and simply said that that is what happened, your sons would probably get twenty years. So much for their predicament."

Stephen lit a cigarette, blew the smoke out over the heads of his listeners and continued.

"Their chances of getting less than twenty years lie in the law's allowing us the opportunity of proving that the circumstances under which the crime was committed were such that they lessen the seriousness of the crime—or in legal terms, reduce the degree of the crime. If the girl led them to believe that she wanted to have sexual intercourse with them, deliberately excited them, urged them on and then changed her mind, there is even a possibility of acquittal. I don't, at this moment, see any positive way to convince a jury that there was no intercourse. So the practical objective becomes to get the boys off with second degree and as light a sentence as possible. I don't mean to rule out the—"

The sound of George Rapp's interrupting voice astonished Stephen, and he struggled to keep his face from reflecting that astonishment.

"You tryin' to tell us right off the bat that our boys are goin' to go to prison?" George said. "What the hell are we payin' you for then?"

The question suffered a loss of intensity in the silence which followed it. It was in no way an uncertain silence, for all uncertainty was dispelled by the expression in Stephen's eyes as he stared at his questioner.

"You're Mr. Rapp, I believe," he said, hoping that there would be no answer. There was not. "Armand is your son." The pause was shorter. "You'll be paying me to defend three boys against the State, which will be trying to send them to prison for twenty years. I have not and will not at any time try to predict the outcome of this trial. Anyone who does is a fool. If I defend these boys and they are acquitted—which I was about to say is not impossible—you'll pay my fee. If I defend them and they go to prison for twenty years, you'll pay my fee. And you will still have got what you paid for: a sound legal defense. You're paying for my services, which are necessary and worth the money regardless of the outcome of the trial. That's quite clear, isn't it, Mr. Rapp?"

"I . . . I want my boy got off," George Rapp said.

"So do I, Mr. Rapp, but if you can find an attorney who'll guarantee it, you'd better report him to the Bar Association."

There was a pause during which the room was utterly empty of movement. Then George Rapp shifted his great weight in his chair and said, suddenly: "Maybe nobody's told you about this here Ida Praul. Mother's a tramp. Girl probably ain't much better."

"If you're suggesting that we attack the girl's reputation," Stephen said, "you'd better also suggest an argument by which we might prove that a whore can be a virgin."

There was another pause, through which George squinted at Stephen.

Stephen went on. "You do understand, Mr. Rapp," Stephen said with heavy sarcasm, "that since the girl was a virgin, we might run into some trouble proving that she had an unsavory reputation? And there isn't any confusion in your mind as to who was raped, is there? It wasn't Ida Praul's mother; it was Ida Praul, who was seventeen and a virgin, although her mother is older and obviously not. If all these things are clear to you now, Mr. Rapp, I'll go on."

Again there was no answer, and Stephen turned his eyes from George to the others and went on. "I believe I was about to say that acquittal is not impossible, which brings us to the manner in which I might go about defending the boys. I will not be held to anything that I'm about to say. Subsequent examination of the defendants—and others—could utterly change the approach to this case. But for now this is how it looks. The reduction of the degree of the crime is a very subtle process. There are circumstances which can positively, legally, accomplish this. If those circumstances are present, the judge will instruct the jury that a verdict of first-degree rape would be improper. Such circumstances do not exist—at least not clearly—in this instance. That leaves the field wide open both for the prosecution and the defense. No verdict is either unacceptable or beyond the realm of possibility. Now, there is one other principal way of reducing the degree of this crime, and that is to convince the jury—not necessarily for legal reasons—that the defendants do not deserve the maximum sentence. That is the approach on which we'll have to rely. We would try to turn the jury's hostility toward the complainant—toward Ida Praul—and its sympathy toward the defendants. The success of this method could result ideally in acquittal; somehow less ideally in a verdict of second-degree rape. Its failure, of course, would result in a first-degree verdict. The sentence in any case is up to the judge. Even in first degree it would probably be an indeterminate sentence—*up to* twenty years, but I doubt that it would be less than ten. That's about all I have to say. Your decision to retain me must be based on implicit trust; if that trust is lacking, I don't wish to be retained. That's your first decision. If you don't mind, I'd like it made now."

Once again the room was utterly still. Slowly, John Taylor turned just his head to look at Jim Beyers. Jim cleared his throat and said, "I think they're all agreed, Stephen, that they want you to take the case."

"If there's any doubt about that in anyone's mind, I wish he'd say so now."

"This isn't . . . a doubt . . . Mr. Hertzog," John Taylor began haltingly. "But there's something I'd like to ask you. I don't really know . . . just how to put it. I see what you mean about Ida Praul's reputation. I mean, if we know what people say about her isn't true, we can't say it anyway in court just because it would help us. But . . . I don't want to seem a fool . . . but is . . . would it be honest to go into court, knowing the boys are guilty, and try to get them off anyway?"

Now Stephen Hertzog could not keep the astonishment from his face. He was even less successful in keeping it out of his voice. "If it weren't honest," he said, "and I could do it, would you want to prevent me?"

John looked at the floor, his face deeply troubled. Without changing his expression, he looked up again at Stephen and said, quite certainly, "No."

"I'm relieved to hear that, Mr. Taylor," Stephen said. After a moment he went on. "I assume then that it's decided. Mr. Beyers will be handling the details. At least one of us will be at your disposal at all times. The first thing to be done when the Judge returns on Monday is to arrange for the boys' release on bail. I don't see any reason why reasonable bail shouldn't be set, but that, of course, is up to the judge. I think that's all I can do just now. You'll be hearing from me in due course."

When Stephen got up, the others did so too. Jim went with him to the door.

George Rapp walked directly to the Taylors and said, "You think that guy's all right?"

"Of course I do," John said curtly, "or I would have said so."

"Huh. Sure hope you're right."

George turned and left the room. Slowly and silently the Schliers followed him. Mary started for the door, but turned to find John standing by the table, holding his hat, his head bowed slightly and the troubled look again on his face.

"John," she said. "Let's go back to Johnny now."

"Sure," he said without looking at her. He did not move. Mary walked back and stood near him.

"I don't think you seemed one bit a fool," she said firmly.

He looked at her, startled, and slowly the expression gave way to a smile. "Thank you, Mary," he said.

Then they turned and went across the hall to join their son.

XIII.

SATURDAY HAD BEEN A BAD DAY FOR PEG PRAUL. SHE HAD TO WAIT AT the hospital until mid-afternoon. It was not until two o'clock that she remembered her one o'clock date with Cal Ulmer. He had promised to take her shopping in the city. It was the first time since she had started to see him regularly, three months ago, that he had offered to buy her anything except drinks and an occasional meal, and she had been very determined about going. She knew, of course, that there was still some uncertainty about the trip. It would depend largely on Cal's mood and his state of sobriety when she met him at the Bridge Tavern. She had planned to be there, however, at twelve o'clock, so that if Cal were to arrive early, she would have some control over what he drank before they left for the city. When, at two o'clock, she remembered the date and there was still no definite word of the result of Ida's examination, she knew the trip would have to be canceled—or, if she had her way, postponed.

She went to a public telephone in the hall of the hospital and called the Bridge Tavern. She knew from the first word he spoke into the telephone that he was drunk.

"Peg?" he said. "Peg who? I don't know no Peg."

"Now, listen to me, Cal Ulmer," she said authoritatively. "You go on home an' wait for me."

"Home?" he said in mock surprise. "What would you be doin' at my room?"

"You know what I mean: my place. You got your key?"

"I threw it off the bridge," he told her.

"Like hell you did. Can't I leave you alone for a minute without you gettin' stinkin' drunk? And what about our trip to the city?"

"Hah! That's a laugh!" he said. "You didn't even show up."

"I had good reason not to. You treatin' me like this when my poor . . . Ida . . ."

"Yeah! I heard! Got laid three times last night. Doin' almost as good as her old lady."

"You shut up, you drunken son of a bitch!" she said. Her regret was immediate. "Go on, Cal honey. Go back to the place and wait for me. I won't be long."

"Don't hurry on my account, Mama," he said. "I got somethin' all lined up right here." And she heard the click of the receiver.

She dialed the Bridge Tavern again, but Cal refused to speak to her. She left a message that she would be there as soon as she could and went back to the waiting room. She found her own fury nearly unbearable when, forty minutes later, she was told not by Dr. McKenna, but by an interne, that Ida's examination and treatment had been completed and that Ida was under sedation and sleeping soundly. She would probably sleep straight through the night, Peg was told, and they thought it advisable not to discharge her until Sunday afternoon. They would make an exception to the regular visiting hours if she wanted to return tonight . . . but at once Peg was striding down the hall, her plastic heels clicking loudly against the marble and her stiff hair bouncing regularly up and down, as if all the hairs were glued together.

She arrived at the Bridge Tavern at three-thirty and found Cal considerably drunker, but not, as he had said, otherwise occupied. Two of the six men standing along the gray-brown path to the dart board (that they had helped to wear in the linoleum), were friends of hers and they spoke to her.

She ordered a drink, which she declared she badly needed, and when Cal refused to pay for it, she did so herself. Then for some time she cajoled and simpered. Next she pleaded, all without the least hint of success. At first she tried to get Cal to go home with her, but when this failed, she proclaimed herself a lady of great pride. She was angry then, but Cal began to ignore her completely. She hit him on the shoulder to get his attention, causing him to knock over his drink. He turned, without excessive emotion, and struck her in the face with his fist, knocking her off the stool on which she had sat.

The bartender said, "All right, Cal. Cut it out!" and one of the men from the dart board picked Peg up. At a nod from the bartender this man helped Peg toward the door as she screamed obscenities at Cal. Gently the man pushed her through the doorway and closed the door. She stood for a moment, screaming foully at the closed door. Then she patted the back of her wiry hair, tugged downward at her tight skirt and clicked plastically up Main Street.

She went directly to Frank Ferraioli's Murray Street Grill, which was never called anything but "Frank's" and which was her favorite drinking establishment. Serafina Ferraioli, who was never, except in anger, called anything but Dolly, was tending bar. She was loudly and profanely angry at Cal Ulmer's treatment of her friend, and gave Peg a piece of beef for her eye. Peg sat at the bar, wetting the beefsteak with her tears, as she related again and again the details of her mistreatment. In one of her many expressions of sympathy, Dolly complained that this latest misfortune, coupled with Ida's tragedy, was almost too much for poor Peg to bear. With a gasp, as if she had suddenly remembered, Peg began a delicious recounting of Ida's story, which for the customers held a touch of novelty not to be found in tales of Peg's mistreatment. And to hear the details of this already celebrated incident first hand—well, at least from someone on the inside—was an exciting privilege.

During the fourth telling of the tale, Peg found herself being consoled by a rather dapper gentleman who, when she finally stopped talking, turned out to be a friend of a friend visiting from the city. He was wearing a silver-gray suit of nubby synthetic silk and a straw hat with a silver and blue band. He wore wing-tipped brown and white shoes, discreetly perforated for foot comfort, and pale blue silk socks which matched his hatband and tie. He had a tiny brown and white moustache which seemed to have been designed to complement his shoes.

It was nearly five o'clock—the stores were beginning to close—when he and Peg, the blue-black spreading beneath the skin of her puffed eye, left Frank's and started for her house. As they passed the Très Chic Chapeaux Shoppe, he pointed out the beautiful hats in the window and insisted she have one. She was so stunned that she stood staring at him for a moment with her one open eye, but then recovered so quickly that at the next moment she clicked into the shop like a shod rabbit.

The salesgirl was initially cold, but her enthusiasm for hats soon overcame her sense of propriety, and finally she sold them what she described as a "chick" little darling of a hat at $6.98.

After this, on the way home, Peg clung so tightly to her companion that he, in embarrassment, loosened her grip once or twice. Once indoors, however, he became in Peg's own phrase, "cuddlier" than she. They "cuddled" and drank far into the evening until on returning from one of her trips to the bathroom, Peg found him crumpled into unconsciousness on her bed. She sat down beside him forming a hazy plan to let him rest for half an hour, but she soon followed him into sleep.

Peg awakened in the early hours of the morning from a dual pain around her eye: a sharp, stinging pain from the cut, and a dull ache from the purple bruise. She got up, stumbling, and undressed. Then with some difficulty she roused her companion from his alcoholic stupor. He had undressed laboriously, folding his suit and shirt and tie and underwear. He folded even his socks, which he put into the perfectly placed shoes beneath the chair. Peg had nearly fallen asleep during this ritual, but at last he came to bed, where Peg found him too gentle, too submissive a lover.

The piercing pain in Peg's eye seemed suddenly duplicated by the ringing of the telephone. The return of reality was at once gradual and too quick: sunlight bordering and peeking through the cracks in the green paper shade; the warmth, the presence of the other body in her bed; the memory of the soft gentleness; the new hat; the drinking; the unconsciousness and reawakening; awakening, yes; the telephone.

"Hullo," she said, her voice so thick with recent abuses that the word could hardly be understood.

"Mrs. Praul, please," a sweet, feminine voice said.

"This . . ." She cleared her throat painfully and had to swallow several times before she could begin again. "This is Mrs.—"

"Just one moment, please."

Peg sighed heavily and looked back at the bed. In the dimness she could see the S-curved form of her gentleman under the sheet.

"Mrs. Praul?" a voice said through the telephone. It was low and harsh, and Peg could not tell whether it belonged to a man or a woman.

"Yeah, this is her."

"This is Mrs. Barton, Audubon Hospital. We are discharging your daughter this afternoon. Dr. Carter asked me to tell you that he thinks it would be wise for you to come and get her."

"Yeah, sure," Peg said. "What time?"

"We rather expected to hear from you before this," the voice said archly. "She'll be ready in a few minutes."

"You said this afternoon. What do you mean—"

"It is now . . . two o'clock . . . Mrs. Praul," the voice said, scanning the perfectly matched syllables.

"Oh . . . sure. I was thinkin' it was about noon. I'll be there soon."

Peg went into the bathroom, washed her face and put on a pink rayon nightdress which was hanging on the door. She came out and went to the bed.

"Charlie," she said, softly. He did not answer. She touched him gently on the shoulder and said again, "Charlie."

The man sprang to a sitting position, mumbling among unintelligible syllables, "Huh? What? Huh?"

"It's me, Charlie, Peg."

"What? Oh, yes," He rubbed his eyes sleepily and said, "What time . . . is it?"

"It's two o'clock, honey. Do you want to go back to sleep?"

"No. No, I'll get up now."

"Why don't you go back to sleep for an hour?"

"What? No, I'm awake now. I'll get up."

"Well, I . . . I have to go someplace for about an hour. You can just . . . laze aroun' an' . . ."

"Go someplace?" he said, opening his eyes wide for the first time. "Where d'you have to go?"

"To get Ida."

"Who's Ida?"

"You remember," she told him. "My baby. The one who got . . . you know. Friday night."

"Oh. Oh, of course. Ida." He pulled back the sheet, then realizing his nakedness, covered himself. "I'll just run along, then. Only take me a . . ."

"Oh, no, Charlie!" Peg cried. "Don't you remember, we was goin' to have a day together. I was goin' to cook you breakfast an' you was goin' to tell me all about your hardware business an'—"

Startled, he said, "I told you about my business?"

"Yeah, sure. An' I got another fifth of Seagrams' an' lotsa beer. We was goin' to have a day together—an' maybe a night, too." She stopped and nudged him with her elbow.

"Well, it's a little late for breakfast, Peg," he said gently, "and if you have to go and get your little girl, I'd just better be getting—"

"Oh, Charlie!"

Suddenly she ran across the room and picked up the new hat. She jammed it straight on top of her head and walked across the room on her toes, her arms extended flowingly, her head cocked coyly in what she believed to be only a slightly exaggerated imitation of the fashion model's attitude.

"Don't you remember my lovely new hat?" she said in a horrible approximation of an English accent.

"Sure I do, Peg. It looks beautiful on you."

"Aw, come on, Charlie. Stay. We had such fun. We could have more."

"I'd like to. Honest. But you have to go and get your little girl and . . ."

Peg did not hear the rest of his protest. She was thinking of the little hat; of his extreme, if unsatisfying, gentleness; of his refined speech; of his nubby suit; of his cuddliness.

"Could you eat some eggs?" she asked, seemingly incongruously.

"What?"

"If you could eat some eggs, I'd fix 'em."

"What about your little girl?"

"Oh, she'll be okay. She's fixed up now—by the hospital. I'll send a cab for her. All the cab drivers is friends of mine. They'll take care of her as good as me. I'll cook you some swell eggs an' . . . an' I'll make you a sour!" she added excitedly. "Ida don't need me to come an' get her. She'll be fine."

He reached out, smiling, and tickled her belly. "Okay, honey. That sounds just okay to me."

Ida was standing next to a tree outside the hospital when the cab went by, and the driver did not see her. She had waited for a short while in the reception hall of the hospital, but she soon became the target of muted and badly hidden attention which drove her to the street. There she aligned herself with the tree and stood very still for nearly an hour attempting to camouflage herself. She had hoped to intercept her mother and leave the scene with a minimum of difficulty. Her plan, like most of Ida's plans, served only to work against her.

The cab driver inquired for Ida at the reception desk. The nurse at the desk had seen her leave and asked the driver if he hadn't seen her outside. As the driver said he had not, the doorman approached the desk and told them that he had noticed her walking down the street. This short sequence of events crescendoed from a simple inquiry to a missing-persons-panic. The aura of sexual tragedy which now surrounded Ida gave rise to a sadly ludicrous manhunt. The nurse and the cab driver and the doorman and two internes and three visitors rushed from the hospital as if it were afire. One of the internes, spitting instructions in a fine surgical manner, sent half the party north, while he, the nurse, the cab driver and one of the visitors went south on Audubon Avenue. Within two minutes they found Ida next to her tree, and the sudden deflation of the panic was abruptly disappointing.

"Ida!" the interne said, more in confusion than discovery. "Ida, what are you doing here?"

Ida was frightened by this excitement. "I'm waiting for my mama," she said, drawing closer to her tree.

"I'm going to take you home, Ida," the cab driver said.

"Where's Mama?" Ida asked.

"She . . . she couldn't come," the cab driver said, and added hastily, "but she's waiting for you at the house."

"Yes. Come with us, Ida," the interne said. "The cab's up here in the driveway."

Ida walked with the cab driver, and the others were a few steps ahead.

The nurse said to the interne, in not sufficiently hushed tones to prevent Ida's hearing, "That woman! She can't even come to get her own daughter. And after what she's been through!"

"Probably too busy shacking up with somebody," the interne said.

"There isn't a decent bone in that woman's body! She ought to be horsewhipped!"

"She obviously couldn't care less whether the kid lives or dies," the interne said. Then with a look over his shoulder at Ida's blank face he hushed the nurse, and they went on in silence.

For the first few minutes of the trip to the Praul house, the cab driver said pleasant things about Peg's eagerness to see her daughter. But since none of them made sense, either to him or to Ida, he soon became silent.

Ida said quietly, "Thank you for comin' to get me. Goodbye."

When the cab had gone, Ida stood for a moment, looking at the bleak red brick house. Then she went around to the back door and went in. Cautiously she pushed open the door from the porch to the kitchen. She heard her mother's incongruously high laughter coming from the front room. Peg pushed back the curtain and came into the room, belting a thin cotton housecoat which she wore over the pink nightdress. She looked up and saw Ida.

"Ida!" she said. "Ida . . . baby!" There was silence. "How . . . how are you?"

Ida did not answer. Peg went to her and put her arms around her.

"Oh, Mama!" Ida cried and, pushing her head against her mother's breast, wept freely. And the tears, soaking through the cotton and the rayon and finally dampening Peg Praul's ample bosom, cleansed from her, in her daughter's mind, all the vileness, all the foul smell of her, all the ugliness that Ida might then have seen. Washed away, too, in that salty torrent were the white-clad nurse and her foolish accusations; the reception hall full of eyes and shaking heads; the recent, now distant lonely morning of motherlessness; gone, all gone with the purifying tears. For Ida believed that she felt her mother's love, the love she needed so desperately that she manufactured it out of the hot grip of those stubby, encircling arms, created it from the simple, animal gesture which had sprung not from Peg's love, but from her confusion. And Ida, so degraded by the years of her mother's neglect that she felt unworthy of love from anyone, stood now in this brief, new illusion, weeping and trembling with the joy of it.

Ida heard the deep, masculine cough from the front room, but it had come too late. Love had preceded it, and made it simply the sound of incidental circumstances which she could ignore in the newly born complacency of her love.

"We got to get you to bed," Peg said.

"I'm all right, Mama," Ida answered.

"Oh, no, honey. You gotta get to bed."

"Yes. Yes, Mama," Ida said, smiling, unable to resist these tender, novel, but now never-to-end attentions of her phantom love. "Yes, Mama, put me to bed."

When Peg had tucked in the sheet, saying, "Now, you sleep, baby." and hurried away from the bed, leaving Ida hungering for her kiss, Ida merely closed her eyes and dreamed of all the kisses there would now be. No need for this kiss or that kiss in the profusion of kisses there would now be. No need, no need, ever again.

XIV.

The Audubon County Courthouse was a neoclassic oasis in a desert of worse than mediocre architecture. The courthouse was in the heart of Harrisville, the county seat. It stood at the top of a landscaped and terraced slope, which on its various man-made levels held green slatted benches and archaic cannon. At the foot of this park was Harris Street. It was lined with simple boxlike structures of brick and stone, some of which were quite old, but no more attractive than the others for their antiquity. Those which had not been built as stores had long ago been converted into stores, so that for half a mile Harris Street was a tasteless profusion of plate glass and neon, interrupted occasionally by the bogus dignity of a pretentious bank building or the hideous angular hodgepodge of a movie theater. Opposite the courthouse, sharing the plateau on which it sat, were a steepled, gray-stone Episcopal church and the county jail.

It was to this spot, four miles from their homes, that John Taylor, Otto Schlier and George Rapp had been summoned to attend the bail hearing for their sons. The call had gone out from the justice of the peace to Magistrate Loomis to Attorney Beyers to them. And, bail having been arranged, the three men left the courthouse with their sons in the awkward silence which always characterized their reluctant meetings.

The three pairs of men began to part company amid mumbled farewells: "See you later," which reminded them that they surely would; "Bye now," which suddenly sounded coy and feminine; and "So long," which seemed far too familiar and convivial.

George and Armand Rapp got into the five-year-old Plymouth which

John Taylor had sold George last year. They started down the hill toward Harris Street and turned left in the direction of home.

"Fine mess you got into," George Rapp said. "Don't you know no better than to do a thing like that?" The question remained as unanswerable as he had intended. "This kinda trouble's worse than knocking her up."

"I don't know about that," Armand answered petulantly.

"You don't, huh, you smart bastard," George said. "Wait'll they send you to jail for a few years. Then you'll know."

"What's so goddamned bad about what we did?" Armand said. "Who's Ida Praul, anyway? She ain't nobody."

"You damn dumb bunny," George said, not looking at his son. "Every day they's women raped all over the country. Hell, they's wives raped regular once a week by their husband. They's ways of doin' it. An' if you ain't bright enough yet to know them ways, then just keep your pants zippered." He paused for a moment, pleased with the soundness of his advice. "An' leavin' her out there on Potts Hill. Jesus!"

"What else could we do?"

"You don't have the good sense to give a girl a ride home after you had her, you deserve to get in trouble."

"She was out cold!" Armand protested.

"I don't care if she was havin' pups, you should have took her home!"

"We took her home like that, her mother woulda had the cops after us before we left her house."

"Instead of the next day, you mean. Dumb bastard! Look, Armand, you put her back in the car; you take her for a ride; you give her a couple o' drinks; you smooch her up a little, like you was fond of her. Make her think you're maybe goin' to take her out again soon. Like you didn't mean it to be just this one time for what you could get off her. She gets to thinkin' how after all, it's over . . . and maybe it wasn't so bad at that. Besides, she's gettin' all this attention—they all love the attention—an' you'll be comin' callin' before too long. She even thinks you'll sure come callin' 'cause she's got this thing to hold over your head. So you take her out once more, maybe even get it again. Let her try to yell rape then. Just let her try!"

"It wasn't like that," Armand said sullenly.

"No, sure as hell wasn't," George Rapp said. "But it ought to been if you an' your friends wasn't such dumb bastards. An' that's another thing: what the hell are you doin' takin' seventeen-year-olds out with you? Bet them two kids never even did it before. What the hell you think you're doin'?"

The guilt of his own inadequacy filled and sickened Armand so that he could not speak.

George shook his huge head from side to side slowly. "The three of you, leavin' her out there on Potts Hill to walk home herself all sore an' prob'ly scared of the dark—all women are scared of the dark. Naturally the first thing she's goin' to do is yell rape. You ought to stay home at night, Armand, and build model airplanes."

"Ain't there nothin' we can do to get out of it?" Armand asked.

"Looks like that's up to that smart-ass lawyer from the city," George Rapp said, "an' I wouldn't trust him as far as I could throw him."

"Jesus! What we goin' to do?"

"Shut up your whinin'," George snapped. "You're as bad as your old lady was, always whinin'."

"Wouldn't make no difference to you if I went to prison," Armand complained.

"No, whatever else you are, you're my own flesh and blood," George told him matter-of-factly. "I ain't goin' to sit around an' watch you sent to no jail. I'll work somethin'. I got friends in town. I'll work somethin'."

George and Armand had reached the bottom of the hill and Harris Street before the others had even parted. Jim Beyers stood with John and Johnny and Otto Schlier stood with his son, facing them.

Rather reluctantly, John said what he thought he must. "Did you drive up, Mr. Schlier? I can give you a lift if you want."

"No thank you, Mr. Taylor," Otto Schlier said in his comic German accent. "Thank you very much and good night."

He turned and started down the hill. Artie followed him without speaking. They walked to Harris Street in silence and crossed the street when the traffic light changed. Even when Artie was walking with his father, he seemed somehow to be following him. They walked past the stationery store and the pharmacy and stood before the haberdashery at the bus stop.

"Papa," Artie said. His father looked at him sadly. "Couldn't we ... couldn't we take a cab, this once?"

Mr. Schlier's brow was lined, and now the lines deepened as he regarded his son and his son's suggestion with characteristic caution.

"Yes," he said, his brow unwrinkling, "yes, perhaps you are right."

Without further discussion, they went around the corner to the taxi stand. Neither of them spoke during the ride home, and they were both acutely conscious of the presence of the driver.

Mr. Schlier's watch repair shop occupied what had once been the living room of the house. No extensive alterations had been made to convert it to a store, and the Schliers still used the front door as the principal entrance to the house. As Mr. Schlier selected the key from his amply keyed chain, Artie stood in dread of the moment when the movement of the door would jingle its brass bell in the darkness, and his mother would hurry to meet them.

The rumble of the heavy sliding doors and the widening patch of incandescent light were accompanied by a lachrymose cry of "Papa? Artie? Artie!"

As they made their way through the still dark shop, Mrs. Schlier covered her face with her hands and turned away, unable to bear the stress of her gratitude and her shame. Inside the small sitting room, Artie turned to his father as if to plead for the words he should say. His father turned to close the sliding doors.

"Artie!" his mother cried again, facing him now and extending her arms.

Artie was taller than she, and she had in recent years grown so fat that the embrace was as awkward physically as it was emotionally. There was a moment of burlesque pantomime as she tried to bend the tall, slender youth around her globular hulk.

Wiping away her tears, she said, "Come. Come, Artie, into the kitchen. I'll fix you some supper."

"I'm not hungry, Mama," he answered.

"You must eat," she said. "Come."

They went into the kitchen where Artie and his father sat at the gleaming chrome and enamel table. This was the only room of the house which had modern furniture. The others were furnished in a way which as closely as possible apprixmated the Schliers' memory of their early homes. The small sitting room just behind the store was kept in cluttered order. The heavy velours furniture looked more inflated than overstuffed, and ornate little tables and cabinets held rococo porcelain figurines. There were two cut-glass vases with pink crepe-paper flowers, and at the end of the room on a good but graceless oak table stood a cherished Meissen clock.

Mrs. Schlier made her way about the kitchen knowingly. She was making sauerbraten for Artie, making in fact, far more food than he would have eaten if he had been hungry. As in moments of crisis some people light cigarettes or pour a whiskey or reach for their knitting, Mrs. Schlier prepared food. Suddenly she leaned on the edge of the sink and cried, "Oh, my Artie. How could you do this? What have we done that you should do this?"

Artie winced and his head hung lower, but Mr. Schlier changed neither his facial expression nor his posture.

Mrs. Schlier went to her son and put her hands on his shoulders. "I'm sorry, Artie! But I do not understand. We have tried to teach you to be good! I don't know where you learned such—"

"Leave the boy alone, Mama," Mr. Schlier said, still looking at the table top.

Mrs. Schlier's surprise was no greater than Artie's. Neither of them had the remotest idea what that man was thinking, but that he should have spoken at all at such a moment was cause for astonishment.

"What? What, Papa?" Mrs. Schlier said, breathlessly.

"Leave him alone," Mr. Schlier repeated. "You try to be nice, Mama, but you only punish him with your crying. He is punished enough."

"Our boy has done a terrible thing, and we must—"

"We must ask ourselves, 'Why?'" the old man said, looking into his wife's eyes. "All my life I thought I never knew somebody who could do such a thing—to take a little girl. Now I find I know somebody—and he is here right in my own house! He is my son that I taught . . ."

"What did you teach me, Papa?" Artie asked quietly.

Mr. Schlier's eyes lowered too quickly, angrily, from his wife's face to the boy's.

"What did you teach me, Papa?" Artie said again. "To sing the Christmas carols in German."

"It is not enough. This I have known for a long time . . . but it was all I had to teach."

"That ain't true," Artie said.

"Could I teach you baseball, take you fishing?"

"You could have taught me the Christmas carols in English."

"We were homesick . . . lonely. . . ." Otto Schlier faltered.

"This is my home. You told me that often enough."

"You . . . were so young . . . always to us . . . you seemed so young."

"And you were . . . you are so . . . old," Artie said. "Is that what you mean, Papa?"

"Too old we were," Mr. Schlier said, shaking his hairless head sadly. "Old and tired with living and with the struggling. It is no time of life for children."

"I knew!" Artie shouted, at once tearful and defensive. "You think I didn't know! I was too late! You didn't want me! Never."

"No, no!" Mr. Schlier said, pleading with his son. "It is not true. We had love for you always. But . . . you were so young . . . a young stranger in our house. And worse it got . . . while you grow up . . . always more distance gets between us . . . until . . . this. Now to myself I say, 'Who . . . who is this one?' "

"Yeah, that's what I was to you, all right," Artie shouted. "A stranger . . . a damn stranger . . . nobody wanted . . . in my own home!"

"A good home it was not," Mr. Schlier said, looking at the floor.

Artie's voice softened as he said, "Papa . . . Papa, I know you didn't—"

"A good home it was not or you could not go out from it and do as you did."

"Papa!" Mrs. Schlier cried.

"Do not hold the boy so, Mama. He does not want to be held."

"Papa, he is my son!"

"He is your son, but you did not know him before, and you do not know him now. Do not hold him so."

"Papa," Artie said in German, "I'm sorry."

"I, too, am sorry," Mr. Schlier said in English. "And I am ashamed. I am ashamed for you and Mama, yes, but mostly I am ashamed for myself. Now, go to bed Artie. We will talk tomorrow."

"But Papa, the sauerbraten . . ." Mrs. Schlier said.

"He is not hungry, Mama. Go to bed, Artie."

Artie got up and patted his mother's shoulder awkwardly. Then he went to the kitchen doorway, where he said good night, again in German, and went up the stairs to bed.

John and Johnny Taylor and Jim Beyers watched the Schliers start down the hill to Harris Street.

"I saw Judge Forsythe coming out of his chambers. Do you suppose he'll ever change, John?" Jim said, into the silence with an attempt at casualness.

"It sure doesn't look like it," John answered.

"You know, I can remember him when I was just a kid. He didn't look a great deal different then than he does now. He's a fine man, too. One of the real old-timers."

"He was a great friend of your father's wasn't he?"

"Yes, indeed. Used to play chess together every Thursday night. Which reminds me that we haven't got together for quite a while—must be a couple of weeks anyway. I'll have Kay call Mary about dinner some night soon. Maybe play some cards."

"That's fine with me. Mary'll be pleased."

"Well, I guess I'll be on my way," Jim said.

When they got to the car, Johnny walked around to the far side, opened the door and got in. John started the motor and they both turned toward the rear window to look for oncoming traffic. They rode in silence through the steadily thinning business district into the strips of row houses.

When Johnny came in from the sunporch, his mother and sister were standing together across the room. He stopped just inside the door and said, "Hi."

After just a moment, Lois cried, "Johnny!" and ran across the room and hugged him. He did not return the embrace, but stood submitting awkwardly.

When Lois released him, Mary said, "Hello, Johnny. It's good to have you home."

"Thanks," he said. He turned to Lois who stood near him now. "How are you, Lo?"

"Fine. How are you?" she asked.

"I'm all right."

"You go and get ready for supper, Johnny," Mary said. "It'll only take me five minutes to get it on the table."

"Okay," he said and went upstairs, grateful somehow to be alone.

He went into his room and simply stood, looking about. He saw the bureau and the chair and the bed, which, he realized suddenly, belonged to his parents, but which, through long use had become *his* bureau and *his* chair and *his* bed. The possessive had a new meaning for him as he stood in the room. These things were indeed his, the personal equipment of his daily life: the desk his father had made for him long ago, the well-filled tie rack, the blue and red high-school pennant, the portable phonograph, the shirt hanging neatly across the back of the chair where he had left it after work on Friday evening. These things were his, and he had recently lost them. He had regained them now, but he might soon lose them again—perhaps forever. At no time until now had the full meaning of this fate struck him. He stood in this precious room, filled with love for these dear objects and paralyzed with fear of the loss of them. The deeper meaning which he had sought in Ida seemed trivial now, seemed not to exist at all, and the act which he had performed with her seemed void and meaningless. He reached out slowly and touched the comb and brush which lay on the bureau. He was afraid that they would disappear at his fingertips. The whole room became suddenly terrifyingly temporary. Nothing seemed to be his. It was as if he had walked into someone else's room where he did not belong and where nothing belonged to him. He had no claim to them now. They were lost to him, lost forever.

He ran into the bathroom where he stood crying softly behind the closed door until he heard his mother calling, "Johnny. Supper's almost ready," and he could not answer for the sudden, violent sobbing.

Supper was an unintentionally somber affair interspersed with little bursts of stilted cheerfulness. The Taylors' preoccupation with ignoring what was foremost in all their minds brought a deadly emphasis to the subject.

"Mr. Simpson expects you at work tomorrow, Johnny," John said after one of the many long pauses in the conversation.

"Are you . . . are you sure?" Johnny asked.

"He phoned your mother this afternoon," John said, "to say it didn't make any difference to . . ."

After a moment Mary said, "Well . . . why ever wouldn't you go in to work?" Only silence answered her question.

No one spoke for several minutes.

"Guess what, Johnny?" Lois said. "I missed Sunday School yesterday."

"It's an ill wind," John said and looked quickly at Mary as if he expected a sharp rebuke.

"What does that mean, Daddy?" Lois asked.

"It's just an expression, Lois," Mary said. "It doesn't mean anything."

"Everybody hollers like mad when *I* say things that don't mean anything," Lois said. "Even when they do—to me, I mean."

"You haven't changed a bit," Johnny said, smiling at Lois.

"Goodness! You haven't been away forever," Lois said, and immediately even she was silenced.

When supper was over John went into the living room and Johnny and Lois helped Mary with the dishes. This was the normal household routine, and they all behaved as if everything were the same as it had been before Saturday morning. But it was not the same, and the terrible difference hung like smoke in the air of the household. Soon they were all in the living room, watching television. They laughed at the comedian and commented on the performances of singers and dancers. They quietly but energetically pretended to themselves that this was a normal evening gathering of the family. No one asked why Lois had not gone to the movies with a friend. No one asked why Johnny was not out somewhere with Artie Schlier. They simply sat, each acting out his own impression of the norm.

"Time for bed, Lois," Mary said, and twenty minutes later, after the inevitable objections and the answers to them, Lois went upstairs.

John got up and turned off the news broadcast and, stretching, said, "Well, guess it's time to turn in." But he sat down again and lit a cigarette.

For a time they sat without speaking. John smoked, Mary leafed through a magazine and Johnny simply sat.

At last Johnny said, "I guess it might be better if we talked about it."

"What is there to say?" John asked.

"I don't know," Johnny answered. "It just seems like we . . . ought to talk about it."

"There are some things that just don't bear discussion," Mary said.

"But, Mother, we can't just sit around from now till October and not . . . not talk about it."

"October?" Mary said, looking up quickly.

"The trial," John said.

"Is . . . is that when it is?" she asked.

"Yes," John said. "Johnny, there'll be enough said about it between now and then. We'll be talking to Jim Beyers and Mr. Hertzog and . . . well, there'll be enough talk about it. There's no point in pushing it."

"I know you're right, Dad, but . . . well, that's not what I mean."

"What do you mean?" John asked.

"It's just that . . . well, we seem to be going out of our way not to talk about it."

"We can't very well discuss it in front of Lois," Mary said, her attention again on the magazine.

"That's what I mean," Johnny said.

"What?" Mary said, an unturned page still in her hand.

"Don't we have to tell Lois something?" Johnny asked.

"You leave that to me, Johnny," John said.

"Sure, Dad, but what are you going to tell her?"

"I . . . I don't know yet."

"It's just . . . I don't want her to think . . ." He looked at the floor. "I guess I just don't want her to know the truth."

"Well, we can't tell her the truth, Johnny," Mary said.

"Somebody will," Johnny said, still looking down.

"I'd hate to think that anybody . . ." Mary began.

"Johnny's right, Mary," John said. "Eventually somebody's going to tell her the truth, so we might just as well do it ourselves. But, Johnny, you leave that to me. I don't want you . . . well, I just don't want you to tell her."

"All right," Johnny said. "I guess I'll go to bed." He got up and went to the stairs. "Good night."

Johnny heard Lois' sibilant signal as he reached the top of the stairs.

"Come on in," she whispered, opening the door wider.

Johnny went into Lois' room and stood as she hopped into a crouching position on the bed. She looked up at him expectantly.

"What do you want?" he asked.

"Well, tell me!" she said, emphatically.

"Tell you what?" he said.

"What happened," she said, wrinkling her face into a painful expression of impatience.

"It . . . it's none of your business, Lo," Johnny told her.

"None of my business?" she said. "Johnny, you're my brother, and they arrested you and . . ."

"Just forget it."

"You've been talking to *them,* haven't you?"

"Well, sure I've been talking to them. What's that got to do—"

"They told you not to say anything."

"You're a nut, Lois. Go on to sleep." He turned to leave.

"Johnny."

"What?" he said, turning back to her.

"Tell me, Johnny."

"Tell you what?" he asked impatiently.

"Tell me what you did to Ida Praul."

"It . . . it's nothing you have to know."

"Yes, I do."

He looked at her for a long time, crouching on the bed in her spotless, unwrinkled pajamas, her blond hair falling loosely around her little face.

"Go to bed, Lo," he said at last.

"Tell me, Johnny!" she pleaded.

"Dad will tell you."

"No, he won't," she answered.

"He will, Lo."

"No, he won't. I've already asked him."

"What . . . what did he say?" Johnny asked her.

"He wouldn't tell me."

"Well . . . he's going to."

"Johnny, if he doesn't tell me, will you?"

"I can't . . . Dad's going to do it. That's all. Good night."

He turned and left the room before she could speak again, but he thought of Lois far into the night as he lay troubled and sleepless in his bed. He wondered, doubtfully, if she would ever understand what he had done. He thought with horror of her victimized as Ida Praul had been, and his crime seemed more monstrous. But then his thoughts, like the last waking thoughts of Armand Rapp and Artie Schlier, turned to himself. He thought of the unbelievable reality of the coming trial; he thought of the shame he had caused and the harm he had done. As his eyes closed, he thought of the price he might pay, and though he slept he dreamed fearfully.

XV.

IT IS THE EXTRAORDINARY EVENT WHICH RIPS AWAY THE VENEER AND exposes the multiplicity beneath a town. As when in 1932 elderly Clement Parsons strangled his wife with a silk stocking and shot himself through the head in their elegant house on upper Main Street, leaving behind him no note, no clue as to his motive, leaving behind him only a will which bequeathed his substantial fortune to his two grown children. Then, out of its heterogeneity, the town had manufactured motives for Clement Parsons' act: a young mistress from the city; a suicide pact born of Mrs. Parsons' malignant tumor and Mr. Parsons' inability to go on without her; insanity which everyone *knew* ran in his family.

As when in 1939 the high school's newly hired male English teacher was found in an exceedingly compromising situation with the choir master of St. Paul's Lutheran Church in the weedy corner of a vacant lot. "Imagine! A man like that teaching our children!" some people had said. A marriage was nearly dissolved when a husband told his wife: "If that's what they want to do, it's their own damned business. But they might have the good sense, at least, to keep it indoors." "Dismiss them? Why, they ought to be put in prison!" a housewife told her neighbor, leaning out of the dining room window. "Less said the better. Let 'em get out of town as quick and as quiet as possible," suggested the postman to the recipient of his first delivery. And insanity, everyone *knew,* ran in the choir master's family.

As when in 1944 young, handsome, popular Jack Harris was picked up by the authorities in a nearby town for desertion from the army. Most people were stunned that a boy like Jack Harris could be a coward. Great sympathy was showered on Jack Harris' father—except by those who felt that Jack Harris' father had probably told him to desert:

"Stayed out of the first war hisself," they said. But they were people whose mortgages had been foreclosed or whose families had been dispossessed by Jack Harris' father. "Poor Jack Harris!" others had said. "Must be more in this than meets the eye to make a kid like Jack Harris do such a thing." "Ought to shoot him for a traitor!" wept a gold star mother. "You know what's wrong with him, of course," confided a woman to a clerk in Hammond's Dry Goods Store. "Why, his Aunt Margaret *died* in the asylum."

But between such incidents the town seemed at peace.

Until once more a moment of violence would awaken it suddenly and, rousing, it would focus its Cyclopean eye on the perpetrators.

As when in this very year Johnny Taylor, Armand Rapp and Artie Schlier raped little Ida Praul.

Without anyone's realizing it, the gaps between the town's myriad factions were bridged by the impulse to communicate information concerning this fascinating catastrophe. No unity was achieved among the factions, for it was only the accidental overlappings of interest which served as a channel from group to group. Mutuality was being preserved when Kay Beyers spoke to Vera Miller, for Vera was a member of Kay's bridge club. But when Vera hung up and her telephone rang again, she spoke to a woman with whom her only common interest was the mutual activity of their daughters.

"Mrs. Miller?" the voice said. "This is Phyllis Preston."

"Oh, good morning. How are you?"

"I'm fine, thank you. I'm calling because I hoped you'd be able to help us out with the Girl Scouts' covered-dish supper next month. Anna Stubinski asked me to be chairman of the committee and I thought you might like to 'volunteer' to join the committee." She laughed briefly and good naturedly at her own inflection on the word "volunteer."

"Oh, Mrs. Preston," Vera Miller began, her voice revealing none of the distaste she felt at being invited to lower the level of her social endeavor, "ordinarily I'd love to, but I'm on the flower committee at church next month and I've made a rule never to do two committees in the same month. I'm terribly sorry. If you'd just called a few days earlier—"

"Oh, don't be silly, Mrs. Miller," the woman said. "I understand, believe me. If you try to do too many things, you don't do a good job on any of them. Maybe you'll be free for the next activity."

"Yes. Have you tried anyone else, Mrs. Preston?" Vera Miller said, and her tone sounded odd to Phyllis Preston.

"Why, no. You're the first. I'd welcome any suggestions you have, though."

"Oh, it's not that. I guess it . . . well, just that it's on everyone's mind. You certainly wouldn't have called Mary Taylor. Her Lois is a Girl Scout, you know."

"Oh, that poor woman!" Phyllis Preston said. "My heart goes out to her."

"Yes. Well, I don't suppose Lois will be doing much Girl Scouting for a while," Vera Miller said, and her lips were parted in preparation for the answer to the question she anticipated.

"What do you mean?"

"Oh, haven't you heard? Poor little thing's on the verge of a nervous breakdown. And it's certainly no wonder."

"Oh, how terrible!" Phyllis Preston said. "Is she at home or in a hospital?"

"She's at home at least for the time being. Dr. McKenna's attending her, I understand. She burst into Betty Allen's house on Saturday in a nervous fit bordering on convulsions. She upset Mrs. Allen's daughter terribly. Then she ran out of the house screaming, and I've heard the police had to bring her home. It's just too awful!"

"Oh, that poor family!"

"Yes. I don't know Mary Taylor well, of course, but it seems to me that she could keep her daughter from running all over town under the circumstances."

"Yes, but you know how children are. You never know what they're going to do."

"But under the circumstances wouldn't you think Mrs. Taylor would be more careful?"

"I suppose so. Oh, the whole thing is just . . . unbelievable!"

"Yes. Well, I'm sorry about the supper. Maybe next time."

"Oh, yes. Thanks anyway. Goodbye."

Phyllis Preston depressed the telephone button with her finger, released it and dialed the number of her sister-in-law, whom she did not like very much, but whom she was forced to see constantly.

"Hello, Sally?"

"Oh, hello, Phyllis," Sally Miles Johnson said with a noticeable lack of enthusiasm.

"Isn't this business about the Taylors just horrible?"

"My God, yes!" Sally Johnson answered. "I don't know what children are coming to these days. Just this morning I put a curfew on my kids. I've always thought I've been strict enough, but now I'm not so sure."

"Oh, but you never know what kids are going to do," Phyllis Preston said.

"That's a lot of bull, if you don't mind my saying so, Phyllis. It's all in the bringing up."

"Maybe you're right," Phyllis said. "I guess if Mary Taylor'd been more careful with Lois, she wouldn't be in such a state."

"What state is she in?"

"Well, I only just heard myself. The poor little thing's having a nervous breakdown. They may have to take her off to a hospital any minute."

"No!"

"Yes. She was running all over town in hysterics on Saturday. Why, the police had to pick her up."

"They picked *her* up, too?"

"Yes. It wasn't the same, of course—not like Johnny, I mean. But that apparently was the only way they could get her home. They have the doctor every day."

"Isn't that awful? Well, it's just like I said: it's all in the bringing up. Parents these days let kids do just as they please, until something like this happens and it's too late. It's John and Mary Taylor ought to be punished, more than the kids."

"I don't know, Sally. You're probably right, but I can't help feeling that you never know what kids are going to do. How's my little brother, by the way?"

"Oh, he's the same as ever," Sally answered. "I've got to go now, Phyllis. I'll talk to you later."

Nor did Sally Miles Johnson replace the receiver when she finished her conversation. She broke the telephone connection with her finger and immediately dialed the number of the factory where her sister was working supervisor of the twenty girls in the packaging room.

After the buzzing and clicking of the switchboard, Sally Johnson heard the familiar voice of her sister say, "Packaging. Miss Miles."

"Gladys, it's Sally."

"Oh, hi ya," Gladys Miles said. "Saw your husband on the way to the plant this morning. He don't look as sick as he says he is."

"Gladys, have you heard about Lois Taylor?"

"*Lois* Taylor? What the hell's happened to her?"

"She just had a nervous breakdown, is all."

"Christ! What else can happen to them people?"

"The police had to pick her up and take her home last Saturday, she was so hysterical. Imagine, out on the streets in that condition! You'd think her mother would keep tabs on her after what's happened."

"That poor kid! I don't care what you say, I feel sorry for both them kids. I worked with Peg Praul years ago, and if her kid's anything like her, you can just bet it was her raped them boys."

"Do you always have to be so bull-headed, Gladys? They had to keep Ida Praul in the hospital overnight, she was so hurt. Does that sound like she wanted it?"

"Maybe not, but I'm telling you, them Prauls are no good. Good thing there's only the mother and daughter left. Look, I got to get back to my table. I'll call you tonight. Goodbye."

Gladys Miles returned to the head of one of the two long, narrow tables at which her girls worked. When she spoke, it was only to the four girls in easy range of her normal tone of voice, but the other noises of the room—the humming of a popular song, the giggling at a joke, the irritated mumbling—gradually quieted as all of the girls were brought into the conversation.

"You hear about Lois Taylor?" Gladys asked.

"Johnny's sister?" someone said.

"Yeah," Gladys answered. "Poor little kid's on her way to the hospital with a nervous breakdown."

"No!" someone said. "What happened?"

"I don't know," Gladys said. "Guess the whole thing was too much for her. She was running all over town on Saturday having hysterics. Police had to bring her home."

"What was too much for her?" a girl at the other end of the table asked.

"Ain't you heard?" the girl next to her exclaimed.

"Heard what?"

"Three kids raped young Ida Praul Friday night."

"No kidding? Who were they?"

"Armand Rapp and Artie . . . what's his name . . . Schlier and Johnny Taylor. It's his sister Lois had the nervous breakdown."

The girl next to Gladys, her assistant for the last eighteen years, said quietly, "I got to make a phone call, Glad. Okay?"

"Sure, Norma. Go ahead," Gladys answered.

Norma Zelinsky pushed her chair away from the table and went to the public telephone in the hall. The number she called was the number of McCaffrey's Bar and Grill on Lincoln Street near the railroad. Lizzie McCaffrey, who was said to be past seventy, though she looked not a day over fifty, had become proprietress of the establishment on the occasion of her father's death.

"McCaffrey's," the harsh-voiced Lizzie said into the telephone.

"Lizzie, it's Norma. You seen Stan yet today?"

"No. It's early for Stan. I ain't seen him since you left here with him Saturday night."

"*I* ain't seen him either. That's the trouble. You know how loaded he was when we left your joint. Well, he wanted to go to the Veterans' Club, and he would've just got in a fight or something, so I wouldn't go. He just ups and leaves me standing on the street and gets in a cab. Imagine!"

"Well, that's Stan," Lizzie said.

"I called him Sunday, but he had just went out to a ball game. I just missed him again last night, too. Well, tell him to call me if he comes in, huh? I'm at work."

"Sure thing, Norma. What's new?"

"Oh. You remember Stan tellin' us about the Taylors Saturday night?"

"Yeah. That's some mess."

"Well, they're going to put the little girl, Lois, in the hospital. Nervous breakdown."

"No!"

"Cops picked her up on the streets Saturday, hysterical."

"Oh, that poor little kid! I still can't get over it: those three young guys raping a girl out there on that hill. I guess they must of done it, huh, or there wouldn't be all this fuss?"

"Oh, sure! They're going to have a trial in October. They must of practically admitted it. Well, I better get back to work. Don't forget to tell Stan, hear?"

Lizzie replaced the receiver beneath the bar, clucking and wagging her head. As she picked up the bottle of whiskey to refill the shot glass of her only customer, she said, "You hear about them three boys raping Ida Praul?"

" 'Course. Who ain't?" said the fat Negro woman who sat at the bar, her steel-rimmed spectacles sparkling occasionally as they caught the neon light from behind the bar.

"Bet you ain't heard about little Lois Taylor though," Lizzie said, her grayed and hennaed head bobbing with the pleasure of anticipation.

"L'il Lois?" the Negro woman said to Lizzie's back as Lizzie rang up the sale on the cash register. "What about l'il Lois?"

"Had a nervous breakdown," Lizzie said, pushing the cash register

168

drawer shut efficiently. "I tell you kids today just ain't the same as kids used to be. Why, I never even thought of thrusting a candle till I was eighteen. And if I got caught, I would've had my ass whipped proper, I tell you. But just imagine," Lizzie said, leaning on the bar with both forearms and relishing the image she was about to project, "them three young studs out there on that hill giving it to little Ida Praul! Ain't that a picture, though?"

The Negro woman picked up her shot of whiskey and drank it. "Ah declare!" she said, and laughing heartily added, "Ah always said any woman reluctant enough so she got to get raped ain't just normal. Mus' be somp'in wrong with her."

Lizzie reached behind her for the bottle of whiskey. "Come on, have one on me," she said, pouring the liquor into the shot glass.

"Ah shouldn't do it, Lizz. Ah got to get on to work. But Ah guess one more won't do me no harm."

"Where you working today?"

"Out to Miz Harkins' place. Tuesdays, Thursdays and Saturdays mah days out there. She de fussiest woman alive," the Negro woman said, deftly raising the shot glass in the air. "Heah's to you," she added and drank the whiskey with a flourish. She slid from the bar stool like an ocean liner getting under way. "Don't you go lettin' none o' dem young bucks in heah, Lizzie," she cackled as she sailed toward the door. "You' honor wouldn't be safe."

She laughed heartily as she made her way to the bus stop, and throughout the trip to the other end of town she giggled whenever her witticism occurred to her. She smiled broadly as she went around to the back door of the Harkins' house, thinking that it was too bad she couldn't say something like that to Mrs. Harkins, but she knew very well that she couldn't.

"Mornin', Miz Harkins," the Negro woman said to the fluffy blond woman in the powder blue peignoir.

"Oh, thank goodness you're here!" Grace Harkins said. "The cook is sick and Mr. Harkins hasn't had his breakfast. He's simply raging! You'll fix some eggs for him, won't you? Just this once. You don't mind, do you? Tell me you don't mind."

" 'Course Ah'll fix 'em. You jes' relax, Miz Harkins."

"Oh, bless you! I'm simply useless in the kitchen. Useless! Mr. Harkins is simply raging," Grace Harkins said, "I was nearly hysterical! I simply forgot you were coming today. Oh, thank goodness!"

"Seems like everybody in town gettin' hysterical."

"What?" Grace Harkins said.

"L'il Lois Taylor runnin' all over town bein' hysterical de other day."
"How in the world did you know that?"
"Everybody know it. Jes' like dey know what her brother do."
"Oh, don't even speak of it! It's too horrible!"
"Sure is. Dey gonna put dem boys in jail for sure. You jes' wait. Come October, dey gonna go to jail."
"October?" Grace Harkins said.
"Dat's when de trial gonna be. An' dem jes' school boys. . . ."

The Negro woman did not finish the sentence because Grace Harkins was no longer listening to her. She had gone to the blue telephone on the kitchen wall and was dialing.

"Kay?" she said. "It's Grace."
"Good morning," Kay Beyers said.
"Is it true that they aren't going to try those boys who did that terrible thing until October?"
"Calm down, darling," Kay Beyers said. "Of course it's true. That's when criminal court convenes. What on earth are you so upset about?"
"Aren't you upset? With three . . . rapists running around town absolutely free? Can't Jim do something about it?"
"Jim?" Kay Beyers laughed. "Grace, darling, they're his clients—at least, in a way they are. What do you expect Jim to do about it? Anyway, I think you're fairly safe, Grace. They only seem to go after little girls."
"Oh, Kay, you're terrible!"
"Oh, don't be silly, Grace."
"But October! Why, they might even let them go back to school! Johnny Taylor and—"
"Oh, my God! I never even thought of that!" Kay Beyers said, suddenly smiling fiercely.
"I think Johnny Taylor's in the same class with—"
"Grace, I've got to hang up. I've got to call Dora Henry."
"Dora Henry?"
"Of course. Her husband's on the school board, ninny."
"Oh, yes."
"I'll let you know what happens. Goodbye."

"Dora—Kay Beyers."
"Oh, hello, Kay. How are you?"
"I'm fine. Listen, Dora, you've heard, I suppose, that they aren't going to try those boys in the Ida Praul thing until October?"

"No, I hadn't heard. I think they should all get the electric chair—and I mean that. How could anyone—"

"Dora, that means that Johnny Taylor and Artie Schlier will probably go back to the high school the first week in September."

Kay Beyers could not see the paleness which spread across her listener's face as the blood drained out of it. She merely heard the slight sucking in of air, which she would have described as a gasp, had it not been so weak a sound.

"I can't believe it. I cannot believe it!" Dora Henry said. "Do you realize," she said slowly, pronouncing each word as if it were a great effort, "that Betty Lou will be right there in the same building with two confirmed rapists? My daughter, right there. And my husband on the Board of Education. . . ."

"Dora, why do you think I called you?" Kay Beyers said quietly.

"It is not going to be," Dora Henry said with the same deliberateness. "It is not going to be. I'll see to it. I'll call Chris at the office. Before this day is over I'll have fixed that. It just isn't going to be, Kay."

"I knew you'd feel that way."

As she listened to the buzzing of the telephone ringing at her husband's office, Dora Henry could feel the slight pain at her fingertip where it had hit so hard against the crescent-shaped stop of the telephone's dial. She forgot that pain as she told her husband's secretary (whom she did not like—with ample reason, had she only known it) that she wanted to speak to him.

"Chris?"

"Yeah," Christopher Henry said, leafing through the crowded pages of a purchasing contract.

"Chris, I want you to listen to me."

"What do you think I'm doing, holding my ears?"

"Do you realize that Johnny Taylor and Artie Schlier will be back in school with your daughter in a mere matter of days?"

"Not unless Betty Lou's been promoted, they won't," Mr. Henry said tonelessly.

"It's the same school, Christopher," Dora Henry said, using her husband's full name as she did only in exasperation.

"What do you want me to do now, close the school?" he asked, blue-penciling a change in the contract.

"I want you to call John Taylor and tell him not to send his son to school next week."

"Dora, there are times—and it's most times—when I don't think you can think your way out of a paper bag."

171

"There's no need for you to be your rude self, Christopher. You—"

"John Taylor has a legal obligation to send his boy to school in September. The truant officer would—"

"The truant officer will not require a criminal to be sent to a school to mix with decent boys and girls. Your own thirteen-year-old daughter will be in that school. . . ."

"Where I guess you think she's going to be screwed in the hall while the teachers are—"

"Must you speak to me that—"

"I can't do anything about—"

"You'll keep those boys out of school. All you have to do is—"

"I don't think either of us has finished saying anything in the last twenty-five years. You never—"

"Christopher. I want it arranged."

"And if I don't arrange it, you'll tell my mother about that thing in nineteen forty-seven."

"I didn't say that."

"You didn't have to. Okay, you sweet, affectionate, considerate bag. I'll arrange it. What are you going to do, Dora, when Mom passes on, and you don't have any power any more?"

"That's not the issue at—"

"No it's not. But someday it's going to be. And I'm going to make up for all the times you—"

"Are you indeed, Christopher? And what about all the times—"

"Goodbye, you frigid old bat." And Christopher Henry hung up and went back to his papers, considering all the while the best course by which to accomplish the purpose his wife had set for him with the weapon of his seventy-two-year-old mother, whose image he had tried to recapture so many, many times in the persons of people who so little resembled her.

Johnny Taylor awoke to the sound of his mother's voice coming from just outside his bedroom door. The smooth protective feel of the sheet lying lightly upon him, the first haphazard sight of the high-school pennant tacked to the wall, seemed to be introducing a quite ordinary day. Then, unaccountably, as in the sudden flick of an optical illusion, the voice, the bed, the room, his very presence became extraordinary. He felt seconds of sheer panic and searched furiously for its source. Then he remembered—with a suffocating calm.

"Okay, Mother," he called. "I'm awake."

He dressed wondering if this was what awakening would always be like now. He felt sure that the shock of his guilt must diminish through repetition, yet he did not truly believe that it could. Nor did he, on this fourth morning of that guilt—although he did not admit it fully to himself—truly believe that he could survive many more such mornings.

He ate breakfast silently, trying to receive his mother's attempts at cheerfulness in the spirit in which they were offered. But beneath the attempt he tried to invent an acceptable excuse for not going to his job at Simpson's. He thought of leaving the house, pretending that he would go to work and simply not going. He thought of telling Mr. Simpson immediately that he could not work for him any more and returning to the house with the deed irrevocably done. He thought for a moment of disappearing mysteriously and completely, never to be heard of again. Yet eventually he got up from the table and reluctantly walked the five blocks to Simpson's store.

"Morning, Johnny," Mr. Simpson said as if nothing had happened, Johnny thought.

"Good morning, Mr. Simpson," he answered.

"Would you put those two cartons of Campbell's soups up on the shelf before you have your coffee?" Mr. Simpson said. He chuckled as he added, "Mrs. Postlethwaite nearly fell over 'em yesterday while she was bruising the tomatoes. I woulda almost wished the lawsuit just to see her go sprawling."

"Okay," Johnny said. He put on a clean white apron and started for the boxes piled on the floor. "I . . . I don't think I want any coffee today, anyway."

"What?" Mr. Simpson said. "I don't want Mrs. Simpson complaining to me all day she makes extra coffee for you and you don't drink it. When you finish with the soup, take your break and have the coffee, like always."

Johnny had nearly finished stocking the soup when Mrs. Simpson, a very stout woman, came into the store from the house behind it.

"Do you suppose Johnny isn't . . ." she began, addressing her husband. "Oh, there you are. Why ain't you been back for coffee?" she asked critically.

"I had to do the soup first," Johnny explained, and added with a sudden interior glow of warmth for the Simpsons, "so Mrs. Postlethwaite wouldn't break her neck."

"Oh, who cares about that skinny old bird?" Mrs. Simpson said. "Come on. Coffee's still hot."

Johnny went around the counter and into the kitchen of the Simpsons' house. After twenty-five years of conducting a grocery business practically in his own living room, Mr. Simpson had bought this house at the corner of Tenth Avenue and Caldwell Street and built a store against its Tenth Avenue side. It was not a large house, but it was adequate for Mr. and Mrs. Simpson, their son, Herbert, who was now in the army, and their daughter, Virginia, who was in Johnny's class at school. Virginia was standing at the sink washing the breakfast dishes when Johnny came into the room.

"Hi, Johnny," she said, turning to him briefly from her work.

"Morning, Ginny," Johnny said, sitting at the enamel-topped kitchen table.

"Did you hear about Grace Porter?" Virginia asked him. "She's not coming back to school next month. Her mother and father are sending her to St. Clement's. How about that?"

"Why are they doing that?" Johnny asked as Mrs. Simpson poured his coffee.

"Well you know Miss Sperlock nearly flunked her in history last year. And the rest of her grades were pretty lousy, too."

"Well, no wonder. She didn't do any homework all winter," Johnny said. "She and Kenny Rimbaud went out together every night in the week."

"If you ask me, *that's* the reason they're sending her to St. Clement's —to keep her away from Kenny Rimbaud. Grace is absolutely livid, of course. But what can she do? Right now she's kicking her feet and screaming she won't go."

"Virginia," Mrs. Simpson said, "you're dripping."

Virginia had paused in her dishwashing to turn to Johnny and stood with her wet and sudsy hands on the edge of the sink. Both suds and water were cascading slowly down the porcelain and falling to the floor.

"Oh, heck!" Virginia said and stooped to wipe up the puddle.

"There's already orders phoned in, Johnny," Mrs. Simpson said. "Virginia will help you get 'em made up."

"Already?" Virginia cried from her squatting position. "They'll be phoning 'em in before we're out of bed next."

By ten-thirty Virginia and Johnny had made up about fifteen orders and Johnny was carrying them out to the station wagon in which he would deliver them. Mr. and Mrs. Simpson were both in the store waiting on customers and answering the phone and the normal atmosphere of friendly industry had returned with the aging of the day as it always did.

Johnny put the last order into the station wagon, closed the tailgate and got in behind the wheel. The weather during most of August had been oppressively hot, but this particular day, with its gentle breeze and mild, pale sunshine, seemed to offer the first indication of a no longer distant autumn. As Johnny drove down the slope of Tenth Avenue toward the eastern edge of town, the air that rushed in through the open window of the car was cool and moist. He saw the big frame house where his Aunt Sarah lived. He drove past the vacant lot where he had once fallen and cut his leg while playing. Next door the Purdy children were playing jacks on the front walk. Old Mrs. Kittinger was sweeping her pavement as she had twice a day for thirty years. For a moment, in the cool, rushing air, surrounded by this congenial familiarity, he had forgotten. The world became again the comfortable, welcoming place it had once been. Then he remembered, just as he had on awakening. His fingers tightened their grasp on the wheel, and all comfort fled.

Johnny stopped before the Beale house and took their boxed order out of the station wagon. He followed the worn cement walk which bordered the house and led to the back door. As he came through the back yard, Alice Beale saw him through the dotted Swiss curtains at her kitchen window. She opened the door even before he had knocked on it.

"Johnny Taylor, you're a fine one," she said, standing back for him to enter. "Mr. Simpson promised me I'd have those eggs by ten o'clock. How am I going to get two devil's food cakes down to the church by this afternoon for the supper tonight if I don't get 'em in the oven? Marjorie Clemens is running this thing and you know how *she* is. Well, sit down, sit down, and have some milk and some of these toll-house cookies. What's the matter, doesn't your mother feed you any more? You're skinny as a rail."

"Thanks, Mrs. Beale," Johnny said, "but I shouldn't stay. I'm late already."

"You sure are," Mrs. Beale agreed. "But a glass of milk'd do you good."

"I shouldn't take the time, honest," Johnny said. "But I *could* eat a couple of cookies on the way."

"All right," Mrs. Beale said. "They're there in the dish. Stick a handful in your pocket. I've got to get these cakes started."

As Johnny put the cookies into his pocket, Mrs. Beale handed him some change from a Mason jar in a corner cupboard and he left as she piled the groceries on the kitchen table in search of the eggs.

When she had finished talking to her husband, Dora Henry went to her desk and wrote a note. The note said PLEASE LEAVE GROCERIES ON

175

STEPS. Simply that. Then she went outside and thumbtacked the note to the kitchen door.

"Betty Lou!" she called before going inside again. "Come into the house this minute and stay there." Dora Henry didn't know whether or not Johnny Taylor was delivering her groceries, but she was taking no chances. Neither did she know that the greatest joy in the life of thirteen-year-old Betty Lou was the twice-weekly appearance of Johnny Taylor, for Betty thought herself to be thoroughly in love with this older man, and he, flattered somewhat by her attentions, never failed to take an extra moment at the Henry household to stand in the back yard talking to Betty Lou. So it was that, with her mother busy on the kitchen telephone extension, Betty Lou simply went outside when, later, she saw Johnny Taylor coming up the front walk with the groceries.

"Mr. Simpson, this is Mrs. Henry," Dora Henry said into the telephone, unaware of her daughter's defection.

"Good morning, Mrs. Henry," Mr. Simpson said. "Your order should be there any minute."

"Yes, that's what I'm calling about," she said coolly. "Who is delivering the order?"

"Who's deliv . . ." Mr. Simpson thought for a moment. "Johnny Taylor's delivering it."

"Mr. Simpson," Dora Henry said icily now, "I have a thirteen-year-old daughter."

There was silence for a moment. Then, "I have a seventeen-year-old one."

There was silence again, for it was Mrs. Henry now who was unprepared.

"The way you take care of your family is your own business," she said.

"And I'd certainly extend that same courtesy to you, Mrs. Henry."

"I will not have that boy delivering groceries here with a thirteen-year-old girl in the house."

"He's the only delivery boy I've got, Mrs. Henry."

Mrs. Henry had not planned it this way, and now she was twisting the telephone wire around her fingers in nervous anger. "Are you arguing with me, Mr. Simpson?"

"No, ma'am," he answered. "I'm just explaining that Johnny's the only one I've got to make deliveries."

"I can't believe that a man of your age . . . of your position would . . . would send a rapist around to make deliveries to your customers where little children are playing . . . and where . . ."

"Mrs. Henry, if the law puts Johnny Taylor in jail, he couldn't deliver groceries for me, but until it does I don't think I have the right to stop him from working for me. And I'm afraid I don't think you have the right, either."

"If you want to lose your customers, Mr. Simpson, that's up—"

"I'm a businessman, Mrs. Henry. The last thing in the world I want to do is lose customers. But I know Johnny Taylor, and I don't see how you can think what you're thinking."

"It's not a matter of thinking. You know as well as I do what happened."

"No, ma'am. I don't *know* what happened."

"All right, all right, Mr. Simpson. But I don't want that boy coming to my house."

There was another silence. "I . . . I hope you mean you'll be coming here to the store to get your groceries from now on."

"What?" Dora Henry fairly screamed. "What did you say?"

"I said, 'I hope you'll be coming—' "

"You mean you're going to go right on sending that boy all over town?"

"Like I said, Mrs. Henry, he's the only one I've—"

Dora Henry slammed the receiver into place and sat staring at it with all her anger focused for the moment on Herbert Simpson. She did not know why she called out for Betty Lou just then. In fact, she found herself wondering what she would say to her when she came into the kitchen from the living room. The problem was solved by the silence which followed her summons.

"Where is that little imp?" she muttered to herself as she stalked out of the kitchen, only half realizing how much better she felt now that there was disobedience to deal with right here at hand. She went to the stairway and called again, and in the ensuing silence she began to realize intuitively what had happened.

Without further hesitation she went to the back door and threw it open. What she saw turned her anger into horror, for she had not heard the innocent conversation which had prompted it.

"Hi Johnny," Betty Lou had said, falling into step with him as he started for the back yard, carrying the box of groceries.

"Hi there, Betty Lou. How are you?"

"I'm fine, Johnny. How are you?" Betty Lou asked, smiling brightly.

"I'm all right," Johnny answered. "Your mother ordered that devil's food cake mix. You're in for a treat," he told her as he always did when he knew there was something she particularly liked in the grocery order.

"Yummy!" Betty Lou said, licking her lips deliciously. "I'll save you a piece."

"Don't go eating too much cake," he warned her with mock seriousness. "Little girls aren't supposed to be fat, you know."

"I'm not a little girl any more," Betty Lou protested. "I'm older'n Lois. I bet you can't even lift me any more."

It was a game which they played regularly, and it was this—the sight of Johnny Taylor standing beside the box of groceries in the back yard, his hands around Betty Lou's waist lifting her in the air—which confronted Dora Henry when she flung open the back door. The two young people in their playful innocence were totally unaware of their observer.

"Oh, no! No! Stop that!" Dora Henry screamed.

Johnny turned, still holding the little girl aloft, and saw Mrs. Henry running toward him, an unmistakable expression of terror on her face. He truly did not know what was wrong.

"Let her alone! Let her alone!" Mrs. Henry screamed, tearing at the little girl's body. Johnny, now more terrified by the suddenness of her unexplainable outburst than Dora Henry was herself, put Betty Lou down, and Mrs. Henry clasped the child to her.

"Betty Lou, did he hurt you?" she shrieked.

"Mommy—"

"Mrs. Henry—" Johnny began.

Still screaming, Mrs. Henry shrunk from him fearfully. "Don't you come near Betty Lou! I'll have the police on you for molesting my daughter!"

"Mrs. Henry—" Johnny began again.

"You're depraved! You should be put away where you can't molest children!"

"But Betty Lou and I—" Johnny began desperately now.

"Get away from here! Get away!"

The woman from the house next door, who had come into the adjoining yard at the sound of Dora Henry's hysterical screaming, leaned on the fence as if she might leap over it. "Dora!" she called. "What's wrong?"

"I found him . . . Johnny Taylor . . . with his hands . . . all over Betty Lou! His hands all over my little girl!"

"It wasn't like th—" Johnny tried to explain.

"You get out of here, Johnny Taylor, before I call the police!" the neighbor said.

"Please listen to me, Mrs. Hen—" Johnny begged in vain.

"You're not fit to be with decent human beings!" Dora Henry cried.

She was nearly in tears of hysteria now. "I'll see to it you're put away!"

"Go on, get out of here!" the neighbor shouted.

"But won't you let me explain? I was just—" Johnny said, his hands extended in supplication.

"Mommy, don't yell that way at—"

"I said get, you terrible boy!" the neighbor threatened.

Johnny's hands dropped to his sides, and he stood staring at Dora Henry in a way that made her—for the first time in this episode—genuinely afraid. Then he turned and walked quietly and quickly from the yard.

Johnny got into the truck and drove away slowly, for there were tears in his eyes. They did not fall, but merely remained in his eyes, blurring his vision. They were tears of anger and remorse and confusion. He drove to the extreme eastern side of town and to the River Road. He followed it past Fourteenth Avenue where the sidewalks ended and it became a country road. It swung westward through the countryside in a wide, gentle arc, which eventually turned back toward the town.

The anger he felt was at the injustice of Dora Henry's accusation and the unfairness with which she had judged him. Was it unfair? he wondered quite suddenly. What he had done to Ida surely did not make him a molester of children, but did it give Mrs. Henry the right to be afraid of him? Did it make him "unfit" to be with little, innocent Betty Lou? He guessed maybe it did. If he knew that somebody had committed rape, he sure wouldn't want that person anywhere near Lois. Maybe the person knew himself that the rape was a single, separate act and that he wouldn't ever harm Lois, just as he, Johnny, knew that he would never harm Betty Lou, but that didn't make any difference to anybody else. It wouldn't make any difference to him if it was some other person and Lois: he just wouldn't take the chance. And Mrs. Henry was right not to take the chance. Oh, Christ, no! It couldn't be like that! There had to be something wrong with that. He knew what he did to Ida was wrong and he was willing to pay for it, but even then he hadn't meant to *harm* Ida. People didn't have a right to think they had to hide their children from him.

The tears had gathered now and he wiped them from his cheek, still driving carefully against their effect. But his anger was replaced by his remorse, a sickening, hopeless regret. Why had he done it? he asked himself. How *could* he have done it? It was as if somebody else, not him, was out on that hillside Friday night. The Johnny Taylor he knew as "I" could not have done what was done out there. And yet because of what was done Johnny Taylor was a boy who made mothers afraid for their little girls. If only it had never happened! If only he had never touched Ida . . . Ida. Here he was, a good breakfast in his belly, driving the grocery truck like always, feeling sorry for himself—and he hadn't even told Ida or her mother he was sorry for what he'd done. Hadn't even apologized. He had just let it go as if he didn't care about what he'd done to poor Ida—just like when he left her on the hillside. But now he wasn't drunk and nobody was pushing him and there was no excuse. What the hell kind of a person was he? All right. He had done it to Ida when she didn't want it, and he had left her lying there, but damned if he wasn't going to tell her—*her* he was sorry. It was Ida who was hurt, Ida who was abandoned, Ida who was . . . raped; and it was Ida he was going to tell how sorry and how ashamed he was.

"Well, we just lost the first one, Ellie," Mr. Simpson was saying, shaking his head.

"I told you it would happen," his wife said. "Who was it?"

"Oh, Dora Henry," he answered. "I just didn't believe anybody would be so—"

"Dora Henry!" she said. "I'm not surprised. She's always been little Miss Straight-Laced, just like her mother—"

"I hope she'll be the only one," Mr. Simpson said absently.

"Well, she won't."

"No, I guess not. I didn't even expect her to be the first. I thought if anybody did it, it'd be—"

He was interrupted by a commotion in the store. The front door had opened, ringing the bell which was attached to it. Even through the tinkling of the bell and punctuated by the slamming of the door, he heard the shrill, unpleasant voice, saying, "Where is your father, Virginia?"

"That's what I've been waiting for," he said quietly to his wife.

"And she doesn't even have the decency to do it on the telephone," Mrs. Simpson answered. Mr. Simpson sighed heavily and went into the store, his wife following.

"Morning, Mrs. Postlethwaite," he said to the skinny, gray-haired woman.

"Herbert Simpson," she said measuredly, "did I or did I not see Johnny Taylor driving your truck down Tenth Avenue as big as life?"

"I guess you did, Mrs. Postlethwaite. He was driving it when I saw him last."

"Have you taken leave of your senses?" she said, her eyes bulging and her wire-thin lower lip snapping shut.

"No, I don't think so, Mrs. Postlethwaite."

"You don't think good, law-abiding, Christian customers are going to stand for it, do you?" she asked without a thought of rhetoric.

"Stand for what?" he asked.

"Herbert Simpson, you're supposed to be a Methodist," she went on. "You come to our church on Sundays, send your children to our Sunday School. You—"

"Mrs. Postlethwaite, I don't want any fuss in the store—"

"You don't want any fuss, don't you?" she shouted. "Then why have you got that wicked, awful boy working for you?"

Mr. Simpson's answer might have been quite different had Mrs. Simpson not seen Johnny get out of the station wagon and come to the front door. She had been an approving bystander as her husband rebuffed Mrs. Postlethwaite, but when she realized that Johnny had seen Mrs. Postlethwaite's upraised arm and gone back to the station wagon, she broke out angrily, "Mrs. Postlethwaite, my husband's right not to argue with you, but you're making it just too hard. I been catering to you and listening to you for more than twenty years now, and as long as it was just gossip, I didn't care. But if you think you can come in here, yelling and screaming, telling us who we can keep on here and who we can't, you're sadly mistaken. I've always known Johnny Taylor to be a good boy, and till somebody proves to me that he isn't, I'll go right on thinking he is. Now, if you want to order something, Mrs. Postlethwaite, we'll be happy to wait on you. If you don't, I'll thank you either to mind your tongue or get out of our store."

A moment later Johnny came into the store and went directly into the kitchen, where Mr. Simpson joined him shortly.

"I'm afraid I won't be able to go on working for you, Mr. Simpson," Johnny said, staring at the table top.

"And why not, may I ask?" Mr. Simpson said sternly.

"It . . . it's going to cause too much trouble," Johnny said.

"Trouble for who, Johnny, you or us?"

"Both, I guess."

"Well, we can take our part of it if you can take yours."

"Mr. Simpson, you could lose customers over it," Johnny said, looking at him now.

"So? Is that the most important thing in the world?"

"No, but you shouldn't have to."

"Lots of things shouldn't be, but they are." He paused for a moment, sitting down at the table with Johnny, then went on. "Look, I don't doubt for a minute that you don't want us to lose customers, but I wonder if maybe you aren't also worried about having your feelings hurt by the way people might treat you." Johnny looked at him for a moment, then turned again toward the table top. "I guess I heard the same story as everybody else. I don't know what you did, but I do know that everybody makes mistakes, some serious, some not so serious. There's going to be a lot of people who won't be able to see how you could have done this—if you did. But if you did, there's just two things you got to learn to do. The first is to be sorry for it, pay for it if you have to. And the second is to hold your head up, even if you're ashamed of yourself. If you quit this job now, you're just hanging your head. If you'll stick it out, we'll stick it out right with you. You'll see; it's the only thing'll shut 'em up. How about it?"

"I . . . okay, Mr. Simpson," Johnny said quietly, knowing that he could not deliberately refuse to try to justify this kind of confidence.

"That's the way to talk," Mr. Simpson said. "Now, let's get back to work or we won't have any customers at all to worry about."

XVI.

As John Taylor drove home from his own work that night, he saw great mounds of billowing clouds, shaded from white to delicate gray to fierce black. They moved from the horizon toward town, dimming the soft gold of the setting sun. By the time he had finished supper, the storm had broken. He stood looking out a living-room window, and he saw the leaves still green on the trees outside the house, and he heard them crying out in the fierce wind and rain that beat them so that they looked in the flashes of lightning as if they might be torn from the trees. Suddenly the doorbell rang, and John went to open the door to the sunporch, where the rain, making the glass panes sing, sounded louder and more threatening. He could see a figure standing in the downpour outside the front door, and hurried to let the visitor in out of the rain.

"Come on in," John said, without knowing to whom he spoke.

The man came in and removed a shapeless felt hat, from which he shook the excess water. The faint light from the living room illuminated the dripping face of George Rapp, and John could not keep the expression of surprise from his face.

"Got a few minutes?" George said. "Like to talk to you."

"Sure . . . sure, George," John said. "Come on in."

"Out here'll do," George told him.

"All right," John said, and his expression silently, but clearly added, *Then say what you have to say.*

George pulled back his still buttoned raincoat and dug laboriously in the back pocket of his trousers. He withdrew a dirty handkerchief and wiped the trickling rain from his face and neck.

"I been thinkin' about the other day down at the Borough Hall,"

George said. John waited. "I don't think you trust this Hertzog fella any more'n I do."

"It's not entirely a matter of trusting him." When John talked to George Rapp, his syntax improved in an unconscious attempt at dissimilation. "He's a good lawyer. That's all I care about."

"Yeah, he's a good lawyer, I guess. But it's like he said: he'll go into court and do what everybody'll say was as good a job as could be done. Then he picks up his money and goes home, an' everybody's happy—except our kids, who'll be in jail."

A flash of lightning clearly revealed John's thoughtful frown. He started to speak, but a loud clap of thunder made his voice inaudible. After a moment he said, "If he does a good job, we'll have no complaint."

"The way I look at it, we'll have a complaint as long as our boys go to jail."

There was something sure, almost compelling about this man's bluntness.

George Rapp went on, "The point is that this guy's goin' to go in there with one thing in mind: to come out with his reputation as good as when he went in. That's the way them guys think, 'cause their next job is goin' to be based on their previous record. Well, I don't give a goddamn about his reputation. That ain't what I want."

"What do you want?" John asked.

"I want a guy who don't talk about what a good job he's goin' to do. I want a guy who says he's goin' to go in an' get 'em off. An' then does it."

"They're guilty, George."

"Of what?"

"Of rape."

"You know Peg Praul?"

"Yes."

"What kinda daughter you think she's gonna raise?"

"That's not the point," John said. "The point is—"

"Yeah. She was a virgin. But how long do you think it'd be before she climbed in the sack with one of her mother's boy friends anyway?"

"Maybe never," John said after a moment. "She might've married."

"You want to bet?"

It was a bet that John would not have taken, and he realized it fully.

"What the hell's all the fuss about, anyway?" George went on. "So the kid got screwed. Like I say, how long would it be before she got it anyway, of her own free will?"

"Don't you think she deserves the choice?"

"Aw, all right. So that's what they took away from her: the choice of pickin' the guy who'd be first. Do you think they should get twenty years for that? Do you think they should get anything for it?"

John did not answer. Almost desperately he was trying to find a way to resist this reasoning.

"So what it boils down to is this," George said, "they took out a girl who looks like a tramp, talks like a tramp and sure as hell is goin' to be a tramp, an' they had a good time with her."

"They held her down to the ground and raped her, George."

"Whose side are you on?"

"What the hell do you mean, whose side am I on? This isn't a high-school debate!"

"No, it's a trial, an' all I want is to see the boys get off. Yours as well as mine. You almost seem like that ain't what you want."

"That's a stupid thing to say!" John was angry, not with George, but with himself, for it had begun to seem that way to him, too.

"Well, what do you want then?" George asked.

"I don't know that you'll understand, but I guess what I want is . . . justice."

"That's good enough for me," George said quickly. "But ask yourself if it's justice to ruin the life of three boys for screwin' Ida Praul."

And John asked himself, over and over and over again, but he was afraid of the answer.

"An' what good's it goin' to do Ida Praul for them to go to jail?" George asked. "It won't make her no virgin again."

"But they've committed a crime," John said, almost pleadingly. "There's a punishment involved."

"I say, 'Get 'em off.' Then I'll take care of the punishment for Armand—an' the justice, too. Maybe you think prison's goin' to teach your boy somethin' about right an' wrong. Well, you're all wrong if you do. All prison's goin' to do is turn him into a bum or a real criminal."

"Look," George Rapp said, "ain't you ever been out with a woman who didn't want to?" Uncomfortable memories stirred inside John. "An' before she ever said yes, didn't you just go ahead an' start? This Ida Praul egged 'em on—even Hertzog admitted that. So it was the first time for her, an' she passed out or somethin'—maybe. How do we know she didn't just lay there an' take it, then start raisin' hell afterwards? Like I said to Armand, if they'd got her back in the car, loved her up a little an' took her home, she prob'ly woulda been too scared to tell her mother, an' none of this woulda happened. An' another thing, what do you want to bet the kid don't really give a damn one way or the other? What do you want to bet it's all that goddamn Peg Praul's behind the whole thing?"

The ring of truth echoed in John's head as if a great, bronze bell trembled vibrantly there. The sound hung and quivered and overwhelmed his thought.

"What . . . what do you want to do?" John asked.

"Well, they's two ways of goin' about it," George said in a more relaxed tone. "It may be that Peg Praul's just after dough. I say let's offer her some to call it off."

"And if she's not after dough," John said relinquishing his insistence on their dissimilarities of speech, "and she yells, 'Bribe!' to Judge Forsythe . . ."

"Who's goin' to believe Peg Praul against you?"

"That's quite a risk."

"What risk? Sure, you went there. Why wouldn't you want to see if there was somethin' you could do for the kid? Not that you're admittin' that your boy did it, but you wanted to see if you could help. What's wrong with that?"

"All right."

"So if she takes the money an' calls it off," George continued, "great. It costs us less than that friggin' lawyer. If she don't, no harm done."

"What's the other way?" John asked quietly.

"The other way's a little more complicated, but I got it all arranged. I know a couple of guys has been to bed with Peg Praul. Kinda regulars of hers."

"I don't see what that—"

"These guys see the whole thing the way we do." John winced at the easy plural. "An' they're willin' to help."

"How?"

"They're willin' to swear on the stand," George went on, "that Peg Praul offered her daughter to them."

"That's going too far. If you—"

"Now listen t'me," George interrupted. "They know they been there on nights when Ida's been on the back porch where she sleeps, so—"

"On the back porch?" John said, incredulously.

"Yeah. So there can't be no alibi that Ida was someplace else on these particular nights. 'Course, they can't say they had her—Ida, I mean—or they'd be gettin' in trouble theirselves. But they can say Peg Praul said Ida wasn't no virgin. Both of 'em'll swear Peg said that. And we'll play on Peg Praul's reputation. The district attorney'll say it's . . . it's some kinda evidence. . . ."

"Inadmissible?"

"Yeah, inadmissible. But that don't matter. You say somethin' about it every now an' then, an' you put Peg Praul on the stand, an' pretty soon the jury gets the idea—inadmissible or not. The point is, you get the jury thinkin' the way we do: it just ain't right to send three decent boys to jail for havin' sex with the daughter of a tramp—'specially when there's some doubt as to whether she wanted to screw or not . . . an' maybe even as to if she was a virgin. The jury just won't convict 'em with all that doubt an' her bein' a tramp. Maybe it don't sound so nice, but nobody gets hurt. An' the boys get off, an' you get a chance to teach 'em, to help 'em. 'Stead of them goin' to prison an' havin' their lives ruined. The boys get off, an' Christ Almighty, John, that's the important thing to me."

"It's the important thing to me too, George," John heard himself saying, and suddenly he knew that it had to be. It would be unnatural if that were not the important thing, the only consideration. Get them off, at any reasonable cost, and this cost seemed now sublimely reasonable.

"I guess you're right, George," John said. "Let me think it over— see if I can come up with anything that might help. You know. I'll call you."

"Be kinda careful about the phone," George said, putting his hat on. "We gotta keep this thing strictly on the Q.T."

"Of course," John said.

"I'll be hearin' from you then?" George asked, his hand on the doorknob. "The sooner the better."

"Sure."

John stood for a moment on the porch, listening to the rain pounding on the windows, not steadily, but in great rushes as the wind whipped it, let it fall freely, then drove it again against the house. He was physically sick with indecision. He wanted almost desperately to do what was right, defensible, moral, but he felt that he should want his son's freedom more.

The boys get off, an' Christ Almighty, John, that's the important thing to me. He almost said the words aloud: What the hell was all this business about honesty and justice and the Prauls and righteousness? Get Johnny off, that was what mattered. Oh, not at the cost of blaming someone else, of letting someone else suffer. But at the cost of a lie, of a bribe, of an act which everyone would consider not quite right, but of which everyone was guilty. Was it any worse than most income-tax deductions, than padded expense accounts, than a tip to a borough fire inspector? Simple greed motivated these universal crimes. But this petty crime which John contemplated was literally to save a life, not from death, but from waste, from uselessness, from utter ruination.

John turned and went into the house.

"I've been waiting supper," Mary said.

"Oh," John answered, not emerging from his thoughts enough even to look at her.

"What did he want?" she asked.

"George? He just wanted to talk . . . about the whole thing."

"What did he say?"

"Nothing worth repeating," John said irritably. "It was just talk."

He ate very little, for nausea crept about in his stomach. When other members of the family spoke to him, he answered almost curtly.

The family had fallen almost completely silent by the end of the meal. John ate two spoonfuls of rice pudding and sipped his coffee. He rose from the table rather suddenly and said, "I'd like to talk to you, Johnny. Would you come upstairs when you're finished eating?"

"Sure," Johnny said with false cheerfulness, but his father was already out of the dining room, walking toward the stairs.

After a few minutes of heavier silence, Mary said, "You'd better go up to your father."

Johnny got up, his reluctance showing in every slow movement. He went up the stairs and knocked on his father's bedroom door. When he went in, John stood at the window where the rain still tapped lightly against the pane. Now and then the horizon glowed with distant lightning, and a distant rumble of thunder could be heard.

"I want to hear about it, Johnny," John said, more harshly than he had intended.

"About . . . about Ida?" Johnny asked, almost incredulously.

"Yes, about Ida."

"What do you . . . what do you want to know, Dad?"

"I want to know what you did," John said and the impatience in his voice further frightened Johnny.

"Well . . . you know what we did, Dad."

"No, I don't. I don't know at all. Tell me." John heard the anger in his own voice, and to explain it he told himself that the time had come for parental indignation.

Johnny and Lois had rarely received direct commands from their father, but when they had the commands had always been obeyed silently and swiftly. Disobedience was unthinkable. But now Johnny stood, his every reflex stiffening in attempted response, yet unable to speak.

"Well, tell me," John said. "After all, I have a right to know. You know, John . . ."—Johnny winced at the unheard of use of his name—"your mother and I have been pretty . . . pretty soft about this whole thing. We know it hasn't been easy for you, but it hasn't been easy for us, either. And then there's Lois."

"Yes, I know," Johnny said softly.

"We didn't commit this crime—you did," John went on. "I don't want you to think that our being nice about it means we don't know what a terrible thing it is. You just take for granted that we're going to think about you and get you out of this whole mess, but you sure didn't think about us when you did it." He wanted to stop, but he did not. "Don't you realize the disgrace and the shame you've caused us? And what about your mother? Don't you realize what this is doing to her? Didn't you realize before you did it what it would do to her?"

He waited, feeling cruel, for the answer he knew could not come. Johnny stood silent, looking at his own feet.

"I think you're taking this whole thing too lightly," John said.

"No, I'm not, Dad," Johnny pleaded. "I'm not taking it lightly at all. Please believe that."

"All right. Tell me what happened."

Still looking downward, Johnny rubbed his hand over his clipped brown hair. Then he looked up into his father's eyes and said, "I can't."

"You can't?" John snapped. "Why can't you?"

"I just can't tell you."

"You mean you're keeping something from me? There's something I don't know?"

"No, Dad, no. It's not that."

"Well, then, what is it?"

"I just can't tell you. I can't tell *you*."

John was stunned by the statement, and his anger grew with his recovery.

"Oh. You can't tell me. Mr. Hertzog seemed to know a hell of a lot about it the other day. You must have been able to tell him something."

"That . . . that's different, Dad," Johnny said, looking down again.

"Different, is it? You can tell a perfect stranger about laying a girl, but you can't tell your own father."

"Dad . . . Dad, please! You know that. You can't talk about that kind of thing to your own father. You know that."

Quite suddenly John was sick and angry and dazed all at once, for he realized that his son had just stated what was for him a simple fact of life—a universal fact. He had not said that he could not discuss sex with his father, but rather that one did not discuss sex with one's father. And John saw, as if in a flash of the recent lightning, the enormity of the boy's ignorant innocence. He had reversed a simple principle of family life: one did not discuss intimate problems with one's parents; it was one's parents with whom one *could* not discuss intimate problems. It was as if Johnny had said, "Everybody knows that." John searched his memory for some past exchange of intimacies between them, and found himself wondering if it had indeed been *Johnny* who had reversed that simple principle. In his desperation he spoke too quickly: "Well, we talk about other things."

"What?" Johnny asked, not flippantly, but truly wanting to know what other things his father meant.

"Johnny, I know we've never talked about sex before," John said softly, knowing that the whole balance of the conversation had shifted, but too concerned to correct it, "but I always just assumed you were finding out about it in a healthy, normal way."

"Well, sure, Dad. I guess I did."

"How *did* you find out about it?"

"What do you mean?"

"Well, for God's sake, you can tell me that, can't you?"

"I'm sorry, Dad. I . . . I didn't know what you meant."

"I mean how did you find out about sex. Who told you? Who . . . who told you how to do what you did to Ida Praul?"

"I don't know . . . it was just how . . . how everybody finds out. Just talking and . . ."

"And what?"

"Fooling around. You know, Dad." Johnny's tone was agonized.

"Fooling around with who?" John drove on, angry with himself and his son and George Rapp and all of this undeserved unhappiness.

"Just with other kids, I guess. I don't know what you want me to say!"

"With other boys? You mean you've been fooling around sexually with other boys?" John was nearly shouting now.

"Not any more. Just a long time ago when I was a kid . . . the way kids do. It doesn't mean anything!"

"It doesn't mean anything? You've been goin' around doing God knows what like . . . like a pervert, and now you've committed rape, and you say it doesn't mean anything!"

"It was a long time ago!"

"Not the rape!"

"No, but the other!"

"Why didn't you come to see me when you were having sexual problems?"

"They weren't problems . . . I mean, I didn't know it was a problem."

"You must have known! Why didn't you come to me, and . . ."

"Why didn't you talk to *me?*" Johnny shouted, unable to stand the meaningless punishment. "If you didn't want me to find out like that, why didn't you tell me yourself?"

"How was I supposed to know you'd do perverted things with other boys?"

"It wasn't like that! It was just fooling around!"

"That kind of fooling around is perverted!"

"Well, maybe it wouldn't have happened if you'd told me ahead of time!"

"A . . . a father can't watch his son every minute. He can't—"

"You didn't have to watch me every minute. You only had to tell me!"

"Johnny . . . Johnny, I didn't bring you in here to argue with you. I just want to know what happened, so I can help you."

"If you want me to, I'll try. But I don't think I can tell you."

"Can you . . . can you tell me *why* you did it?"

"I guess . . . I just wanted to find out what it was like."

"I can understand that, Johnny. But couldn't you have waited . . . at least until it was with a girl who wanted to?"

"I guess I couldn't . . . imagine it like that. Out there on the hill with Ida it was . . . it seemed like that was the way it ought to be."

"Where did you ever get an idea like that?" John said softly and in wonder.

"I don't know," Johnny answered, shaking his head and looking away.

"Johnny, you don't believe I gave you that idea?"

"No, Dad. But . . . but you never gave me any other idea. We just never talked about it."

"No. No, we didn't, did we?"

They stood for a moment, each feeling something very like pity for the other.

"We'll talk about it some more later," John said. "Tell your mother I won't be downstairs again. I'm going to bed now. I guess I'm pretty tired."

"Okay, Dad," Johnny said.

"Johnny . . . I got pretty sore a few minutes ago . . . said some things I didn't mean."

"You have a right to be sore, Dad."

"But I said some things I didn't mean. Just forget it."

Johnny left the room and closed the door behind him, wondering which were the things his father hadn't meant.

He went into his own room then, looked out the window and saw that the rain had stopped. He changed into a plaid sports shirt, bluejeans and white tennis sneakers. He went downstairs and called to his mother in the kitchen, "Mother, Dad says he's going to go to bed now."

"To bed?" she said.

"Yeah. I'm going out for a while."

"Oh. Oh, all right. Don't be late."

Johnny left the house and turned toward Main Street, but suddenly without hesitation and without realizing that he had made the decision, he reversed his direction and was walking through the darker east side of town. Lights were on in most of the houses, and through the sheer ecru curtains at many of the front windows he could see men sitting in easy chairs holding before them the spread of an evening paper or sitting before the pale blue flash of a television set. Almost without exception the women were still in the kitchen, probably finishing their nightly chore with the wiping off of table tops and the closing of cupboard doors. He thought how similar all this was to what used to be the routine of his own home and wondered if that routine would ever be reestablished. Oh, the same things went on, he realized, but they were marred now by their terribly careful conversation, by mysterious visits by people who didn't even come into the house, by private conversations like the one he had just had with his father. How could his father expect . . . well, no use thinking about that. His father was upset, just like Mrs. Henry was and all the others. After all, it was his fault. Well, he had to go ahead and do the only thing he could think of to do: he had to see Ida Praul.

But how would he go about that? he wondered. He had decided against any contact with Mrs. Praul, and if he telephoned she might answer. Anyway, he doubted if Ida would agree to see him—or would even talk to him.

Johnny walked south of Main Street until he was two blocks from Ida's house. At the corner of Third Avenue and Caldwell Street he would have to turn east to go there, and he stopped for a moment with his body turned in that direction. Then he walked on. He stood in the shadow of the Dietrich Elementary School across the street from the

Praul house. He did not know if Ida was at home or, if she was, whether or not she would come out.

He lit a cigarette and leaned against a tree. He had set no time limit on his waiting. He had nothing to do, really. He didn't feel like being with anyone—he wasn't even sure at the moment that he wanted to see Ida. But he waited. After nearly forty minutes the door of the house opened and he could see Peg Praul silhouetted in the rectangle of light. She seemed to be looking down the front steps and to her right. Then in the faint periphery of light from the house he saw Ida emerging from the narrow alleyway between the buildings. He heard Peg's voice, but could not make out the words. He did not hear Ida's answer at all, but when he saw her start down Third Avenue toward Poplar Street, he stamped out a freshly lit cigarette and started after her.

He crossed the street diagonally and caught up to Ida just before she reached the corner. "Ida," he called gently.

Ida turned, startled, and was even more frightened as she recognized Johnny in the light from the street lamp. She uttered a quiet cry and covered her mouth with both her hands.

"Ida, don't be scared," Johnny said. "I . . . I want to talk to you." She stood absolutely still, not removing her hands from her face nor changing her nearly terrified expression. "Honest, Ida. I only want to talk to you. I won't do anything." Still Ida did not move or speak. "Couldn't I just walk along with you for a way? And just talk to you? Please, Ida? Don't be afraid."

Slowly Ida took her hands from her face. "Johnny . . ." she said.

"What, Ida? There's no reason to be scared, Ida. Come on, let's just walk a little way."

She looked at him for a moment during which some of the fear drained from her face. Then she turned to her original direction and they walked together. They turned north on Poplar Street which was only five blocks long. Old, luxuriant maple trees lined both sides of the street and made it dark and quiet and remote, for everything except the pavements and the trees and the earth from which the trees grew and the asphalt road seemed, in summer at least, to be outside the physical existence of the street. Houses, yards, sky, the rest of the town seemed excluded from this leaf-domed sanctuary.

"Where you going, Ida?" Johnny asked when they had walked a short distance.

"Up to Rodenbaugh's to get Mama some cold cream," Ida said, and her reluctance and fear still sounded through the mundane words. "It's closest—Rodenbaugh's."

"Yeah, I guess it is," Johnny said. "Ida, I wanted to tell you . . . that I'm sorry about what happened. That must sound awful." She didn't answer. "But it's true. I'm sorry and . . . and ashamed." Still she did not speak. "Are you all right, Ida? I mean, you're not hurt, are you?"

"I'm all right, I guess."

"I don't know what I'd do if you were hurt. I certainly didn't mean to hurt you."

"No. I guess you didn't."

"I guess that's what I wanted to say."

"Johnny," Ida said as if she did not intend to go on. "When . . . when you say you're sorry, what do you mean? Sorry because of jail and all?"

"Well, I am, of course, but I don't mean that when I tell *you* I'm sorry. I mean, I'm sorry that . . . that I . . . I did it when you didn't want me to, when I had no right to."

"Would you have a right if I wanted you to?"

"Gee, Ida, I don't know."

"Do you . . . do you like me, Johnny?"

"Well, sure I like you, Ida."

"Sometimes I think most of the kids don't like me."

"Oh, Ida . . ."

"Sometimes I think none of 'em like me. Nobody."

"Aw, that's crazy. Why shouldn't they like you?"

"I don't know," Ida said, looking about at nothing in the darkness.

"What about Virginia Lukens? She's a friend of yours."

"Yeah. Sorta. I don't think she sees me when she can be with anybody else."

"I'll bet that's not true," Johnny said, making himself very uncomfortable, for he firmly believed that it was true.

They had reached the end of Poplar Street, and Ida stopped in the darkness of the trees and the shadow of the Odd Fellows Hall. "Maybe," she said. "You got lots of friends, don't you?"

"Some. No more than you, I bet."

They were silent for a moment, and Johnny's discomfort grew. He suddenly regretted having come to see Ida, but he felt, too, that he owed her these moments of discomfort.

"Aside from bein' sorry," Ida said suddenly, "how do you feel about . . . about what happened?"

"Well . . . what do you mean, Ida?"

"It . . . it was the first time for you, too, wasn't it?"

"Yes."

"Did you . . . did you . . . like it?"

The memory of the physical act of sex sprang into Johnny's mind as if lightning had suddenly lit up the darkness under the tree, and his body responded to that memory so quickly, so strongly that he was filled with revulsion for both himself and for Ida.

"Did you, Johnny?"

"Yeah . . . I . . . guess I did."

"I wish . . ."

Johnny waited for a moment, and said, "What, Ida?"

"I wish . . . I wasn't unconscious when you did it. I wasn't completely," she added hastily. "I mean, I remember you doin' it . . . part of it." Johnny was deeply embarrassed now and did not speak. "Did you mean it when you said you liked me?"

"Sure I meant it," he said, and he spoke too quickly, too forcefully, but Ida did not hear the anger in his voice.

"I thought . . . I hoped," Ida began haltingly, "you liked me special . . . and that was why you did it."

He would have lied, for he did not want to hurt Ida, but the lie would have meant a commitment which he was in no way prepared to fill— or even capable of fulfilling. "I . . . like you," he said.

"Maybe I woulda . . . let you do it . . . if it was just us . . . and we was alone. I might've." Johnny was not at all sure what she wanted him to say to this. When he said nothing, she asked, "Do you think a girl should . . . I mean, let a fella if she likes him special and he likes her?"

"I don't know, Ida. I guess it depends."

"On what?"

"Well, I guess it's mostly up to the girl."

"I don't know if I would or not. I mean if I liked a fella special. If it was you and me, would you want me to?"

"I don't know, Ida," Johnny answered in an agonized tone, produced largely by his struggle to protect Ida from the truth which he now desperately wanted to give her.

"I guess . . . if we was goin' steady . . . if it was special between us . . . I guess I would let you. Would you want to?"

"Gee, Ida . . . I don't—"

"We could, you know. I don't go with anybody, and I know you ain't got a steady. We could go to parties together and dances and I'd come to all the basketball games— I do anyway, of course, but I mean I'd wait for you after like the girls do when their steady's on the team." The words were rushing from her now, and her uncontrolled excitement was at once confusing and repellent to Johnny. "And maybe Mama would let me give a party, and you could invite all your friends and . . . oh, it'd be fun, Johnny!"

"Yeah, but . . . well, you don't just . . . you know, make up your mind like that. It's something that . . . that just happens. You know."

"It's happened to me, Johnny. A long time ago. I like you an awful lot." He did not, could not, answer. "And there'd be . . . the other thing . . . the thing I'd let you do. Whenever you wanted, Johnny. Just you, though. Never anybody else. You wouldn't want me to, I know. You'd want me just for yourself, wouldn't you?"

"Ida . . . I don't want to go steady with anybody."

"Even if I'd let you . . ."

"I don't want to go steady. I just . . . we better go on. Your mother'll be wanting her cold cream." He turned from her as if to go, but she did not follow immediately. He turned back to her.

"You don't have to tell me right now," she said.

"Come on, Ida. We better go."

She started toward him, and together they walked west on Eighth Avenue. "You could let me know tomorrow or the next day if you want," she said.

"Ida, I don't want to go steady, honest. Not with anybody."

"Is it . . . is because you already did it with me?"

"Oh, Christ, Ida! No, it's not that at all. I just don't want to go with anybody."

"That's not true," she said sullenly. "You just don't like me. You just—"

"Ida, that's all wrong. You have to feel . . . well, like you said, special toward somebody to go steady. And I don't feel that way about anybody—it's not just because it's you."

"Oh, but Johnny," she said, and her tone was openly imploring now, "if we was together a lot and if you could do what you wanted, I know you'd get to feel that way about me. I just know you would!"

"Either you feel that way or you don't. You can't make yourself feel that way. Ida, I don't want to . . . to be mean to you or anything. But . . . it just wouldn't work. It wouldn't. We better not go on to Main Street together. I'll leave you here. I . . ."

"Oh, Johnny, don't go yet. Walk me home after I come out of Rodenbaugh's."

"I ought to get home, Ida."

"Well, will you call me tomorrow?"

"I don't think it'd be a good idea."

"You're just goin' to go on home?"

"Yes."

"Wouldn't you just call me, Johnny? Even if I'd . . ."

She did not finish. They had reached the corner and stood in the light from the street lamp. He could see the tears in her eyes and the utter hopelessness in her face. He realized then that he had seen that expression on Ida's face before. He realized that it was the way that she always looked, that only the tears were unusual, and they gave the expression a new meaningfulness. "I have to go now. Thanks for talking to me, Ida. I'm glad you did." He stood for a moment as if he might say more. Then he turned and walked away from her. He did not turn around, for he was sure that she was still standing there, watching him. He went directly home and went to bed. He lay awake most of that night, wondering many things. He wondered whether or not he would have had the right, if Ida wanted him to do it. To have the right did he also have to want to? Could the body want to all by itself whether the mind wanted to or not? Did he owe Ida both that act and the pretense of his love? Was it right for him, having already hurt her so much, to hurt her again with his refusal? But had she the right to bribe him with sex? He did not know when he stopped wondering and went to sleep. He saw the gray light at the windows, dimly offering shape to the high-school pennant on the wall. Then there was nothing.

XVII.

WHEN HIS SON HAD LEFT HIM, JOHN TAYLOR HAD UNDRESSED AND GONE to bed. He did not sleep, as he knew he would not, even late in the night when he was truly tired. He had gone to bed simply because he did not know what else to do. He had to retire to someplace within himself where he had never consciously been before, and he did not know how to get there. Bits of his discussion with George Rapp echoed in his mind, and all the arguments which that discussion had aroused within him returned, crying out for consideration. But an infant phantasm came to haunt him: it was the new-born specter of Johnny's ignorance. It whispered softly inside him, accusing and threatening. And it insisted again and again, each time more firmly, on George Rapp's plan.

When Mary came upstairs he pretended to be asleep. As he heard each familiar movement of her preparation for bed, his mind predicted the next one. Soon she was in bed, and after a long time, he knew from her breathing that she was asleep. Then his restless thrashing could begin again.

He was preoccupied and irritable during the day, and unable to work. He went to the telephone to call George Rapp a half dozen times, but each time he found something to attend to instead. So late in the afternoon, he went into the small office at the back of the lot and dialed the number of the steel company where George Rapp worked.

The operator switched the call to the shop. John could barely hear the voice above the noise of the plant. George came to the phone and said that he would go outside and call John back in five minutes. The five minutes seemed infinite to John, but at last the phone rang.

"It's me," George Rapp said.

"I've decided to pay that visit that we talked about," John said.

"Fine."

"There's only the question of the amount," John said.

"Oh. What do you think?"

"I don't know."

"Well, I can get together about five hundred, I think," George said. "Can you match it?"

"Yes. You think that's about right?"

"Okay," George said. "Let me know what happens."

"I'll call you."

"Good luck."

After dinner that night as it was growing dark, John told Mary he was going for a walk. She did not believe him, for he never took walks, but she did not question him. It seemed no more strange than many other things about his recent behavior.

He slowed the car as he neared a drugstore. He considered calling Peg Praul before he went to her house. In the end he decided that while he might take her by surprise, if he did not call, he didn't want to risk dropping in when there was someone else there.

He went into the drugstore and called Peg Praul.

"Mrs. Praul?" he said.

"Yeah."

"This is John Taylor."

"John Tay—well! What do you want?"

"I'd like to talk to you if you're not busy."

"What about?" she asked.

"I'd rather tell you in person. May I stop in to see you in a few minutes?"

"I don't know if . . . well, all right."

"You are alone, aren't you?"

"Ida's here, but that's all."

"All right. I'll be right over. Thank you."

Five minutes later John knocked lightly on the front door of Peg Praul's house. She answered the door and looked straight at him without speaking. Then she stood back to let him in.

"Sit down," Peg said.

As he did so, John could not prevent the surge of erotic images induced by this room of such wide and ill repute. It was small, crowded with furniture whose ugliness was heightened by the utter lack of relationship each piece bore to the others. John sat in a wine-colored velours armchair. Threads, broken by long use, tangled in the crocheted ecru antimacassar. Behind this chair was a small floor lamp with a pleated shade of flesh-colored rayon. The only other light came from a table by the bed where there was a small lamp with a flared and ruffled shade of once pink silk. The bed, of heavy, dark wood, was covered by a pink chenille spread.

"How is Ida, Mrs. Praul?" John asked.

Peg sat for a long moment twisting the noisy charm bracelet on her wrist. Then she raised her head and looked at John guardedly.

"The doctor says he guesses she'll be all right."

"I'm glad to hear that."

"I'll bet you are," Peg said, looking again at her jewelry.

"Mrs. Praul . . ." John began.

"Why do you keep callin' me that?" Peg asked. John stared at her in surprise and confusion until she added, "Was a time you called me Peg. When we used to see each other at dances around town. Or don't you remember that?"

"I remember," John answered. "It's just that it was a long time ago."

"Yeah," Peg said. "We ain't gettin' any younger, are we?" There was a slight wistfulness under the coarse language and manner. "Must be more than twenty years," she added.

"Yes, I guess it is."

And John did remember, in that softly diffused way in which memory brings back the distant past. Dances held in the gymnasium of the old high school, at the Horace Butler Fire Company, the American Legion Hall, in the loft over Pud Bailey's store, at the Odd Fellows Hall, all compounded into one fluid memory in which faceless people laughed and talked and danced in colorless clothes. Then color and detail returned again, and he saw Peg Praul, an ugly face, smiling its ineffectual and self-conscious smile. Even then her reputation had not been good, and that was nearly all he had known of her, that and that she was homely. Homeliness and age are not incompatible, and John thought now as he looked at Peg Praul that it is not so bad to be old and homely, but to be young and homely must be a terrible thing. Then his memory was over.

Peg Praul, too, was remembering. She remembered the dances and thought of them now as her carefree, joyful youth. The intimate pain of them did not return with their memory, for she had taken the pain with her. She had let each day slip into the past, but had clung to her pain, taken it with her into each new day. She remembered the dancing and the bootleg drinks and the smoke and the noise and the countless brief erotic episodes which culminated all of those evenings; but only the joy and the pleasure returned with them. She remembered how attractive John Taylor had been. Even now, she thought, looking at him, he was desirable.

"You haven't changed very much," she said.

John laughed quietly. "Oh, I guess I've changed as much as anybody."

"What did you want to see me about?" Peg asked, serious again.

"Well . . . I wanted to see how your daughter was and . . ."

"And what?"

"I . . . I wanted to ask you why you're doing this."

"Why I'm doin' what?" Peg asked, both angry and puzzled.

"Why you want to take my son into court," John said.

For a moment Peg was stunned. "For what he did to my daughter, that's why!" she shouted. "What the hell do you mean asking me—"

"Don't get upset," John said quickly. "I understand that. I do, honestly."

"Then why in the hell—"

"But have you asked yourself what good it's going to do?" John went on. "What good it's going to do anybody?"

"What d'you mean, what good it's goin' to do?" Peg asked.

"I know what a terrible thing this is, believe me. I wouldn't want to trade places with you, but I don't think you'd want to trade with me, either."

"What's that got to do with it?"

"First of all, we don't know what really happened out there on that hill."

"My daughter got raped, that's what happened!"

"I don't mean to say anything against your daughter—"

"You better not!" Peg interrupted.

"But who knows what was said or what was done out there? They're all just children, and—"

"Armand Rapp's no child."

"Armand Rapp isn't my son. What you say is true. Maybe he was more responsible than anybody else, but I don't think a court is going to recognize that. Johnny will suffer just as much as Armand."

"But not as much as my baby."

"Is that what you want? To make them suffer like Ida?"

"Sure, that's what I want," Peg said bluntly.

"That's revenge."

"I don't care what the hell you call it, it's my right by law."

"You mean it's Ida's right."

"Don't you try to double-talk me," Peg said.

"I'm not trying to double-talk you. I just meant that Ida is the one who was wronged. I wonder if she cares about seeing that the boys are punished."

"Ida's just a kid. What she cares about don't matter. *I* care about it."

"It's not going to do Ida any good to punish them."

"What the hell did you come here for anyway?" Peg asked, vehemently. "Did you come here to ask me just to forget about what happened? Do you think I'm goin' to let them young bastards get away with this just because one of 'em's your son? If that's what you came here for, you get the hell out right now."

John was virtually certain that nothing could deter Peg from her revenge. But if he left now without trying George Rapp's plan, he could never be sure that it might not have worked. Dismally he realized that he would have to make her the offer, somehow.

"Mrs. Praul . . . Peg . . . I know that things haven't been so good for you . . . over the years. . . ."

"You're goddamn right they haven't!" she cried, "And nobody's goin' add this to all the rest!"

"Well . . . I thought of something that might make it easier for you if you were willing to settle this thing out of court."

"If what?" she fairly screamed at him, and though he knew he must, he was genuinely afraid of going on.

"If you would agree not to go on with this I could see my way clear to . . . to let you have a thousand dollars to help—"

"You son of a bitch!" Pegs said quietly. "You goddamn son of a bitch! Offerin' me money to let them go, after what they did to my little Ida!" Her voice was still quiet, out of sheer astonishment, for she was not bright enough to have foreseen the bribe. "You get outa here!" she said, her voice rising now. "You get outa here before I get the cops after you! Yeah, that's what I'm goin' to do! You just wait till I tell the cops what you done!"

"Mrs. Praul . . ." John started, desperately.

"Get out, you son of a bitch! Get out! Get out!"

She sprang from her chair and in an instant stood banging her fists against his head and shoulders. John took her by the arms and pushed her back across the room. Her body hit the edge of the bed, and she crumpled across it, still screaming profanely. As John pulled the front door closed behind him, he saw Ida come through the curtain into the room, looking frightened, but not surprised.

He got to his car quickly and drove away from the house. He tried not to think, that is, tried not to put his thoughts consciously in order. Over and over he heard Peg Praul's voice screaming and cursing. He felt her fists pounding him. Beneath this consciousness thoughts of what he had said and images of the ugly little room ran like a subterranean stream. He drove on, without seeing where he was or knowing where he was going. Dimly he realized that his racing thoughts were preventing the admission of his self-loathing.

He drove across the bridge and up into the hills and stopped at a spot where he knew he would be alone. He parked the car and sat with his hand covering his eyes. What had he done? What stupid, terrible thing had he done, he wondered. If Peg Praul went to the police. . . . How could he have done such a thing? It was a mistake, an awful mistake, but he had done it to save his son, and that was honorable. Honorable. Trying to bribe a whore whose daughter had been raped, was that honorable?

He flicked on the ignition and started the car. He turned onto the highway and brought the car up to the fifty-mile-per-hour speed limit, his jaw set, his hands firm on the wheel. Then his speed, like his resolve, diminished, and as he finally parked the car in front of his house, he knew with a sad resignation that if Peg Praul should call him, having changed her mind, he would probably go to her in the middle of the night with the money.

He went into the house, took off his hat and coat and wearily threw them over the arm of a chair. Mary had been watching television. She got up now, turned off the set, and stood before it expectantly, her hands folded in front of her, but she did not speak.

John crossed the room and sank into his easy chair, putting both hands to his forehead. He sat that way for a long time, with Mary watching him, afraid now to speak.

John put his hands on the arms of the chair and sighed heavily. "I've done something stupid, Mary. Stupid and dangerous to Johnny." He waited but she said nothing. "I . . . I tried to bribe Peg Praul into dropping the prosecution. That means she can go to the police or the district attorney or anybody she wants and tell them that Johnny Taylor's father tried to bribe her—which he would not have done, of course, if he wasn't sure his son is guilty."

Mary uttered a faint cry. "Oh, John, why did you do it?"

"I did it to help Johnny!" he shouted. "Why the hell do you think I did it?" Then more quietly, "It seemed like such a good idea when that goddamned George Rapp suggested it. 'Who's going to believe Peg Praul against you?' he said. Just everybody, that's who."

"Oh, John, didn't you think of that before?"

He looked at her for a moment. "Yes, Mary," he said sarcastically, "I thought of it and went to Peg Praul anyway."

"But bribery, John!"

"Wouldn't you bribe for him, Mary?" John asked.

"I . . . I don't know," she answered.

"Holy Christ, Mary, you're the boy's mother! What do you mean, you don't know?"

"I guess . . . I would."

"If that bribe had succeeded you'd be all love and kisses right now. So would Jim and even Hertzog. But it didn't succeed, so now I'm just a stupid, dishonest bastard!"

"I didn't say that."

"No. Nobody'll say it. They'll just think it and let show in their eyes."

"You were only trying to help."

He looked at her wearily, almost disgustedly, and said, "Yes, Mary, I was only trying to help." He sighed, got up and went to the telephone. "I've got to see Jim."

When John got to the Beyers' house, Jim answered the door. He was wearing an old jacket with frayed sleeves and flannel slacks. He's still young looking, John thought as Jim stepped back to let him enter. The gray threaded so evenly through his black hair did not really give an impression of age.

When they came into the living room from the small foyer, Kay was sitting at the desk writing letters. She rose when John came into the room.

"John, I haven't had a chance to tell you how sorry I am," she said, extending a hand in sympathy.

"Kay," Jim said, "you needn't talk as if someone had died."

"I understand," John said. "Thank you, Kay. I hope we'll be able to work everything out."

"I hope so," she said, but her voice was tinged with elaborate doubt.

"Let's go downstairs, John," Jim said.

"Sure," John answered, following.

"Excuse us, Kay, will you?" Jim said out of polite habit, not waiting for the requested permission.

The two men went down the stairs to the lower level of the Beyers' split-level dwelling, the "family room." Jim's two children—David, who was seventeen and Seth, fourteen—were lounging there in what seemed to be extreme lethargy, David lying on a window seat reading, while Seth was changing the records on the phonograph.

"Boys," Jim called as he and John came into the room, which was pine-paneled and had gay denim curtains at the windows.

"Oh, hi, Mr. Taylor," Seth said, turning from the phonograph.

"Hello, Mr. Taylor," David said, looking up from his book.

"Hello, fellows," John said, smiling at them both.

"David, you wouldn't mind reading your magazine upstairs, would you?"

"Uh . . . no, Dad. No."

"Seth."

"Huh?" Seth grunted without turning around.

Jim winced at the absence of the "Yes, sir" he had hoped to elicit. "Just run along, please. Find something to do—elsewhere."

"Oh, sure, Dad. What's the conference?" Seth asked.

"Seth. Just go. All right?"

"Sure. Sure, Dad. See you later, Mr. Taylor."

The boys left the room. Jim went to the bamboo bar at one end of the room and stepped behind it.

"Like a drink, John?" Jim asked.

"I could use one," John said, crossing the room to sit on one of the four bamboo bar stools. "Nice kids," he added, looking after them.

"What's the trouble?" Jim asked, handing John his drink and settling on a fifth bar stool which was kept behind the bar for the bartender's convenience.

"Oh. I . . . I've done something very stupid, something you're not going to like."

"Okay, Longjohn . . ."

John smiled at the high-school nickname.

"Out with it."

"I'm afraid it's very serious, Jim," John said, and Jim sobered with him. "George Rapp came to me a couple of days ago with what seemed at the time to be a pretty good idea."

"George Rapp's never had a good idea—or even an idea," Jim said. "I should think you'd know that."

"I suppose I should. Anyway, he suggested that I go to Peg Praul and—" John took a deep breath and let the words ride out on the expulsion of air "—ask her to accept money to drop the prosecution."

Jim's drink was in midair as John finished the sentence. The glass clunked heavily on the bar. "You didn't do it?" he asked, his forehead wrinkled in apprehension.

"Uh . . . yes . . . I'm afraid I did."

"Oh . . . my . . . *God* . . . John! How *could* you have—"

206

"Been so stupid? I don't know, Jim," John said, looking into his drink, "but I did it."

Jim put his elbow on the bar and put his head into his upheld hand. "John . . . John, do you know what you've done?"

"I . . . think so."

"I'm sorry. I didn't mean to be . . . schoolteacherish. I have no right to be. I know you were only doing what you thought was best. But Holy God, John! Well, come on. Tell me about it. Everything—from the first minute George Rapp came to you until now."

Jim listened to John's account of the bribe in seeming suspended animation, which grew out of his attempt to be professional. When John had finished relating his retreat from the Praul household, Jim said, "Well, Longjohn, you really did it."

"I'm ashamed, Jim," John said and thought immediately of Saturday afternoon outside the Borough Hall. "It's funny, I was ashamed of Johnny and what he did when we came out of the Borough Hall Saturday, and I was ashamed to let you know I was ashamed. Now I'm ashamed and I don't mind letting you know. Maybe something's happening to me," he added with a little laugh.

"A hell of a lot's happening to you, John," Jim said and took a large swallow of his drink. "Look, boy, I know what I think about all this, but it would be better to hear what Steve Hertzog thinks. Let me give him a call right now."

Jim picked up the telephone extension at the end of the bar. When the telephone was answered the background noises of a party reached Jim. He asked for Stephen, and after a moment heard Stephen's voice, obviously on another extension. The original one had been replaced in its cradle and there was quiet.

"Stephen, I'm afraid we're in trouble."

"You mean *more* trouble?"

"Yes. At George Rapp's suggestion, John Taylor tried to bribe Ida Praul's mother into dropping the charges."

"Why, the stupid son of a bitch!"

"Yes. He's right here."

"I don't care if he's on an extension, he's still stupid. For Christ's sake, what'd she do?"

"Threw him out—threatening to go to the police."

"Well, that wouldn't do her a hell of a lot of good. She'd be better off going to the local newspaper. Look, Jim, don't do anything. I was planning on coming up tomorrow to have a talk with the boys. Would you set it up with them, please. If there's any immediate trouble about the other thing, call my office. They'll get me out of court if necessary. Otherwise, just sit tight."

"All right."

"And tie Taylor up, will you? Nice and tight."

"I'll be careful."

"I'm not worried about you. Tell *him* to be careful. See you tomorrow."

"Good night," Jim said and hung up. "He's a hard man, John."

"I suppose he's pretty mad."

"He wasn't exactly pleased. It's just that . . . well, it's the worst thing a client can do to a lawyer—especially a criminal lawyer—trying to help without asking first. Almost invariably things get messed up."

"I'm sorry, Jim."

"I know you are. Forget it. Just don't do anything—*anything* else. Don't look so glum. Come on, let's have another drink."

"Okay," John said, pushing his glass across the bar toward Jim. "Jim, I know going to Peg Praul was bad for the case and all that, but . . . well, if you knew Peg Praul *would* take a bribe, would you tell me to go to her?"

Jim paused in his drink-making. "I . . . I'm not a criminal lawyer, John."

"Neither am I," John laughed.

"I'm sorry," Jim said, joining John in the quiet laughter. "I didn't mean to be evasive. Yes—I guess I did mean to be evasive. It's a hard question to answer."

"Suppose it was David instead of Johnny who was involved. Does that make it any easier?"

"Harder," Jim said without hesitation.

"Does it really?"

"What do you mean?"

"Well, I'm not asking you if you approve of bribery. I guess I'm not even asking if you approve of bribery if it works. I'm asking you if you'd bribe somebody to keep your son out of prison."

"I . . . I don't know."

"Well, it seems to me a father's answer to that question ought to be yes."

"Does it, John? Suppose the girl were Lois instead of Ida Praul, and suppose further that the boy were David. Would you approve of my bribing somebody to keep David from his just punishment?"

"Lois wouldn't have led anybody on the way Ida Praul—"

"Ah, just a minute. We aren't sure that Ida did, and even if we were, are you proposing that that gave Johnny and the other two boys license to rape her?"

"No, of course I'm not."

"Anyway, we were dealing in absolutes, I thought. Does the moral justification of bribery rest in the nature of the motive?"

"Does the end justify the means?"

"Exactly. And the answer, unequivocally, is no."

"I'm not sure."

"I am."

"Wait till your boy's facing a prison sentence."

"Does that change it, John?"

"I only know what I had to do."

"We've kind of got away from the question, 'Would I bribe somebody to keep my son from going to prison?' In effect I'm answering two questions: no, the end does not justify the means; yes, I probably would bribe to keep my son out of prison."

"I think you're trying to make me feel better," John said, twisting his glass on the bar.

"You mean you think I wouldn't commit bribery or perjury or anything else to save David or Seth?"

"That's why it's so hard, Jim," John said looking up earnestly. "If you condone bribery or perjury you have to condone theft or murder or rape."

"There's a thing called practical morality—"

"No, there's not."

"—by which one says, 'I would lie or cheat or steal to save my son from prison, but I would not murder or rape or commit arson to save my son from prison.' "

"But they're all wrong."

"Yes. But you felt compelled to bribe Peg Praul to save Johnny. Really compelled."

"Yes."

"Yet would you murder her to save him?"

"N—no."

"Practical morality."

"Moral backing and filling."

"Perhaps. Now, suppose the girl were Lois and the boy were David. Do you think that would stop me from trying to save David?"

"I . . . I guess not."

"It wouldn't. And if you could circumvent the bribe, you'd do it. Right?"

"I . . . yes."

"Out of revenge?"

"Certainly not. Because David would have committed a crime and he'd deserve to be . . ." John stopped, looking almost puzzled.

"You see, John. It all depends on where you sit. Do you think I wouldn't like to be able to say to you that if David were to rape a young girl, I wouldn't lift a finger outside the allowances of the law to save him? Do you think I don't wish the whole world operated on that principle? And do you think I don't know that the world never will until men like us take it upon ourselves to make their own lives operate on that principle? I know all of that full well, as well as I know that I'd bribe until my pockets were empty to keep my son out of prison."

"I don't feel any less guilty," John said, tilting his glass and lining up its edges with his line of vision.

"There are other considerations too."

"Such as?"

"If Johnny had set out to rape Ida Praul, tricked her into a lonely spot, knocked her out, raped her and left her there, I don't think you'd be so willing to bribe to save him."

"Jim, I wouldn't say this to another living soul. I don't know what those boys—including Johnny—had in mind when they started out. Apparently Ida went with them willingly, but you know what happened. They held her down, Jim, while Armand Rapp raped her. Then they left her lying there. That's pretty close to what you said."

"I don't think it was quite like that," Jim said. "We certainly don't know for sure."

"I'm afraid there isn't much doubt."

"Let's give Johnny the benefit of whatever doubt there is."

"I hope the jury will."

"Stephen will see to that."

"Anyway, if I get your meaning, you're saying that whether or not it's right to bribe depends on the seriousness of the crime?"

"Not quite. I'm saying that whether or not Johnny deserves to be punished depends on the seriousness of the crime."

"I thought that was what all that degree of the crime business was for."

Jim laughed, this time heartily. "You're teaching me law, Longjohn, and you're absolutely right. But what we're discussing is affecting the outcome of a trial *outside* the processes of the law, as with bribery. If I thought my son were or would become a hardened criminal I might not be willing to bribe or—"

"Do you really believe that? Don't you think you'd still want to get him off, and then get him some kind of psychological treatment or something? But get him off first?"

Jim look troubled now. "Yes . . . I suppose so."

"Hell, Jim, George Rapp said that to me. Get 'em off first, he said. And you can go further than that. You can say that prison would turn a decent boy into a criminal, so there's an excuse for getting him off any way you can."

"The law assumes that a rapist is not entirely a decent boy."

John looked down at the top of the bar and said, "Thanks for that, too."

"John, I didn't mean Johnny. Look, the law makes allowances for every single eventuality we've discussed. A defendant can be pleaded legally insane. If there are mitigating circumstances such as Ida's leading on the alleged attackers, it lessens the degree of the crime and the punishment is less. The law is wise, John; it allows for all of these things. What we've been talking about is putting ourselves above the law, and as a lawyer I cannot advocate that under any circumstances. As a father, I know I'd bribe to keep my son out of jail—and goddamn the law."

"And morality. . . ."

"And goddamn morality. You've demonstrated it yourself tonight. You're a decent man, John, yet you had to try to bribe Peg Praul. You just had to when you tried to balance years of prison for Johnny against one dishonest act which would hurt no one. You can be academic about this kind of think for just so long. Academically you can bring yourself to an absolutely ironclad decision, but when the time comes to act, you do what you have to do."

"You mean you know what's right, but you do what seems best?"

"Sometimes, I think. Yes."

"Maybe you're right, Jim."

After a moment Jim said, "Have one for the road?"

"I think I'll make the last one my road drink," John said. "I guess Mary'll be waiting, and I need some sleep. Thanks, anyway."

XVIII.

It was after she had made Johnny's bed while she was smoothing out the spread that Mary stopped, still bent over the place where her son slept, but utterly motionless as she considered the astonishing fact that it was mid-morning of the fifth day after Johnny's arrest. Could it be only Thursday? she asked herself. Was it really only four days ago that she had gone to Borough Hall to visit her imprisoned child? Was it merely the day before yesterday that George Rapp had stood on the sunporch during that terrible storm? Was it just last night that John had sat in his easy chair, his hand covering his eyes in preparation for the awful confession he had to make? It seemed to her that there had been a great wedge of years jammed between Ben Summerfield's visit and this quiet moment in Johnny's bedroom. It seemed longer to her than her childhood. It seemed longer than her marriage. No lifetime seemed long enough to encompass those four short days. If a person could be always that conscious of time, she thought, why, life would seem endless. She wondered if that would be a good thing, if it would be even bearable.

She ran her hand across the last wrinkle in the spread, turned and went outside the room. As she reached the bottom of the stairs, Mary saw through the door and the sunporch windows the large, familiar figure with the slow, ponderous, almost hulking walk on the pavement just outside the house. It turned at the front walk, and Mary went out onto the sunporch and opened the door.

"Aunt Sarah," she called. "Hello."

"Morning, Mary," the woman said between deep, labored breaths.

Mary merely waited then during the slow progress toward the house. She did not go to her aunt, did not take her arm, did not offer assistance.

She merely waited, for Aunt Sarah, who was seventy-two, did everything slowly but she did everything herself and refused to be helped. In these last ten years everyone had become accustomed to waiting for Aunt Sarah. Everyone waited silently and without apparent apprehension as Aunt Sarah hauled her bulk through the low, narrow door of an automobile; as in well-defined stages she lifted herself out of a living room chair and laboriously made her way to the dining room. Aunt Sarah Jennings, the youngest and last of the four Jennings sisters, was not fat, nor was she feeble. She was five feet eleven inches tall. The human mechanism had simply slowed with age and arthritis, and rather than expose her thousand daily physical struggles with haste, she disguised those struggles with her slow, deliberate movements. Mary had often wondered how Aunt Sarah managed to keep her hair, once blond but faded now to the exact color and sheen of cornsilk, in the wide, perfect ripples of the marcel in which she had worn it for the last forty years.

Everything about Aunt Sarah was like that marcel. She was always immaculate. Her pale, thin lips were almost straight, and beneath them were two gleaming rows of tediously perfect false teeth.

"Haven't seen you for a coon's age, Mary," and Aunt Sarah was in the house.

"It has been a long time, Aunt Sarah," Mary said, and she closed the door very slowly, giving Aunt Sarah time to cross the sunporch before she followed.

In the living room Aunt Sarah took off her black straw hat and handed it to Mary. Then, her black leather purse dangling from her arm, she crossed the room and lowered herself into the small occasional chair which she found she had the least trouble getting out of.

"Can I get you something, Aunt Sarah?" Mary asked. "A cup of tea?"

Aunt Sarah was breathing less heavily now. "Glass of ginger ale if you have one, Mary. Got a little gas, and ginger ale's just the thing."

"Of course," Mary said. "Only take a minute."

A moment later Mary returned carrying the glass of ginger ale. "There you are, dear," she said, handing it to Aunt Sarah.

"Thank you," she said and added before Mary had even got to a chair, "Came to talk about Johnny." Talking was the only thing that Aunt Sarah did not do slowly.

"Oh," Mary said quietly. "John doesn't think it's a good idea to talk about it," she said, grateful now for John's advice.

" 'Course I see his point," Aunt Sarah said, "if he means gossipy neighbors. But he certainly don't mean me. I'm the boy's great aunt," she explained quite unnecessarily.

"I think he means it just shouldn't be discussed, Aunt Sarah."

"Well, people *are* talking about it," she said and lowered her eyes to the ginger ale, which she sipped, holding the glass with both hands.

"Yes, I guess they are," Mary answered.

"Neighbors told me," Aunt Sarah said. "Would've thought you'd of called and told me yourself, Mary."

"It was . . . such a shock, Aunt Sarah," Mary told her. "I guess I haven't done just right in every instance."

" 'Course it was. That's why I ain't really mad at you. Wouldn't of come if I was."

"Thank you, Aunt Sarah."

"How's the kids?"

"Lois . . . well, she's been very upset. She doesn't understand, of course. I mean, we haven't told her. I just don't know what to tell her, Aunt Sarah."

"You better tell her the truth, Mary. She's going to hear it anyway."

"I suppose so," Mary said, trying to keep the conversation as uncomplicated as possible.

"Got yourself a lawyer?"

"Yes. Jim Beyers arranged it. A man from the city."

"City fella, huh? Well, maybe it's best." There was another pause and more sipping of ginger ale. Then, "Your sister called me this morning."

"What did Agnes want?" Mary asked.

"It was about . . . about supper Sunday. We was all to go over to their house to supper on Sunday, you know."

"Yes, I know. What about it?"

"Now, don't you go getting upset with Agnes. It ain't her doing. . . ."

"What about it, Aunt Sarah?" Mary said again, sitting up stiffly in her chair.

"Well, Fred don't think it's a good idea for the children to get together right away."

"Why not? What did Agnes say?"

"Just that. Now, look here, Mary, poor Agnes is so upset herself she didn't even know what to say to you. There's no use you getting all het up over—"

"My own sister!"

"It ain't your sister, it's your brother-in-law."

"Well, it's obvious Agnes agrees with him or she wouldn't let him—"

"Mary, think about it yourself. They don't know what to tell their young ones any more'n you know what to tell little Lois. But you get them all together, you're going to have to tell them something."

"Why? Why does everybody have to talk about it? Why can't everybody just let the court decide, and just keep still themselves until then?"

"You can't stop people talking, Mary. And kids is worse gossips than grownups. Agnes' children are sure to hear something about—"

"Or have they heard already?"

Aunt Sarah carefully put her glass on the table beside her, turned back and looked directly into Mary's eyes. "All right. I ain't going to lie to you, Mary. Agnes' little Sally—and she's only eight, mind you—came home from the park yesterday using words about Johnny she couldn't possibly understand."

"What words?"

"I don't see it makes any difference. The point is you get them kids together and there'll be talk among them that—"

"And how are we supposed to explain to Johnny that his own aunt and uncle won't have him in their house?"

"Oh, Mary, it ain't they won't have him in their house. It—"

"Isn't it, Aunt Sarah? What else is it? Are John and I going to be the only ones who'll stand by Johnny?"

"They'll stand by him, Mary."

"How? By not having him to supper? Why don't you tell me what Agnes said?"

"It ain't Agnes. It's Fred."

"All right, then, tell me what Fred's really afraid of. If we went there, the children wouldn't be alone for a single minute. We'd be able to stop any conversation in an instant. So it's not that, is it, Aunt Sarah?"

The old woman looked at her niece for a long moment, then she sighed and said, "No, Mary, it ain't. Fred says if Johnny did what he done, it ain't proper for him to be with other children. That's it in a nutshell."

Mary stared at her, hurt and angry and confused all at once. "And you, Aunt Sarah. Do you feel that way, too?"

" 'Course I don't," she snapped. "I'm only here for Agnes' sake. What can she do if Fred feels that way?"

"She could insist."

"With Fred Schreiber? Be like talking to a wall. I know it ain't right, Mary, but that's the way it is. I just don't want contention between you two. Not when it ain't Agnes' fault."

"What ever will we tell Johnny?" Mary said, her hand going to her mouth.

"I don't know, Mary. I suppose he'll guess the truth, whatever you tell him."

"Yes. He'll know."

"I wish we could spare the boy that."

"And John. I doubt if John will ever speak to Agnes and Fred again."

"A fat lot of good that'll do anybody."

"It's his way. And I'm not sure I blame him."

"Never was any love lost between your John and Fred Schreiber. Never thought much of him myself, to tell the truth."

They were silent then for a few minutes, until Mary said, "You'll stay to lunch, won't you, Aunt Sarah? Won't be much, but you're welcome."

"If it's no trouble, yes, I will, Mary."

"No trouble at all."

"Where's little Lois?"

"In her room. I'll call her. She always loves seeing her Aunt Sarah."

Aunt Sarah stayed most of the day and Mary got no housework done. It was just after four o'clock as Mary and Lois stood in the doorway watching Aunt Sarah inching her way down the street toward her home.

For the first time he could remember John came home to find that dinner was barely under way.

"What's happened now?" he asked.

"Oh John, it's Agnes and Fred, my own sister . . ."

"Agnes and Fred?" John said, stopping in his progress across the kitchen. "What about Agnes and Fred?"

"They . . ." Mary paused, unwilling to strike this latest blow so seemingly thoughtlessly. "Aunt Sarah was here this afternoon."

"What about Agnes and Fred?" John said ruthlessly, for now his anger spilled over and flowed through the room like a flood, ready to drown even the innocent bystander.

"They . . ." Mary began again and realized as she hesitated that she must go on now. "They canceled supper next Sunday." She was truly afraid then as she watched his eyes narrow and harden in their expression.

"Because of Johnny?" he said, and though his lips moved, his teeth did not part when he spoke. Mary put her hand to her mouth and nodded. John stood looking at Mary as if it had been she who had canceled the invitation. Then he crossed the room and picked up the telephone, but as he was dialing the front door opened and Johnny came into the room.

"Hi, Mother," he said, and when his father turned, the telephone in his hand, Johnny said, "Hello, Dad."

Neither parent answered Johnny's greeting. They merely stared at him, each with a quite different expression, but both of which Johnny interpreted as looks of anger.

"What . . . what's the matter?" he asked, standing by the door, a baffled look on his face.

"N—nothing, dear," Mary said.

"No, Mary," John said, replacing the telephone.

"John, don't—"

"No Mary," he repeated loudly. "Can't you see that that's what's done this to all of us?"

"John, please don't—"

"Can't you see you're lying to keep from saying something unpleasant, not just to protect Johnny? You can't protect everybody from the truth, Mary, or pretty soon you stop believing in the truth. That's what's happened to us. We've been sitting around for years talking about the weather, laughing at some little joke, passing on some local gossip. But we never say anything to each other. That's a hell of a way to teach kids to live, Mary, but that's what they've learned from us. How long has it been since we used the word love between us, Mary . . . or even made love? What's wrong, is it something to be ashamed of? You've never talked to Lois about sex, and the one time I tried to talk to Johnny I found out he'd learned his lesson so well he just couldn't bring himself to talk to me about it. What's wrong, are we ashamed of that, too? Are—"

"John!" Mary almost whispered. "Not with Johnny here. . . ."

"Not with . . ." John started, looking amazed. "Mary, six days ago Johnny was out on that hill laying on top of Ida Praul! He knows about sex, Mary! Can't you understand that? He knows how he came to be born; he doesn't believe in the stork any more. He's a human being, Mary. He's an adult. You can talk to him! You can tell him you don't feel good because you're having your period, and he'll know what you mean. You don't have to be ashamed of it, and make him ashamed because you are."

"Oh, John, stop it!" Mary said through the fingers spread across her mouth. "Why do you want to say such filthy things in front of Johnny?"

"My God," John said, drawing his hand across his forehead. "You don't understand, do you? You haven't got any idea what I'm even talking about! Mary," he said, taking a step toward her, "we've got to start talking to each other—all of us. Not talking just because we happen to be in a room together, but because we want to say something to each other. That's the way people learn things—learn about each other. We've got to . . ."

He saw then how frightened Mary looked, and he understood how frightened she truly was. He stopped talking for a moment, looking into her eyes. Then he said, "Mary, just tell us about Agnes and Fred. Tell us—Johnny and me—about Agnes and Fred. Come over and sit down, Johnny. Your mother has something to tell us. It concerns us both, and it's something I think is going to hurt you, but nobody can do anything about that. Come over and sit down."

As Johnny crossed the room, he realized that he did not like what was going on, but he also realized for the first time in many years that he liked his father.

"Go on, Mary," John said when Johnny had sat down. "Just tell us."

Mary looked from one to the other of these men, who, even through her confusion, she knew she loved. "I don't . . ." They both looked at her when she paused, and their looks were soft and, to her, strangely loving. "We . . . we were supposed to go to your Aunt Agnes' and Uncle Fred's for supper next Sunday." She watched them then, to be sure they understood that much. "Aunt Sarah came by today to tell me that they don't want us to come because . . ."

"Mary," John said with an unnatural quietness, "if you don't tell him that, you might just as well not tell him any of it."

They could see in her eyes that she understood. ". . . because they don't want Johnny to be with their children . . . his own cousins." Her voice was flat and expressionless.

After a moment Johnny said, "Couldn't . . . couldn't the rest of you go without me?"

There was a silence then which John found unbearable, and so he said, "Johnny. Johnny, the rest of us don't *want* to go without you. Not there or anywhere else."

Then for a precious, fleeting moment, though John and Mary and Johnny Taylor were still alone, the Taylors were not.

Their supper was eaten in an uneasy quiet with only Lois not fully understanding why. John could barely eat for struggling with the problem of explaining their quietness to her. He did not find a way. As they were eating dessert, Jim Beyers telephoned to tell John that Stephen

Hertzog would be at Jim's house at seven o'clock. John said that he would be there, and did not return to the table.

John arrived at Jim's house before Stephen, and Jim took him immediately into the room with the bamboo bar. They had taken only the first sip of their drinks when Kay brought Stephen into the room.

"Mr. Hertzog's here, Jim," she said, coming down the stairs before the guest.

"Stephen," Jim said. "How are you? Come and have a drink."

"Hello," John said as Stephen crossed the room and Kay lingered at the bottom of the stairs.

"Hello," Stephen said to both men, his eyes resting for a long moment on John.

"Thank you, Kay, for showing Stephen in," Jim said quite deliberately.

"Oh, you're welcome," Kay said gaily. "I'll see you boys later," she added, waving them a casual goodbye.

"What'll you have, Stephen?" Jim asked when his wife had gone.

"Scotch, please," Stephen said, sitting on a stool next to John.

There was a short but noticeable silence as Jim got the drink for Stephen. It was ended when Stephen Hertzog turned his head directly toward John and said, "I think you'd better tell me, Mr. Taylor, every single detail that you can remember that in any way relates to your attempt to bribe Mrs. Praul."

John took a mouthful of his drink and then haltingly, but without interruption, told Stephen of George Rapp's visit to him and of his own visit to Peg Praul. When John had finished, Stephen took his eyes from John's face for the first time and looked at Jim expressionlessly. Then, looking again into John's eyes, he said, "You goofed, Mr. Taylor."

"Yes, I know," John said.

"Do you?" Stephen asked. "Do you really know what you've done? For everybody's best interests there shouldn't be any doubt about it, so I'm going to tell you what you've done. You have publicly admitted that you believe your son guilty. You've lived in this town all your life, I believe, Mr. Taylor. So you must know even better than I do that between here and Harrisville there's nothing but a network of small towns so close together that they're interlocking. I'm sure you have friends, possibly relatives, in one or more of those towns. The Harrisville paper is the major newspaper in every town in a ten- or fifteen-mile radius of Harrisville, and this trial is front page news on that paper. Do you think we're going to be able in October to find one prospective juror in this county who doesn't know every juicy detail of this lovely scandal? It's bad enough that when they run out of gossip they'll make things up, but to give them this kind of ammunition, to forearm and prejudice every prospective juror with the knowledge that you tried to bribe Mrs. Praul is practically suicidal. Even though it can't be brought into the actual trial, it—"

"It can't?" John asked in uncontrollable surprise.

"No, it can't—unless, of course, Johnny knew about it. With the knowledge and consent of the accused it would become evidence. Otherwise it's inadmissible for the very reason I've been trying to explain: it's information of the most prejudicial nature possible. Johnny *didn't* know about it?"

"No," John said.

"All right. Then if the district attorney should introduce it as evidence—which he won't, he won't have to—I daresay I'd demand and get a mistrial. And then we'd have the dubious privilege of starting all over. But don't be encouraged by any of this, Mr. Taylor. The jurors aren't going to admit knowing about this. Hell, last year in that city council scandal I saw a normally intelligent male juror stare into the judge's eyes and flatly deny that he knew who was mayor. Yes, he'd lived in that city for ten years. Yes, he read both the city newspapers. Yes, he'd read them both two days ago. No, he didn't see the mayor's name in two-inch headlines. You know goddamn well they're lying, but you can't do anything about it. And suppose I ask the judge to question a juror about the bribe. 'What bribe?' he'll say. 'I see nothing in the indictment about a bribe. Are you trying to prejudice this jury, Mr. Hertzog?' So first of all, we can't ask about it; second, if we did they'd lie; and third, we're going to have a prejudiced jury in any event. Our best hope is that there'll be at least as much prejudice for us as against us—a possibility made entirely remote by your bribe attempt, Mr. Taylor."

"What if it comes up, Stephen?" Jim Beyers said. "I mean locally, you know, just among friends."

"Deny it."

"What if it comes up with somebody we know knows the truth?" John asked.

"I can't imagine any circumstances under which you couldn't flatly deny it, but if for some reason you have to say something, say that you did it out of the fear of scandal and the general unpleasantness of the trial. You panicked at the image of your son's being subjected to a criminal prosecution for so heinous a crime as rape. You went without thinking—because you were scared, as any father might be—to Mrs. Praul with an offer of money if she would spare your son. It's not very convincing, but it might help some."

"Could . . . could I ask you a question?" John said.

"Certainly. What?"

"I understand that it's not going to come up at the trial, but . . . but if it were going to come up and I'd have to testify about it, what would you want me to say?"

Again Stephen looked at Jim Beyers and from Jim back to John, but as he did so, he considered his answer, and when he finally spoke it was slowly and carefully. He was too able and experienced a lawyer to underestimate an adversary. And somehow, he sensed, John Taylor was at this moment an adversary. Stephen had no fear of matching wits with this less well educated and probably thoughtless man, but he knew that their differences made it more difficult for him to see a question from John's point of view. He proceeded with caution.

"Since it won't come up," he said, "the question is entirely academic. I don't think there's any advantage in academic discussions between us, Mr. Taylor. Do you?"

"If I didn't think there was some point to the question, I wouldn't have asked it," John said.

This was the kind of aggression which Stephen simultaneously did not expect but managed to be prepared for. "Perhaps if you told me what you think the point is I could better answer the question."

"I didn't go to Peg Praul to see if I could help," John told him. "I went to offer her a bribe. I guess maybe I was panicky, and I was certainly worried about Johnny, but I didn't go to see if I could help. What I'm asking you is whether—I mean if it were going to come up in court—whether you'd say I went there just because I was panicky if you thought you could get away with it."

"Get away with it, Mr. Taylor?"

"Yes."

"In other words," Stephen said, beginning to understand, "you want to know if I'd be willing to put forward to the jury an advantageous untruth if I were certain that it would not be discovered to be an untruth."

"Yes."

"Or more simply, you are questioning my ethics."

"Yes."

Jim Beyers, who had been turning his glass round and round on the bar, stopped turning his glass and looked over the heads of the two men as if there were something of great interest at the far end of the room.

"That's sort of unusual," Stephen said calmly. "As a rule, the question arises from the opposite point of view: the client is afraid that too strong a sense of ethics on the part of his attorney will interfere with the proper performance of his duty—will impede the attainment of the obvious goal, acquittal. Here we have a client who is concerned about too weak a sense of ethics on the part of his attorney. Should we perhaps extend the parallel and assume that you are no longer interested in an acquittal?"

"Maybe I'm just wondering if in the long run a strong sense of ethics wouldn't help to get an acquittal," John answered, and his own surprise at the words was at least as great as Stephen's.

"If that's what you're wondering, Mr. Taylor, you're a rare bird," Stephen said. "But since you brought up this whole damned thing, let's be objective about it. There are going to be things said during the course of this trial that may not seem to you to be strictly accurate. For example, we can't go into court and tell the jury exactly what the boys have told me about dragging Ida from the car, or about your son and the other boy holding Ida down while Armand Rapp raped her. You understand that we can't say that, don't you, Mr. Taylor? Because if we're going to say that, we might just as well plead your son guilty of first-degree rape."

During the silence that Stephen intended for the absorption of the full effect of his statement, John said, "Are you telling me that if we go into court and tell the truth, Johnny will be found guilty?"

"I'm telling you the truth is that your son raped Ida Praul and that our job is to mitigate that truth."

"Mr. Hertzog," John began, and there was an effective contrast in the quietness of his voice, "you're a lawyer and I'm sure a good one. I'm not fool enough to think I can beat you in an argument. But you asked me not so long ago if I'd want to prevent you from doing something dishonest that would get the boys off, and I said no. All I'm trying to do now is find out if . . . if maybe I shouldn't have said yes."

Stephen Hertzog looked at John for a long time, and John could see that something was taking place in Stephen's eyes, a pale and subtle expression of what was taking place in his mind.

"You've been having quite a struggle with the truth, haven't you?" Stephen said.

"Yes."

"Well, that's one thing about you I can understand and respect."

His voice was quiet now and as nearly friendly as John had ever heard it. "But, you see, you've just recently had it thrust upon you; it's a struggle I've been involved in most of my life. And I don't really see any end to it."

"That must be terrible," John said.

"Sometimes it is."

Quite suddenly these two utterly dissimilar men had fallen into a conversation which was so deeply personal, so based on a profound mutual experience that Jim Beyers sat, marveling at the sense of exclusion he felt.

"But don't be too hard on yourself," Stephen went on. "Don't try to make it black and white or you'll find it impossible to go on living."

"But it is black and white," John said.

Stephen smiled faintly. "No, Mr. Taylor. The truth is a spectrum. It's every shade of every color, and it's an infinite number of tones of every shade. It's red and blue bleeding together in indivisible purples. It's yellow: chartreuse and lemon and straw and gold, just as it's green: emerald and grass and olive. It can be as brilliant and multicolored as a sunset, and it can be as muted and indefinite as the color of fog. But black and white . . . well, there are degrees of those, too."

"But a man has to choose," John said.

"Yes, but like the truth, the choice is relative, not absolute."

"I find that difficult to accept."

"Difficult? You don't know what difficulty is until you've tried living with the truth the other way."

"Yes. I'm finding out," John said.

Stephen looked at him for a moment with unmistakable sympathy. Then he sighed lightly and with an air of changing the subject, said, "The time will come in this trial when, out of necessity, you will be largely relieved of the responsibility for the honesty of the necessary decisions, because whoever your attorney is, he will have to make those decisions quickly and firmly and without conference. But, unfortunately for you, we haven't got that far yet, and there is a major decision for you to make now. If I am going to go on representing your son, you must leave the ethics of that defense entirely in my hands, without question and without criticism. If you want to share the responsibility for the ethics of your son's defense, you can get yourself another lawyer. Which is it to be?"

"I didn't mean to give you the idea that I was critical of—" John began.

"Which is it to be, Mr. Taylor?"

John looked at him, frankly annoyed by his rudeness. "I want you to go on representing Johnny."

Stephen looked at John for a moment as if he did not quite believe him. Then he said, "I'm glad. I want to represent your son—not because he's your son, but because I believe a conviction for first-degree rape would be a subtle but grave miscarriage of justice. And I intend to prevent it."

"Thank you," John said after a moment.

"But please—please don't do anything—not anything again without consulting either Jim or me."

John smiled rather sheepishly and said, "I won't."

Before they went to the Taylors' home where Stephen was to interview Johnny, the three men talked for a short time of other things, and even John Taylor, who was not given to such delicate observations, realized that there was a new and pleasant ease in their conversation. It was evident even to Kay Beyers, who stood listening to every word of their conversation just outside the family-room door.

XIX.

As quickly as possible the Taylors resumed the routine of their lives as if Johnny's arrest had been a minor, momentary interruption, but the pervasive difference they had felt on the night of his homecoming persisted. They pursued that routine with an unnatural vigor which made them all self-conscious, and an air of strained normality fell over the household. Frances McGovern visited from next door with her usual regularity, innocently blasphemous and profane as ever. She did not mention Johnny's case; she did not pry; she did not offer the bits of gossip she had heard. Beatrice Lowell, who lived on the other side of the Taylors, appeared on Friday morning with an angel's food cake she had just baked. It was ostensibly a return of a favor: Mary had done some shopping for Beatrice several days ago when John had driven her to the Grangeville shopping center. It was also Beatrice Lowell's tactful vote of confidence, and Mary knew it. Irma Loomis insisted that Mary and Lois come across the street for lunch at her house that same Friday, and having expressed her hope that everything would turn out all right, proceeded to be her usual hospitable and cheerful self, without another word about Johnny. Jenny Morrison was so ostentatiously cordial that Mary was not sure what to think. Old Mrs. Chambers hurried—as best she could—into the house when she saw Mary coming up the street to avoid speaking to her, whether from embarrassment or malice Mary could not tell. Other neighbors, on less intimate terms with the Taylors, called their usual hellos from porches or open windows to which housekeeping chores had brought them while Mary was similarly engaged, but Mary could not help wondering if some of these greetings were not, perhaps, a little more forced, more or less cheery and natural than usual.

Neither Mary nor John telephoned Agnes and Fred Schreiber, Mary's sister and brother-in-law. They had their usual Sunday supper at home, and the others did not know that Mary sat listening for the telephone, hoping but not really expecting that Agnes would call to say that they were still expected and were now very late. Her hopefulness had turned to sullenness as she cleared the table when supper was over.

Hers was not the only nervous silence. To some degree all of them, and particularly John, felt apprehensive about tomorrow, which was Labor Day, the day of the annual picnic of the Businessmen's Association at Fairview. John was vice-president of the Association and their absence would have been glaringly conspicuous, but their prospective attendance under the circumstances seemed to them hardly less so. However, the following morning the four Taylors, sportily dressed, with lunch baskets packed, reluctantly got into their car and drove to Fairview Amusement Park.

They turned off the main road toward the cool, shady grove where the picnic tables were already beginning to fill up. Children scrambled off and onto the stationary benches attached to the long, crossed-legged wooden tables. All was laughter and swimming suits and chattering and plum-colored pickled eggs and thick sandwiches and huge black flies and ants and thermoses and all of the other elements of picnicking.

As they got out of the car and unloaded their equipment, John paused and looked over the grove. The choice of a table would be important. He saw that the Beyers family shared a table with Chris and Dora and Betty Lou Henry. The Simpsons and the Morrisons had come together, probably in the Simpson's station wagon, and were together at a table. He saw Will Ziegler, there in his official police capacity, watching them in a not unfriendly manner. Will waved and John waved back. The Schliers (Otto Schlier was the Association's newest member) were there, too, at a table by themselves at the very edge of the grove. Then he saw that Fred Collins and his family had just arrived and were setting up a table on the other side of the grove. Fred, after World War II, had taken over the haberdashery his father had established. John's father had always bought his shirts from Fred's father, and John was both a customer and a friend of Fred's. He steered the family toward their table.

"Got room for us?" John called, after taking a deep, bracing breath which no one saw.

"John! Mary!" Fred Collins called back. "This horde of mine's getting bigger all the time, but we still got room. Come on over."

They all exchanged greetings then, and for one terrible moment during a sudden silence they noticed that little Butchy Collins, aged ten, was staring almost fearfully at Johnny. Fred Collins picked up a paper cup of grape juice, stuck it into his son's hand and said, "Drink up, Butchy, and I'll race you to the lake." Immediately everything returned to as nearly normal as it could be.

Johnny and Lois wanted a swim before lunch, and Lois wondered for a moment, though she did not ask, why Johnny took her to the stoniest part of the lake shore where no one else was swimming. They encountered many other children on the way to and from the lake, but the holiday spirit was strong, and only the cheeriest greetings were exchanged.

After lunch Johnny walked across the grove and approached the Schliers' table. "Hello," he said to the parents and added, "Hi ya, Artie."

Mr. Schlier looked at Johnny for a moment and said, "Your mother and father, they are well?"

"Yes, sir," Johnny answered. "Thank you." Mr. Schlier looked as if he were going to say something else, but when he did not after a long time, Johnny said, "You want to go over to the Midway, Artie?"

Artie looked at his father for a moment, then answered, "Sure." Then he turned again to his parents and said, "I won't be long."

Johnny listened to the dry crunching of the gravel as they walked in silence. After a moment Artie said, "What do think's going to happen?"

"What do you mean?"

"To us," Artie said.

"I don't know."

"I'm scared, Johnny," Artie said, kicking at the loose stones.

"Yeah, I guess I am, too."

"Geez, are you?"

"Well, sure I am. Why wouldn't I be? You just said you were."

"Yeah, but . . . I just thought maybe you wasn't."

"Well, I am, I guess. Want to go on the Thunderbolt?"

"No, I . . . I don't feel like it."

They walked past the whizzing, zooming Thunderbolt as one set of cars sped down the steepest incline with a deafening metallic roar. The high, thin scream of a happily terrified girl was faintly audible above the noise.

"I heard we could get twenty years," Artie said.

"Artie, do we have to talk about it?"

"Well, what do you want to talk about?"

"I don't care, but not that."

They walked on past stands where the great gambling wheels clickety-clicked their good and bad luck as the stopping-arm picked against the nails.

"Ever been in Bluebeard's Palace?" Johnny asked.

"What?" Artie said.

"The fun house, over there," Johnny said, nodding and pointing across the midway. "It's great. They've got a tilted room with all stripes that makes you—"

"I don't feel like it," Artie said.

They stopped on the wooden bridge which spanned the artificial lake where adults and some children (*Fifteen or Over Unless Accompanied by an Adult*) drove tiny motor boats through the wood-divided lanes.

"Want to get one?" Johnny asked.

"Aw, they're tame," Artie said.

"They're not so bad," Johnny said, but they walked on. They stopped again at the octagonal pavilion where at night a five-piece combo played until two o'clock A.M., but where now a dimly glaring juke box blared a popular record. Young men and women, mostly over twenty, danced or sat about drinking sodas or beer and holding hands. After a moment Johnny and Artie moved on. Johnny took Artie by the arm as they were passing a shooting gallery where the calling of the barker and the shots and the ringing of the hits silenced the mechanical noise of the gliding animals so that they seemed curiously to be moving under their own power.

"Bet you can't get the best out of twenty shots," Johnny said.

"Yeah, and you'd win, too. My mama wouldn't even let me have a BB gun. I never learned to shoot anything."

"That doesn't mean anything. Come on, try it anyway."

"Aw, I don't want to, Johnny."

"Why the hell did we come over here if you don't want to do anything?"

"It's just . . ."

"Just what, Artie?"

"Just I'm so worried."

"About the trial. And you want to talk about it," Johnny said as if repeating something that Artie had just said.

"Yeah."

"All right, we'll talk about it if it'll make you feel any better. But I don't see what there is to say."

"What did the lawyer tell your father about what he thinks we'll get?"

"The same thing he told *your* father, I guess. I don't think he even knows, Artie. Nobody does yet."

"Will they put us back in jail during the trial?" Artie asked.

"I don't know. Maybe it'll be the county jail in Harrisville."

"Geez, the county jail!" Artie said, his eyes narrowing in fear.

"What difference does it make which jail?"

"But the county jail, Johnny!"

"Maybe this is making you feel better, but it's not doing the same thing for me."

They walked in silence for a short time then, and Johnny stopped to buy a bag of popcorn. They resumed their walk, still silent, eating the popcorn from the white, foil-lined bag.

"How do you feel about it, Johnny?" Artie asked slowly without looking at Johnny.

"About what?"

"What we done."

Johnny did not answer immediately. He thought for a moment that he wouldn't answer at all. Then he said, "I sure wish we hadn't done it."

"Christ, yeah!"

"And I guess I'm sorry for it."

"Yeah, that's what you just said."

"No. They're not the same thing." Artie looked at him questioningly. "I wish we hadn't done it so we wouldn't be in the trouble we're in. But I'm sorry . . . sorry because I know it was wrong, I guess. Aren't you?"

"Well, sure," Artie said.

"Are you . . . are you ashamed of it, Artie?" Johnny asked, crumpling the popcorn bag and throwing it into a wire trash container.

"Ashamed?"

"Yeah," he said, wanting at last, without knowing it, to share his own shame.

"Well, I guess there's guys we know wouldn't've been able to."

"Yeah," Johnny said, kicking violently at a half-crushed paper cup on the ground before him, "guys with some damned sense in their heads."

"Yeah, but I mean there's guys we know would've been too chicken to do it."

"You're not ashamed, are you?"

"Well, sure I am."

"Why do you have to say everything I say? Why do—"

"What do you me—"

"Why do you have to say you wish we didn't? If I say it, you say it. If I say I'm sorry, you say you're sorry. If I'm ashamed, you're ashamed. If you're not ashamed, just say so."

"I am, Johnny—"

"Why don't you once in a while say something all by yourself? Go on, tell me how you feel about it, Artie. You wanted to talk about it. Tell me."

"I just did, Johnny. I said I wish we—"

"Aw, forget it!" Johnny said, waving the words away with a pawing gesture toward Artie. "I'm going back to Bluebeard's Palace. I'll see you." He turned immediately and walked away from Artie into the crowds of strollers.

"Johnny . . ." Artie said, turning to follow. But he merely stood and watched Johnny blend into the crowd until he could see him no longer.

Johnny did not go to Bluebeard's Palace. During their walk they had come round to the other side of the lake where the trees went directly to the shore line and there was no swimming. He turned onto one of the narrow macadam side streets of the park where the stands and booths thinned until the street was bordered by open field. Then the street merely stopped, and ahead of him was the wood. He went on across the short stretch of high grass and into the wood, his anger with Artie rising steadily until he wondered why he had even made friends with him. He sure didn't have to, he thought. He could have just left it the way it was. The way it was?

Johnny had not always been popular. He was a slightly better than average student. He worked only hard enough to maintain his position. He'd always had friends . . . no, acquaintances really, but he had felt merely part of the crowd. Then he made the basketball team in his sophomore year and found the emphasis on teamwork, which was to him a new way of life. A way of life based on cooperation without intimacy. It was intimacy which Johnny Taylor had been made to feel incapable of and which he was afraid to seek among his peers.

The beginning of his junior year Johnny had just come out of the wooden and glass doors of the boys' entrance to the high-school building. He turned up the collar of his heavy knee-length coat against the slowly falling snow. He was still on the top of the steps when he saw them standing beneath the unsheltering, leafless arms of the big oak tree on the corner. There were three members of the basketball team and Artie Schlier. They stood in a small circle, jacketed, muffllered and gloved against the cold, huddling and stamping lightly for warmth. When Johnny reached them, one of the boys was saying, "Aw, c'mon, Artie. Gimme a butt."

"No. Why the hell should I?" Artie said, exhaling a mixture of cigarette smoke and vaporized breath.

"Boy! Are you a kook!" one of the others said.

"Go to hell," Artie replied.

"Get this creep, Johnny," the first boy said. "He's got a pack of butts in his pockets and he won't even give us one."

Johnny looked at the boy, then at Artie for a long moment, and said, "Why the hell should he? Don't you guys ever buy your own butts?"

There was a brief, stunned silence during which the whispering descent of the snow could be clearly heard.

"Aw, the hell with him," the first boy said. "I was going to get some on the way home anyway. C'mon. You coming, Johnny?"

"No. I . . . I gotta wait for somebody," Johnny said.

"So long, Kraut," the boy said to Artie.

"See you later, Johnny," the others said as they started across the street.

"Yeah, see you," Johnny answered.

When they had gone Johnny and Artie stood for a moment in awkward silence.

"You want a butt?" Artie asked, reaching into his pocket.

"No, I got some here," Johnny answered withdrawing his own cigarettes.

After another moment, Artie said, "Boy! Them guys are bums!"

"Aw, they're all right," Johnny said.

"Maybe you think so," Artie replied.

"You just don't know 'em."

"They don't know me, either," Artie said quickly.

"They won't either if you won't even give 'em a cigarette."

"That's okay by me. Who needs 'em?"

"You don't, huh?"

"No."

"Okay."

"Which way you walking?" Artie asked. "You going home?"

"Yeah, I was," Johnny answered, "but I have to go downtown some time. Might as well go now if you're going that way."

"Yeah, I'm going home."

"Okay, I'll walk you."

By the time they parted at the corner of Second Avenue and Main Street, they had arranged at Johnny's suggestion to meet that evening and go to the movies. They did not go to Fordyce's where the "crowd" would be after the movie, for although Artie suggested it, Johnny declined. They simply went for a walk and talked with a lessening awkwardness. Artie came to the Taylors' house the next evening, where he and Johnny did their homework in algebra. The weather had become intensely cold, and on the following night Johnny and Artie went coasting on the steep hill of Eighth Avenue, which the police had roped off from traffic for the sledders' safety. The snow was packed hard and the runners of the sleds soon wore fine twin trails on its surface, which glistened in the faintest light. The darkness and the heavy clothing made it hard to distinguish one sledder from another, and keeping mostly to themselves, Johnny and Artie found it unnecessary to speak to any of the others. On the next night, which was Friday, the program at the Bijou Theatre had changed for the weekend, and they went there again. After the movie Artie again suggested that they go to Fordyce's, and this time Johnny said, "Yeah. All right, let's go."

The "crowd" was indeed there, as they were in full force nearly every Friday night, sitting and standing at the soda fountain, leaning against the candy display cases, sitting sometimes eight strong in booths designed for four. Everyone, including a few people whom Artie did not even know, spoke to Johnny, and one or two added an unenthusiastic greeting to Artie. They stood at the end of the counter and ordered Coca-Cola. From time to time Johnny went over to a booth or to someone farther along the counter in answer to a friendly summons, but each time he came back to stand silently with Artie. Once a boy from the junior class stopped to talk to Johnny. He did not in any way recognize Artie. It was as if he did not know that they were together.

They left after a short time, and outside, as they walked on the soot-stained snow, Artie said, "You like all them, don't you?"

"Sure," Johnny answered, "they're all right."

"They're all dumb bastards," Artie said.

"That's a stupid thing to say. Some of them are dumb, and some of them are bastards, but they aren't all dumb bastards."

"They're a bunch of phonies," Artie said.

"Look, just because they don't like you, it doesn't—"

"What do you mean they don't like me? Any of 'em say so?"

"No, nobody said so," Johnny said with a slight air of irritation, "but I didn't notice them falling all over you."

"Who wants 'em to?" Artie said.

"All right, so you don't want 'em to. That doesn't mean they're dumb bastards or phonies."

"Just because they're your friends doesn't mean I have to like 'em, either."

"I didn't ask you to."

"All right."

"But I'm not asking them to like you, either," Johnny said, looking straight ahead.

"I didn't ask you to," Artie answered.

"All right. Then that's the way it is."

They saw each other almost every day then. Occasionally Johnny went to a party or a dance or some other social gathering to which Artie was not invited. He did not discuss these with Artie, and he did not suggest to any of his hosts that Artie be included in these activities. A few times they doubled-dated, but Artie had difficulty getting a date and even more difficulty in going through the amenities which made dating pleasant. By a tacit mutual agreement they soon abandoned double-dating.

Johnny recognized that his popularity suffered somewhat from his association with Artie. He accepted the fact on the same level of unconsciousness on which he had decided to befriend him, and on that level, too, he had predicted the measurable waning of his popularity. The prediction had been so accurate that he was filled with a discomforting sense of having played it safe.

Johnny found Artie difficult for only a short time, for Artie's gratitude was immediate, though his ability and willingness to express it were somewhat slower in manifesting themselves. Once these preliminary obstacles were overcome, however, Artie turned all of his frustrated desire for friendship toward Johnny, and the resulting loyalty and affection were so strong as to draw Johnny into an intimacy which he had never known before—and which Artie truly believed to be Johnny's gift rather than his own creation.

Neither of the participants in this friendship really understood either his own or the other's contribution. Yet it continued and its purpose was served in spite of their mutual ignorance of that purpose.

At that moment Mary was packing those items of the picnicking equipment which she knew would not be used again that day, and saying to John with rather too much apprehension, "I wonder where Johnny can be?"

"Oh, now, Mary, he's just off somewhere over in the amusement area. He'll be back."

"Hey, John," Fred Collins called from a short distance. "I've still got half a thermos case full of beer bottles over. Let's get working on it."

"Aw, come on, Fred," John said approaching the thermos and looking into it. "We've got half the afternoon left. I could drink that much myself in that time."

"Here," Fred Collins said, deftly lifting a cap off one of the bottles with a small opener, "we'll make it a contest."

John laughed and lifted the open bottle high in the air.

"John, how you doing?" a voice said from behind him.

John turned to find Christopher Henry smiling at him. "Why, Chris, where you been keeping yourself? Haven't seen you for I don't know how long. Come on, have a beer."

"I've had plenty thanks. Hi, Fred."

"Hello, Chris," Fred Collins said.

"Like to talk to you, John," Chris Henry said in his slow, easy drawl.

"Well, sure, but have a beer."

"No, I mean . . . it's kind of private."

John's face darkened as he stood looking over the neck of his beer bottle at Chris. "What do you mean, private?"

Chris Henry looked quickly at Fred Collins and said to John, "Now, I can't admit I want a used car right in front of everybody, can I?"

"Oh," John said, not brightening very much. "All right, if you'll have a beer, I'll talk to you about a car."

"Best offer I've had in my life," Chris said.

Fred opened a bottle of beer and handed it to Chris, and John and he eased away from the tables.

"Is this purchase really so personal, Chris?" John asked, smiling again.

"It's kinda personal . . . and kinda delicate, John."

John stopped then, but they were far enough away that they could talk in private. "What is this, Chris?"

"John, you've got to realize that this has nothing to do with you and me." Even in emotion Chris Henry spoke slowly, lazily.

"No?"

"Not a thing," Chris Henry said, and John stared at him. "I'm president of the school board. Job I never much wanted, but I've been doing it so long I feel I just can't stop." Chris Henry waited for an amiable smile which did not come. "It's not always pleasant, John. I've got something unpleasant to tell you right now." Still John did not speak or move. "John . . . school's scheduled to start on Wednesday—that's just two days away. Look, John, the board met Friday night and they're all agreed."

"They?" John asked.

"All right, we. We just don't think it's in Johnny's best interest for you to send him back to school till after the trial."

John was silent for a long moment, then he said, "Whose idea was this?"

"John, don't try to make a personal issue outa this. It doesn't make a particle of difference whose idea it was."

"Then just explain to me how it's in Johnny's best interest to lose over a month of school."

"Maybe we can arrange to have one of the teachers give him some tutoring in the evenings. We could—"

"That's not an explanation," John said sharply.

"There's no need to be nasty about this."

"Just tell me why it'd be good for Johnny."

Chris looked at him almost coldly. The look changed to a near smile, and he said, "John, you know how kids are. Who knows what kind of things they might say to him? I'm sorry to say, most folks aren't taking this thing too well, and the kids might've heard things from their parents that—"

"I don't expect people to take it very well. I just expect them to wait till the trial's over till they form an opinion. And that includes the Board of Education."

"Folks have a right to their opinions, John."

"Not if they're going to persecute my son with them, they haven't."

"Persecute your . . . oh, now, John. I said it was in the boy's best interest that—"

"Yeah, I heard you say that. But I haven't heard you explain it to my satisfaction."

"John, it may not be your satisfaction we're after," Chris Henry said extremely politely, as if he were merely conveying the information.

"All right, Chris, I'll tell you frankly: I don't agree with you about this and I don't approve of it."

"And I'll tell you frankly: in the long run it doesn't make much difference whether you approve of it or not."

John stared hard into his eyes for a moment. "I thought you were asking me not to send my boy back to school."

" 'Course I am. I've known you a long time, John. 'Course I'd ask you first as a matter of courtesy."

"First," John said, nodding slightly as he remembered the nature of the man he was talking to. "What's second?"

"Let's not even have to talk about that," Chris Henry said mildly.

"We don't have to talk about it if I do what I'm told, is that it?"

"More or less," Chris said and there was nothing mild about it.

"Johnny's going to be tried in a court of law. He's accused, all right, but the accused are innocent until proved guilty, and until he's proved guilty he's going to take advantage of every right this town has to offer him, and that includes going to school. As far as I'm concerned that's the end of it." John turned and started back toward the tables.

"John," Chris Henry said rather quietly, and John stopped, knowing well that if Chris Henry had a hand in this, that was surely not the end of it. He turned back to Chris. "Those boys can't go to school."

"I want you to know that I'd bust you right in the mouth if I didn't know it'd mean more trouble for me than I'm already in."

"That's right, John, you don't want any more trouble. Keep the boy out of school."

"Go to hell."

"You keep him home, John, nice and quiet and nobody'll even notice. You give us any trouble, you'll have a big fat goddamned public legal battle on your hands. 'Boys' Own Neighbors Don't Want 'Em with Their Children' the papers'll say. Think that kinda thing'll do you any good in court?"

"I may sock you anyway."

" 'Father of Accused Rapist Socks Head of School Board.' No you won't, John. You'll just keep your boy out of school."

"I don't know what I'm going to do about this, you son of a bitch. I don't even know what I *can* do about it," John said in quiet rage. "But Wednesday morning when those school doors open, Johnny's going to go through them like every other kid in town."

"You're wrong, John. Think it over, and you'll see that."

"I'll think it over, all right. Just remember, Chris, I won't be thinking it over alone." He turned then and hurried back to the table. "Is Johnny back . . .?" He saw Johnny sitting at the end of the table. "Help your mother get these things in the car, Johnny. And go over there and get your sister. We're going home."

"John," Mary began, innocent in her surprise, "we're supposed to have supper in the restaurant over by the pavil—"

"Mary . . . we're going home."

At the first signs of their departure the attention of most of the picnickers became riveted on them. In a matter of minutes, Jim Beyers was at the table.

"John, what's wrong? What are you doing?" Jim said, almost whispering.

"We're going home!" John said angrily.

"What's happened?" Jim asked.

John stopped his furious activity then, and said, "Chris Henry and the school board are going to try to keep Johnny from going back to school."

Mary stiffened and closed her eyes, but she made no sound.

"Holy Christ!" Jim said, quietly angry at Chris Henry and the school board and this new crisis and everything connected with the case. "John, you're making it worse by leaving like this."

"I can't help it, Jim!" John said loudly. Lowering his voice he said, "If I stay here I'll . . . I just can't help it. I've got to get out of here. It's too late anyway. Look."

Jim looked over his shoulder and saw that there was barely a movement in the entire grove. Even as far away the Schliers' table, people were staring.

"I guess you're right," Jim said. "I'll follow—without the family—as quick as I can. We've got to get in touch with Stephen."

"That's what I was thinking."

"All right. As long as you've started, you'd better get out of here as fast as possible. I'll be along."

The car was already loaded and Mary and Johnny and Lois were waiting in it. John took one last look around the table to be sure they had taken everything. Then quite inadvertently he looked up across the grove. They were facing him as the congregation of an alfresco hymnsing might face their minister. There was no movement. He could hear the carnival noises in the distance, the buzzing of insects, the crying of a baby and the breeze stirring the leaves overhead. Out of his anger he might have said something to them at that moment, but at the next moment he was frightened, terribly frightened. He turned, joined his family in the car and drove away from the picnic.

In his anger and his fear John drove home rather too fast. There was not a word spoken during the drive. Mary and Johnny and Lois felt both curiosity and anxiety to varying degrees, but they waited for the rare anger of the head of their house to abate. Still silent, they got out of the car and began unloading the picnic equipment. There was a strange sadness about the still half-filled thermos, the hastily and untidily packed baskets, the folding chairs which had not quite got unfolded in the cool, peaceful, oncoming twilight.

When everything had been cleaned and put away ("A place for everything, and everything in its place," Mary always said), John asked the others to come into the living room and sit down. "I told you the other day that we were going to discuss things from now on. Well, I don't guess there's much to say about this particular subject, but I'm going to tell you what's happened anyway." John paused for a moment and looked out the living-room window. Turning back to them, he said, "The school board doesn't want Johnny to go back to school until after the trial. They have no right to keep you from going back," he said, feeling the necessity of addressing Johnny now, "but they're sure going to try even if . . . if it means going to court over it. Well, I'm just as determined to see you go back with the other kids on Wednesday. And, by God, I'm going to see to it!"

"Dad, maybe it'd be better if I didn't go back," Johnny said.

"What?" John said strongly.

"Well, if they don't want me to go . . ."

"You have every right to go. You understand that don't you?"

"Yes," Johnny said quietly.

"I hope you're not afraid of facing the other kids."

"I was willing to until this happened."

"Now you have an excuse not to, is that it?" Johnny did not answer. "Look, Johnny, there are a lot of good reasons for you going back." Johnny looked at his father questioningly. "The first one is it's your right to go. The second one is that we can't let people like Chr—well, people walk all over us. You mustn't ever do that, not when they're taking away your rights. And another thing—and it's important—it'll be better for you . . . in October if you've been back in school. I mean, it'll be better than if you don't go back voluntarily or if we let them keep you out."

"You mean keep up a front, Dad?" Johnny asked with just the faintest tinge of sarcasm.

"It's a lot deeper than that," John said sternly. "What are you going to do, run away from people for the rest of your life? You've got to hold your head up, Johnny, in this town and everywhere else."

"That's what Mr. Simpson said," Johnny told him.

"Well, Mr. Simpson was right. You've got to go back to—"

"John, I . . . I don't like saying this in front of the children, but it seems to be your way of doing things lately. So I'll just say it. It might be too late otherwise. It might be . . . awful for Johnny at school."

"Yes, it just might be," John said neither with nor without sympathy. "Johnny's going to have to take his chances. I'm not giving you a choice, Johnny. I'm going to do everything I can to get you back there, and if I succeed, you're just going to have to go."

"I . . . I guess I'd go anyway, if I could."

John looked at his son softly and tried to select the proper phrase of the many that were running through his head. *That's the spirit, Johnny!* or *That's the way to talk!* or simply, *Fine, Johnny!* It did not please him that he found them all embarrassing. He said nothing. And in the silence the telephone rang. "I'll get it," John said.

He crossed the room and picked up the telephone. "Hello."

"It is Mr. Taylor?" Otto Schlier's voice said.

"Yes. Mr. Schlier?"

"It is. I am still at the picnic. I thought, in this case, better it is that I spend the money to telephone," he said, not wanting John Taylor to think him extravagant. "Mr. Beyers has told me of the school board."

"Oh. It's a damned bad thing to have happen, but don't worry about it, Mr. Schlier. Mr. Beyers and I will see to it that the boys get back to school."

"Yes. Mrs. Beyers has told me of that, too. I think better we should let the school board have their way. I do not—"

"What?" John said. "You'd agree to keep the boys out of school?"

"*Ja.* Yes," he corrected. "This is a bad thing they have done. . . ."

"Yes, and they may have to pay for it, but not by staying out of school."

As the conversation went on, the doorbell rang and Mary let Jim Beyers into the house.

"Artie I would like to keep home," Otto Schlier was saying.

"Schlier?" Jim asked John quietly. John nodded. "Tell him Hertzog will talk to him tomorrow. Ask him not to do or say anything about this."

"Mr. Schlier, I can't agree with you about this. I think it's best for everybody if the boys go back. But Mr. Hertzog will explain all that to you tomorrow. He can do it better than I can. Will you wait till then? I mean, will you just not do anything about it till then? Till tomorrow?"

"If you wish me to I will. It is terrible, terrible."

"I know, Mr. Schlier. And thank you for cooperating. Goodbye."

"Poor old Schlier," Jim said. "I think he's taking this harder than . . ." He stopped abruptly, looking at Johnny and Lois. "Oh, I'm sorry."

"It's all right, Jim. We were just talking about the whole damned thing. Why try to keep it from them?"

"Well, time is certainly of the essence. We only have one day to straighten this whole thing out. I'll call Stephen right now."

Jim put through the call and was told by Stephen's answering service that he was at his club. Jim called the number and got the reception desk of the club. The desk clerk said, "Mr. Hertzog? I believe he's on the tennis courts. If he's not I'll have him paged. It may take a little time."

It was nearly five minutes before he heard Stephen's voice. "Stephen, sorry to break in on your holiday, but I'm afraid it's important. The head of the local Board of Education just announced to John that they're going to try to keep Johnny Taylor and Artie Schlier out of school, when it opens on Wednesday."

"Christ!" was all Stephen said for a moment. "Don't they know they can't do it?"

"I know they haven't a legal leg to stand on, but Chris Henry—he's head of the board—he's head of Jeffers Oil and Chemical Corporation here, he has connections in every part of this town. With the right pressure in the right place, he might be able to pull it off."

"Connections, has he?" Stephen said quite calmly. "Connections in your illustrious borough and he thinks he can keep a boy out of a school that is ultimately under the jurisdiction of the State. Why, the pompous bastard! I'll come up there and show him some connections that'll put his ass right out of office overnight. If I can't just talk him out of it, that is."

"You don't know Christopher Henry," Jim said.

"And you don't know Stephen Hertzog. We can't let this thing get into litigation, Jim. I don't want to get an injunction."

"I know."

"Arrange for me to see him tomorrow."

"Okay."

"Call me first thing, and I'll try to arrange my day around it."

"I'll call you as soon as I can get in touch with Chris."

"All right. Talk to you then. Goodbye."

Mary and Lois were in the kitchen starting supper preparations when Jim finished. Only John and Johnny and he remained in the living room. Jim turned to John and said, "Well, if we had his confidence, we'd all go back to the picnic."

"What'd he say?" John asked anxiously.

"Well, in addition to saying that he could get Chris Henry kicked off the school board—that ought to give you some satisfaction—he said he'd come up here tomorrow and . . . well, take care of it."

"Take care of it?" John said.

"John, the problem is this: the Board of Education doesn't really have a case. But with Chris Henry's connections he might be able to stir up quite a fuss. There would also be a public controversy—in the press, I mean. Between those who think the other children shouldn't be . . ." Jim stopped.

John looked over at Johnny. He turned back to Jim and said, "It's all right Jim. Go on."

"Well, those who think the other children shouldn't be subjected to the influence of . . . of anyone accused of this particular crime. Of course, that's pre-judgment and is against the whole basic principle of the legal system. That won't make any difference to those who feel that way. Then there'll be others who'll feel that the boys are being persecuted. I should think they'd be in the majority, particularly out of town where they are not directly involved in sending their children to this school and the decision would be a less sensitive one. We'd win that battle too, over-all, but the less public opinion that's stirred up, the better. Stephen's idea is to settle the whole thing with Chris Henry tomorrow and avoid both extremes. From the way he talked, I'd say he must have ways of doing it, but I assure you I don't know what they are."

"I guess we'll just have to wait and see," John said.

"Will you stay and have supper with us, Jim?" Mary asked, coming in from the kitchen.

"Thanks, Mary, but I've got to go back and pick up Kay and the kids." He got up then and started for the door. "There's no point in worrying too much about this, John—and Johnny. I guess Stephen can handle it."

"I hope so," John said.

As Jim started his car, he admitted to himself that he was less confident than he pretended to be with John Taylor. There was really no way of knowing, but he had known Chris Henry for a long time, and he knew that there was no underhanded trick that wouldn't occur to him or that he would not subsequently execute. And he had the advantage of knowing his way around town far better than Stephen. Even if Stephen did have influence in higher places, would such higher-ups be willing to involve themselves in a potentially explosive situation just to oppose a relative nobody like Chris Henry?

When he got back to the picnic grounds he found his family completely packed and ready to go. "Where in the world have you been?" Kay said angrily as he approached them.

"I'm sorry to have been so long. It was business," he explained as he picked up a picnic basket to take to the car.

"Well, it was damned inconsiderate of you to leave me sitting here. You know very well we have people coming back to the house for dinner. How could you just run off like that?"

"Kay, I told you I was going," he said.

"You didn't tell me where, although it was perfectly obvious unfortunately not only to me, and you didn't tell me how long—"

"What is that supposed to mean?" Jim asked.

"I know you don't like me to meddle in your affairs. . . ."

"My *business* affairs," Jim corrected.

"That's why I haven't said anything before this. But if you're going to make such a public display of your misplaced sympathies, I feel it gives me the right to express my opinion. You certainly don't think I approve of your . . . alliance with the Taylors in this awful mess, do you?"

"I hadn't really considered it, but considering it, I would expect you to, yes." They had reached the car, then, and David and Seth immediately got into the back seat. "Kay," Jim said quietly before they had got into the car, "I really don't think you ought to express such opinions in front of the kids."

"Jim, I don't need or want your approval for everything I do," she answered and got into the car, slamming the door.

"What was all the fuss about, Dad?" David asked as Jim drove down the main road toward the gate of the park.

"What fuss is that, David?" Jim asked.

"This afternoon . . . at the picnic. You know, the Taylors."

"It's something that I'd prefer you didn't concern yourself about, David," Jim told him.

"Everybody else seemed pretty concerned."

Jim shot a quick glance over his shoulder at the boy. "David, I'm perfectly willing to talk to you about what has happened to the Taylors in a general way, although I'd rather you didn't discuss it with anyone else. But you mustn't ask me to discuss it specifically. What you asked me was a specific question, and since I'm involved as an attorney, it would unethical for me to answer. Do you understand that?"

"Sure," David said, as if the explanation had been entirely unnecessary.

"Incidentally, you know Johnny Taylor, don't you? I mean, he's in your class at school?"

"I see him around."

"What do you think of him?"

"Johnny Taylor," Kay said icily, "is a subject that *I* won't have discussed with the children. It's disgusting."

"Kay, the boy is innocent until—"

"Jim, would you mind driving faster? I told you we have people coming in."

"There's a speed limit on this road," Jim told her.

"Oh, damn the speed limit!" she said. "Why do you have to be such a puritan about everything?"

"Obeying a law designed for the safety of everyone on the road is hardly being a puritan."

"You know what I mean," she said irritably.

"No, I don't know what you mean, and I won't have the boys thinking that disobedience of the law is a simple matter of choice or expediency."

"Then I fail to see how you can hold Johnny Taylor up to them as an example," she said smugly.

"Hold him up as . . . ? Kay, you know perfectly well that I wasn't doing that. I merely—"

"Are you inferring that you know he's guilty?" she asked.

Jim was quiet for a moment, staring straight ahead at the road. "I know that you are guilty of the worst kind of distortion of the truth. I'm sorry to have to say that in front of you, David and Seth, but you must understand that I'm not merely 'sticking up' for Johnny Taylor because I'm involved in his case. The laws say that he's innocent until the State proves him guilty. And nobody . . . *nobody* has the right to judge him. That concerns you directly, David. You've got to decide how you'll behave toward him, and your decision must be based on the assumption of his innocence. You'll be coming into contact with him at school, and you—"

"Maybe," David said, smiling slyly.

"Oh," Jim said. "You didn't have to ask me what the 'fuss' was about."

"It sort of got around after you left, Dad," David said.

Jim looked at David in the rear-view mirror until David slid out of his area of vision. "And I suppose you took an active part in its 'getting around'?"

"People kept coming over to us," Seth said. "They think we know all kinds of things because you're their lawyer."

"How well I know," Jim said. "That's the whole point, Seth. It's because of your connection with me that—"

"Jim, would you *please* hurry," Kay said.

"Damn it, Kay, Mae's prepared this whole dinner party. You have absolutely nothing to do but bathe and dress before people arrive. Will you stop trying to hurry me?"

None of them spoke for a long time, and as the silence steeped, Jim became more and more aware that it was a divided silence. He felt himself an island of muteness against the continental mass of the other three speechless humans in the automobile. He found it necessary to control the impulse to drive faster in spite of his discussion with Kay of the speed limit, and he wondered as he eased the pressure of his foot on the accelerator why he felt this compulsion to hurry. Then he slowed the car so markedly that he could hear Kay's irritated sigh, for he had realized that he was anxious to escape this proximity with his family, and he was frightened by the realization.

He thought of John Taylor suddenly and of what must have been his helpless astonishment on learning of Johnny's crime. How detached from, how ignorant of his son John Taylor must have felt at that moment. And how alone. No more alone than he, Jim, felt at this moment. He felt for a blinding instant that he would not have been surprised to hear David blurt out a confession of a more shocking crime than Johnny Taylor's, for he was certain now that he knew even less of David than John knew of Johnny.

No, he did not know this boy, and he knew Kay less. But they knew each other, he was sure, in a forceful, unassailable exclusion of him that was amoebically enveloping Seth. He did not know what to do about it. He was driving very fast again, admitting, accepting the escape from them and wondering in his now frantic silence how far away that escape might eventually take him.

They got out of the car at their house, and Kay rushed upstairs to get ready for the dinner party. David and Seth departed to the family room with nearly as much dispatch, and Jim found himself standing alone in the living room. After a moment he followed the boys into the downstairs room.

Neither boy spoke to him when he came into the room. David was in his prone reading position with a copy of *Sports Illustrated* and Seth as usual was at the phonograph. Jim went to the bar to make himself a drink.

"Anybody want a Coke?" he asked.

"Yeah, I'll have one," David said, and added directly into his father's staring eyes. "Thanks."

"Me too, please," Seth said.

Jim fixed his own drink and the two Cokes and said, "Come and get 'em."

Seth went to the bar and David called to him, "Bring mine, too, huh, Seth?"

"Yeah, sure, Laziest-Man-In-Town," Seth said. "We have to have an early dinner," he told his father. "I don't like to eat early. Besides, then I have to eat with just *him*. He's boring."

"That's no way to talk about your brother," Jim said.

"Oh, it makes no nevermind to me," David said, putting down his magazine. "I like to eat early, anyway. It makes the evening longer. I'm supposed to make myself scarce because of the party."

"What . . . what *do* you think of Johnny Taylor, David?" Jim asked him.

"Mother doesn't want us to talk about it," he said.

"I asked you a question, David. Kindly answer it."

"Okay," he said in a tone which conveyed, *It's your funeral.* "I don't really know him very well. I see him around . . . at school, at parties sometimes. I don't bother with him much."

"Any particular reason?"

"No, but under the circumstances, I should think you'd be glad to hear it."

"I'd like a little less flippancy from you, young man," Jim said. "I'd say you must have some reason."

"Well, for one thing, he hangs around with that creep, Artie Schlier."

"What's wrong with Artie Schlier?"

"He's a creep."

"Come on, David," Jim said irritably. "I'm asking you to talk to me like an intelligent human being, which you are. Don't talk like a moron. What's wrong with Artie Schlier?"

"*He* talks like a moron," David said, and added quickly, "He's stupid, he's standoffish, he's second-rate, he's lower class, his father barely speaks English. . . ."

"What has that to do with it?"

"Come on, Dad, there are social levels, castes in this town just like there are everywhere else."

"And Artie Schlier is beneath your social level?"

"Yes, he is. Look, Dad, if a guy's lower class and he does things to be—well, like everybody else, that's different. If he gets decent marks or plays football or tries to make friends, that's one thing. But if he comes from a lower-class family and just doesn't do anything about it . . . well, tough."

"David, it's *people* who count—what they are, not their social level that counts."

"I haven't noticed you inviting Mr. Schlier to dinner."

"Otto Schlier and I have nothing in common. If we had, I wouldn't let his 'social level' prevent my inviting him."

"That's what I'm saying, Dad," David said. "If Artie Schlier did things like everybody else, fine."

"It's not quite the same thing," Jim said. "What you want is for Artie Schlier—and apparently everybody else—to conform to your standards. And even then, I suspect unless his 'social level' suited you, he wouldn't have much of a chance."

"Johnny Taylor gets invited around, and his social level isn't so hot," David said quite without meaning to.

"His what?" John said leaning forward over the bar, staring at his son in genuine surprise. "Listen, you little snob, every member of the Taylor family is just as good as every member of this family. Don't ever let me hear you say such a thing again!"

"Dad, I didn't say they weren't as good as we are, I just mean they're different in a way. You and Mother talk better than Mr. and Mrs. Taylor. You've been to college, and Mr. Taylor hasn't. You're a lawyer and Mr. Taylor is a merchant. . . ."

"David, if you were merely pointing out differences in our backgrounds I'd agree. People tend to band together in groups according to their common interests, and education, religion, income—all those things heighten that tendency. But that's not what you're talking about. You think you're better than other people because of those differences in background and, boy, you couldn't be more mistaken. And it's an attitude we're going to have to do something about changing." David did not answer, and Jim heard his own emptiness in the silence. "I'd still like to know why you dislike Johnny Taylor."

"I didn't say I disliked him, Dad."

"Well, do you?"

"No," David said, screwing up his face in an attitude of indifference. "If I see him in Fordyce's we say hello. I meet him at a dance, I say, 'How are you?' and maybe I dance with his date. I guess I just don't have much in common with him, either. Besides, he's not exactly a sparkling character."

"And you are, I suppose?"

"More'n him," David said, confidently.

Jim looked at him and shook his head. "David, I want to ask you a question that I'd like you not to tell anyone I asked. I expect you to respect my confidence. Were you surprised by all this business about Johnny?"

"Well, sure. Weren't you?"

"Our surprise is likely to be on different levels. Of course, a thing like this is always surprising, shocking, in fact. Just an accusation of such a thing involving people you know is shocking."

"And this is more than an accusation."

"I wasn't kidding about what I said in the car, David."

"But everybody in town knows they did it, Dad," David said, frowning.

"They are innocent until proved guilty."

"Sure, legally," David said.

"Legally as opposed to what?" Jim snapped.

"What do you mean?"

"Legally as opposed to what, morally, actually?"

"I don't know about morally," David said, "but they did it, actually."

"What do you mean, you don't know about morally? Do you approve of what they're accused of doing?"

"That's their business, I guess," David replied easily.

"It's your business to make a decision that applies to yourself and to the community in general," Jim told him sternly.

"I guess you don't know much about Ida Praul," David said, picking up the *Sports Illustrated*.

Jim stared at this tall, slender boy with blond hair of the exact shade of his mother's, stared in wonder at his subtle rudeness and his patronizing attitude.

"David, put down that magazine." David stared at his father in mock amazement. "One doesn't simply start reading in the middle of a conversation."

"I was reading when you came in," David said, with the maddening logic of adolescence.

"And you stopped reading when I came in," Jim said, "and started talking." David closed the magazine and threw it on the table next to his chair. Then he folded his hands and stared into his father's eyes. Jim debated for a moment the wisdom of making an issue of this brazenness, but decided not to interrupt the pursuit of the other issue. He went on: "I find it shocking, David, that you have no opinion as to the morality of this thing."

"Well," David replied, "it's like I said: you don't know much about Ida Praul."

"What has Ida Praul got to do with it?" Jim said, demandingly.

"A lot, I think."

"Just because you think that Ida Praul—"

"Dad," David said, grimacing. "Seth's here."

"I wasn't about to say anything that Seth can't hear," Jim answered angrily. "Were you?"

"All right. I won't."

"I should think you wouldn't under any circumstances," Jim told him. "David, I guess I haven't had a talk with you for too long a time. I wasn't aware that you'd abandoned even a pretense at respect for me."

"Dad," David said, unfolding his hands, "I didn't do anything disrespectful."

"Your attitude is disrespectful," Jim said firmly.

"I didn't mean it to be," David answered, a bit sullenly.

"All right," his father said. "The point is that Ida Praul's reputation, which by the way has little basis in fact, has nothing to do with what I'm asking you. You don't seem to think there's anything very wrong with . . . with what allegedly was done." He was conscious of avoiding the word. Perhaps, he told himself, it was, after all, because Seth was here.

"Of course I think it's wrong," David told him.

"Well, why didn't you say so when I asked you before?"

"Because . . ."

"Why?"

"You don't want me to talk about Ida Praul."

"All right, if you must, talk about her."

"I don't think there's anything so wrong in what happened as long it happened with a girl like Ida Praul."

"What do you mean, 'a girl like Ida Praul'?" Jim barked.

"She's a tramp."

"That does not justify this alleged rape!"

"Wow!" Seth cried. "Just like a courtroom."

"Seth," Jim said, "if you want to stay in the room, either contribute something constructive or sit quietly."

"Okay," Seth said.

"Am I to judge from your attitude," Jim continued, "that if it were with a girl you think is a tramp, you would be sufficiently free of moral compunction to be involved in such a situation yourself?"

"With a dog like Ida Praul?" David asked, flippantly.

"The physical appeal of the girl is *really* beside the point," Jim said in exasperation. "Answer my question."

"Dad, if you want to know if I would commit rape, the answer is no."

"I'm asking you if you approve of rape under what you seem to be outlining as the right circumstances."

"No, I don't. It's against the law. How could I approve of it?"

"Now we're back to the legal aspect. I mean morally."

"No, I don't approve of it morally."

"You know," Jim said, "I'm not at all sure I believe you."

"Dad!" David said, laughing slightly and rather inscrutably.

"He's a regular sex maniac, Dad," Seth said.

"Seth!" Jim said in extreme annoyance.

"All I meant, Dad, was that if I know Ida Praul, she was probably asking for it," David said.

"And all I meant," Jim said, "was that that doesn't give a man license to commit such a horrible crime."

"Then I guess we agree."

"I hope so, David," Jim said. "Incidentally, *do* you know Ida Praul?"

"Even less than I know Johnny Taylor," David said, smiling. "I just see her around. And she sure has a rep!"

"Even I know about her, Dad," Seth agreed.

Jim looked at them both thoughtfully; then he said, "All right. I'll see you later."

Jim went upstairs, then, knowing that he had not not reached his son, but had engaged in a contest with him—and lost. He found Kay seated at her vanity table, putting on makeup.

As he unbuttoned his sport shirt, he said, "Are you aware that our elder son has turned into a rude little snob?"

"David?" Kay said, turning slightly toward him. "Other parents tell me he has better manners than any child they know."

"Probably has," Jim said, "when he's out to make a social impression. He doesn't seem interested in impressing his father."

"I'm sure you're exaggerating, Jim," she said, turning back to her mirror. "Besides, a little snobbishness is a healthy sign."

"Sign of what?"

"Of a normal ego, I'd say."

"The only thing wrong with David's ego is that it's swollen," Jim said, dropping his shirt on a chair. "Who's coming to this dinner, anyway?"

"Oh, the usual crowd," Kay answered as she delicately featherstroked her light eyebrows with a pencil.

Jim turned to her suddenly and said, "Something just occurred to me. Mary Taylor invited me to stay for supper while I was there. Didn't you invite the Taylors?"

"No. Should I have? We don't always, you know."

"When we're having the usual crowd, we do. Why didn't you invite them tonight?"

She turned to him with lipstick on only one lip, and said, "Jim, don't be an idiot. You know perfectly well why I didn't invite them."

"So will they."

"I suppose so," she said.

"It's not hard to see where David learned his rudeness."

"Jim, would you want them here making everybody uncomfortable with everybody avoiding the subject and—"

"I suppose you intend to make it the main topic of conversation."

"You know it'll come up."

"And I'll put it down."

"Suit yourself—if you want to be a bore." She turned around again, pressed her lips together, then put a Kleenex between them and pressed again.

"You don't give a damn about how the Taylors will feel about not being asked, do you?"

She turned to him again, quickly now, and the Kleenex still hung ridiculously from her mouth. She pulled it away hastily and said, "I haven't particularly wanted the Taylors in this house for years. I know that you and John are close, so I've put up with Mary. But I certainly don't consider her a pal of mine."

"Not of the right social level?" Jim asked, mockingly.

"Don't be an ass!"

"But that's it, isn't it?"

"Yes! It's part of it. She's a frigid old prude who—"

"Frigid?" he said, leaning toward her. "*You* are calling someone else *frigid?*"

"We . . . won't . . . go . . . into . . . that," Kay said and turned away again. "Mary Taylor is a mousey little housewife. You know they can afford a servant—at least a cleaning woman. Do you know what Mary Taylor said to me when the subject came up? She said—"

"When you brought the subject up," Jim said.

"She said, 'I've always felt it's my job to get the men off to their work and give them a spotless house to come home to. And the extra money we save can always go toward the children's education.' Now, I ask you!"

"Maybe they need the money to educate the children."

"You know that isn't true, James Beyers."

"All right, so she wants to do her own housework. Who the hell cares?"

"As long as the men have a 'spotless house to come home to' who the hell cares who makes it spotless?"

"All right. I agree with you, but you've got to allow other people the privilege of their own attitudes."

"She can have her attitudes. I just wish she'd have them in someplace other than my house."

"You're impossible, Kay. You're an impossible snob. I guess David gets all his 'qualities' from you—and not by inheritance."

Kay had no particular answer to this, so she merely turned and cast her husband what she considered an inscrutable glance and turned back to her mirror.

"Who *is* coming to this formal dinner of yours?" Jim asked, taking his robe from the closet.

"It's our dinner and it's casual. Oh, the Allens and the Harkins and . . . oh, there's another thing. It's just a very good thing I didn't invite the Taylors. How would you like to sit through an evening with the Henrys and the Taylors in the house on this particular evening?"

Jim stopped with the robe in one hand as if it were still hanging from a hook. "Chris Henry is coming here tonight?"

"Well, of course, he is."

"Don't you realize that it's my job to try to stop this vicious plan of his—which you obviously know all about. How long have you known about it, Kay?"

"I choose to ignore that question. Jim, what you have to do at the office is one thing. What you do in your home is quite another."

"I happen to think Chris Henry is a son of a bitch for starting this thing. I don't particularly want him in my house."

"Well, it's too late now. They're coming."

"Maybe I should have accepted the Taylors' invitation."

"Oh, Jim, stop it!"

"I'm serious. I'm not sure I want to be at this dinner party."

"If you'd feel more comfortable about it, darling, don't come."

Jim stared at her back for a moment. She tried not to look at his reflection in the mirror. "You mean that, don't you, Kay?"

"I'm just trying to make you happy."

"My presence or absence in this house doesn't mean any more than that—to you or to the children."

"Oh, Jim, don't be silly."

"Stop that goddamned powdering and look at me, Kay!"

She whirled around and there was an incongruous expression on her face, which with its unbrushed powder made her look like a badly made-up mime.

"You have everything you want, haven't you, Kay?" he said. "Your own loyal friends to come to dinner, your bridge club, your telephone to chatter on, complete control of the children, a damned attractive income, a husband to front for you . . . just about everything. And you don't pay a thing for them."

"Don't I?" she said, throwing her head back slightly so that she left a faint trail of powder in the air.

"No, you don't. But don't count on the permanence of that arrangement."

"Are you threatening me?"

"Yes, I think I am."

"With what?" she said with an effort at defiance.

"I'm not sure," he said quietly.

"If you're thinking of taking a mistress, Jim, don't. I wouldn't take it well."

"How typical of you," he said and stood shaking his head and looking at her in a way that made her feel something like shame. She turned away from the look. She heard the bathroom door close, and she knew that he was gone. She smiled into the mirror at what she considered to be the lack of drama in Jim's exit. But the smile faded quickly and left her with a new uneasiness.

XX.

The following morning Jim Beyers got to his office early. He reached Stephen by telephone at nine-fifteen and told him that Chris Henry would see him any time after ten o'clock. Stephen said he would meet Jim at Jim's office in time to see Chris Henry at eleven. Then Jim phoned Chris Henry to set up the definite appointment and called John Taylor to reassure him.

Jim did not tell Stephen exactly how the appointment had been arranged, only because he felt—and he was quite right—that it would not interest Stephen. Chris and Dora Henry had been the first to arrive at the Beyers' dinner party the night before, and Jim had taken Chris directly to the bar in the downstairs room. He had fixed him a drink and said, "Chris, I want you to see Johnny Taylor's attorney tomorrow."

"Now, what good's that going to do, Jim?" Chris Henry had said. "All it's—"

"I want you to see him."

"It's only going to be a big legal hassle that those boys would be better off without."

"I just want you to tell me you'll see him, tell me what time and stay off the subject for the rest of the evening," Jim had said.

"It's a subject people want to talk about, Jim."

"Well, they're not going to talk about it in my house. Now, will you see him or not?"

"If John Taylor's going to be so pigheaded about it, I guess I'm going to have see him sooner or later. Might as well be tomorrow," he said in his casual manner.

"What time?"

"Got only one definite appointment tomorrow morning. Nine-fifteen. Shouldn't take long. Let's say any time after ten."

"I'll tell him."

"You sound pretty hot about this, Jim. Just doing a job or what?"

Jim had stared at Chris Henry over his half-raised drink and said, "I have no compunction about telling you I think you're a son of a bitch for starting this thing—or if somebody else started it so is he and you're a son of a bitch for going along with it."

"Pretty strong language, Jim," Chris Henry said calmly.

"It's a pretty vicious plan."

"Better be careful, Jim, about calling names. I didn't start it, and you don't want to just go calling 'son of a bitch' out in the air when you don't know who you're calling it to."

"Who did start it?"

"Now, Jim, you know I'm not going to tell you that."

"I think I'd rather you'd didn't. Let's not say any more about it."

And Chris Henry had smiled, enigmatically, Jim thought, and Jim did not like that smile.

Stephen arrived at exactly ten-forty-five and together they drove down Main Street, across the railroad tracks and pulled up outside the Jeffers Oil and Chemical Corporation. They went up in the elevator to Chris Henry's office, where his secretary let them in immediately.

"Chris Henry," Jim said, "Stephen Hertzog."

The two men shook hands without speaking and Chris pointed to the two large leather armchairs before his desk. They sat down.

"I understand, Mr. Henry," Stephen began, "that the local school board plans to make an effort to prevent John Taylor, Jr., and Artie Schlier from returning to the *public* high school when it opens tomorrow."

"You understand right, Mr. Hertzog," Christopher Henry said, leaning back in his swivel chair and making a steeple of his hands, fingertips together.

"Why?" Stephen asked.

"Bad influence on the other children," Chris Henry said blandly.

"I'm sure the Board of Education has competent legal counsel. You must know that you haven't a leg to stand on."

"The board's intent is to keep those two boys from going back to school till after they're tried. If they get off, we can assume they're innocent. Fine. Let 'em come back to school. If they're found guilty, we were right in the first place and they don't come back to school at all. There is, to say the least, Mr. Hertzog, some doubt as to if they're innocent, and as long as the doubt exists I don't . . . that is, the board don't want 'em thrown together with other children till after the trial. As I say, that's our intent, and legs to stand on or no legs to stand on, we can accomplish that."

Stephen Hertzog smiled at Christopher Henry in a way that made him uneasy. "I appreciate your bluntness, Mr. Henry. And I'm going to return the favor. I assume you are going to use your illegal influence on the judiciary to keep me from getting an injunction. An influence I do not doubt you wield. Without similarly powerful interference in opposition, you could then delay further legal procedure until after the trial, when the issue would be decided, as you pointed out, by the guilt or innocence of my clients. If you persist in this plan, I guarantee you that I will retaliate in two major areas. First, I will use my own influence, which, if you will check through your own channels, you will find begins in the governor's mansion, to bring this 'affair'—I hesitate to call it a case—to immediate litigation, during which I shall not only get the boys back into school within two weeks by having this mess thrown out of court, but will expose your illegal influence, and the exposé will include you and every person in the chain of that influence. I needn't explain the obvious consequences of such an exposé either in terms of your position on the Board of Education or in terms of your position as general manager of the local Division of Jeffers Oil and Chemical Corporation. Your twenty-two thousand five hundred dollars a year, your five hundred shares of Jeffers stock as well as your stock option would surely be jeopardized in spite of your thirty-three years with Jeffers and your admirable rise from the cooper shop to this office. The world is truly small, Mr. Henry. I had a rather hurried breakfast this morning with H. Sandford Jeffers—who, I believe, is president and chairman of the board of Jeffers O. and C. and from whom I did *not* get the elements of your brief dossier—whose teen-age son and some cronies became involved some time ago in the theft of an automobile. It was not a difficult case, so I don't deserve much credit for having won the boys an acquittal. At breakfast Mr. Jeffers told me what a dim view he takes of abuse of personal liberty. But regardless of Mr. Jeffers' opinions, if you choose to disregard them, I shouldn't think such an exposé would earn you any particular popularity with those other "influential" people in Audubon County who will be exposed. Second, I will have a reporter from every major newspaper in every major city in this end of the state standing outside that school at nine o'clock tomorrow morning, when, I assure you, Johnny Taylor and Artie Schlier will make an attempt to enter it.

"Here is a list," Stephen went on, handing Christopher Henry a sheet of paper, "of those cities and those newspapers with the names of their managing editors and the telephone numbers at which they may be reached. They have been alerted to the situation down here and are awaiting the result of this meeting. To ascertain that fact, you have only to telephone them. The prevailing attitude among them, Mr. Henry, is that a fundamental democratic process is being abused by the Board of Education and that two young high-school students are being deprived of their basic rights. This kind of persecution is not of interest merely to the people in a town of twelve thousand. There is no limit to the potential interest in this issue, and you can trust that I will see to it that that potential is exploited to the fullest. If you think I'm trying to buffalo you, Mr. Henry, make the telephone calls I suggested. Check my connections in the state capitol.

"You won't want to make a decision in this matter without legal counsel, I know. I should imagine Mr. Beyers and I will lunch now somewhere nearby and be back in his office shortly before one o'clock. I'll be leaving town at one o'clock sharp. I expect to have heard from you by then. That's all I have to say to you, Mr. Henry, and I can't think of anything you might have to say at the moment that would be of any interest to me. One o'clock. Goodbye."

Stephen rose and left the office and Jim Beyers, as if he were somehow attached to Stephen by a string, rose and followed him.

"I'll be damned!" Jim said when they had reached the car.

"How about that lunch?" Stephen said.

"I'm buying," Jim answered and they drove to the Manufacturers' Club on Main Street. They got a table immediately and ordered dry Manhattans. "May I ask you a question that I hope won't annoy you?"

"Sure," Stephen said.

"You . . . *weren't* trying to buffalo Chris Henry, were you?"

Stephen laughed robustly and said, before the laughter had quite subsided, "No." More laughter. "No, I wasn't."

"Well, in any case, that was a pretty dramatic performance."

"That's exactly what it was, my boy," Stephen said. "Drama. We had to scurry pretty frantically to get that information on Henry this morning—and last night, I might add. But the presentation wasn't decided upon until after that first little speech of his. He's *not* very difficult to size up. The drawl, the absence of subjects to go with his verbs, the portly serenity. This is a man who usually creates one of two reactions: futile anger or docility. And the way to handle either is with that comfortable superiority of his. The one thing to which Mr. Henry is not accustomed is drama. I went into that office planning to give him the old one-two. You know, the 'All right, Buster. Now I'm going to let you have it. Get on that phone and get your attorney down here.' That kind of treatment. It wouldn't have worked. This will."

"Are you really that sure?" Jim asked.

Stephen thought for a moment. "Yes. Your Mr. Henry has some rather shady political friends, but they're people who'd be aware of my political connections, which are just as good as I said they were. I can do all of the things I told Henry I could, and he can find out very quickly that I can. And I did defend Sandy Jeffers' son, did have breakfast with him, and although he isn't about to can Henry because he's a legal obstacle in a case of mine, he'd be very likely to can him if he got involved in a brouhaha that turned out the way this one probably would. Yes, I think we've licked Mr. Henry."

"But how in the hell did you find out all of those things in so little time?" Jim asked, his tone a mixture of amazement and admiration.

"Jim," Stephen said, drawing out the one syllable to imply that Jim ought to know, "I'm a criminal lawyer. It's not as if *you* had started out to dig up that stuff. I have a beautifully efficient organization all set up for no other purpose. I have only to push a button at any time of night or day to start it working. One phone call yesterday before I went back to the tennis court and we were hot on Henry's trail."

"I've never seen Chris Henry licked before," Jim said. "I must say, I enjoyed it. It was worth the trouble just to see the expression on his face."

"The enjoyment goes out of it after a while," Stephen said. "Nice club for a town this size," he added, looking about the mahogany-paneled room.

"How about another drink? After all, it's a kind of premature victory celebration."

"Okay, but I hope after my little paean of praise to Stephen Hertzog it doesn't turn out to be too premature." When Jim had ordered two more drinks, Stephen said, "Jim, what ever made you settle in a town like this?"

"It's my home. I've lived here all my life."

"I know that, but what made you *stay* here?"

"Just that it's my home, I guess."

"It's none of my business, and I don't usually give a damn enough to pry, but when we were at school you were as close a friend as I've ever had. What . . . what happened to that brilliant career everybody predicted for you?"

"I guess they were wrong."

"No, that's the point. They weren't wrong. You could have had it. There must be a reason why you didn't."

"Stephen, I didn't know you cared!"

"As I told you, I don't as a rule, and one more crack like that and you can stick your wasted career."

Jim looked at him quite seriously. "That's just what it was, I guess. Wasted."

"What happened?"

Again Jim was silent for a moment. "You've never been married, have you?"

"No. Is that what happened, your marriage?"

"Partly. There's no simple answer to a question like this. It's all the unpredictable, uncontrollable, interrelated things that happen to a man. But Kay was certainly a big part of it. We were married right after I finished school, you know. We'd had two summers together when we were in love, and that can be misleading. Especially when the girl—and her mother—have had you picked out for years. Stephen, you don't have to listen to this, you know. I—"

"Have you observed my asking questions to which I don't want the answers?"

"All right. If there was such a thing as a good family in town mine was it. The depression had hit us pretty hard financially, but we still had the name and some money. It's hard to believe, but it has to be true. All the things that Kay and I had in common during those summers, she pretended. I'm not the misunderstood husband talking out of vengeance. No, she understood me too well. After we were married all those things just disappeared. Gone. I've often wondered why, if she could pretend them so well, she couldn't really have them. But . . . well, I didn't even notice for a while they were gone. That was one of my mistakes. I had everything I wanted: an education, a wife, a home and ahead of me the eagerly awaited brilliant career. I threw myself into it with such abandon that I guess I neglected Kay. At least, one of the few things we agree on is that I neglected her. But I was busy. Kindly do not laugh at my naïveté."

"Just go on. I won't laugh."

"Well, I was going to reform this festering little town of ours. You wouldn't believe there could be so much graft, so much dishonesty, so much corruption in a town of twelve thousand people. This poor, rotten little town has been run by the same political machine for nearly sixty years, and there isn't one bar that isn't open after hours; there isn't one appointee in the borough who wasn't appointed out of patronage, political or otherwise; there is always a minimum of six establishments running illegal wire services, crap tables, card games; there is one flourishing brothel; and the burgess is never available to hear such complaints because he's always either in one of the card games or at the brothel. Well, I was going to clean it up. I was going to become a member of the town council on a reform ticket and shine the town up like a nice red apple. The next stop for me was to be the office of the district attorney of Audubon County, and from there it was the state legislature. There was even a time, and I've never said this aloud before, when I saw myself in the governor's mansion. That was another mistake: I should have told Kay about that. Being the governor's wife would have appealed to her, though she hasn't the imagination to conceive of it herself. But I never told her about any of it. She never seemed very interested."

"You might well have made it, you know."

"Maybe. But I'll never forget Burgess Moriarity's face when I told him what I was going to do. He looked up at me with that round, red, fat, Irish face and said, 'Now, is that what you're goin' to do, Jimmy me boy?' Then he smiled that irresistible smile, and said, 'Well, would you have a mind to be coverin' five hundred dollars at about three to one that says you won't be succeedin'?' I must have looked duly shocked, because that was the only time in his life I'd ever seen him become serious. He said, 'Jimmy, take some advice from an old man who knows. When a municipal government is as corrupt as this one is, it's because it's the way the people want it. Sure an' they're all reformers at heart. The card players want the bars closed on time, and the tipplers want the horse rooms shut, and the fornicators don't approve of the drinkin' an' gamblin', an' you give your brother a job in the Borough Hall an' he wants you to fire your cousin, and the Baptists want you to stop the Sunday movies, but the Catholics won't support 'em because Mass is only in the mornin'. Half the town council is in favor of buildin' a housin' development out along the pike for the Negroes because they own the land out there; the other half is havin' none of it, because they own the Lincoln Street slum where the Negroes live now. And they're all good Christian people, Jimmy me boy. They're all willin' to live side by side with their neighbors' vices rather than interrupt their own. I won't be makin' a move to stop you, Jimmy; I won't have to. They don't want your reforms.' And, of course, he was right."

"How long was it before you found that out?" Stephen asked.

"It was quite a while, and I had made an absolute ass of myself before I did. I campaigned as if I were after the Presidency. I was asked to speak everywhere: the churches and the Rotary and the Kiwanis and the American Legion. Everyone was for me and my reform movement. It became the respectable thing to do. That is, it was respectable to *appear* to be for me. The returns were embarrassing. I avoided people for some time after that."

"And that stopped you, huh?"

"It wouldn't have stopped you, would it?"

"I don't know. If you want to reform a city of two hundred thousand people, I'm your man. But a little burg like this where everybody knows what's going on and just doesn't care . . . seems to me they deserve it."

"You wouldn't have tried here, would you? You'd have got out."

"Right."

"Well, I suppose I should have. But I was defeated, Stephen, politically and emotionally. I might have gone somewhere else then, if it hadn't been . . . well, I turned to Kay then, and she just wasn't there. Maybe if I'd included her from the beginning, I wouldn't have had to turn to her. She might have been there with me. When I tried to talk to her about it, she said, 'You didn't really expect to be elected, did you?' It seemed to me my world had collapsed."

"It had."

"Yes. I had no marriage, no career, no home. I didn't think I could fight the battle for a career against the dead weight of an unsuccessful marriage—it was pretty unsuccessful in other areas by then—nor did I think I could make the marriage work in the face of a shattered career. So I didn't do either. I'm very much ashamed now that I just let it ride, both of them, all these years. But David—my oldest son—had arrived by then, and we wanted more children. Kay had her friends and family here. So did I. I knew I could make a comfortable living in town and . . . it just sort of fizzled out. Just like that."

"You're right," Stephen said, " a waste is exactly what it was."

"Yes. I don't know how much better I could have done, but I could have done better."

"May I tell you what I think was your biggest mistake?"

"Please do."

"When the political thing fell through, you should have pulled up stakes and got out. This was your home—and your family, your girl were here. All right, you came back and it didn't work from a career point of view. That was the time to take your wife—if she'd go, and leave her if she wouldn't—and go on to bigger and better things. If you had started a career then, you'd be at the peak of it now, or very nearly. But you're young enough to start again under the right circumstances."

"Kay wouldn't have gone then. You certainly don't think she'd go now. I'm not even sure I'd want her to."

"Maybe that's not part of the right circumstances. How do you feel about starting again?"

"I . . . I haven't thought about it for so long, I don't know how I feel."

"I wish you did."

"Why?"

"The idea must either basically appeal to you or repulse you. Which?"

"It'd be crazy . . . but I might just have a hell of a good time."

"Got any money?"

"Enough."

"Enough to cut your income in half for a couple . . . three years?"

"Probably. Yes."

"For the last couple of years I've had a number of people—people of the H. Sandford Jeffers caliber—urge me to go into corporate law. I have no intention of abandoning my present practice, but I'm going to expand the activities of my office to include corporate business. I know a dozen guys, Jim, with so much experience that they're better qualified than you, but I don't know anybody I think would eventually become as good as you might. I'm not talking about a partnership—a junior partnership at best. Maybe not even that for a while. But there's no limit to where you could go if you have the ambition and the brains to make up for the time you've lost. It's a risk. I'm willing to take it if you are. Think it over."

"It . . . it's something of a surprise."

"To me too. Such an offer hadn't occurred to me until a very short time ago—like half an hour. For better or worse, I make decisions fast. There's no hurry. I'm not even going to start things moving for another month. I *would* like to know if you're interested at all."

"Yes," Jim said firmly. "Yes, I'm interested as hell."

"Good. We'd better have some lunch and get back to your office. Wouldn't want to miss Mr. Christopher Henry's call—not for anything in the world."

XXI.

CHRISTOPHER HENRY'S ONE-SENTENCE CAPITULATION ("I GUESS you've got what you wanted, Hertzog, but I don't think your methods are a hell of a lot better than mine"), delivered at precisely 12:55 P.M., cleared the way for Johnny's return to school. John's announcement of the news just before supper on Tuesday night was met with unenthusiastic approval by Johnny, for now that the moment was nearly at hand he was uncertain and apprehensive. He stayed at home that night and watched television as did the rest of the family. They spoke little and retired early.

As Johnny rose from the breakfast table the next morning, ready to start for school, his mother said, "Johnny, aren't you going to wait for Lois?"

"Wait for Lois?" he said. "I never did before." It was true: Lois went to school with her friends and Johnny with his.

"Don't you think it might be a good idea this morning?" Mary asked.

"No, Mother," Johnny said. To his mother's unyielding expression he said, "Everything's got to be just like always, Mother."

Reluctantly Mary said, "All right. I'll see you at lunch time."

"Okay. So long. So long, Lo."

Johnny waited on the corner for Jimmy Morrison to come out of his house across the street. He had not waited more than two minutes when Jimmy appeared and waved a greeting from the front steps as he descended them.

"Well, here we go again," Jimmy Morrison said as he approached Johnny.

"Yeah, I can hardly wait," Johnny answered.

"This must have been the shortest summer on record," Jimmy said, starting up the hill toward Main Street. "Where'd it all go to?"

"Seems like we just got out of school last week, doesn't it?"

"It sure does. Hey! There's old Vince Gottlieb, waiting as usual," Jimmy said, seeing another of their morning group waiting at Elm Street.

"All ready for the torture?" Vince Gottlieb said as they neared him.

"Not ready, but present," Johnny said.

"How ya doing, Johnny?" Vince said.

"Okay, Vince."

"I thought they wouldn't let you out of junior year," Jimmy said to Vince.

"None of the teachers could stand me again, so they just sent me on," he said.

"Hey, wait up!" a voice came from behind them.

"Late again," Vince Gottlieb said when he turned around. Then he called to Barney Santantonio, who was running toward them, "You think we're going to start out all over again waiting for you every morning, you're nuts."

"Hey, Barney!" Jimmy Morrison called to him. "Come on, boy! Get the lead out!"

So it was and so it would be: at almost every corner someone joined them until they were twelve strong and the twelve soon blended into the streams of boys and girls who filled the streets that converged on the high school. The conversation of any group of boys could nearly have been interchanged with that of any other group of similar age. The girls were no more exclusive. The one notable exception to this observation occurred as Johnny's group came in sight of the high-school building. And the exception was a silence rather than a statement.

"Well, there she is," Barney Santantonio said.

"Yeah," Vince Gottlieb agreed, "it's back to prison."

It was then that the silence occurred. It was Johnny who broke it. He said, "Yeah, isn't it."

And a curious thing happened: the others began to laugh, and Johnny laughed with them. They laughed almost all of the rest of the way to school.

In the classroom, not only Johnny, but many of his fellow-students as well, sensed an embarrassment on the part of certain teachers. Some of these teachers were men, some women, but always when it was there, the students knew it. Yet it did not make the students uneasy, for without realizing it they had in some mysterious way joined forces in a quiet rebellion against the parental and scholastic authority which had tried to chastise one of their own kind. Whether rightly or wrongly they did not always agree, but they were all but unanimous in their resentment against the penal spirit which had attempted the chastisement. Those who had been forbidden to speak to Johnny and Artie spoke to them. The graciousness of their fellow-students raised them almost to the verge of celebrity, and those who would have had it otherwise did not say so.

"How . . . was it?" Mary asked casually when Johnny and Lois were seated for lunch, and she was at the stove with her back toward them.

"How was what, Mother?" Lois said, buttering a piece of bread.

"School?" Johnny asked. "Same as always. What's for lunch?"

Mary could not know that for this precious time they had both truly forgotten.

"Nothing . . . nothing happened?" she asked.

"Janet Diesenderfer fell down the stairs," Lois said, "but she wasn't hurt. Of course, she has all that beef for protection."

Mary suspected for a moment that they were deliberately keeping it from her. Then she began to wonder if it could be true. "No one said any—?"

"Oh . . . that," Johnny said glumly.

"Oh," Lois said.

"No, Mother. Nobody said anything to me. You, Lo?"

"No. Nothing," Lois answered and took a bite of her bread.

"Well," Mary said, which always for her changed the subject. "We have creamed dried beef on toast and lettuce and tomatoes and some nice strawbery Jello for dessert." She looked at them wonderingly for a moment, then turned away and began serving lunch.

The other two school days of that week were much the same as the first. On the third day there were two casual references to Johnny's predicament. ("I hope you'll be around for the basketball team, Johnny. The team'd sure miss you." And, "Hey, Johnny, you got a date for the Tri-Hi-Y dance on October twenty—oh. Sorry, Johnny.") Such references were inevitable, Johnny understood, and he took them in his stride. The effect of school on Johnny Taylor was, if anything, therapeutic. This seemed to be true of Lois, too, but it soon became apparent that the therapy was effective only during school hours.

When she was not in school, Lois was at home. At such times she was not at Girl Scout meetings, in which she seemed to have lost interest, she was not doing homework at a friend's house, she was not at the movies: she was at home, and as near to John Taylor as she could manage to be. She hovered about him expectantly almost every minute that he was in the house, and when he wasn't at home and Lois was, she was in her room.

The Saturday after school started was a warm, quiet day from which autumn seemed to have retreated, inviting the return of summer. Lois had breakfast early with her father. Then she went to the store for Mary and, when she returned, went to her room.

At precisely twelve-fifteen she came downstairs and said to her mother, "May I make myself a sandwich for lunch now? I'd like to go out for a walk."

This was the first time since Johnny's arrest that Lois had asked just to go out, and Mary was concerned.

"Lois . . ."

"Yes?"

"You . . . you haven't seen Beatrice Crowley for ages. Why don't you call her and see if she'd like to come to lunch? This is the last weekend they have their bungalow—"

"They've gone to the lake," Lois said. "Besides, I'd rather go for a walk. May I?"

"Why . . . of course you may."

Lois made her sandwich and ate it in no apparent hurry. When she had finished, Mary said, "I'll do those dishes when I do my own, Lois. Don't you bother with them."

"Oh, thank you, Mother," Lois said. "I'm going now. Goodbye."

"Where are you going, Lois?" Mary asked with as little concern as she could manage.

"For a walk," Lois answered, turning back to her mother.

"Yes, I know, but I meant . . . well, where? In case I should . . . want you for anything. You know."

"I don't know exactly, Mother," Lois said. "Just for a walk. I won't be too long. Goodbye."

"Goodbye," Mary called as Lois stepped into the sunporch. She heard the front door close, and she turned to see Lois crossing the lawn in a direct diagonal line, with none of the casual uncertainty of the stroller.

Lois went to the corner, turned left and walked to the north edge of town, where the community athletic field and tennis courts were. She pushed open the door that was cut out of the high wooden fence and went inside. There were several welcoming cries of "Hi, Lois," and "Hey, Loey, where you been?" She saw, as she had known she would, Brandon Davis playing on number three court. He was about to serve but, hearing the commotion, turned and called, "Hi'ya, Lo!" She waved to Brandon and went to the bench against the fence, where two of her girl friends eagerly made room for her.

"Where's your racket, Lo?" one of the girls asked.

"I didn't bring it," she answered. "I didn't feel much like playing."

"How have you been, Lo? We've missed you," the other girl told her.

"Oh, I've been fine," Lois said.

A small group of boys and girls of various ages had begun to form in front of Lois, partly because they were truly fond of her and partly, it could not be denied, out of curiosity.

"Hey, Lo, you've been ruining my game, staying away like this," one of the older boys said. "You know you're supposed to play against people who are better than you are, and you're the only person around here who can beat me."

There was silence for a moment. Then a girl of seventeen said, "Why don't you borrow a racket, and you and Jenny and Gladys and I can play a set of doubles on number three when Brandon and Tommy are through?"

"No, thanks. I don't really feel like it," Lois said. "Maybe tomorrow if you're going to be here."

"Sure," the girl said.

The girl on Lois' left suddenly moaned and said, "Oh, the agony of it! How I hate being back in school!"

"Oh, it's not such agony," the girl on the other side said. "Frankly, I was bored with the summer."

"Bored?" her companion screamed. "Bored with swimming and tennis and sleeping late and no homework and . . . oh, you're a kook!"

"We of the intelligentsia enjoy school," the other girl said. "Don't we, Lo?"

"I can take it or leave it," Lois said. "But I guess I'm sort of glad to be back."

The group before them had dispersed now, and Lois had a clear view of the courts. She looked out across the cracked, red-brown clay which held the sun's heat like a kiln and watched Brandon Davis. He was playing fiercely as he always played, and perspiration had soaked his white, short-sleeved shirt and the belt line of his khaki shorts. His skin was sun-darkened to a color very like that of the clay courts, and his normally wavy brown hair was clipped to a length of less than an inch, and, like the hair on his arms and legs, had turned slightly golden from exposure to the sun. He played tennis well and a month before his fifteenth birthday would easily win the Community's Club's Junior Championship. Even in the savageness of his game, his lithe body seemed to move easily, gracefully, with absolutely geometric coordination.

Brandon had drawn sixteen-year-old Tommy Ridley to the net and now lobbed his return over Tommy's head to land six inches inside the base line. Tommy slammed his racket against the net in momentary anger at his loss of this second set six-four, but recovered to smile at Brandon and shake his head in mock disgust. Brandon went around to the far side of the court, and together he and Tommy walked to the corner of the fenced-in rectangular enclosure, where there was a water faucet. They stood on the little slatted platform by the faucet and drank and splashed themselves with the cold water. Then they walked back to the benches and stood near Lois and her friends.

"Nice shot, that last, Bran," Lois said.

"Thanks," Brandon Davis said.

"Pure luck," Tommy said, smiling as he leaned his racket against the fence.

"Where've you been, Lo? We missed you," Brandon said as he stooped and pulled a small carrying case from under the bench.

"Oh, I've been home mostly," Lois said.

Brandon took a package of cigarettes from the case, gave one to Tommy and they lit them. "Want to play a set later, Lo?" he said.

"It's silly for me to play with you, Bran," Lois replied. "I get so tired of six-love, six-love, six-love."

"Aw," Brandon said in mock sympathy, "I'll let you win one set just because you're so beautiful."

"You wouldn't let me win a set if I was Gina Lollobrigida," Lois said, squinting into the sun.

"That's what you think," Brandon said, winking rather coyly.

"Maybe I will be a Gina Lollobrigida someday," Lois said. "Who knows?"

"I think you are one already," Brandon told her. "I think you have hidden charms."

Lois' smile began shyly, but as it broadened, she looked up into his face, and in spite of the sun opened her eyes wide and stared into his. She found his large brown eyes friendly and warm and appealing. The last faint traces of uncertainty left her as Brandon returned her look.

Lois and Brandon sat there talking for a long time. They talked to Tommy Ridley and the two girls and to other friends who came by after Tommy had moved on and the girls had gone to play tennis. But between these arrivals and departures, they talked to each other, sometimes laughing very privately, sometimes murmuring almost secretly. They sat with their bare legs touching, and their conversation was full of awkward, uncertain innuendo. It was mid-afternoon now, and the clay courts radiated their excess heat and refracted light into the quivering beginnings of mirages. Insects hovered by the ear and hummed intimately before zooming on into the hot haze of the day. The hollow plops of batted tennis balls fell suddenly into an even, monotonous rhythm. The flesh, like the texture of the day, was moist and warm and pliant.

"Want to go for a walk, Lo?" Brandon said.

"Yes."

They left the courts and walked north through a thin line of young trees which bordered the old abandoned Catholic cemetery. Holding hands they walked among the tombstones, which tilted crazily with the erosion of the earth, as if disturbed by some raucous debauchery of the dead. Weeds thrust themselves brazenly into the air, and brilliantly orange meadow lilies stared above them.

"Where are we going, Bran?"

"Just for a walk."

They went to the front of the cemetery and out of it through the high iron gate. They crossed the Pike and walked for a short distance along the pavement which lay before a line of large, widely separated houses. They turned and went down across the sloping lawn between two of the houses to a path which led through the waist-high foliage into the wood beyond. Deeper into the woods they went, where the path, at first dappled with shade and sun, became cool and dark. They passed a pond whose utterly still, brown, stagnant water cast a reflection of the overhanging trees which, except for a lessening of intensity, was a nearly perfect image. Just past the pond there was a sudden thickening of the wood.

"Maybe we ought to go back, Bran," Lois said.

Lois did not know quite why she had come here. She did know that from the moment she had seen Brandon Davis on the tennis court she had wanted to be with him. Or, she suddenly thought, watching him turn to face her, had she gone to the tennis courts, knowing he'd be there?

"Do you want to go back, Lo?" he asked, facing her, a golden slash of sunlight across his otherwise shaded face.

"I . . . I don't know," she said. "Do you?"

"Not . . . not for a little while, I guess."

"Okay," she said.

Brandon turned and continued along the path until it turned toward the pond. From there it led to a clearing of trampled brown grass, a bathing spot for local boys, and simply stopped.

"Let's go this way," Brandon said, turning toward the thicker woods where there was no path. When he took her hand to guide her, she felt that he was trembling, and his trembling reassured her.

She followed him without speaking until, behind the branches of several luxuriant saplings, they came upon a tiny, leaf-walled forest room. Brandon stopped and turned around, confronting Lois expectantly. She stood entirely still, feeling a new kind of fear. But it was not fear of Brandon, and since there was nothing else to be afraid of, she decided that it wasn't fear at all. He took a step toward her, and without touching her with any other part of his body, pressed his lips against hers. They stood for a long moment, trembling together now, in a tight-lipped passion. When they stopped kissing, Brandon sat down on the cool, damp earth and looked up at Lois as nearly imploringly as he could. As she looked down at him, she felt that he looked so helpless, shaking very slightly but visibly, his brown eyes damp as the earth, his brown hair darkened in the dark of the forest, that she dropped to the ground beside him.

"You . . . you've kissed boys before," he said as if to relieve himself of guilt.

"Yes," she said. "But it wasn't like this."

"No," he agreed quietly.

"It was just at parties where you did it because you were playing a game or something. And once coming home from the movies . . . Brandon, there's more, isn't there?"

"Sure," he said in an utterly futile attempt to resume his vanished savoir-faire.

"What?" she asked. "What is there?"

"Lois . . ."

"You know, Brandon."

"But I . . . I never did . . . anything."

"Could we . . . kiss again?"

"Yes."

He kissed her, this time placing his hands on her shoulders, and she responded as if in some well-rehearsed pantomime, by placing her hands stiffly on his waist. But soon the stiffness was gone. Soon the academic gesturing gave way to the soft fluidity of genuine desire, and they lay together, forcing the contact of their bodies—lips and arms and legs—wherever the flesh was bare.

"Lo," Brandon whispered.

"What?"

"There's more."

"Yes."

"Do . . . do you want to?"

"Oh, Brandon, I'm afraid!"

"Me too. But I . . . I think I want to."

"Yes. I want to find out. I want to know."

"I . . . we have to get undressed, I think."

"Oh, Bran! What if somebody sees us!"

"I don't think anybody comes in this far—except maybe in summer. Lo, do you want to go?"

"No."

She stood up and in a moment Brandon did too. Their enormous curiosity with each other's bodies slowed their undressing. He saw the untanned areas of Lois' upper body which he had never seen before. And Brandon's bare chest and arms seemed now to Lois barer than they had ever been at the lake. Soon they were completely naked and he moved toward her again. He kissed her and she slid into his arms.

"Oh, Lo, are you sure?" he asked miserably.

"Yes," she said, and his ear felt the shape of the words on her lips.

He kissed her again, and she pressed her mouth against his, opening it instinctively. "Yes," she said again into his open mouth. "Yes."

They melted toward the earth, their lips, their bodies still together, their eyes open wide and staring into each other's. Then Lois' eyes closed slowly and Brandon knew. Her cry rang out into the forest, and frightened birds fluttered from the trees. But she clung to him and thwarted his retreat.

Brandon was almost comically protective toward Lois as he took her home. He helped her through the woods as if she were decrepit, and once on the streets again, he assisted her over every curbstone. She accepted his attentions seriously and gracefully. They did not talk of their experience, but silently shared a new awareness, a new sense of responsibility. At her suggestion, Brandon left her two blocks from her house with a solemn promise that he would call her the next day.

Lois had walked barely a block after leaving Brandon before she was stricken by his absence. The sense of sharing, made so nearly tangible by his presence, faded as she drew away from him. His nearness had created an outlet for the welling emotion she felt, and now without him, she feared she would burst with the need to communicate her discovery. There were moments during the next few hours when she was afraid that the need would overcome the obvious necessity for secrecy, but with noticeable self-control she resumed the routine of her life until it was time to retire.

When Johnny came upstairs to go to bed, she hissed through her partially open bedroom door for his attention.

"What do you want?" he asked from the doorway.

"Shhhh," she hissed again, waving for him to come into the room.

"What's the matter with you?" he asked, closing the door to insure the privacy which Lois' attitude made mandatory.

She was kneeling on the bed, just as she had during her last talk with him, and the similarity made him instantly uncomfortable.

"Can't you tell?" she asked, kneeling upright for his inspection.

"Lo, do you want to tell me something?" he asked. "I'm too old to play games with you."

"Johnny!" she said delightedly.

"Look, if you put me through all this, and it turns out you've dyed your hair or something silly like that I'll—"

"It's nothing silly." Johnny waited. "I know what you did," she said. "But I don't understand . . ."

"You what?"

"I know what you did," she said, pronouncing the words clearly and with great emphasis in her impatience with him.

"You mean Dad told you?" he asked, knowing somehow that that was not what she meant.

"No," she said, again impatiently. "I told you he wouldn't tell me, and he didn't."

"Lois, what are you talking about?"

"I wanted to find out, and now I know," she said brightly as if the simple statement made everything clear.

"Lois . . . Lois, just tell me plain what you're talking about."

Lois sighed irritably and said, "I decided I was only going to wait so long for somebody to tell me, then I was going to do something about it myself. Well, I did this afternoon, with Brandon Davis."

Johnny stared at her for a moment and said, "You . . . you did what?"

"Oh, Johnny, you know what!" she said, almost angry at his lack of joy.

"Holy Christ!" Johnny said quietly. "Lois . . . you didn't let him . . .

go all the way?" Lois stared at him in utter confusion. "Well, did you?" he shouted suddenly.

Lois did not answer, and Johnny turned and started for the door.

"Johnny . . . where are you going?"

"Where do you think I'm going? Downstairs, to tell them!"

"To tell . . . Johnny, no!"

"Lois, don't you realize what you . . . Holy Christ, you don't, do you? You don't have any idea!"

"Johnny, don't tell them!" Lois begged.

"I have to tell them!" he said. "It isn't a game or something. You're only thirteen years old! My God, thirteen years old! Something has to be done!"

"What?" Lois asked, fearfully.

"I . . . I don't know," Johnny said, his confusion almost as great now as hers. "I don't know, but something!"

He looked at her crouched on the bed, pale and delicate.

"Lois," he said, "I've got to tell them." And he left the room.

By the time he reached the living room, his astonishment and confusion had turned to anger—anger with himself, with Brandon Davis, but above all with his father. John was sitting in his easy chair smoking and watching a sportscast on television. He seemed to Johnny monstrously complacent.

"Dad, turn off the television set."

John recognized the urgency in his son's voice and started from his chair, but Mary said, "Johnny! That's no way to talk to your father."

Johnny ignored his mother and in the sudden silence of the television set said, "You didn't talk to Lois."

"You mean . . . about what we discussed?"

"That's what I mean."

"No . . . no, I didn't, but listen here, Johnny, you can't—"

"Well, you don't have to bother now."

"What are you talking about?" John said after a moment.

"Why the hell didn't you talk to her, Dad?" Johnny said, desperately.

"Johnny, tell me what you're talking about."

"She waited for you to tell her . . . then she went out and . . . she and Brandon Davis . . . did it this afternoon!"

"Johnny, what are you saying?" Mary asked in a low, breathy tone, as if he were telling some obvious and horrible lie.

"Johnny . . ." John said, smiling a weak, sick kind of smile. "Johnny . . . your sister's only a child. She's thirteen years old. What kind of foolishness . . ."

"Ask her," Johnny said.

"Ask her?" John said. "Why, I can't . . . can't even suggest such a thing to Lois."

"No?" Johnny said. "You going to pretend it hasn't happened just because you can't bring yourself to talk about it? Dad, that's exactly why it did happen."

"I don't believe it," John said.

"Then call her down here and ask her," Johnny said.

He looked at his son for a moment, then went to the stairs and called, "Lois. Lois, come down here, please."

After a moment Lois came down the stairs silently and without expression.

"Lois," John said, sternly, "did you . . . is it true, what your brother has told us?"

Lois looked squarely at Johnny and said, "No."

"Lois . . ." Johnny began.

"I made it up," she said.

"Lois, tell them the truth!" Johnny said.

"How could you have told such a terrible lie?" Mary said to Lois.

"What made you say such a thing?" John added.

"You believe her, don't you?" Johnny said to his father, incredulously.

"Of course I believe her," John answered. "It's so ridiculous that—"

"Call Brandon Davis and ask him," Johnny said.

"Now, stop it, Johnny," John said harshly. "You can't just call people up and accuse them—"

"I'll call him," Johnny said, starting across the room.

"Johnny, don't!" Lois cried.

"Johnny!" his father shouted.

"You don't want it to be true, so you're not even going to try to find out," Johnny said. "Why would she tell *me* if it wasn't true? You know in your heart it is, but you won't admit it—even to yourself." There was no answer from John, and the room was utterly still. "Lois, if you don't tell them the truth, I swear to God I'm going to call Brandon and tell him you told me about it."

The muscles of Lois' face had become tight and hard in her continued attempt at expressionlessness. She stared at her brother stonily. Johnny went on to the telephone and dialed information, not waiting to look up the number.

"Would you give me the number for Timothy Davis on West Twelfth Avenue? . . . Thank you."

He put his finger on the button of the phone and turned to his sister. "Lois . . ."

When she did not answer, he began to dial the number.

"Johnny, don't!" Lois cried.

With his hand still on the dial, he said, "Tell them."

Lois looked at her father as the tears came into her eyes.

"Lois," John said, "Lois . . . it's true?"

"Yes," she said, almost inaudibly, and the tears streamed down her face.

Johnny put down the receiver and stared at it, unable to look at Lois.

There was no sound at all in the room then, until John said very quietly, "What shall we do?" Then he said again, in exactly the same tone and volume, "What shall we do?" The silence surrounded him again, and after a moment he said dazedly, "I'll . . . I'll have to call the Davises."

"Oh, Daddy, don't!" Lois wailed.

It occurred to John then that he should be cursing Brandon Davis for violating his daughter, but it occurred to him, too, that Brandon Davis could not be more than fourteen years old, and the reality of their sexual act escaped him. Then all reality seemed to depart from him, and he could not feel anger or shame or regret or astonishment, although the words occurred to him. He felt only that somehow, as in the bursting of a bubble or the ending of a dream, what was would no longer be. He looked at Mary, who sat, staring at Lois, with her hand on her mouth; and he knew that she was even further from reality than he.

"Daddy, please, please don't call Brandon," Lois pleaded.

"Don't you know what he's done to you?" John said, and the sound of his own voice brought the truth rushing upon him like a gigantic wave.

"But I wanted him to! I told him to!"

"Oh, my God," Mary said quietly. "What has happened to us?"

"Lois . . . go upstairs and get dressed," John said, not looking at her.

"Daddy . . ."

"Not another word," he said, turning to her. "Go upstairs and get dressed."

Mary got up and took Lois by the hand. At the bottom of the stairs she paused and said as if in a daze, "You'd better call Dr. McKenna." Then she led Lois upstairs.

"Yes. Yes, I'd better do that," John said as if to himself as he stood staring at the telephone. Then he picked it up and dialed the doctor's number. "Dr. McKenna? . . . Can you see Lois right away? . . . I'd rather not tell you on the phone. . . . I'll tell you when we get there. . . . Yes, we'll bring her right over. Thank you."

When John hung up, he found Johnny staring at him. He turned from the stare and went into the kitchen. He drank a glass of water and stood by the sink, waiting until he heard Mary and Lois on the stairs. He went into the living room and straight to the front door.

"We shouldn't be long," he said to Johnny, but Johnny did not answer.

Dr. McKenna's office was at his home. He had left a light burning at the side door, which was the door to his waiting room. He heard the Taylors' car and was standing at the door as they approached. They entered without speaking.

"What's the trouble, John?" the doctor said rather grimly.

John looked at Dr. McKenna, sighed and said, "Lois . . . had sexual intercourse this afternoon, and we'd like you to examine her."

Even the parental, long-suffering Dr. McKenna was not prepared for this. His eyes widened and his chin dropped as he stared at John as if he thought John was raving. John stared back rather challengingly. The doctor's eyes went to Mary as if she might inject a note of sanity into the situation, but she looked away, tight-lipped. The doctor's eyes found Lois, who must surely be mad if her parents were not, staring at her feet.

"You say Lois had . . ." The doctor shook his shoulders as if a chill had come over him, but the movement was intended to help him collect himself. He would not have himself outdone in aplomb by non-professionals. "Yes . . . well," He looked at all three of them again. "Who . . . who was it, John?" he said, leaning forward anxiously.

"It was Lois, Dr. McKenna," John said. "Would you examine her?"

"I mean, who was the man?" the doctor said irritably.

"Would you mind if I didn't tell you that?"

"Mind? Of course I'd mind! Look here, John . . ."

"Dr. McKenna, we don't want this thing to get all over town. . . ."

"What? Are you implying that I'd talk about it? I'm a doctor, John Taylor. I have an oath, and I haven't violated that oath in—"

"All I meant was that the only people who have something to lose by talking about this are Lois, the boy and the four parents. If they're the only people who know, there's no danger of it getting around. Can't we just leave it at that?"

"I have a right to know," Dr. McKenna said. "I'm the exam—"

"Damn it, I'll take her someplace else!" John said, turning toward the door.

"Wait!" the doctor said. John turned back, his hand on the doorknob. "All right. Come on in here, Lois. You'd better come, too, Mary." And the three went into the examining room.

In a shorter time than John expected, Dr. McKenna returned. John stood up as if to receive dire news.

"Lois is perfectly all right. No damage. And you know, of course, that at her age and with only one occurrence, there is practically no chance of pregnancy. So don't worry about that. I've explained that to Mary."

"Thank God!" John said. "Doctor, it's good to have someone we can trust at a time like this."

The three got into the car without speaking. John drove to Rodenbaugh's Pharmacy and stopped the car. "I'm going to call the Davises," he said.

"Oh no, Daddy!"

"Not another word, Lois," John said and got out of the car.

A few minutes later John and Mary and Lois stood on the porch of the Davis home. John rang the bell, and Brandon's mother, Martha Davis, came to the door. Her face was openly troubled.

"I'm John Taylor," John said.

"Yes, I . . . I know. Come in."

Timothy Davis was standing in the large, air-conditioned living room, wearing slacks and an old and comfortable sports jacket. He was a small man with only a fringe of hair at the sides and back of his head. He had large brown eyes, made larger by his strong, rimless glasses.

"Would you mind telling me what this is all about?" he said as they came into the room.

John was annoyed by his tone, and he said flatly, "It seems that your son Brandon and my daughter Lois had sexual intercourse this afternoon."

Mrs. Davis' indicated offer of a chair stopped in midair, and Mr. Davis' eyes grew larger than John would have thought was possible.

"Are you out of your mind?" Timothy Davis said. "Brandon is fourteen years old."

"And Lois is thirteen," John said. "I think we'd better have a talk with him."

"This is Lois?" Mr. Davis said. "You wouldn't tell a lie about a thing like . . . I'm sorry, Mr. Taylor. I didn't mean to . . . to sound accusing . . . but . . ."

"I know just how you feel," John said. "But I do think we'd better talk to Brandon."

"Of course," Mr. Davis said. "Martha, would you get him?"

Mrs. Davis had clearly not recovered from John's initial statement. She looked at her husband blankly for a moment, then with a slight shake of her head, said, "Yes." No one spoke while she was gone or when she returned. They stood waiting in silence for Brandon. If there had been any doubt in any of their minds, Brandon's expression would have dispelled it finally. He did not know when he came into the room that the Taylors were there, and when he saw them, his face displayed a certain guilt that can be registered only by the recently innocent. His gaze came last to Lois, and his look of accusation brought new tears to her eyes.

"Brandon," Mr. Davis said, "do you know why the Taylors are here?"

"I . . . I don't . . ." Brandon looked at Lois miserably, and she began to cry audibly. "Yes," Brandon said weakly.

"Then it's true?" his father asked.

"Yes," Brandon said.

"I . . . I think we'd all better sit down," Mr. Davis said.

With monumental reluctance Lois and Brandon alternately related the details of their afternoon together, and even as these details spun a web of undeniable reality, the tale had for the adults a quality of fantasy. The act seemed beyond the realm of possibility, yet its perpetrators stood before them documenting it with an innocence which only contributed to its incredibility. When there was no more to be said by the children, the Taylors and the Davises sat looking at each other speechlessly, hopelessly.

"I don't see . . . what's to be done," Mr. Davis said.

"No," John said, and feeling that it was inadequate, said again, "No."

"I wish I could . . ."

"There's nothing," John said. "We'll just have to deal with it separately. We'll be going now."

As the Taylors started for the door, Brandon said, "I'm sorry."

John turned and looked at him blankly. Then he turned to the older Davises and said, "Good night." They left and drove home in silence.

They found Johnny sitting at the kitchen table. He had made coffee and sat toying with his empty cup. Mary took Lois upstairs to bed with a nearly acknowledged, belated overprotectiveness. Beyond saying hello, Johnny barely spoke to any of them. John poured a cup of coffee and sat at the table with his son.

"When are you going to tell her?" Johnny asked.

"What?" John snapped, tense now from the strain of the evening.

"When are you going to tell Lois about . . . what I did?"

"This is hardly the time to discuss it," John said wearily.

"According to you, there's never a time."

'What do you want me to do, run upstairs and talk to her right now?"

"If you don't talk to her by tomorrow, I will."

John stared at Johnny, and both fatigue and anger showed in his eyes. "I don't know who you think you're talking to, Johnny," he said. "And I certainly don't know what makes you think that your own behavior gives you the right to start teaching others—particularly your father—how to behave. You've made enough of a mess of things already."

"I hope you're not including Lois in that," Johnny said.

"I don't see why I shouldn't. You certainly don't think this would have happened if it wasn't for you."

"I guess you'll deny that you had every chance to prevent it."

"Just what the hell do you think being a parent is?" John said, pushing his cup away and leaning angrily toward Johnny. "Do you think you can cause or prevent anything your children do? Do you think it's just a matter of feeling responsible every time your kids make a mistake?'

"No, but—"

"You're supposed to have a sense of responsibility, too, you know," John went on. "Everybody's responsible for himself. Even Lois at thirteen is supposed to have a sense of right and wrong—or else she's an imbecile. You can't do anything you damn well please and just point at your father and mother and say, 'They're the ones to blame.' "

"All right!" Johnny shouted. "But you can't point at us, either, and say we're strangers, and you haven't any idea why we do what we do or why we are what we are."

"The more I see of the two of you the more I'm convinced that you *are* strangers."

"If we are, that much is sure your fault. You couldn't even talk to Lois—even when she had the guts to ask you to. In seventeen years you didn't say a word to me about sex, then you just stand me in front of you and tell me to start talking."

"As long as you're in such a talkative mood now, maybe you can tell me how you and your friends could hold a little girl down on the ground and rape her."

Johnny's eyes were filled with tears. He said, "No, I can't tell you that, because I don't know. But I can tell you now how I found out about sex. I was told that a man filled a woman up with pus from his penis, and when she got sore and swollen like a boil, a baby was squeezed out. Oh, I didn't think that for long, but while I did, I used to lay awake thinking of you doing that to Mother. The next thing I was told was a little better than that, and the next thing was a little better, until I was able to piece together what I thought was probably the way it really was. I know you're not responsible for the way I found out. You're only responsible for the fact that you didn't tell me—just like you didn't talk to Lois. And if I go out and rape somebody, that's not your fault, either—but you're not going to have to pay for it—I am." And Johnny left the room and ran upstairs.

When Mary came downstairs, she found John on the open back porch, standing among the buckets and mops and brooms that she kept there. He was leaning on the railing, staring at the sky as if he might be trying to count the stars.

When he heard her behind him, he said, "Mary, I'm afraid I've gone through my life just trying to mind my own business and pretending that whatever anybody else did, he was just as separate and alone as I was. And that's not the way it is. Everything you think or say or do is part of everybody else, everywhere. Have you ever wondered what would have happened if you hadn't done something, or if you'd done it some other way or time? Everything is hopelessly tied up with everything else. Oh, I know you can't control all those things, but it seems to me that it's every man's job to look ahead as far as he can and try to be sure that what he does is going to cause good. And if he can't see ahead, he ought to try to be sure that the things he does are good in themselves. Yeah, that's the way it seems to me now. It's a little late."

"John, you can't punish yourself for—"

"Oh, I'm not punishing myself, Mary. But look at our own lives. Somewhere along the way we lost our love . . . no, we shut it out; we shut it out over trifles. And when we did that, we shut it out from the kids, too. I don't mean affection; we love our kids. But the talk, the being together, the knowing each other, the understanding; we shut them out. And because of it, something happened to Lois and Johnny, and something—maybe the same thing, maybe something different—but *because* of it, something will happen to Lois' children and Johnny's children. Maybe it's a little late, Mary, but it's not too late. We've got to start doing something about it."

"What . . . what can we do?"

"I'm going to learn to talk to them, Mary. Oh, I know I've been trying recently, but never about anything . . . deep. But God knows, the kids tried to talk to me, but I always found some excuse. Just now Johnny tried, and all I could do was accuse him and insult him. Even that was easier for me than talking to him. But I'll learn to talk—to Johnny if there's time, but certainly to Lois." He turned to Mary for the first time since she'd come downstairs. "I may even learn to talk to you again."

Mary was deeply embarrassed, but she was pleased, too, and felt a faint but certain response within herself.

"That would be . . . nice, John," she said. "I think I'll go up now," she said in her own desperate escape.

"All right," he said. "I'm going to stay here for a while. Good night." He stayed outside for a long time. Then he went to bed, more aware of his hope for the future than of his despair of the past.

XXII.

JOHN'S SLEEP WAS SO SOUND AND SO DEEP THAT WHEN HE AWOKE next morning with the thought of Lois in his mind, it seemed for an instant as if he had not been asleep at all. He shaved and dressed quickly and on the way downstairs, tapped lightly but firmly on Lois' door.

"Get out of bed, Lazybones," he said, sticking his head into the room, "and we'll go for a walk."

"For a walk?" Lois said, skeptically, sitting up in bed.

"Yes. Hurry up," John said and closed the door, smiling.

Before John had finished his breakfast, Lois came into the kitchen, dressed and ready for the walk.

"Sit down," John said, "and have something to eat."

"Why don't we go for our walk first?" she answered.

"Okay," John said, gulping his coffee.

"Walk?" Mary said.

"Yes. Lois and I are going for a little walk," John explained.

Mary simply said, "Oh," and turned back to the stove.

Outside John and Lois heard the intimate noises of the day's beginning. For a few moments they walked in silence, listening.

"Lois, do you remember the Sunday a couple of weeks ago when we went for a ride?"

"Yes," Lois answered.

"I tried to have a talk with you that day and I couldn't. It wasn't your fault in any way; it was mine. I'd like to try to tell you why I couldn't talk to you."

John did not speak again immediately, and Lois did not rush him. They simply walked in the morning sunshine, which had not yet become uncomfortably warm.

They were approaching the end of the block when John said, "I think that very often children don't realize what a responsibility it is, raising a family. There's such a lot to be taken care of. There have been times when all kinds of problems seemed to crowd up on me, and certain things just didn't get done, things that should have gotten done. One of the things I let go was being close to you and Johnny, being able to really talk to you. That was very wrong, and I can't tell you how much I regret it."

"You're close to us, Daddy," Lois said.

"Oh, I don't mean that I don't . . . don't love you; I do, just like I know you and Johnny . . . feel the same about me. But we haven't done enough things together, haven't gotten to know each other really well. That's why I couldn't talk to you that time about . . . about what Johnny did."

"I understand, Daddy," Lois told him.

"Do you, Lois?"

"Sure. But I think I've felt it more with Mother than with you."

"Well, that may be. You see, there are other problems, too. Household problems and problems between your mother and me that have kept us both from knowing you better. They're quite complicated problems, Lois. If you just realize that everybody's life is complicated—and your mother and I are no exception—you'll see that problems are bound to come up between us all. But if we all try to understand each other and are honest with each other, we'll always be able to work out the problems."

"Just like democracy, huh?"

"Exactly like democracy. We all have opinions and we all have a vote. We put them all together and decide what's best for all of us, and that's what we do."

"It hasn't been that way up till now, has it?"

"No, it hasn't, Lois, but it's going to be that way from now on."

"What about Mother?"

"What do you mean?"

"Well, do you think she'll go along with this democracy stuff?"

Trying not to smile too fully, John said, "I think so, if you try to remember that it's probably going to be a little harder for her than for the rest of us, and make allowances."

"I guess I can do that—otherwise I can't very well expect any allowances to be made for me sometime when I find something hard to do."

"You understand perfectly," John said. He was quiet again for a moment, then he said, "I guess it's a little late to tell you about what Johnny did, but I'd like to try."

"I'd like to hear, too," Lois said, "and I'll try to understand."

"Lois, what you did yesterday is one of the most important acts of life, so whatever you do, you mustn't take it lightly or think of it as just something that happened. It has two purposes: one is to produce children, and the other is . . . this is very hard to explain, Lois. You . . . you must have felt something toward Brandon . . . before . . ."

"Well, at first I just wanted to find out what Johnny did. I knew Brandon knew and I . . . I guess I went with him, hoping he'd show me. But then all of a sudden I *wanted* to do it . . ."

"That's what I mean, Lois. God put that . . . that desire in us, and satisfying that desire is the other purpose of sex. But it's only really satisfying, it's only really good when it happens with somebody you love. That's why it should be reserved for a husband and wife. They should keep it just for each other. If you let it happen any time you feel like it, it's cheapened, and doesn't mean anything any more."

"Like a birthday," Lois said thoughtfully.

"What?"

"Well, if you had a birthday every week, it wouldn't be nearly so . . . so special as it is when you only have one a year."

"It's very much like that, I guess. It's also the whole secret of life, Lois; that's another reason why it's so important. It makes it possible for mankind to . . . to go on generation after generation so that science can advance and . . . cities can grow. It's the thing that keeps the whole human race from dying out. So you can see how important it is."

"Yes."

"But, Lois, you do understand that it was wrong for you and Brandon to do what you did yesterday? I don't mean there's anything wrong with . . . with sex itself; it was just wrong for you to do it so early in life. Life has a wonderful way of arranging things, Lo. When you're very young, your natural interest is in toys and games and ice cream and very simple, innocent things. When you get a little older and you start going to school, your interests broaden, and you start to meet people and . . . well, somehow your life fills up with school and friends and all the things that it should fill up with. Then when you get to be just about your age, life starts to awaken a knowledge of sex inside you. Both your body and your mind have lots of growing yet to do. And you have your education to finish—college if you want—and there'll be dates and dances and parties and . . . well, there'll be lots of things to fill up this part of your life. And it can be a wonderful part of your life. Don't spoil it, Lo, by trying to crowd sex into it so early. It's too early, and it can throw your whole life out of balance. Do you understand that?"

"Yes, I think so, Daddy. You mean that there's a time for doing that, and it's wrong for me to do it until my time comes."

"That's exactly what I mean. Your time will be when you're in love and married and want to raise a family. I think your mother will be going into all of this with you in more detail—and very soon. There are lots of things you should know that she can tell you better than I can."

"But what about Johnny?" Lois asked, hearing a note of finality in her father's voice.

For a moment the old stigmas sprang into John's mind, but he had gained too much ground now to turn back.

"Well, I told you before that sex can be a beautiful thing when it happens between two people who love each other and desire each other. It's a thing that two people must share. I guess Johnny didn't know that . . . and that's partly my fault. I should have explained things to him . . . just like I'm trying to explain them to you. But I didn't and . . ."

"Tell me," Lois said quietly.

"It's very hard for me, Lois. What your brother did was bad . . . it was a terrible thing, but I don't want you to feel . . . well, there are probably lots of people who would do what Johnny did if the circumstances were the same, but the circumstances never come up for them. They did for Johnny, and he wasn't prepared; he didn't know. I'm not trying to make excuses for him. He shouldn't have done it under any circumstances, but if you try to remember that he truly didn't know how bad it was, you'll be able to understand it better."

"I'll remember."

"Johnny and the boys he was with wanted to do with Ida Praul what you and Brandon did yesterday, but Ida didn't want to. They . . . forced her to do it against her will."

Lois' face became troubled.

"That's not only morally wrong," John went on, "it's against the law. It's a crime, a serious crime, to force anyone into a sexual relationship. You see, it goes back to what I said about . . . about sex being an important act. You can steal money and you can trespass on somebody's property . . . and they're crimes, too. But a crime that involves sex is . . . is special because of the . . . sacred nature of sex. When it comes to sex everybody has a very special privilege, granted by God, and when you violate that privilege, you violate something direct from

God himself. And that's why it's so terrible. It's a crime against society and man and God . . . all at once. But what I want you to understand, Lo, is that Johnny didn't realize all of that. He knew it was wrong, but he didn't really understand the nature of the crime. So you mustn't condemn him."

"I won't condemn him, Daddy," Lois said, "but will they know in the court that he didn't understand?"

"I guess that's what Mr. Hertzog will try to explain to the jury."

"If they knew that, maybe they'd let him go."

"Maybe, Lo, but we mustn't count on it."

They had walked in a circuit of several blocks, and now were approaching the house. The breeze had already begun to fail, and it was warm and humid.

"It was a nice walk, Daddy. Thank you," Lois said as they turned into the front walk.

"Lo . . . I hope you know that any time you want to talk, if you have any problems or questions . . . I'm ready and willing to talk them over with you."

"I'm afraid it'll keep you pretty busy, but you asked for it."

"Indeed I did," John said, smiling. "Indeed I did."

They went into the house then and to the kitchen. Mary was washing dishes at the sink.

"Where's Johnny?" John asked.

"He's upstairs," Mary said. "You two were a long time. How was your walk?"

"Marvelous," Lois said, sitting at the table to await her breakfast.

"Some more coffee, John?" Mary asked.

"Yes, I will have a cup, Mary," John answered, sitting across from Lois.

"Do you know what I think?" John said. "I think it'd be a good idea if we all four got dressed up and went to church this morning."

"To church?" Mary said.

"Yes. Why not?"

"Well . . . all right . . . if you want."

Mary poured the coffee for John and started to cook Lois' breakfast.

"Daddy told me about Johnny," Lois said absently.

"Oh?" Mary said, glancing at John almost suspiciously.

"Yes," she said, lifting the glass of orange juice Mary had put on the table. "I understand the whole thing now."

"Do you?" Mary said, failing completely in her attempt at casualness.

"You know, even after what Brandon and I did, I didn't understand why Johnny was . . . well, in such trouble."

"Lois . . ." Mary began.

"But now that I understand it all, I feel so much better."

Mary put Lois' eggs before her and said, "Lois, eat your breakfast."

"Yes, Mother," she answered. After a moment she added, "Gee, I hope the Davises are as nice to Brandon about this whole thing as you've been to me."

"Lois!" Mary cried, turning to her angrily. "Your father apparently didn't make you understand that you shouldn't be talking about this at all."

"Mary . . ." John said.

"But as long as you are talking about it, I hope you don't think the result of the whole horrible mess is that we're going to be nice about it."

Lois was stunned by Mary's sudden vehemence. "Mother . . . I . . ."

"I don't see how your father could fail to realize that it's heartbreaking for me to have my daughter behave like a . . ."

"Mary, that's enough!" John shouted.

"No, it's not enough," Mary said quickly. "After a thing like this happens you tell me you're going to have a talk with her, and she comes back talking about it as if it was the most natural thing in the world, instead of something unspeakable."

"Daddy . . . I don't understand . . ." Lois said haltingly.

"I thought your father was going to make you understand. Well, I can see he didn't. And it's time somebody did."

"Shut up, Mary!"

"Oh, yes! You tell me to shut up. I'm not supposed to say anything unpleasant. I don't suppose you told her what the immediate aftermath of this thing could be—even at her age. And I don't suppose you told her she'd be marked for life . . ."

"Lois . . . Lois go on upstairs . . . please."

Without speaking, with only a dazed look at her mother, Lois got up from the table and went to her room.

"Mary . . . goddamn it, Mary!" John said in a desperate attempt to control his anger. "Have you completely lost your mind? Talking to Lois like that . . ."

"I'm wondering if *you've* lost your mind. Or are you deliberately trying to turn your daughter into a tramp—just because you don't seem to object to them?"

"Mary, will you just try to be rational about this?" John asked, trying himself to retain some degree of sanity in spite of his rage. "We know Lois isn't pregnant. Dr. McKenna told you that it would be almost impossible, so what point is there in suggesting to her that she might be? And absolutely nobody knows about this. The Davises aren't going to run all over town telling people. Why in the world do you want to tell Lois she'll be marked for life? Mary, you—"

"What's going to keep her from doing it again? Being nice about it and telling her there's nothing wrong with it?"

"I don't want her to go through life thinking there's something wrong with sex."

"No, you don't. I think you'd rather have her be a tramp. Well, I won't stand by and let that happen. If she's frightened of getting pregnant, she won't do it again."

"This is a hell of a time and that's a hell of a way to tell her about pregnancy!"

"Now you're going to tell me I should have talked to her before—just the way you should have talked to Johnny."

"Yes," John said firmly. "We're both very much at fault, but we're not going to do any good by fighting with each other. All I want to do is help Lois—keep something terrible from happening to *her,* too."

"It already has."

"Mary, it certainly isn't the way we would have wanted it, but if we help Lois now, we can keep it from turning into something terrible."

Mary looked straight into John's eyes and said, "No. What has happened has happened, and it's already terrible. And I don't think we could have prevented it by talking to her. There's something unnatural about a thirteen-year-old girl deliberately leading a boy into the woods to have sex with him."

"Mary, don't you understand that when we refused to explain to Lois about Johnny, we practically forced her to find out for herself?"

"No, I will never understand that," Mary said flatly. "She could have asked someone. . . ."

"She did. She asked Brandon Davis."

"Or even if she had gotten physically sick with confusion or . . . or went through half her life ignorant and frightened, I could have understood that. But there must have been something else . . . something in her nature that made her take that way out."

"Mary, you don't know what you're saying. . . ."

"Oh, yes I do, and we've got to make her understand what an awful, awful thing she's done."

"To understand, yes, but not to be frightened and confused. And I've tried to make her understand. You've got to help me, Mary."

"I can't help you to do something I think is so wrong!" She turned away from him and clenched her fists before her. "God in Heaven, how could those children come to such filth?"

"I'm afraid it was through us, Mary," John said quietly. "Because we gave them nothing to keep them from it."

"How can you believe that?"

"I find it easier to believe than that there's anything wrong with Lois' nature," John said quietly. "And there's another thing, Mary. You see, I don't think it is filth. You do. You always have. That's something I'm afraid they did get from us—whether we gave it to them deliberately or not."

"I don't believe that," she said, still turned away from him.

"I was hoping you would, because I'm going to do something about it—with or without you."

She turned and faced him. "It'll have to be without."

"All right, Mary," he said, feeling a great loneliness which he did not show. "But I forbid you to talk to Lois about this—or Johnny either, for that matter. I'll take care of it myself—somehow. But at least give me the benefit of not having you working against me."

"All right," she answered. "But I certainly can't take any responsibility for what happens."

"When have you, Mary?" John asked, and in the silence that followed he left the room and went upstairs. He knocked gently on Lois' door.

"Come in," she said.

John went into the room and said, "Lois, all of this . . . this trouble over Johnny and then over you has been an awful shock to your mother." She was looking at him quite blankly. "Try to understand that she's very upset. I . . . I wouldn't talk to her about it any more for a while."

"Is it true . . . what she said downstairs about being marked for the rest of my life?"

For a moment John weighed the choices: he could discredit Mary or he could explain her remark in a way that would at once—he could only hope—inform Lois and leave intact whatever respect she had for her mother. He saw before him years of trying to instruct Lois in matters of which he now felt less than certain, and simultaneously trying to protect Mary and to keep her influence from reaching Lois. He was not sure that it could be done at all, and he was less sure that he could do it. He felt incredibly tired.

"No, it wasn't true, Lois," he said wearily. "Your mother was wrong. You're no different now than you were two days ago. You know a little more, maybe, and you must be very careful to use the knowledge wisely, because it is only a little bit of knowledge, daughter— a very little bit."

"Are we . . . going to church, Daddy?"

"No . . . I guess we'd better forget about that."

He went into his bedroom and looked out the window. In the face of problems and even of failure he had always managed finally to muster a certain determined resilience, a sense of challenge. But now he felt only a numbing spiritual fatigue and, beneath that, a seeping, black fear for everything he had so recently thought secure: his son's future, his daughter's immediate happiness, and his own marriage.

XXIII.

DURING THE NEXT TWO WEEKS JOHN SUFFERED A GROWING DISAPpointment. He had hoped, as one does at the outset of a project, for immediate action. He had watched closely for an opportunity to instruct, to guide, to be close to his children, but he found none. He saw them briefly at breakfast, briefly at lunch on those days when he lunched at home and again somewhat less briefly at supper and during the evening. And always, unless he deliberately arranged it otherwise, Mary was there, unwittingly threatening, impeding, creating embarrassment, which only John felt, by her very presence.

Lois stayed home less since her experience with Brandon. She resumed her Girl Scout activities, she visited friends to watch television or do homework (sometimes both simultaneously), she went to the movies with friends. Johnny seemed to have little homework, having mastered the technique of fulfilling only the minimum requirements of any assignment and finding time to do it during the school day. He went to Fordyce's nearly every night, where he frequently did no more than sit with his friends until it was time to go home. His situation became less and less a novelty to his peers, and this allowed him, like Lois, to resume the comfortable if boring routine. Also resumed was the pattern of emotional isolation to which all of the Taylors had subscribed for so long that only a conscious effort, which John alone seemed willing to make, or another crisis could break. John made himself supremely available to Johnny and Lois in readiness for such a crisis, but they seemed to have no need of him. He began to wonder if, indeed, they *would* come to him at such time. He could not know that he had not really long to wait for an answer.

John and Mary seemed to each other even more distant, perhaps only because they now acknowledged the distance. They spoke little, and then only out of necessity or unwillingness to endure the silences, which occurred not out of animosity, but out of their new awareness of their differences. The only outward change in their lives was the suspension of the bimonthly exchange of visits with Agnes and Fred. Frances McGovern and her husband came over to play cards, and John and Mary went there one night and watched television, drank highballs and had a late snack of coffee and sandwiches. The Morrisons had a Saturday night party which John and Mary attended briefly and without incident. Clint and Helen Staley had three other couples, including John and Mary, for drinks and food and canasta in their basement recreation room.

The principal difference in the lives of all of the Taylors was that now each day was tinged with the muddy color of waiting.

Granted that fundamental difference, it was an ordinary evening at the end of an ordinary day in late September. Lois had come home from a Girl Scout meeting and gone to bed. Mary had retired immediately after her ten-thirty television program. John sat watching a rather incongruously sultry weather-girl offering elaborately contrived forecasts. He was also waiting, as he did every night without admitting it to himself, for Johnny to come home.

John heard the opening of the front door with his usual unrealized sense of relief and prepared for the regular rhythm of the closing of the door, the footsteps across the porch, the opening and closing of the living-room door. But this rhythm was abruptly shattered as Johnny burst immediately through into the living room and stood at its center, looking down at his father.

"I thought you said we were going to talk things over," Johnny said.

"I did and I meant it, Johnny. What's wrong?"

"Well, it's gotta work both ways, Dad."

"Will you sit down, Johnny, and tell me what's wrong?"

Without sitting down Johnny said, "Why didn't you tell me you tried to bribe Ida Praul's mother?"

Johnny's accusation had little significance for John, coming as it did with the more meaningful realization that Johnny knew about the bribe at all. John sat for a moment, stunned by the implications of this new knowledge. "Where . . . where did you hear about that?"

Johnny misinterpreted his father's hesitancy as guilt. "It doesn't make any difference where I heard it, why didn't you tell me about it?"

"Johnny . . . just a minute. Give me a minute to think. Sit down, Johnny. Please sit down."

After a moment Johnny turned and sat across the room from his father. John's confusion began to clear somewhat, and he saw that if he was to get Johnny to discuss the sources of his information, he would first have to settle what was to Johnny the more important issue.

"Johnny, I was doing what Mr. Hertzog told me to do. We certainly would have told you before the trial, but for now Mr. Hertzog didn't want *anyone* to know about that. That's why it's so important that you tell me who told you."

"Is it . . . true?"

"I'm afraid it is. Johnny, I was just trying to do what I thought was best for you. It was foolish and it was wrong, but I really thought at the time it was best. I'm not making excuses. I was wrong and I know it."

"I . . . understand, Dad. I guess it wasn't an easy thing for you to do."

He found it difficult to say, and knew, therefore, that he had to say it. "Thank you, Johnny."

"It won't be very good for us . . . at the trial . . . will it?"

"No, it sure won't. And I apologize to you for that. It won't come out in the trial, but if everybody knows about it beforehand, I think it'll be just as bad as if it did."

"It was Bobby Huntsinger who told me about it," Johnny said. "He heard his mother and father talking about it after supper tonight. They didn't know he could hear them, of course. Somebody told Mrs. Huntsinger on the phone. Bobby didn't know who."

"Was he the only one that knew?"

"He was then. I left right after he told me, but I guess they all know by now."

"What . . . what did he tell you, Johnny?"

"Just that you went to Mrs. Praul and offered her a lot of money to call off the trial and that she fought with you and threw you out of the house. And . . . and that she went to the district attorney about it."

"I . . . I don't know how this could have happened," John said. "I guess I'd better call Jim Beyers."

He went to the telephone and dialed Jim's number. "Hello, Jim? I didn't wake you, did I?"

"John? No, I was just on my way up to bed. Anything wrong?"

"I'm afraid so. Johnny just came home and told me that the young Huntsinger boy—you know, Nat Huntsinger's boy—told him about me going to Peg Praul. Said he heard his mother and father talking about it. Carol Huntsinger heard it from somebody on the telephone."

"I was afraid this would happen," Jim said.

"But, Jim only you and I and Stephen . . . and Mary knew about it."

"And Peg Praul," Jim said.

"Of course," John said quietly. "I completely forgot about that."

"I don't see that we can do anything about it. It certainly isn't going to do us any good to have everybody in town know about it. There's no telling how far it could spread."

"Christ!" John said. "Can't anything *good* happen to us?"

"I'm afraid things haven't gone too well, John. But there's no point in worrying. We still have Stephen Hertzog, and if you could have seen him function in Chris Henry's office, you'd feel a great deal better."

"Yes. Well, I'm sorry to have bothered you unnecessarily, Jim."

"Don't be silly. You were right to call. I'll give Stephen a ring in the morning and let him know about it. But, as I said, I don't see what we can do."

"Pretty stupid of me," John said to Johnny when he had replaced the phone. "Completely forgot that Peg Praul's probably the one who told people. I'm . . . I'm sorry about all this Johnny. It's my fault. I . . . I'm sorry."

"*Your* fault?" Johnny said, smiling weakly. "Seems to me I had a little more to do with it than you."

"I guess you have a point there."

"Well, I'd better get to bed, I guess."

Johnny had reached the bottom of the stairs when John said, "Johnny." The boy stopped and looked at him. "Would you . . . like a highball before you turn in? Might help us both to sleep."

Johnny did not even try to hide his surprise. "Why . . . why, sure, Dad."

"You get the ice," John said, "and I'll do the honors."

"Okay," Johnny said, starting for the kitchen. And without looking at his father he said casually, "Thanks, Dad."

The next morning Jim Beyers called Stephen Hertzog and told him of his conversation with John.

"I'm not surprised," Stephen said rather wearily. "It was almost inevitable. It's hard to say how much public opinion can hurt us, but it isn't going to do us any good."

"I know," Jim said.

"There's absolutely nothing to be done, of course."

"Not a thing," Jim agreed.

"I was going to call you later this morning. I have an appointment with the district attorney late this afternoon in Harrisville. I thought if there was anything you wanted to see me about I could stop on the way from there."

"No, there's nothing."

"I'll be in town anyway. I'm going to see John."

"Oh? Anything in particular or just another interview?"

"Something in particular. Something I don't much like doing. I confess to not having thought much of John Taylor when I met him, but I've rather got to like him over this past month—even admire him."

"I've known John for a long time," Jim said. "He's not the brightest fellow in the world, but he's one of the decentest men I know."

"I guess that's the word: decent. Well, whatever it is, I like it, and it makes me feel like a heel to have to tell him what I'm going to."

"What's that?"

"That I'm going to base the defense of his son at least partially on his inadequacy as a parent."

There was a pause. "I see what you mean," Jim said quietly. "Is it the only way?"

"I think it's the best way," Stephen answered. "I've learned a lot about Johnny Taylor in these last three or four weeks of talking to him. And through him I've learned almost as much about his father."

"Do you really believe John bears that much responsibility?"

This time the silence was Stephen's. "I'm afraid I do," he said. "It makes me almost glad I have no children of my own."

"Well, I don't envy you the job."

"I have a feeling I'll be invited to dinner. . . ."

"Supper," Jim corrected him.

"Yes, excuse me. Supper. John and Mary have asked me almost every time I've been up there. I think I'll accept this time. Anyway, if you want me around six o'clock, that's where I'll probably be."

"Okay, Stephen. Maybe I'll talk to you then."

Stephen left the city at three-fifteen for his four o'clock appointment with Joseph F. Cardamone, the district attorney for Audubon County. Although Stephen had been to the county courthouse before, it had not been during Mr. Cardamone's incumbency, and he had not met the present district attorney. He found the office with no difficulty. When he announced himself to the secretary in the outer office, he was asked to have a seat. The secretary informed the district attorney of Mr. Hertzog's presence, returned to the outer office and said, "The district attorney will see you in a few minutes."

Stephen waited, far from patiently, for fifteen minutes, during which time a variety of people entered and left Mr. Cardamone's office. One of them, Stephen guessed correctly from his familiar manner, was an assistant district attorney. This young man entered the office for the second time and after a few minutes came out and said to the secretary, "Okay, Gloria." He came through the gate in the low railing and said to Stephen, "He'll see you now. You can go right in."

"Thanks," Stephen said and went into the office. Stephen's first thought was that the room was not very impressive. His second thought was that neither was Mr. Cardamone, and this immediately put him on his guard. Stephen preferred to deal with obviously impressive people from whom there would be few surprises.

"Hello, Mr. Hertzog," Joseph Cardamone said, rising and extending his hand.

"Nice to meet you," Stephen said, shaking hands.

"Have a chair," Stephen sat down. Mr. Cardamone sat, leaned back in his swivel chair and said, "Quite a case, isn't it?"

"Might be," Stephen said.

"Might be, indeed, with you handling the defense," Mr. Cardamone said. "I've watched your career pretty closely. Everybody has, I guess. I'm looking forward to this."

"I hope that's a compliment," Stephen said.

"It is. You've never seen me before, but I've seen you. I took a day off couple of years ago to go watch you defend August Whipple. Temporary insanity. Difficult plea."

"Unless, of course, it happens to be a fact."

"Even then. I'm indebted to you to the tune of five bucks. I bet Haviland Curtis—the fellow just left the office, assistant D.A.—bet him five bucks you'd get Whipple off. Thanks."

"You're welcome," Stephen said, smiling. "What are the odds on this one?"

The district attorney laughed, and during his laughter the telephone buzzed. "Excuse me," he said. "Yes, Gloria? . . . All right. Put him on. Just take a minute," he said to Stephen. "Hello. Yes, hello, Judge. . . . They haven't even been served yet, Judge. I know that, but—"

Stephen was grateful for the opportunity to observe Joseph F. Cardamone. As he watched and listened, Stephen realized that had Cardamone's birth taken place a generation earlier, he would have become a factory worker, perhaps, or a barber or a candy store owner. But the generation into which he had been born had shed all of the Italian traits that older members of the family and an innate chauvinism lent it.

Yet the influence of that blood and of that chauvinism was strong. It had caused him as a child to learn simultaneously two languages, neither of them well. He struggled at college to overcome this obvious liability. It was a struggle that was never to end. Even now it was necessary for him to make a ceaseless effort to keep from falling into a blunt, graceless English which was his natural means of communication. Sometimes, just as his language seemed most fluent, he would lapse suddenly into one inelegant, vernacular phrase, then regain his poise and go on as he had before. Stephen had not yet determined just how much legal ability lay beneath this façade of provincialism.

"All right, Judge. I'll take care of it. . . . Yes. . . . Yes. Goodbye. Sorry, Mr. Hertzog."

"Perfectly all right," Stephen said.

"Now. To the business at hand. I don't suppose you're going to plead them?"

Stephen laughed quietly. "Would you?"

"I don't know," Cardamone said. "Doesn't seem to me you have much of a case."

"Well, I'm glad to hear that."

"Oh, I think I know just about how you'll approach it."

"I'm not so glad to hear that."

"Of course, I could be wrong."

"Yes."

"Ah, you *are* a slippery customer, aren't you?"

"I've heard my legal technique described more flatteringly."

"If you plead 'em, I think I can get 'em ten to fifteen."

"How generous."

"Think you can do better than that?"

"We'll see."

"They did it, you know."

"Did they indeed?"

"You know they did." Stephen smiled, but did not speak. His silence was not one of disadvantage. "What kind of deal did you expect me to offer you?"

"Just about the kind you did."

"And what kind do you want?"

"I don't want a deal, Mr. Cardamone. You asked me to come here."

"You certainly don't expect me to get 'em five to ten on a plea."

"I wouldn't accept it if you could."

"You wouldn't accept five to ten?"

"Not when there's a chance of acquittal."

"Acquittal? Are you serious?"

"I'm rarely otherwise, Mr. Cardamone."

Cardamone said, leaning forward, "If you can go into court against me with three defendants who committed first-degree rape and get 'em an acquittal, I might just resign as district attorney."

"That would be a shame. I'm sure you're a good one."

"Thanks." The district attorney looked at Stephen for a long moment. "You think they're innocent?"

"Their plea will be 'not guilty.'"

"And no deals."

"Not on this one."

"Well . . . good luck, Mr. Hertzog. I think this might just be fun."

"Same to you, Mr. Cardamone. I hope you enjoy it."

As Stephen left the office he was glad that Joseph F. Cardamone had not offered five to ten; it would have been difficult to turn down.

As Stephen had predicted, the Taylors had invited him to dinner as soon as he called to say that he wanted to see John. He arrived at the Taylor house shortly after five o'clock, just as John was parking his own car. They went inside and had two drinks while they waited for dinner. Stephen's very presence in the house put a heavy emphasis on the Taylors' predicament, and there appeared the old dilemma of further stressing their trouble by avoiding the subject completely.

Johnny was the most acutely affected, because Stephen was a symbol of his guilt. His deep silence was contagious, and Lois, who had begun dinner chattering, soon fell silent too. Mary, with characteristic escapism, was the most successful at this game of self-deception. She talked brightly and steadily—sometimes almost inanely—throughout dinner. Each time she went into the kitchen to bring food or to take it away, a silence of both relief and discomfort hovered over the table. And each time she would fly back into it like a noisy bird, seemingly oblivious of the fact that there had been a silence at all.

At last dinner was over, and while Mary and Lois cleared the table, John and Stephen sat together in the living room, smoking. Johnny asked to be excused and went to his room.

"Why don't we go for a walk, John," Stephen said, pressing out his cigarette. "I think it might be a good idea to have our talk away from the house."

"Whatever you say," John answered. Then he got up and went to the kitchen doorway. "We're going out for a little while, Mary. We won't be long."

"Oh," Mary said, and added, "Oh, all right." She could not quite conceal the curiosity in her tone.

It was that time in late September when one is likely to be suddenly aware that the days are much shorter than in midsummer.

After a moment Stephen said, "The trial begins in just a little more than two weeks."

"Yes," John said quietly.

"I've just about worked out the defense strategy," Stephen continued, and John heard a certain heaviness in his voice. "I think I'd better tell you about it."

"All right," John said.

"I don't think you're going to like it."

"Why not?"

"It isn't very . . . flattering to you."

"I guess I can take that—if it's going to help Johnny."

"We won't know whether it is or not until that jury comes in with a verdict," Stephen told him. "But I think I've worked out the only valid defense there is. It's been my experience that the most valid defense is always the best one."

"Then I guess that's it," John said.

"If you understand the problem," Stephen said, "you'll understand what I have to do."

"Okay."

"The first question we must ask ourselves," Stephen began, "is, 'What are you trying to prove?' We certainly can't prove that the boys didn't have sexual intercourse with Ida Praul for the simple reason that they did have—and that fact can be ascertained in court. We can try to prove, but we cannot be sure of proving, that their intercourse with Ida did not constitute rape, because the penetration was not against the will of the alleged victim. There is still doubt in my mind that Ida Praul did not want to have sexual intercourse with these three boys, but the prosecution has to *prove* that she didn't, and until the prosecution succeeds in that proof, the jury must by law assume that she did want to—at least by inference, for they must assume the boys' innocence until they are proved guilty. So technically there is always doubt as to whether Ida was a willing participant in an orgy or the unwilling victim of a rape—and we must take advantage of that doubt." Stephen was quiet for a moment, as if considering a choice of words. He was in reality simply giving John time to digest what he had already said, for he knew quite certainly how he would go on. "John, we must . . . minimize the boys' use of force."

"Minimize it?"

"If the boys are going to agree in court that they dragged Ida from the car, that two of them held her to the ground while the third raped her, that while she was in a resultant state of semi-consciousness the other two proceeded as well to rape her, that they then left her alone and injured on that hillside—well, we might just as well plead them and—I mean change our plea to guilty—and ask for leniency because of their ages. Rapp almost certainly wouldn't get it. Johnny and Artie might."

"I assume that's what we're *not* going to do," John said.

"You are correct," Stephen answered. "We're going to do our utmost to create the impression that Ida was not unwilling to become sexually involved with the boys, and that it is impossible to determine at what point—if at any point—she became unwilling."

"Is . . . is that true?"

"I *do* know, John. I *do* know that this girl spoke and behaved lewdly—led them on—during the time immediately preceding the alleged rape. I know that she tried to create the impression that she was experienced sexually. I know that her actions were deliberately of a nature which would excite the boys. Would you like to tell me whether this poor, lonely little girl merely wanted attention and used the only way she knew to get it? Or did she actually want to have sexual intercourse? She might have feigned her protests out of some pseudo-moral compunction which she felt would justify the act. It could be either way, and to defend the boys we must assume the latter. On the basis of that assumption, the boys must not admit that they dragged her from the car or that they held her down while Armand had intercourse with her."

"You mean, they must not tell the truth," John said quietly.

"Ida will do that," Stephen said. "The boys will say that Ida seemed to be pretending to resist, that she was coy and coquettish. They will even admit that at the last moment they did hear some unintelligible muttering on Ida's part—which could be interpreted as cries of passion as easily as cries of protest."

John looked shocked. Stephen went on, "This isn't going to be a pretty trial, John. It will be necessary to maintain that what Ida now describes as being pinned to the ground was in reality the result of all three boys trying to caress and make love to her—it may sound distasteful but it does not constitute rape. It's going to be Ida's story against the boys'. The jury is free to believe whichever story seems to them the most credible."

"I see."

"There's something else you may not see," Stephen said, and his tone was even more serious than it had been. "In this age of psychoanalytical awareness, every schoolboy knows that people are inclined to believe what is least painful for them to believe. We must make it easier for the jury to believe that the boys are innocent than that they are guilty. I've seen juries bring in absolutely unacceptable verdicts out of sheer sympathy with a guilty defendant. Now we're back to the original question: What are we trying to prove? First, that Ida Praul is the 'bad seed' of Peg Praul, if not in a hereditary sense, certainly in an environmental one. Second, that she was a willing participant in this act, not a victim of it. Third . . . John, if we are going to tell the jury that this was not rape, then we must, to convince them completely, tell them what it *was*. If we are to tell them that it was not an act of violence, then we must tell them it was an act of ignorance—an ignorance which stems from the total lack of enlightenment by the parents. If we are going to explain that Ida Praul's background led her to tempt these boys into sexual intercourse, then we must explain that the boys' backgrounds were unusually, monstrously naive, of such distorted sexual focus that it will justify their inability to resist that temptation. We must psychologically shift the jury's sense of blame from these innocent children to the guilty parents. Unable to punish the parents by law, the jury will be reluctant to punish the children."

"For Christ's sake, how can you do that, Stephen?"

It was a moment before he answered. "I don't know. But if I can do it, those boys are going to get the lightest sentence possible under the circumstances. I don't expect an acquittal, John; you may as well know that. But there are other factors, more against than for success. I reserved decision until I'd talked with your district attorney. I'm convinced that he's not the most imposing adversary I've ever faced. I don't think he is going to know how to cope with the latter part of this approach. That's in our favor, of course. Against us is the lack of precedent for this approach. And you'll probably become a little tired of hearing the words 'inadmissable' and 'irrelevant.' Everything depends on how much of this kind of testimony and oratory I can get admitted, or at least heard. Forsythe may go on sustaining objections to such evidence and charging the jury to strike it from their minds as well as having it stricken from the records, which, of course, they cannot do entirely. He'll recognize the unethical attempt to have irrelevant evidence heard, and eventually he'd cite me for contempt if I didn't stop. The question is, *when* will he get that tough? If by some near miracle he agrees that such evidence is relevant, it might come off even better than I hope. But that's a slim chance. John, I know—maybe only intuitively—but I *know* this is the way to do it."

After a moment John said, "You're the lawyer, Stephen."

"I may have to paint you as pretty much of a failure as a parent," Stephen told him.

"I gathered you would," John said sarcastically. "I . . . I wish all the aspects of the case were as sound as that one."

"John, you mustn't—"

"You're not going to pretend that you don't believe that I'm largely responsible?"

"No," Stephen said. "No, I'm not. Do you want to hear the kind of thing I'll probably be saying?"

"No . . . I don't think so," John answered. "I guess I've found out pretty much for myself lately. Is there anything else?"

"No. Shall we go back?"

"Okay."

They had come quite a long way from the house, and they walked about half the distance back in silence. Then John said, "You don't have any children, do you?"

"No," Stephen said, suddenly and needlessly on guard.

"It's a great joy," John said, "and it can be . . . terrible."

"Yes."

"Where do you think I went wrong?" John asked.

"That's an impossible question to answer. And it's not a fair question to you. I think the question ought to be, 'Where did things go wrong?'"

"Just uncontrollable things, huh?"

"Probably as many uncontrollable ones as controllable ones," Stephen said.

"Let me try to tell you what I think," John said. "I think that it was my marriage that went wrong, although I'm not sure just where. Mary and I used to talk, used to plan, but somehow we just stopped that sort of thing. Things were . . . not going right between Mary and me, but the one thing we never *could* discuss was sex, and so I didn't know how to straighten it out. I . . . blamed Mary for that, I guess to give myself an excuse for . . . doing what I did. Of course, that was years ago. I know that it wasn't just Mary who couldn't talk about sex; I hid my own embarrassment under hers. If we'd tried to talk it over—if we'd *learned* then to talk things over, maybe when the children were growing up we could have talked to them better. Our life has been like a big party where nobody says anything meaningful or serious. You just tell jokes or gossip a little, keep it light and gay, no arguments, no contention—but also nobody really gets to know anybody else. If you do it long enough you get to the point where any kind of serious talk embarrasses you. You forget how to understand each other."

"It may surprise you, but without his telling me any of it, I knew almost all of that just from talking to Johnny. I hope you don't think I was prying, John. I felt that I should get to know Johnny, so we just talked at random sometimes. He's very young for his age. In telling me how he felt about something that happened years ago at home, he'd reflect such a clear image of you and Mary that it was impossible not to know that something had gone wrong with your marriage. It wasn't difficult to know what it was. And it was almost the same with Artie. From his tension, his terrible defensiveness, it was possible to form a surprisingly accurate picture of his home life."

"I guess it all gets to them somehow, doesn't it?"

"It certainly seems to," Stephen said, "one way or another."

"Even things that are far beyond them."

"Yes."

"So many things can go wrong. I know Mary; if we were to discuss this whole thing tonight, she'd say, 'I gave you everything a wife can give; I don't know what more I could do.' She doesn't even know what it was that she didn't give me. I think it's possible for a man or a woman to have a blind spot, to fail somewhere without even knowing it."

"Of course it is, but that's where communication comes in. When a blind spot is causing a failure, the one who doesn't have the blind spot comes to the other, and they try to work it out."

"What if the blind spot's so blind that you can't see through it, even then?"

"I guess . . . then you're in trouble," Stephen said. "John, I'd like say something to you that I hope won't offend you. I think you've let life force you into patterns—maybe even into a marriage—that have been wrong for you."

"I don't guess there's much doubt about that," John said.

"For reasons that I certainly can't entirely explain, I've chosen almost everything in my life very carefully. My career, my not having married yet, just about everything."

"Believe me, Stephen, don't be offended, but I think that sounds . . . complacent, I think that's the word. Things can go wrong so unexpectedly, so suddenly. At least, they seem sudden whether they are or not."

"You're right, of course, but I have difficulty applying that to myself.

I think it's part of the reason that I'm a little scared about getting married and having children. You can't be very deliberate about children."

"Or anything else," John said.

"Maybe not."

They were both silent until they reached the house. Then John said, "Here's the old homestead. Come on in and have a drink."

"Thanks, but I can't, John. I have to see both the Schliers and George Rapp before I go back. I'll just come in and say good night to Mary."

"Okay," John said.

"I hope you know that I'll be doing my best for Johnny—not just because I'm being paid and because I think I owe it to myself always to do my best. I know Johnny now. I don't think he deserves to go to prison."

"That . . . that's about the most reassuring thing I've heard since this whole mess started. Thank you, Stephen. Come on. Let's go in."

XXIV.

They had known that Johnny would have to leave now. Mary had packed a small bag for Johnny, and they had had supper, most of which had gone uneaten. When Mary told Lois to go to her room afterwards, John had quietly countermanded the order. Then the four Taylors had sat in the living room. Mary, red-eyed and wiping away each tear as quickly as it appeared; John, somber and unintentionally severe; Lois, looking pitifully confused and tremulous; and Johnny, dazed and openly frightened. They had spoken less and less as the time drew near until finally they sat in complete silence. Finally, the time came, and John and Johnny had left and Mary and Lois had cried together, yet separately.

Next morning John bathed and dressed and went downstairs. Mary was already in the kitchen, wearing one of her good dresses, of dark blue silk with an apron over it. As John sat at the table, he said, "Mary, are you sure you want to go?"

"Yes," she answered.

"Mary, you know what Stephen said. They'll only be picking a jury and they can't possibly finish today—maybe not even tomorrow. It's only going to be a strain on you. Why don't—"

"I want Johnny to see me there every day—to know that I'll be there every day, no matter what."

"All right, Mary. Have it your own way."

Lois came downstairs and they had breakfast together. Mary and Lois washed and dried the dishes.

"It's time for you to go over to Frances', Lois," Mary said.

"All right, Mother," Lois answered.

"Now, be a good girl and don't get in Frances' way."

"Yes, Mother."

"I'll stop in to get you as soon as we get back."

"Yes, Mother."

They left the house together, Lois going next door and waving goodbye from the steps as John and Mary got into the car. They drove away from the house and all the way to Harrisville without speaking. John parked the car a block from the courthouse. When John had locked the car, he turned to Mary and their eyes met for a long, long moment. Then she took his arm and they started down the street.

They made their way up the long, wide stone stairs toward the portico of the courthouse, which was supported by high Ionic columns. Just inside the oak doors was a round hall with the Office of the Recorder of Deeds on one side and the Bureau of Licenses on the other. A great flight of marble stairs rose from the center of the hall to an upper gallery where there were four green leather, brass-studded doors marked Courtroom A, Courtroom B, Courtroom C, and Courtroom D. From the gallery two long, dark corridors led to the other two, larger courtrooms designated E and F. It was in Courtroom E that Criminal Court proceedings were usually conducted, and it was toward this room that John and Mary made their way, John looking serious and troubled, Mary, pale and expressionless and calm.

Just outside the courtroom they encountered a cluster of people, a few of whom they had known for years; others were elderly attendants, bailiffs and court clerks, whose faces were to become newly and irrevocably familiar. Some, like themselves, were relatives of the defendants; some were merely spectators, who came daily with the enthusiasm and loyalty of a fan club. And, as was always to be the case, there were one or two new faces, arresting and offensive in their complete lack of involvement. From this group came a constant, quiet, solemn murmur. Mary could not understand or forgive what was to her their sacrilege.

The Taylors exchanged good mornings with Stephen Hertzog and Jim Beyers and, strangely, Mary thought, with District Attorney Cardamone, who smiled at them briefly as they were introduced, then went into the courtroom.

Stephen began to say something, but a bell rang, signaling the beginning of the session, and he said, "We'd better go in."

One of the old men moved toward the green leather doors, preparing to close them. Conversations were brought to a hurried end. After a deep last puff, cigarettes were stamped out on the marble floor or deposited in the sand-filled urns. Then, a common gravity descending upon all—the interested and the disinterested, the worried and the unconcerned, the participants and the spectators—they shuffled slowly into the hallowed hall where justice made her home.

In the opposite wall from the entrance to the rooms were four windows, stretching to the top of the room, which was two floors high. Just inside and to the left of the entrance was the jury box, enclosed by low walls of the same grayish-green marble with which most of the room was lined. Within this enclosure were twelve chairs of dark wood and green leather which the members of the jury occupied in the same order during each day of the trial. There were two more of these chairs just outside the jury box, for the two alternate jurors. At the front of the room and across almost its entire width was a long, high table of solid marble which fronted the bench. At either end of this massive structure and attached to it was a small, low-walled enclosure, higher than the floor of the courtroom, but lower than the bench. The enclosure nearest the jury was the witness stand, and the other, on the far side of the room, was used by the judge when conferring with the attorneys. Opposite the jury box was a bank of chairs reserved for the press. The wide area between held two long tables, each with chairs, at which sat the defense and prosecuting attorneys. The tables were close together to allow for easy conferences. All of this was contained behind a brass and black wrought-iron fence which separated the area from the spectators' benches.

As John and Mary entered, they could see that the Schliers were already there, sitting near the front of the spectators' benches. George Rapp was sprawled on the aisle seat of the last row. Peg Praul was in the first row of the far section. They nodded to the Schliers as they took seats in the row just in front of them. They saw then that Ida Praul, the district attorney, and an assistant were sitting at the prosecution table. As Mary was observing this scene, the great green doors swung open, and two uniformed policeman escorted Johny and Artie and Armand into court. She gasped almost inaudibly and covered her mouth with her handkerchief. John took her arm and squeezed it reassuringly. When the boys were seated at the table, the court clerk stood and said to the already orderly group, "Order! Order in the Court! Everybody rise!"

With an echoing rumble the assembly rose, and from his chambers in the left-hand corner of the room Judge Forsythe entered, his white patrician head held high above his black robes. He strode across the room and took his seat in the high-backed leather chair. The clerk looked about the room, then at the big clock over the doors and said,

"It is duly noted that at ten-five o'clock on this eighth day of October in the year of Our Lord . . ."

Mary heard no more. She had slumped against John, not in unconsciousness, but in a gray-hazed attempt to shut out everything around her. By the time the clerk had reached ". . . and in the presence of all other required persons, this court is now in session," Mary could see and hear again, but what she saw and heard meant little to her.

"Mary!" John whispered. "Are you all right?"

After a moment she looked up at him and said, "Yes. Yes, I'm all right."

District Attorney Joseph F. Cardamone was on his feet then, saying, "Your Honor, due to the youthful age of the complainant, the prosecution would like to request that her mother, Mrs. Margaret Praul, be allowed to sit at the prosecution's table."

Judge Forsythe looked at the district attorney, then at the attorneys for the defense and said, "The court has no objection if that is agreeable to the defense."

Stephen rose and said, "No objection whatsoever, your Honor."

The assistant district attorney came through the gate in the dividing fence and escorted Peg Praul to the table as the district attorney stood thoughtfully surveying the courtroom.

Judge Forsythe said, "The court would like to remind the attorneys for the defense and for the prosecution that this is not the only case to be tried before it. The court recognizes the importance of an impartial jury, but urges you both to use your best efforts to select such a jury within a reasonable period of time."

This was not the last time in the next three days that the court was so to urge the defense and the prosecution. Over and over the men and women of the panel were examined, and over and over jurors found to be acceptable to the defense were challenged by the prosecution, and vice versa.

At four-ten on the third day, Judge Forsythe peered over the rims of his spectacles, his thick white eyebrows raised in an expression of mingled displeasure and relief at the selection of the second alternate juror in this already difficult trial. The last juror had been a woman, as were only two other members of the panel. She was a thirty-two-year-old housewife from Fairview, the mother of two children, a non-militant Protestant and a member of the Book-of-the-Month Club. She was also, Stephen Hertzog noted, well and revealingly dressed in a shirtmaker dress. Stephen saw in her a distinct physical awareness, indicated by the way she touched her hair, crossed her legs, and ran her fingers lightly across her lips thoughtfully before answering a difficult question. She was the best of the three women jurors he had allowed on the panel, Stephen thought, and the other two were not bad.

"It reinforces my faith in mankind, Mr. Hertzog," Judge Forsythe was saying, "to find that you really do, after all, believe that the defendants have fourteen qualified peers among their countrymen. I had begun to doubt it." His gaze shifted to the large, silent clock over the doors of the room. "Since it is now ten minutes after four, I see little point in continuing this session." The eyes swung back to Stephen and thence to Mr. Cardamone with a steely expression that dared the attorneys under some unknown but horrible punishment to suggest otherwise. "Court is adjourned until ten o'clock tomorrow morning."

There was noise then and some shuffling about, but everyone remained approximately where he was until the defendants were led by their police guard from the front of the courtroom to the door. From there they would be taken through a corridor to a back elevator and down to the street floor to await the arrival of a second guard, and then across the street to the county jail. As resolutely as Johnny refused to look toward his family as he left the courtroom each day, Mary insisted on watching every step of his slow and torturous progress toward daily imprisonment. Mary was in this watchful attitude when Stephen and Jim approached.

"Well, so far, so good," Stephen said.

"What?" Mary said, wondering what he meant.

"It's a good jury from our point of view," Stephen told them. "An average age of about thirty-eight, which is as young as I've ever seen a jury. It's as intellectual a group as Audubon County is likely to present in a jury pool. No Negroes—they're what I call 'rape-sensitive.' There are only three women—women are likely to take rape a little more personally, a little more seriously than men—and the women we have, I think, have a healthy respect for the sex instinct. There's only one childless juror, which at least gives both sides an equal chance to exploit their parenthood. There are no religious fanatics, unless, of course, there's some secret psychopathic avenger hidden in there somewhere, and that's not very probable. I have a feeling we have a favorable group."

"I was really trying to pay attention," Mary said, "but I had no idea you were arranging all that."

Stephen laughed. "I wish Cardamone had had no idea; we'd have a jury of twelve twenty-one-year-old boys."

"But don't be disheartened," Stephen said. "We have a good start. I want to talk to Cardamone for a minute. I'll see you tomorrow." He moved off toward the prosecution table, and John and Mary and Jim started down the long corridor.

Already John and Mary had fallen into an agonizing routine—the silent drive home, the nearly silent supper, the increasing meaninglessness of television-watching, the fitful sleeplessness until exhaustion brought equally fitful sleep, then breakfast and the return to the courthouse.

On the fourth day of the trial Mary walked up the stairs to the courthouse without looking to either side, as if she were quite accustomed to being there. She had found that it added measurably to her already severe distress to note the physical circumstances of Johnny's trial. Her attendance at the trial had taken on an unreal, dreamlike quality. To the observer she seemed to remain untouched, but her consciousness was shattered again and again by the reality of a hundred little events, a sudden movement by Johnny, a familiar voice behind her, or merely the strained sound of her own breathing.

John and Mary took their seats, and Mary grasped the back of the bench before her, prepared now for Johnny's entrance. The defendants were brought in and seated. The court was brought to order. The clerk noted the time and date and place and the presence of all the required officials. The judge peered about the room over his horn-rimmed glasses, which seemed sharply anachronistic to the archaic grandeur of the large Episcopalian head.

Without speaking, the judge rose and went to the far end of the bench. Mr. Cardamone and Mr. Hertzog followed automatically, and the mechanics of justice began. As the three men conferred, John looked at the faces of the twelve people who held the fate of his son in their hands. Even in their extraordinary role they were ordinary looking people. Any of the nine men might have been one of John's salesmen or an assistant manager at the bank or an office employee at one of the steel companies. One of the women looked a lot like Jenny Morrison, he thought, and a second looked younger than she probably was, while the third might have been a schoolteacher. Men and women just like him and Mary, with the same kind of lives and homes and children. Except for one new and essential difference, he thought: they now had the power to put his son in prison.

John did not see and did not realize that in all groups of human beings there are leaders and followers. He could not foresee that in this group of twelve there would be three persons, representing three different preconceived attitudes toward this trial, who would lead the others to or away from the possible verdicts. Although the woman from Fairview was only thirty-two, she had two sons, one nine and one seven. She had seen the defendants for the first time just yesterday, but twice when she had looked at them her fertile and intelligent imagination had caused Johnny Taylor and Artie Schlier to disappear and she saw in their places her two sons, advanced slightly in age, but unmistakably her sons. She was Janet Somers McNaughton, formerly of Boston, and she had been educated in a small but exclusive New England girls' school, which she had disliked because she had always, even as a preadolescent, got on better with men than with other girls. This did not prevent her always being in the upper 10 per cent of her class, nor did it prevent her being the most popular girl in her class—at least with the nearest prep school or college. She had been a virgin when she had married Gerald McNaughton II in 1950, but it was due, as she always said, "more to good luck than good management." Now as the wife of the young vice-president of McNaughton Woolen Mills, Inc. she lived a happy, comfortable, well-balanced life in a ten-room stone house in fashionable Fairview. She disliked Peg Praul on sight, felt sorry but not responsible for "that pathetic little Ida," distrusted the district attorney, found Stephen Hertzog enormously attractive, hated Armand Rapp and hoped that her sons (the eldest of whom had begun to look to her faintly like Johnny Taylor) would never come into contact with such a brute. Had she been asked to decide without evidence, she would have acquitted the defendants, even Armand.

Janet McNaughton sat in the last chair in the second row of jurors. In the first chair of the first row, since he was foreman, sat Robert R. Dickinson, who was vice-president and manager of the Farmers' Bank and Trust Company. He was a short man (five feet seven) with graying black hair, parted in the middle and waved ever so slightly just once on each side of the part. He was fifty-three years old and had smiled for so much of his life that his face, even in complete repose, retained vestiges of that expression. He had rather large teeth, and his nearly perpetual smile occasionally revealed the glintings of the metal fasteners of an expensive but antiquated dental bridge. Mr. Dickinson lived in Hawesport, a small town five miles north of Harrisville. Little of a civic nature was done in Hawesport without the consultation or active participation of Mr. Dickinson. He was a prominent member and substitute minister of the Hawesport First Presbyterian Church and substituted in emergency at all of the other Protestant churches in the town. He was qualified for this task by the fact that his father had been a Presbyterian minister. His mother had been a prostitute, reformed by Mr. Dickinson's father, who had spent the last twenty years of her life in Hawesport secretly drinking herself to death. Mr. Dickinson's rise to banking prominence had begun nearly thirty years ago when he had exposed the bank's head bookkeeper, who had embezzled two thousand dollars and had managed in nine months to put back only $435 of it. It had all been pretty clear sailing from there. He had had a secretary by the time he was thirty and had been sleeping with her since he had been thirty-two. The only person in Hawesport who knew this was Mrs. Dickinson, who didn't mind since sleeping with Mr. Dickinson or anyone else disturbed her concept of her role in the church. Mr. Dickinson's secretary relieved her of the necessity of fulfilling her wifely function. Mr. Dickinson deeply felt it was his civic duty to decide against anyone who could become involved in so unseemly a crime as rape and would have so decided in this case even without evidence.

One chair to Mr. Dickinson's right sat Ira Bickford, whose hair was the color of cumulus clouds and whose face had the quality of a topographical map in red and pale brown. Mr. Bickford was a retired surveyor, who, in December of 1929, at the age of thirty-one, had given up a musical career when his suddenly nearly penniless and ailing father had offered to educate him sufficiently and quickly in the business of surveying in order that he might support his mother and invalid sister. This Mr. Bickford's father had done and then died. Mr. Bickford's mother lived to the fine age of ninety-two and expired quietly. His sister still lived, principally to listen to Mr. Bickford play the cello as he did each evening. He had not really played very well since the early nineteen-thirties when his large hands had hardened and cracked from exposure to sun and wind and rain, but he played, and his sister had never in her restricted life heard such beautiful music. Mr. Bickford looked upon the defendants and upon Ida Praul and her mother and upon Judge Forsythe and Stephen Hertzog and Joseph Cardamone as equally innocent of any guilt, just as he looked upon his sister and his mother and his father. That human beings were capable of guilt, he knew. And he also knew that sometime in the very near future he would become convinced that someone was telling the truth and someone was not. It was a decision that he could not yet make, and had he been asked to, he would have withdrawn from the situation and gone home to please his sister with the beautiful if limping music he made with his cello.

Although the jury would eventually be required to weld its individual opinions into the decision of a unit, those opinions were to vacillate wildly hour by hour, sometimes minute by minute, until that time. A word or a facial expression or a reaction on the part of a witness could be enough to rout the separate elements of an entrenched opinion and send them scurrying. Yet a poll of Mrs. McNaughton, Mr. Dickinson and Mr. Bickford at any given moment of the trial would have produced an accurate picture of the jury's position at that moment. No one knew this, of course, and so the interested parties were spared the anxiety which the knowledge would have caused them.

It was after eleven o'clock when Joseph F. Cardamone rose to present his initial argument. He approached the jury in a thoughtful manner as if considering for the first time what he was about to say to them. "Ladies and gentlemen of the jury, the People will prove in this trial that on the night of August twenty-third of this year, the three defendants perpetrated upon the person of Ida Praul the crime of rape in the first degree." He paused and looked into the faces of the jurors. "There's nothing complicated about this case, nothing vague. There are no extenuating circumstances to weigh. It's as simple a case of first-degree rape as I've ever seen. To couch the situation in simple terms, three boys invited this seventeen-year-old virgin to go for a ride with them in a car. To this much she agreed. Then against her strenuous objections they drove to a lonely spot in the wooded hills outside of town. There all three of them forced their immoral attentions on her as she struggled to resist. They forced her, virtually dragged her, from the car to a convenient spot on the hillside. While two of them immobilized her, held her to the ground, the third raped her. She fell into unconsciousness and while she was in that state, the other two raped her. Then, as if this brutality, this complete lack of human decency were not enough, they abandoned her on that hillside in the dark of night and drove away in their automobile."

The district attorney paused again, walked toward the defendants and looked at each one. Then he turned back to the jury. "Sexual penetration, however slight, against the will and without the consent of the victim, constitutes rape under the law, ladies and gentlemen. You will hear a physician testify to the physical damage caused to Ida Praul by the penetration of her body. You will hear him testify to the presence of male sperm in her body. There can be no doubt about the penetration. You will hear this poor little girl's own account of the savage manner in which these men rendered her unable to prevent that penetration. The law clearly states, ladies and gentlemen, that unconsciousness on the part of the victim constitutes her lack of consent, even if the attacker is not *responsible* for that unconsciousness, and in this case, that responsibility certainly falls heavily upon the defendants.

"So we will see that beyond the merest shadow of a doubt, this is in a legal sense first-degree rape. But there is more than that, ladies and gentlemen. There is a crime against morality, a crime against nature, a crime against the community which has nurtured these men. Be not misled by the youth of the defendants, or by sympathy for them. We will prove beyond a reasonable doubt that they committed each of the acts charged in the indictment. At the close of the evidence we will ask you to return a verdict of guilty of the crime of rape in the first degree."

Josph Cardamone looked at the jurors for a moment as if he might see the effect of his argument in their faces. He turned then and resumed his seat.

"The attorney for the defense may proceed," Judge Forsythe said, and after a moment Stephen rose and walked to the jury box.

"Ladies and gentlemen," he began, "the defense contends and will clearly demonstrate that there has been no rape in this case." He stopped speaking and looked at the floor as if to allow time for this statement to be absorbed. "Rape must be 'against the will and without the consent of . . .' There is the key to what happened to these four young people on the night of August twenty-third. Ida Praul deliberately and of her own free will sought to excite these boys by her lewd language and behavior, sought their sexual attentions, and, having ultimately received those attentions, sought, out of her own guilt, to escape the blame for her promiscuity by charging these boys with rape. The defense will further prove that the complainant has long been known for lasciviousness of speech and behavior, and that her behavior on the night of August twenty-third was not unusual. The defense will prove that what the prosecution chooses to call rape was in reality a sexual experiment in which four ignorantly curious young people participated willingly and after which they felt varying but violent degrees of remorse. The defendants' remorse sent them fleeing in panic from the scene; the remorse of the complainant sent her into this courtroom, charging the defendants in order to clear herself. This—" Stephen hesitated—"unpleasant . . . trial is not the result of viciousness on the part of any of these mere children. It is a result of their sexual confusion, as you will see in the course of this trial. If through this due process we increase our understanding of these young people—and, therefore, possibly of all young people—we will have gained a great deal. But let us not forget that justice is our primary goal, and in pursuit of that goal, ladies and gentlemen, I ask you to remember the phrase, 'against the will and without the consent of the victim. . . .' For the consent of this alleged victim was truly there, and in the presence of that consent there can be no rape in any degree. And there can be for the defendants only acquittal."

There was a pause in the proceedings then as the district attorney went to the bench and conferred with Judge Forsythe. Janet McNaughton watched the district attorney walk to the bench, and her first thought was of collusion between him and the judge. She scoffed at herself and put this thought out of her mind. She could not put out of her mind, however, the clause, "It is a result of their sexual confusion." She remembered in how many adolescent situations her honor had been saved by mere accident or by the gallantry or the inexperience of her partner. She believed every word which Stephen Hertzog had said.

The only word of Stephen's argument which Robert R. Dickinson remembered really clearly was "viciousness," and he asked himself what right Stephen Hertzog had to judge, to decide who was vicious and who was not. He remembered nearly all of the district attorney's argument and joyfully felt the spirit of vengeance which he was sure he had heard in the words. Yes, truly it was his duty to punish these fiends to the fullest extent of the law.

Excellent speakers, thought Ira Bickford, realizing that each attorney had taken just about the only course open to him under the circumstances. He sat back calmly, ready, now that he knew what these two men were going to try to prove, to have one of them prove it.

"Is the prosecution ready to call its first witness?" Judge Forsythe was asking. Mr. Cardamone had come back from the bench and was whispering to Stephen.

"Yes, your Honor. The prosecution calls Virginia Lukens," Mr. Cardamone said as he returned to his table for a last glance at his notes.

A frightened-looking girl of sixteen with pale, lusterless, blond hair rose from the first row of spectators' benches and walked toward the witness stand. Though she looked very much as if she would have to be helped before she reached her destination, at last she entered the marble enclosure and was sworn in.

Virginia Lukens said "I do" utterly inaudibly.

"Miss Lukens," Judge Forsythe said, "you'll have to speak up."

Miss Lukens looked as if she would cry.

"Would you tell the court your name," Mr. Cardamone said.

"Virginia Lukens," she answered, again inaudibly.

"I'm afraid you'll have to talk a little louder," Mr. Cardamone said.

"And would you please address your remarks to the jury," the judge said. "They're the ones who must hear you."

Miss Lukens repeated her name.

"Would you tell us in your own words what you did on Friday night, August twenty-third of this year?" Mr. Cardamone said.

"Was that . . . the night . . .?"

"Yes, Virginia," Mr. Cardamone said quietly, "that was the night of the crime."

"May I suggest, your Honor," Stephen said, "that Mr. Cardamone refer in future to the alleged crime?"

"I don't see that that is particularly important, Mr. Hertzog," the judge replied.

"Your Honor, if the jury is to assume the innocence of my clients, they must assume that there has been no crime—until the People have proved otherwise."

Judge Forsythe raised one shaggy, white eyebrow, which quivered for a moment as he stared at Stephen Hertzog. Then the eyebrow fell and he said, "You have already impressed that on the jury, Mr. Hertzog, but all right. Will you please refer to the 'alleged crime,' Mr. Cardamone."

"Would you tell us where you were on that night?" Mr. Cardamone said.

"I went to the movies with Ida Praul," Virginia answered.

"Then what did you do?"

"We went for a walk."

"Yes, what else?"

"Well, we didn't finish our walk, because Ida stopped to talk to some boys, and I went on home."

"What boys?"

"Them," Virginia said, nodding toward the defendants.

"Can you tell us who they are?"

"Armand Rapp, Johnny Taylor and Artie Schlier."

"Do you know them?"

"Yes."

"Then why didn't you stop to talk, too?"

"Because Armand Rapp was there and he has such a terrible reputation."

Stephen jumped to his feet. "Objection, your—"

"Sustained, sustained. The jury will wholly disregard the last answer."

"What did you do then, Virginia?"

"Well, I waited a couple of minutes, but Ida stayed with them, so like I said, I went on home."

"Your witness, Mr. Hertzog," the district attorney said.

Stephen rose and walked quite slowly to the witness box. He stood rather close to the girl and said, "Virginia—you don't mind if I call you 'Virginia,' do you?"

"No," the girl said, smiling faintly.

"Virginia, how well do you know Armand Rapp?"

"Well . . . I know who he is."

"Oh? Do you speak to him when you meet him on the street?"

"Oh, no!"

"Have you ever spoken to him?"

"No, sir!"

"Ever been introduced to him?"

"I wouldn't even want to."

"Then, Virginia, you don't really know Armand Rapp, do you?"

"Well . . . no, I guess not."

Robert R. Dickinson turned, as casually as he could manage, and looked at the other jurors much as he might have looked at the congregation of the Hawesport Presbyterian Church. His opinion of Armand Rapp was confirmed, and he had no intention of striking it from *his* record of the trial. Janet McNaughton did not see Mr. Dickinson turn. She was preoccupied with the formation of a vague but forceful picture of Armand Rapp's rape of Ida Praul.

"Now, Virginia, do you know the other two boys, Johnny Taylor and Artie Schlier?"

"Yes, sir."

"And you speak to them?"

"Yes, sir, they're nice boys."

"Virginia, why did Ida stop to talk to these boys?"

"Well, they called her over."

"Oh, and Ida went and you didn't?"

"Yes."

"Did you say anything to Ida before she left you?"

"Oh, yes, I told her not to go."

"Indeed? Would you say that you insisted?"

"I sure did."

"But Ida went of her own free will, against your admonitions, against your insistence?"

"Yes, she just wouldn't listen to me."

"Thank you, Virginia," Stephen said and turned away. "No more questions."

When Stephen returned to the table, Mr. Cardamone got up and went to Stephen's chair. Jim Beyers leaned toward the two men. The district attorney's assistant simultaneously leafed through a stack of papers and spoke quietly to Peg Praul. Judge Forsythe watched for a moment, then turned his attention to a thick file of typewritten papers. Wizened minor officials of the court took the opportunity to cluster by the doors in carefree conversation, their nonchalance being the badge of their officialdom. These were the worst moments, John thought, and there were many of them, when nothing seemed to be happening, when the whole world stood wastefully still and all you could do was wait.

After several minutes, Judge Forsythe said in his most effective monotone, "May we get on with it? Will the prosecution call its next witness?"

"Yes, your Honor," Mr. Cardamone answered, and after a few more whispered words, went back to his chair. He spoke for a moment to his assistant, then to Peg Praul. "The People call Chief of Police Benjamin Summerfield."

Ben Summerfield, immaculately uniformed as he was only in court, rose and went to the witness stand. He was elaborately questioned as to the circumstances under which he had apprehended the defendants and as to the most minute, irrelevant and meaningless events which occurred at Borough Hall immediately thereafter. When Mr. Cardamone had finished his examination, Stephen Hertzog went through a second recital of this testimony, reinterpreting this or that detail in favor of his clients. After a lunch break of an hour and a half, the whole maddeningly tedious procedure of the arrests was repeated.

This monotonous testimony, which was bound to bore the disinterested, had a curiously strong effect on those who were involved in the trial. Involvement, for most of these people, was so new that their sense of novelty nearly overcame their sense of reality. The appearance of arresting officers and such phrases as "taken into custody," "incarcerated," and "out on bail" created a picture of crime and punishment such as they had only seen on television or read about in thrillers. Their involvement now became involvement in the committing of a crime and, therefore, with criminals, and Janet McNaughton and Ira Bickford were made uncomfortable by a new awareness of the course to which their responsibility might compel them.

It was four-thirty-five when court was adjourned until ten the next morning.

On the second day of the trial, after the inevitable droning delays, the district attorney called as the people's next witness Dr. Francis X. McKenna.

"Dr. McKenna," Mr. Cardamone said when the doctor had been sworn in and identified, "you were called to the Borough Hall on the morning of August twenty-fourth?"

"Yes."

"For what purpose?"

"To examine and treat Ida Praul."

"And what did you find in your examination?"

"I found evidence of male sperm which indicated she had recently had sexual intercourse."

"What else did you find?"

"There was severe damage to the tissue around and in the vagina."

"Would you say, doctor, that this damage could have been inflicted by a sexual assault?"

"Yes."

"Would this damage have been inflicted by one attacker?"

"It would be impossible to determine that with any certainty," Doctor McKenna said, "but the extent of the damage would surely be commensurate with a multiple rape or rape more than once by the same man."

"Was there any other evidence of rape?"

"There were cuts and bruises about the legs and feet and arms, and the patient was limping from a sprained ankle. She was also in shock. She kept muttering, 'They raped me.'"

"Is it therefore your professional opinion that Ida Praul was the victim of rape?"

"It most certainly is."

"Your witness, Mr. Hertzog."

Stephen sat at the table for a long moment staring at Dr. McKenna. Then he rose and started toward the witness stand, saying, "Dr. McKenna, do you know the legal definition of rape?"

"I do," the doctor answered.

"You know, then, that there must first be penetration, however slight?"

"Yes."

"And that this penetration must be against the victim's will?"

"Yes."

"It is medically not only possible but relatively simple as a rule to determine whether or not there has been penetration, is it not?"

"It is."

"Would you explain to the court by what medical process you determine whether or not that penetration is against the will of an alleged victim?"

"Why, by . . . by the damage to tissues of the sexual organs, damage that is not inflicted by normal sexual intercourse."

"Is it not possible that such damage as you found in examining Ida Praul could have been inflicted through inexperience, through ignorance rather than violence?"

"It's unlikely."

"Is it possible?"

"Yes . . . yes, it's possible."

"As a matter of fact, it's entirely possible, isn't it?"

"I don't know what you mean by the qualification."

"I mean that if you were to hear someone say, 'It is entirely possible that the female genitals could suffer severe damage during sexual intercourse among inexperienced or sexually ignorant people,' you would not be inclined to contradict."

Mr. Cardamone was on his feet. "Your Honor, I object! The attorney for the defense is—putting words into his mouth!"

"Overruled," the judge said, eyeing Stephen.

"Is it entirely possible that the female genitals could suffer severe damage during sexual intercourse among inexperienced or sexually ignorant people?"

"I object, your Honor!" the district attorney shouted.

"On what grounds, Mr. Cardamone?" the judge asked.

"It assumes a state of facts not in evidence," Mr. Cardamone answered a trifle incredulously.

"The witness has been asked a hypothetical question, a medical one, to which he is at liberty to answer, Yes or No. You may answer the question, Doctor."

The doctor looked at the judge, then at his questioner. "Yes, it is . . . but it's not likely."

"Doctor, when you examine a patient who is suffering from contusions and lacerations about the arms, legs and feet, do you immediately diagnose sexual assault and begin making out a police report?"

"That's a ridiculous question," the doctor said.

"Your purpose as a witness," Stephen said quickly, "is not to evaluate the questions, but merely to answer them."

"Of course I couldn't diagnose sexual assault—unless there are other indications as there were in this case."

"But when there are no other indications, cuts and bruises become signs of violence, but not necessarily sexual violence?"

"Yes."

"They can occur separately with no sexual connotation?"

"Of course."

"And when they occur in conjunction with indications of sexual assault, may I ask what irrefutable logic leads you to the conclusion that they must—I say *must*—be in some way connected?"

"They usually are."

"That's hardly irrefutable logic. Is it not possible for cuts and bruises to appear in conjunction with signs of sexual penetration without their having any intrinsic connection with that sexual penetration?"

"Yes, it's possible," the doctor said irritably.

"And is it not *im*possible to determine merely by medical examination whether or not such indications are in any way connected even though they appear in conjunction?"

"It's logical to assume—"

"Is that what you've been doing, Doctor, assuming?"

"Of course not."

"Did you not assume that the cuts and bruises suffered by Ida Praul were inflicted in connection with her alleged rape?"

"Yes."

"Is it a fact that you are basing your conclusions on the fact that Ida Praul told you she had been raped?"

"More than that. I examined the girl. I saw the condition she was in and it is obvious she was raped."

"That is for the jury to decide. By your own statement, you cannot prove it by medical examination. You were called here to testify as to the results of your examination of Ida Praul. Your factual testimony has been that she suffered damage to the tissues about her vagina from sexual penetration, that she suffered cuts and bruises about the arms, legs and feet, that when you examined her she was in shock."

"But she said she had been raped."

"Your Honor, it is perfectly obvious that Dr. McKenna's conclusions are based on hearsay. They are incompetent and I move that they be stricken."

"Dr. McKenna is testifying as a medical expert. It is perfectly proper," Cardamone shouted.

"Order!" Judge Forsythe shouted, "Order! Order! The recorder will read the doctor's original testimony and I will rule on the motion."

The recorder rose and read the transcript without interruption until "Question: Would you say, Doctor, that this damage could have been inflicted by a sexual assault? Answer: Yes."

"I object, your Honor," Stephen said. "The witness has testified subsequently that the damage he found could have been inflicted by other forms of sexual penetration than assault."

"Dr. McKenna," the judge said, "could you clarify your testimony on this point?"

"It is unlikely, but possible, that such severe damage could have been inflicted through ignorance or accident."

"The jury will note that Doctor McKenna's previous testimony is so qualified. Will the recorder proceed?"

The recorder read on until "Answer: It would be impossible to determine that with any certainty, but the extent of the damage would surely be commensurate with a multiple rape or rape more than once by the same man. Ques—"

"Objection, your Honor," Stephen said. "The doctor is still assuming the rape which it is incumbent upon the People to prove." His voice became weary as he said, "He ought to have testified, commensurate with multiple rape or multiple sexual intercourse with inexperienced or ignorant people or sexual intercourse more than once by the same inexperienced or ignorant person."

"Sustained," the judge said equally wearily. "The jury will so note."

The recorder read: "Question: was there any other evidence of rape?"

"Objection," Stephen said. "I request either striking the word 'other' or altering the question to 'other evidence of *possible* rape.'"

"The recorder will enter, '. . . other evidence of possible rape,' without the italics read by Mr. Hertzog."

The recorder read: "Answer: There were cuts and bruises about the legs and feet and arms, and the patient was limping from a sprained ankle. She was also in shock, she kept muttering, 'They raped me.'"

"May I question the witness on this point, your Honor?" Stephen asked.

"Yes."

"Dr. McKenna, would you consider it wise to take literally anything said by a patient who is in shock?"

"No, I would not. I merely testified as to what she said."

"Yes, notably without an opinion, this time," Stephen said. "Is it not true that the mind of a shock victim is hazy and confused, and that any statement of such a victim would be unreliable?"

"That is true," the doctor said.

"That's all, your Honor," Stephen said, sitting down.

"You may step down, Dr. McKenna," the judge said. "Go on, Mr. Cardamone."

Cardamone again conferred with his assistant and with Peg Praul. "The prosecution calls Mrs. Margaret Praul."

Peg Praul went to the stand with an assumed assurance, but she was visibly shaky. She wore a neat but tasteless gray dress and, secure in the knowledge that its source was her secret, the utterly inappropriate little hat which Charlie had given her.

After the technicalities, the district attorney began, "Now, Mrs. Praul, I know this is difficult for you . . ."

Stephen flashed a sardonic glance at Jim Beyers.

". . . but would you tell us in your own words what happened on the morning of August twenty-fourth of this year?"

Peg Praul raised a bone-dry handkerchief to her bone-dry eyes, then said, "I was sleepin' when I heard my little Ida callin' me."

"What time was this?"

"It must have been about six o'clock. When I got out of bed an' saw her standin' there, all hurt and bleedin', my heart nearly broke. I took her into the kitchen an' started cleanin' her up. She was all full of dirt an' grass an' everything. Well, I started cleanin' off all those cuts, an' askin' her questions at the same time."

"Did she tell you what happened to her that night?"

"My poor little baby didn't even know the right words to tell me what happened. She kept sayin' 'They did it.'"

"After that you took her directly to the Borough Hall."

"Yes."

"What happened then?"

"Well, we waited at the Borough Hall till they brought them in, the ones there who did it," she said, gesturing toward the defendants.

"Objection, your Honor," Stephen said.

"Sustained," Judge Forsythe said. "Mrs. Praul, you may testify only as to what you did or what you witnessed. The court is not interested in your opinion as to the guilt or innocence of the defendants."

Peg looked flustered. "Did anything happen while you were waiting?" Mr. Cardamone asked.

"Just Ben Summerfield took down Ida's story. Then they brought them—the uh, defendants—in one by one. Then Dr. McKenna came in an' took Ida across the hall an' examined her. Then he said she been raped and called the ambulance. We got in the ambulance an' went to the hospital."

"What happened at the hospital?"

"Nothin' much. I just waited around till the afternoon. They told me Ida was okay. She was sleepin', they said. An' I went . . . on home."

"No more questions. Mr. Hertzog?"

"Mrs. Praul," Stephen said, walking toward the witness stand, "you have testified that at about six o'clock on the morning of August twenty-fourth you heard Ida come into your room and call your name."

"Yeah."

"Would you tell the court what you did on the night of August twenty-third?"

"That's irrelevant, your Honor," Mr. Cardamone said.

"Indeed?" the judge said, looking over his spectacles at Mr. Cardamone. "How do you know? You haven't heard yet what she did. Go on, Mrs. Praul."

"I . . . I didn't do much of anything."

"I didn't ask you how much or how little you did of whatever you did. Just tell us, please, how you spent the evening—or the night."

"I . . . I entertained a . . . a friend."

"A gentleman or a lady?"

"That *is* irrelevant, your Honor," Mr. Cardamone said, standing and throwing his pencil down on the stack of papers before him.

"Oh, Mr. Cardamone, be still for a minute!" Judge Forsythe said. "If this testimony proves to be irrelevant, we'll strike it, but you'd have to be even more prescient than district attorneys usually are to know whether it is or isn't."

"Was it a gentleman or a lady, Mrs. Praul?" Stephen asked again.

"It was a gentleman," Peg Praul said almost brazenly.

"Was Ida at home while you were entertaining?"

"No, she went out."

"And what time did your gentleman leave?"

"I object, your Honor," Mr. Cardamone said heatedly. "The phrase 'your gentleman' is a deliberate attempt to connote . . . something prejudicial and other than . . . the truth." Joseph F. Cardamone, realizing the grave error into which Stephen Hertzog had led him, stared at his adversary with something very close to hatred. The hatred might have been merely anger had Stephen not been smiling faintly in return.

Understanding fully that Mr. Cardamone deserved this tactical defeat, Judge Forsythe delivered his official reprimand. "I suppose that the phrase 'your gentleman' conveys a meaning, at least in a literary sense, which in this case, we do not know to be either accurate or inaccurate. Objection sustained."

"At what time did your guest leave?" Stephen asked with enormous satisfaction.

Peg Praul, who had understood none of this exchange, said, "I don't know. Maybe twelve."

"Mrs. Praul," Stephen said, "the future of three young men depends on the accuracy of every answer given in this trial. You must try to be as accurate as possible. Do you remember at what time your guest left?"

"No."

"May I assume that it was not before midnight?"

"Yeah, I guess it was later than that."

"Is that as close to the exact time as you can determine?"

"Yeah."

"All right. Your guest left at sometime after midnight. What did you do then?"

"I . . . I went to bed. It was late."

As he stared at Peg Praul, Stephen's eyebrows were lowered in a deep frown. He turned this same look to Judge Forsythe and then to the jury. "Would you tell us *exactly* what you did from the minute your guest left until you went to bed?"

"You mean . . . everything?"

"Everything."

"Your Honor, I object," Mr. Cardamone said.

"Overruled."

"Everything, Mrs. Praul."

"Well . . . I went to the bathroom . . . to clean up an' all . . . an' . . . an' I went to . . . turned out the light an' went to bed."

For a dangerous instant Stephen felt almost sorry for Peg Praul in her utter ignorance of his motives. Resuming his low-eyebrowed expression, he said, "Did you know at that moment where your daughter was?"

"Sure," Peg said immediately, "she was out on the porch in . . ."

In the silence there was an instant of unknown accord among Janet McNaughton, Robert R. Dickinson and Ira Bickford.

329

"No, Mrs. Praul, she was not on the back porch. But did you go to see whether or not she was?" Stephen said.

"Well . . . sure . . . I checked."

Joseph F. Cardamone threw down his pencil again.

"And seeing that at some undetermined hour of the early morning your seventeen-year-old daughter was not at home, what did you do?"

"I was . . . worried."

"And what did you do?"

Peg Praul stared at her questioner, exhibiting all of her worst and best qualities, much like a helpless gray-brown rat in a trap.

"And what did you do, Mrs. Praul?" Stephen repeated.

"I called the po—"

"You called whom?"

"I called a friend . . . to ask if they seen . . . Ida."

"Oh? And had your friend seen Ida?"

"No, they didn't."

"And did you panic then over your daughter's unaccountable absence?"

"Sure," Peg Praul said eagerly, "I was scared."

"And what did you do?"

"I . . . I waited up for her."

"You waited up for her?" Stephen said, his tone frankly unbelieving.

"Yeah!" Peg said, prolonging the syllable in a marked effort at conviction.

"The court is under the impression from your previous testimony that you—may I ask the recorder to read Mrs. Praul's testimony as to her actions after her guest left her home?"

In a lugubrious tone the recorder read, "Well. I went to the bathroom to clean up an' all an' I went to—turned out the light an' went to bed."

"You weren't lying when you said that, were you Mrs. Praul?" Stephen asked.

"No! I ain't no liar."

"Then your testimony is that when your guest left, you went to the bathroom, looked in on the bedroom of your absent daughter, telephoned a friend to ask if the friend had seen your daughter and then went to bed. And the next testimony you are able to give is that your daughter woke you at six o'clock that morning?"

Peg Praul stared at Stephen Hertzog. "Is that your testimony?"

Into the silence Judge Forsythe said, "Answer the question, Mrs. Praul."

"Yeah," Peg Praul said almost inaudibly.

"You did not telephone the police as to your daughter's whereabouts?"

"No."

"You did not telephone any of the local hospitals to see if she had been in an accident?"

"No."

"Was it customary for your daughter to be out until the small hours of the morning without your knowing her whereabouts?"

"No. No."

"You merely telephoned one friend?"

"Ye—yeah."

"Did you not care enough to make further inquiries?"

"I object, your Honor."

"I withdraw the question," Stephen said. "Mrs. Praul, when your daughter *finally* returned to your home that morning, and you began to administer a kind of first aid because of her obvious injuries, she told you of what she said was the attack upon her by the defendants. Is that correct?"

"Yeah."

"You have testified that you became fearful that she might be more seriously hurt than you had suspected at first. Is that correct?"

"Yeah."

"And being fearful of that possibly more serious injury, what did you do?"

"I took her right away to the Borough Hall."

"Is there a medical staff at the Borough Hall?"

"What?"

"Is there a medical staff, are there medical facilities, at the Borough Hall?"

"They got a . . . a . . . police doctor."

"Is he in residence at the Borough Hall?"

"Is he . . .? I don't know what you—"

"You don't know what I mean? I mean, Mrs. Praul, that you have *testified* that you were fearful of serious physical injury to your daughter. But did you call a doctor or take her to a doctor?"

"N—no."

"Did you take her to a hospital?"

"No."

"Did you make any attempt to secure medical attention for your daughter?"

"I . . . I took her to the Borough Hall."

"And at what time did Dr. McKenna arrive?"

"I . . . I don't . . . I'm not sure. It wasn't very—"

"According to the police report, it was eight-thirty-five A.M. when Dr. McKenna arrived. Had you requested a physician before then, Mrs. Praul?"

"Well, sure . . . I . . ."

"You did, Mrs. Praul? Then you are in disagreement with the official police report, which states that it was Magistrate Harry Loomis who finally requested the attendance of a physician. Did you ask for a doctor, Mrs. Praul?"

"I guess . . . I guess I was too upset."

"Did you ask for a doctor?"

"N—no."

"In other words, you sat in the Borough Hall for a little more than two hours without trying to get a doctor for her?" Stephen asked very slowly. "Have you any concern at all for your daughter's welfare?"

"I object, your Honor!" Mr. Cardamone shouted.

"I withdraw the question and leave this jury, as good parents, to draw their own conclusions. No more questions."

"I object!" the district attorney shouted again as Stephen returned to his chair.

"Strike the last remark of the attorney for the defense," Judge Forsythe said. "You will refrain in the future from making prejudicial remarks for the benefit of the jury, Mr. Hertzog."

At this moment Ira Bickford's eyes accidentally met those of Robert R. Dickinson, and Mr. Bickford's eyebrows went up and his brow wrinkled in an expression which was meant to convey no more than interest. He was again admiring Stephen Hertzog's cleverness, but was also aware that although he had certainly reached no decision in this matter, he would never again think of Peg Praul as innocent. He did not, however, recognize this feeling as a loss of sympathy with the prosecution.

In answer to Mr. Bickford's inscrutable expression, Mr. Dickinson smiled suddenly and surprisingly, as if by being observed in thought and without his smile he had been caught napping. The thought that had so distracted him from his external concern was that Peg Praul was the one to be punished. He *did* realize the loss of sympathy with the prosecution, but Peg Praul was such inflammable fuel for the fires of hell that Mr. Dickinson could not resist.

"I think this might be a very good place to pause for lunch," Judge

Forsythe was saying, "unless you have some objection, gentlemen." Neither Stephen nor Mr. Cardamone spoke. "Well, then we will recess for lunch until one-thirty."

When Stephen reached John and Mary, John said, "You certainly tore into Peg Praul, didn't you?"

"There are times, as I'm afraid you'll soon see, when you have to do that just for tactical reasons. But I must say with Peg Praul it was too easy. Come on, let's have some lunch." They went to the restaurant in the Valley Forge Hotel on Harris Street.

The jury went to lunch, too, in the same restaurant, and under the watchful eye of the uniformed policeman who accompanied them, they discussed the food, the weather, their gratitude for the comfortable chairs in the jury box, the cost of living and the gradual discovery that two of the male members of the jury were fourth cousins. They did not discuss the fact that Stephen Hertzog had so roused their interest, that Janet McNaughton was blithely convinced that the boys would go free, Robert R. Dickinson was out of sympathy with the prosecution, and Ira Bickford had begun to wonder if those two younger boys, at least, were capable of rape.

Part of the afternoon session was consumed by the examination of the staff doctor from Audubon Hospital who had treated Ida. Stephen wrung from him the same qualifications which he had got from Dr. McKenna. When this was over, the district attorney said, "Your Honor, the People's next witness will be the complainant, Ida Praul. I'm afraid my examination may consume quite a lot of time. I wonder if it wouldn't be better to adjourn until tomorrow so that we could go through her testimony without interruption."

"It's not all that late, Mr. Cardamone," the judge replied. "Why don't you begin, and if you run a little late, we'll all just go along with you. I'd like to see this trial brought to as speedy a conclusion as possible."

"All right, your Honor. Then I call Miss Ida Praul."

Cardamone had been afraid from the expression on Ida's face that she might refuse to take the witness stand, but after a moment or two spent in looking helplessly from him to her mother, Ida rose and went, shamefaced, to the front of the courtroom.

Ida swore inaudibly to tell the whole truth, and then stood trembling visibly as Mr. Cardamone approached her.

"Would you tell the court your name, Ida?" he said.

"Ida Irene Praul," she whispered.

"You'll have to speak a little louder, Ida, so that the jury over there and Judge Forsythe, too, can hear everything you say. All right?" Ida nodded. "Now, tell them your name again."

"Ida Irene Praul," she answered audibly but hoarsely, and she quickly cleared her throat with an unpleasant sound.

"Virginia Lukens has testified that on the night of August twenty-third of this year you and she went to the movies. Is that true?"

Ida nodded again.

"Miss Praul," Judge Forsythe said, "you must answer the questions more loudly so that we can hear you. You mustn't merely nod or shake your head."

"Yes," she said loudly, staring at the judge in near terror.

"You started for a walk after the movies. Is that right?" Mr. Cardamone continued.

"Yes."

"What happened during that walk, Ida?"

"We . . . just talked."

"I mean, how did the walk end?"

"We met some boys outside Fordyce's Candy Store," Ida said.

"You both met them, Ida?"

"No, just me."

"Ida, you'll have to be very careful to tell us exactly what happened. Would you tell us now exactly what happened when you got to Fordyce's Candy Store."

"When we got just a little past there, some boys . . ."

"Which boys?"

Ida looked at the defendants with so sad an expression that it was clear that she felt she was doing them a disservice. "Them," she said, "Johnny Taylor, Artie Schlier and Armand Rapp."

"All right, Ida. Go on."

"They called me over."

"All three of them?"

"No, it was Armand."

"Ida, that's what I mean when I say you must be very careful. If one of the boys said something to you, you must tell us which one. You mustn't just say 'they'—unless, of course, you mean 'they.' "

"All right. Well, after a while I went—"

"What was it that Armand said to you?"

Ida surprised everyone by looking even paler than she had before.

"I don't know," she said.

"Are you sure, Ida?"

"I can't say that!" she whispered.

Mr. Bickford's image of innocence returned to him in full force.

"Your Honor, much of the testimony from here on will be of an indelicate nature. Understandably, a girl of Ida Praul's tender age who has been through so horrible an experience may well have difficulty in speaking out about such things in open court. I request that I be allowed to repeat any part of her testimony that, due to her shyness and to emotional strain, is inaudible."

"I object, your Honor," Stephen said in a decidedly deprecating tone. "Both the district attorney's remarks and this entire theatrical procedure are designed to influence the jury. I request that the phrase 'who has been through so horrible an experience' be stricken and that the district attorney's request be denied on the grounds that it is prejudicial."

"Your objection to the district attorney's phrase is sustained," Judge Forsythe said. "The remark will be stricken. Mr. Cardamone, if you will instruct the witness to do her utmost to testify for herself, the court will permit you to assist her during her lapses. However, you must keep to the normal method of questioning. Proceed, Mr. Cardamone."

"Will you tell us, Ida," the district attorney said, "what Armand Rapp said to you?"

Ida whispered to Mr. Cardamone, and Judge Forsythe sighed heavily.

"He said, 'Where did you get that sweater with the bumps on it?' Is that right, Ida?" Mr. Cardamone said.

"Yes," Ida answered, hanging her head.

"Your Honor, this is ridiculous," Stephen said getting to his feet. "Subsequent testimony will reveal that this tenderly youthful witness felt no compunction at saying things which would make a sailor blush. I do not see why—"

"I demand that that remark be stricken from the record!" Mr. Cardamone shouted. "The attorney for the defense has no right to cast aspersions—"

"The theatricality of your strategy gives me license to—"

"Gentlemen!" the judge shouted. "You are in a court of law and you will conduct yourselves accordingly. Mr. Hertzog, I have already ruled on your objection. You in turn will refrain from disparaging the witness, and you will refrain from references to testimony not yet recorded. Now we will proceed in order, gentlemen."

"Ida," the district attorney began, "if Armand Rapp made such a vulgar remark to you, why did you go over to talk to him?"

"Oh, I didn't go to talk to him. I went to talk to Johnny—and Artie. They don't have a dirty mouth like Armand."

"What happened then?"

"Well, we talked for a little while. Then they asked me to go for a ride with them."

"Who asked you?"

"I . . . I guess it was Armand . . . but Johnny asked me, too."

"Did they ask you to go for a ride to any particular place?"

"Just around town."

"Around town. There was absolutely no mention of leaving the limits of the borough, was there?"

"No."

"There was no suggestion that you drive to any lonely spot—or that you stop anywhere at all?"

"No, just around town."

"When did you first realize that these men—"

"I object, your Honor," Stephen said. "We do not refer to minors as men. Two of them, at least, are boys—children."

Judge Forsythe said, "Try not to work your way down to 'tots,' Mr. Hertzog. Objection sustained."

"When did you first realize that the defendants intended to leave the borough limits?"

"I object, your honor," Stephen shouted. "It has not been established that there was any premeditation involved in the route chosen by Armand Rapp."

"The route was discussed and deviated from by will," Mr. Cardamone said.

"By will, but entirely spontaneously," Stephen said.

"Mr. Hertzog," the judge said, "you have no more right to suggest spontaneity than Mr. Cardamone has to assume premeditation. Both the question and the objection will be stricken."

"When did you first realize, Ida, that the defendants were not merely driving around town?"

"When we were on the bridge."

"And what did you say?"

"I told Armand to take me back—take me home."

"And he did not?"

"No, he just said we were just goin' for a little ride."

"Did you insist that he take you home?"

"Yes, I kept tellin' him to take me home. I had to get home."

"And each time he refused?"

"Yes."

"And the others?"

"They said we was just goin' for a little ride, too. No. No, that's not right. Johnny said that maybe they ought to take me home."

"But in any event, they did not take you home?"

"No. They turned off the main road onto a bumpy dirt road. Armand said it was a short cut back to town. But it wasn't."

"He deliberately led you to believe that he was taking you home by a short cut, when in reality he had turned onto a dead-end road?"

"Yes," Ida answered quietly.

"When did you discover that the road didn't lead back to town?"

"When Armand stopped the car. I asked him why he stopped and he said it was because the road didn't go nowhere."

"And then?"

"That's . . . when it happened."

"When what happened, Ida?"

"That's when they started."

"Miss Praul," the judge said, "will you try to speak a little louder?"

"What did they start to do?" Mr. Cardamone asked.

"They . . . put their . . . I can't, Mr. Cardamone!" Ida said, and tears glistened on her cheeks.

"I'm afraid you'll have to tell us, Ida," Mr. Cardamone said softly.

"They . . . held me against the seat . . . and . . ."

"They held you against the seat?" the district attorney asked loudly.

"Yes."

"And what did they do to you?"

"They . . . they put their hands on me . . . all over!" Ida said and burst into open sobbing.

"The jury didn't hear that," the judge said.

"The witness said: 'They put their hands on me . . . all over.'"

Mr. Cardamone waited for a moment, looking at Ida with great concern. The jury, too, watched her until their watching what should have been this private agony embarrassed them. Then some turned their eyes to the defendants, each of whom had found some trivial preoccupation (the manipulation of a pencil, the traceable grain in the wood of the table, unmanicured fingernails) to divert his attention. Janet McNaughton had begun to relate her responsibility for her sons—and, therefore, to some measure, for all sons—to a new responsibility for Ida Praul. Mr. Dickinson was caught between the temptation to smile, which he felt would appear callous, and allowing righteous wrath to show on his face. He chose the latter, and John Taylor cringed, seeing his face change.

"Try to be calm, Ida," Mr. Cardamone said. "Did all of them do this?"

"Yes," Ida sobbed, "all at once."

"All three of them at once pawed and mauled you. . . ."

"I object," Stephen shouted, springing to his feet. "The district attorney is putting words into the witness's mouth. She did not say 'pawed' or 'mauled.' "

"Objection sustained."

"How long did this . . . putting on of hands . . . last?" Mr. Cardamone asked.

"I . . . I don't know. I was awful scared. I kept askin' 'em to take me home."

"Do you think it might have been ten minutes—or fifteen?"

"Yes."

"Both?" Stephen asked.

"You are out of order, Mr. Hertzog," the judge said.

"Your Honor, the witness did not answer the question. Nor was the question properly asked. If the witness doesn't know how long it was, she doesn't know."

"Mr. Hertzog," Judge Forsythe said, "when the court hears an improper question, it will so rule. I admonish you strongly against further attempts to usurp the powers of the bench."

"I certainly did not mean to do that, your Honor."

"If you have an objection in the future—and we feel fairly sure in our expectations thereof—you will properly phrase it as an objection, not as an instruction to the court."

"Yes, your Honor."

"Ida," Mr. Cardamone went on, "do you have any idea how long you were in the car once you had stopped?"

"I guess . . . maybe ten minutes."

"And you were pinned against the seat during that time?"

"Yes."

"Did you struggle—try to get away?"

"Yes, but they were stronger than me."

"Indeed, they were. Before we go any further, Ida, is there anything else you want to tell us about what happened in the car? Were the 'boys' doing anything else?"

"Oh, they were drinkin' from a whiskey bottle."

"Did you drink any whiskey, Ida?"

"No, I don't do that."

"All right, Ida. The boys held you in the car and put their hands all over you. Then what happened?"

"They took me out of the car and—"

"They *took* you out of the car?"

"They held me and . . . and pushed me out of the car."

"Did they force you out of the car?"

"Yes."

"And then?"

"They . . . forced me through some weeds . . . to . . . to the hill."

"Could you describe how they forced you?"

"Two of them . . . I guess it was Armand and Artie . . . they took me by the arms . . . and . . . and kind of dragged me . . ."

"And you resisted, struggled?"

"Yes . . . but Armand grabbed my neck and—"

"Grabbed your neck? How?"

"With . . . his thumb and fingers . . . and squeezed . . . so it hurt me bad." Janet McNaughton's shoulders sagged somewhat as she imagined the pressure on her own neck. "Then I think . . . Artie went away somewhere, and then I was on the hill with Armand . . . and Artie and Johnny came up and were standin' there, too."

"They forced you from the car and dragged you to the hill. And you struggled and resisted physically with all your strength?"

"Yes."

"Did you say anything?"

"I asked them not to do anything to me . . . to let me go . . . take me home. I told 'em I . . . I never done it before."

"You told them you'd never done it before? They knew that in advance? You were pleading with them?"

"Yes."

"Your Honor, may I suggest that Mr. Cardamone be content with the witness's description of the scene?" Stephen said. "He has been constantly rephrasing her answers purely for dramatic effect."

"The district attorney is so instructed," Judge Forsythe said.

"You were on the hill with all three of the defendants. Were you standing?"

"Yes."

"What happened then?"

"Armand hit me on the legs."

"Hit you on the legs?"

"Yes, behind the knees . . . to make me fall down. Then . . ." Ida began to cry again, and Mr. Bickford's large, rough hands clasped each other, like two animals of the same species seeking mutual protective warmth.

"Yes, Ida, you fell down. Then what?"

"They jumped . . . on top of me."

"We didn't hear that," the judge said.

"Say it again, Ida," Mr. Cardamone said.

"They . . . they jumped on top of me."

"Who jumped on top of you, Ida?"

"I guess . . . Johnnie and Artie. I can remember . . . Armand standin' over me. One of them was . . . holdin' down my legs, and the other one . . . was . . . holdin' my arms."

"So you were lying on the ground, helplessly pinned down by Johnny Taylor and Artie Schlier?"

"Yes."

"And then?"

"I can't," Ida said.

"You have to, Ida."

"Armand . . . got on top of me . . . and he did . . . it to me."

"The witness said: 'Armand got on top of me and he did it to me.'"

There was a new stillness in the courtroom.

"What happened then?"

"I . . . I don't remember too clear. I felt . . . it hurt awful bad."

"I trust that the jury did hear that," Mr. Cardamone said. "Go on, Ida."

"I . . . must've fainted. I can't remem—oh, I can't, Mr. Cardamone!" she wailed and hid her face in her hands. The spectators murmured loudly, and the jury, almost as a group, shifted in their chairs. Jim Beyers looked at Stephen and shook his head slightly.

Stephen whispered, "It could be worse."

"I don't see how," Jim answered.

Mary Taylor's fingernails cut deeply into her palms. John stared expressionlessly at the back of his son's head. Mrs. Schlier's bulk shook with a quiet sobbing as Mr. Schlier comforted her silently. Only George Rapp seemed to be asleep in the last row of the benches.

"It won't be much longer, Ida," Mr. Cardamone was saying. "Try to go on."

"Armand . . . got up after . . . after a while. I . . . I don't know how long it was . . . I fainted or . . ." she sobbed again.

"Yes, Ida. And then?"

"Then . . . I guess Artie . . . did it."

"The witness said: 'Then I guess Artie did it.' Were you conscious then?"

"I woke up . . . and he was doin' it to me."

Mr. Cardamone turned toward the jury, looked into the eyes of each juror, shook his head and turned back to Ida.

"John Barrymore," Stephen whispered audibly.

"What happened then, Ida?"

"I was layin' there . . . awake, I guess, but I couldn't move. Then Johnny . . ." Suddenly she wailed, "Johnny did it to me, too!"

The wail sailed like a child's paper airplane out through the silent courtroom.

"Ida," the district attorney said, "Ida, do you remember what happened then?"

"The last I remember . . . was hearin' their voices gettin' . . . quieter. They must've gone away then."

"They went away and left you lying on that hillside?"

"Yes. I laid there all night. I don't know . . . if I was awake or not. Part of the time, I guess I was. I don't know. When I saw the sun comin' up, I got up and started . . . down the hill."

"Were you in pain while you were there?"

"Yes," Ida said quietly.

"And you got up when you saw the sun?"

"Yes. I guess . . . I fell, goin' down the hill. My ankle hurt bad. But I got to the bridge, and I went on home to my mama."

Cardamone turned to the jury and then back to the judge.

"I have no further questions, your Honor."

Slowly and effortlessly, Stephen put down the pencil he had held during most of Ida's testimony and got to his feet.

"Your Honor," he said, "I realize that it is rather late, and yet I wonder if it would not be kinder to the witness to continue with my cross-examination—which will not be as long as the prosecution's examination—and have it done with. I think she might well spend a more restful night if the entire procedure were behind her."

Jim Beyers winced, for he knew well that Stephen's real motive was to cross-examine Ida at her most vulnerable.

"Your Honor," Mr. Cardamone said, "I think the witness has been through enough for one day. I suggest that we adjourn until tomorrow."

After a moment Judge Forsythe said, "I am, of course, in sympathy with both points of view. But taking the larger picture, Mr. Cardamone, it seems to me that the wheels of justice move slowly enough as it is. It would expedite this trial to finish the cross-examination today, and I think the broader purposes of justice would be best served. Proceed, Mr. Hertzog."

Stephen knew quite well that his decision, which seemed a minor victory, could only antagonize an already hostile jury. From Mr. Dickinson to Mrs. McNaughton they regarded Ida's story as clear and simple truth, and they resented, were shocked by, what they knew must be Stephen's attempt to mitigate and lessen the effect of that truth. In their view such an attempt was further victimizing this innocent victim.

Stephen moved slowly to the witness stand and said, "Ida, you feel well enough to go on for a few more minutes, don't you?"

"Yes," Ida said.

"Now, then, your description of the events that occurred once the car had stopped was remarkably detailed. I feel, though, that your description of the events—and the conversations—which occurred before that was a little sketchy. It was almost as if there were some things you weren't telling us."

"Objection, your Honor," Mr. Cardamone said.

"Sustained."

"Ida, after Armand made the vulgar remark about the sweater with the bumps on it," Stephen said so matter-of-factly that the vulgarity nearly faded, "what did you say to him? Do you remember?"

"No."

"Ah, no," Stephen said genially. "Did you not ask him what it was that he wanted to tell you when he called you over to him?"

"I . . . don't . . . yes, I guess so."

"Did you ask him more than once what he wanted?"

"I guess . . . I did. Yes."

"And what did he tell you?"

"I'm not sure."

"Oh, I think it was fairly memorable, Ida. Try to remember."

"I . . . I can't . . . say it," Ida sobbed.

"I'm afraid I can't say it for you, Ida," Stephen said gently. "You'll have to tell us."

"It . . . it was . . . a joke."

"A joke? Do you remember it?"

"Your Honor," Mr. Cardamone said, "this is entirely irrelevant."

"Irrelevant?" Stephen shouted, turning suddenly, fiercely on the district attorney. "I intend to demonstrate that this girl spoke and behaved lewdly with the sole purpose of sexually exciting the three boys in her presence! If that is irrelevant to the issues of this trial, I do not understand the issues!"

It couldn't be! Mr. Bickford told himself.

There was a silence during which Judge Forsythe's countenance became deeply solemn. He looked at Mr. Cardamone and said, quietly, "Objection overruled."

"Ida," Stephen said quietly, "would you tell us the joke?"

"I . . . I can't remember," Ida said, with tears streaming down her cheeks.

"I think you can, Ida. Try."

"It was . . . about a . . . a traveling salesman . . ."

"Yes. Go on, Ida."

Ida's quiet, breathy gasps were the only sound in the courtroom.

"He . . . he spent the night . . . with . . . with the farmer's . . . daughter. . . ."

"Yes, Ida. Go on."

She was crying now, and her eyes were closed, but her voice came through the sound of her weeping as if another being were speaking from inside her.

"The next morning . . . the farmer asked her . . . what happened. . . ."

Ida stood for a moment, crying loudly, without speaking.

"And what did she say?"

"She said . . . 'He let me play . . . with his . . . dolly.' And . . . the farmer asked her what . . . the dolly was like. And the daughter said, 'It was . . . it was an awful funny dolly . . . It didn't have any . . . any arms or legs. . . .' "

Ida leaned on the marble wall of the witness box and wailed, and the wail chased the words into the silent air of the courtroom.

"And what did you do when you heard this . . . joke, Ida?"

"I don't know," Ida said in a long sustained cry.

"Yes, you do," Stephen said very quietly, looking at the floor.

"I . . . laughed."

"And did Johnny Taylor say, 'That's not so bad, Ida?' "

"Yes," Ida answered. Her voice was loud and clear, for it had reached the level of her crying.

"And did you answer, 'No, not really, I guess. I know lots worse'?"

"Yes."

"When there was some conversation about your sitting on the pipe railing, did Armand Rapp say to you, 'Come on up here and sit on *this* pipe?' with an obviously obscene double meaning?"

"Yes."

"And did you recoil from this obscenity and leave the presence of these boys?"

"No."

"And when they suggested that you sit in Armand's car with them, did you not say that you knew what could happen if you did, and that you'd been in cars with boys before, and that you only sit in cars with boys that you wanted to sit with? And did you not, having said all of these things, fully understanding their sexual implications, get into the car with the three boys of your own free will?"

"Yes. Yes."

"And did you not brag to Armand Rapp that you could show him what a man and a woman do together?"

"Yes."

"And did you not agree immediately to go for a 'little ride'?"

"Yes."

Stephen looked at Ida with apparent sympathy and pity, then turned abruptly to the jury and said, "With all due respect for the complainant, I submit to the jury that this is hardly a classic picture of the reluctant virgin." Then he went to his chair and sat down.

Over the sound of Ida's sobs, Judge Forsythe said, "If you have no further questions, Mr. Cardamone, I suggest that Mrs. Praul help her daughter from the stand." The district attorney shook his head weakly.

Court was immediately adjourned until nine o'clock the next morning.

The jurors did not move immediately. Ira Bickford was not sure now that the proof he had so complacently expected would ever be forthcoming. Robert R. Dickinson was frustrated by the absence of a clearly deserving object for his punishment. Janet Somers McNaughton wished that she had not volunteered for jury duty. The clear and simple truth which they had snapped at so eagerly (for only a clear and simple truth would make their responsibility entirely bearable) had become a labyrinth out of which they knew they might never find their way.

Stephen and Jim Beyers, too, sat nearly motionless at the table until the courtroom had cleared except for them and John and Mary. Then Stephen rose and walked toward them, Jim following.

Stephen looked directly into John's eyes and said, sourly, "Not very pretty, was it?"

"Stephen . . ." John began.

"I have to keep telling myself that she *did* say those things, that they *are* part of the trial, that it's my duty to my clients to expose her. Well, maybe I'll feel better about it when Cardamone gets hold of the boys."

"I have a feeling we're ahead," Jim Beyers said.

"There's a good chance," Stephen said.

"Are you leaving, Jim?" John asked.

"Not just yet. I'll call you when I get home," Jim said. He had seen Mr. Cardamone approaching them.

"Nicely done, Mr. Hertzog," Cardamone said without a trace of humor.

"I suppose you're going to tell me," Stephen said, "that you would have let the opportunity pass because you're such a nice guy."

"Like hell I would," Cardamone said. "I said nicely done, and that's what I meant, but you don't expect me to be happy about it, do you? See you tomorrow," he said and walked down the hall.

"I think he likes you," Jim said, watching the district attorney's progress through the corridor.

"It's called grudging admiration and I always consider it a half-insult. Well, let's leave the marble halls of justice."

They said good night outside the courthouse and parted.

As Jim was walking toward his car he heard a feminine voice which he knew, calling his name.

"Jim. Jim Beyers," it called. "Over here," it added as he looked about.

On the other side of Green Street he saw Betty Allen, standing by her car with the key already inserted to unlock the door. She beckoned eagerly, and Jim crossed the street.

"It was exciting today, wasn't it?" she said in a confidential tone. "Your friend Mr. Hertzog really tore that terrible little Praul girl to absolute shreds!"

"I'm afraid it was necessary, Betty," Jim said.

"Necessary? It was just too . . . exciting. It makes Perry Mason seem dull."

"I didn't even see you in court," Jim said.

"Oh, I was there. I've been just furious for days. I had planned on being here every day, but wouldn't you just know Nancy would pick just this time to come down with a virus. I wanted to get a nurse to stay with her so I'd be free to come to the trial, but Fred absolutely forbade it." She smiled and tapped Jim on the shoulder coyly. "Said my public-spiritedness was just idle curiosity, and he'd be damned if he'd pay a nurse just to indulge me. So Nancy went back to school today and here I am, just aching with disappointment at having missed so much."

"It isn't all that theatrical, Betty."

"Oh, you're just used to it. But for us lay people it's just too . . . exciting. How much longer do you think it'll be?"

"Not very much. Another day or two probably."

"Damn! Well, at least I haven't missed all the exciting parts. When will the district attorney question Peg Praul about the bribe?"

"About the—"

"Oh, come on, Jim. You know it's all over town. Everybody knows about it."

Jim looked at her, seemingly dispassionately, for a moment. "It won't come up, Betty. It isn't evidence."

"Isn't evidence? Why, it's practically admitting—"

"Only if it were made with the knowledge and consent of the accused would a bribe be evidence. If that kind of thing were permitted, your worst enemy could go out and try to bribe somebody if you were accused of a crime, just to prejudice a jury. The whole incident simply has nothing to do with the case."

"Well, Kay told me it'd be practically fatal when it came out in court."

"Exemplary proof that Kay doesn't know what she's talking about. And I wish she'd stay out of these things."

"Oh, Jim, she must have thought it would come up. . . ."

"I don't care what she thought. I told her it was inadmissable as evidence."

"Well, she must have told me about it before you told her that. She—"

"She couldn't have. She didn't know about it. She heard it for the first time while we were at the club, and I told her immediately that it couldn't be introduced in court."

"You must be mistaken, Jim. Kay wouldn't deliberately lie about it."

"Well, whether you like to think so or not, she did deliberately lie to you. Because at the time she heard about the bribe attempt, she also heard about its irrelevance to the trial. And that was a couple of days after the Labor Day picnic. We had gone to the club to—"

"Now, you see, you are mistaken. She knew about it long before that. It was in August I think. Yes. Yes, it was on Nancy's birthday. I was just finishing cleaning up after her birthday party when Kay called. You were busy in some kind of conference with Mr. Hertzog and John Taylor and Kay said you . . ." Betty Allen's voice dwindled into silence as she saw Jim's expression darken to one of intense suspicion. "Have I put my foot in it?" she said with belated caution.

"I think," Jim began slowly after a moment, "you've done me a great favor."

"Now, Jim, don't say anything to Kay that will get me in Dutch. I could be wrong about—"

"No, you're not wrong. And I don't think I'll even discuss it with Kay."

"Oh, Jim, what difference does it make when she found out about it? Everybody was talking about it as soon as—"

"No, everybody wasn't talking about it, Betty. Not until Kay called you—which seems to be a better way of spreading vicious stories than putting them in the *Times*."

"Jim!" Betty said in exaggerated surprise.

"She called you the night after it happened—when nobody knew about it. She called you after she had obviously eavesdropped like the compulsive, sneaking meddler she is. And I can't think of a closer 'bird of a feather' that she could have started with."

Jim turned away then and left Betty Allen nearly open-mouthed as she stared after him.

Jim did not go home then. He went to a quiet bar at the north end of town, where he slowly got quite drunk, which did not prevent his doing a great deal of very sober thinking.

XXV.

THE NEXT MORNING JIM MET STEPHEN AND JOHN AND MARY IN THE hall outside the courtroom. "Good morning," he said.

The bell, warning of the opening of the session, rang as they greeted Jim. As he and Stephen started for the defense table, Stephen said, "You look a little rocky this morning. What's the matter?"

"I had a hard night," Jim said unenthusiastically. "What do you think Cardamone's going to do now?" he asked, changing the subject.

"I don't see what else he can do but rest his case," Stephen answered, "and wait until I call the boys. He'll have his chance then. I see a group of strange ladies back there. He may be going to try to undo yesterday's damage with character witnesses."

"There's not much more to do then, is there?" Jim said.

"Just win the case," Stephen said, smiling.

The defendants were brought in and Judge Forsythe entered and took his place on the bench. When the mechanics of opening the session were done, Mr. Cardamone rose and said, "Your Honor, members of the jury, the People have offered a very clear picture of the events which occurred on the night of August twenty-third last. You have heard in the victim's own words how she was brutally assaulted by the three defendants. Her testimony ties in with and is completely supported by the testimony of the professional men—the physicians who examined and treated her—and by the only witness to the events immediately preceding the assault. Her mother's testimony as to Ida Praul's physical and mental condition upon her return to her home on the morning of August twenty-fourth further supports the truth which this poor little girl has told. That essentially is the People's case. But in view of the vicious personal attack upon Miss Praul by the attorney for the defense—"

"I object, your Honor," Stephen said. "I made no personal attack. I merely evoked testimony from a witness which was entirely relevant to this trial."

"Sustained," the judge said.

"In view of the testimony which defense counsel evoked late yesterday—testimony which could easily be misinterpreted by the jury—I wish to introduce character witnesses who will testify as to the good name of the complainant. I call Mrs. Irwin Bates."

A great, fat ball of a woman rose and waddled to the witness stand. Her size made one wonder if she were suffering from a glandular disorder. In spite of this, she wore a dress of a huge royal blue print and a blue felt hat.

When Mrs. Bates had been sworn in she gave her name and address.

"Your house is directly next to the house occupied by Mrs. Praul and her daughter?" Mr. Cardamone asked.

"Yes," Mrs. Bates replied in a voice which was unpleasantly high-pitched.

"And do you know the complainant?"

Mrs. Bates's excessively round face became utterly blank.

"Miss Praul, Ida Praul," the district attorney said. "Do you know her?"

"Oh, my yes! Known her since she was born."

"And what do you know of her reputation and good name?"

"Oh, Ida's a good little girl. Dotes on her mama. A good, quiet little girl, all the neighborhood knows her as."

"You've never seen or heard her, in all the time you've known her, do anything lewd or obscene?"

"Oh, my no!" Mrs. Bates answered, seeming shocked at the question.

"Thank you, that will be all, Mrs. Bates. I call Mrs. Conrad Ertz."

The parade of neighbors of the Prauls continued for half an hour. Each swore on the Bible that Ida was a good, quiet, little girl. This procession was followed by a smaller one of three of Ida's girl friends, who testified with varying degrees of enthusiasm to Ida's good reputation. When this was over, Mr. Cardamone informed the court that the People rested its case.

There were then twenty-five minutes of conferences—between the prosecution and the defense, the prosecution and the defense and the judge, and finally between the defense attorney and his clients. Then Stephen said, "Your honor, I call Armand Rapp."

Armand took the stand and was sworn in, while Jim whispered to Stephen, "You're going to start with him?"

"When that jury goes out," Stephen answered, "I don't want Armand to be their freshest memory of the defense." He went to the witness stand and said, "Will you tell the court your name?"

"Armand Rapp."

"Will you tell the court what you did on the night of August twenty-third?"

"Well, after I had supper with my . . . father, I went out and met some guys I knew."

"Where did you meet them?"

"On a corner where we hang out sometimes. Then we all went to Fordyce's candy store, and—"

"Did you stop anywhere on the way?"

"Yeah," Armand answered reluctantly.

"Where, Armand?"

"We . . . stopped at a liquor store and bought some whiskey."

"Did you all buy whiskey?"

"No, just me an' another guy."

"Then what did you do?"

"We went to Fordyce's."

"Yes, and then?"

"Well, the other guys wanted to go over to a club they go to, an' I didn't want to. So they left."

"And while you were discussing this, were you drinking?"

"Yeah."

"Go on, Armand."

"Well, Artie and Johnny come in by this time, an' I called 'em back to the booth an' asked 'em if they wanted a drink."

"And did they join you?"

"Yeah. We had maybe two drinks, then we went outside and sat on the railing." He was silent for a moment, and Stephen waited. "Well, that's when Ida came along with the other girl. An' I yelled to her."

"I believe the previous testimony as to what you said when Ida joined you was accurate?"

"Yeah."

"Armand, you surely don't talk that way to every girl whom you know, do you?"

" 'Course not. Just the ones I know like it."

"How did you know Ida Praul liked it?"

"I talked to her before."

"And did you tell similar stories to her on those other occasions?"

"Yeah. I only talked to her a couple of times before. I told her jokes, an' she laughed."

"And these jokes were of a lewd nature?"

"Kinda."

"There was on this occasion, too, an exchange of lewd and bawdy remarks in which Ida Praul participated willingly and apparently with enjoyment?"

"That's right."

"After about fifteen minutes of such conversation, I believe you invited her to sit with all three of you in your automobile. Is that correct?"

"Yes."

"What happened when you got into the car?"

"We just went on talkin' like we was."

"Did you ask Ida what she had done on those occasions—about which she had already spoken—when she had sat in automobiles with boys before?"

"Yes, I did."

"And what did she say?"

"She said, 'What do you think I did?' "

"Your Honor," Mr. Cardamone said, "This is irrelevant, this whole line of questioning."

"Mr. Cardamone," the judge said, "provocation on the part of the alleged victim can be an intrinsic part of any prosecution for rape. Mr. Hertzog's questions are entirely in order."

"Thank you, your Honor," Stephen said. "Do you remember what you said to Ida then?"

"She said she could show me a few things. An' I asked her what. An' she said, 'Like what a man an' a woman do together.' "

"Ida Praul said that she could show—not tell you, but *show* you—what a man and a woman do together?"

"Yeah."

"Your Honor," Mr. Cardamone interrupted, "it has been testified by a licensed medical doctor that Ida Praul was a virgin on the night of the crime. What diff—"

"This testimony, your Honor," Stephen said, "is meant to reveal simply what Ida Praul said. If her remarks tend to contradict the truth, it would seem to me to be evidence of a sexual intent."

"Objection overruled. Continue, Mr. Hertzog."

"What happened then, Armand?"

"I asked her if she wanted to go for a ride."

"And her answer?"

"She said, 'Okay.' "

"Did she seem in any way reluctant?"

"No."

"When you started over the bridge, did Ida voice any objection to leaving the borough limits?"

"Well, yeah. Kinda."

"What do you mean?"

"Well, she was objectin' to me drivin' too fast—which I wasn't. An' she said she wanted to go home."

"And how did you regard these objections?"

"Naturally I thought she was just sayin' it. Else why would she of got in the car?"

"What happened then?"

"We drove up the highway off the bridge to a dirt road I know, an' I turned off."

"Did you tell Ida that this was a short cut home?"

"Yeah."

"Even though you knew that it wasn't?"

"Yeah."

"Why did you do that?"

"Well, it . . . it was just like a game. You know, you want to kiss a girl, you don't just up an' say, 'I want to kiss you.' You ask her, an' she says, 'No.' You know she's goin' to say no, an' she knows it, but it don't mean nothin'."

"Your Honor, I object," Mr. Cardamone said. "Armand Rapp was asking for something quite different from an innocent kiss. He was—"

"He was being led to ask for something else by the obscene conversation of the complainant."

"Gentlemen," Judge Forsythe said, "you will address such remarks to the court, not to each other. The business about the kiss seems to me a perfectly harmless simile, Mr. Cardamone. However, Mr. Hertzog, you will encourage the witness to testify as to the facts without likening them to other incidents or concepts."

"Yes, your Honor. When you got to the end of this dirt road, Armand, what happened?"

"Well, we did like Ida said—with our hands."

"And what did Ida do?"

"Well, she squirmed a little."

"Did she resist these advances?"

"Well . . . it was . . . we . . ."

"Did she resist these advances, Armand?"

"We was all . . . kind of on top of her at once. She didn't seem to be resistin'."

"Then what happened?"

"We got out of the car and walked up the hill."

"You got out of the car and walked up the hill?"

"Yes."

"You didn't force her? You got out of the car and went to the hill?"

"Oh, I had my arms around her, an' she was wigglin' some. But I wouldn't call it forcin' her."

"We're not interested in the witness's opinions of what he did, your Honor," the district attorney said. "Let him answer the question."

"Armand," Stephen said, "did you force her to the hill?"

"No," Armand said.

"Will you tell us what happened then?"

"Well, we all laid down on the ground together . . . an' . . . an' then . . . it just happened."

"What just happened, Armand?"

"While they . . . Johnny and Artie . . . was lyin' there foolin' around. . . . I did it."

"While Johnny and Artie were caressing Ida, you had sexual intercourse with her?"

"Yes. They went away after a while."

"Did Ida Praul resist you while you were having sexual intercourse with her?"

"No."

"Armand, did you know at the time that you began that act that Ida Praul was a virgin?"

"No."

"Did you believe that she was not?"

"Yes."

"Why did you feel that way?"

"Your Honor, is it of any consequence what the witness thought of or assumed about the virginity of the complainant?" Mr. Cardamone said.

"It concerns the reputation of the complainant, your Honor," Stephen said, "and that is certainly relevant."

"Objection overruled."

"Why did you feel that way, Armand?"

"Well . . . I don't care what them ladies said earlier . . . everybody knows about Ida Praul."

"I object, your Honor!" Mr. Cardamone shouted. "Ida Praul was a virgin before the vicious assault on her. That eliminates the possibility of there being any truth to her alleged bad reputation. This whole shameless attack on an innocent little girl should be stricken from the record."

"Your Honor," Stephen said, "I intend to demonstrate that Ida Praul's language, which was boastful and lewd, and her behavior, which was grossly indiscreet if not downright promiscuous, have caused her to have a nearly universal reputation in her town for immorality. The assumption that she was not a virgin remains an assumption, but an understandable one. The fact that she was a virgin in no way affects the fact that she has and had earned a wide and bad reputation."

The two attorneys stood looking up at the judge, waiting almost breathlessly for this critical ruling. Judge Forsythe sat, looking from one to the other, in an attitude of thoughtful calm.

"Gentlemen," Judge Forsythe began, "the reputation of the complainant is relevant in this case. I believe, Mr. Cardamone, that counsel for the defense has the right to try to prove the existence of such a reputation. You may go on, Mr. Hertzog."

"What is it, Armand," Stephen said, "that everybody knows about Ida Praul?"

"That she'd do it with anybody who came down the block."

"Do what, Armand?"

"That she'd . . . have intercourse."

"They can't *know* that, Armand, because since Ida Praul was a virgin, that cannot be true."

"Well . . . it seemed to be true."

"Why did it seem to be true?"

"Because she was always talkin' dirty with boys."

"I object, your Honor," Mr. Cardamone said. "That's hearsay."

"Sustained."

"Armand, you may only tell us what you have heard Ida say, not what other people have told you. You have testified that on two other occasions you have had lewd conversations with Ida Praul."

"Yes."

"Your Honor, I would like to interrupt this testimony to call five other witnesses who will testify to having had similar conversations with the complainant."

"You may do so," Judge Forsythe said sadly.

"You may step down, Armand," Stephen said. "I call Kenneth Rimbaud."

Kenny Rimbaud rose in the back of the courtroom and walked shyly to the stand.

"What is your name?" Stephen asked.

"Kenneth Rimbaud."

"How old are you, Kenneth?"

"Seventeen."

"Do you know the complainant?"

"Yes, we're in the same class at school."

"Have you ever had a conversation with her?"

"Yes."

"More than once?"

"Yes."

"How often?"

"Maybe five times."

"Were any of these conversations of a lewd or obscene nature?"

Kenneth Rimbaud looked at the floor, regretting at the moment that he had agreed to testify. "All of them were. I . . . I don't think I ever talked to Ida Praul about anything else."

"Do you remember any of these conversations?"

"Not word for word."

"What did they consist of, generally?"

"Mostly . . . mostly dirty jokes."

"And how did Ida Praul react to these jokes?"

"She'd always laugh. And usually she'd tell me a couple."

"Did you ever make an immoral suggestion to Ida Praul?"

"A . . . a couple of times."

"And what did Ida Praul answer to your suggestions?"

"She said . . . I was too young for her."

"During one of these conversations did you touch Ida on the breast?"

"Y—yes."

"Just once?"

"No, twice."

"And how did she react to this?"

"Well . . . the first time she pushed my hand away, but she stuck around for it to happen again. The second time . . . she let me go a little longer. Then she pushed me away again."

"Did you get the impression from her speech and behavior that she was probably a virgin?"

"I sure didn't," he answered, still looking downward.

"Thank you. That's all."

"I would like to cross-examine, your Honor," the district attorney said, going to the stand. Then to the witness, "Were you ever entirely alone with Ida Praul? I mean, on a date or anything like that?"

"No," the witness answered.

"You never kissed her or caressed her?"

"No . . . except that one time."

"That could hardly be called a caress. Then you will admit that you had no right to assume anything about her virginity?"

"I . . . I guess I didn't."

"All right. That's all."

Kenneth Rimbaud returned to his seat. The testimony of the next four teen-aged witnesses seemed like echoes of his testimony. A strange, repellent atmosphere of boredom fell over the courtroom as these boys impeached the good name not only of Ida Praul, but of youth. Yet the impeachment of Ida Praul's good name was inescapable. Armand Rapp's testimony thus far had been ineffectual. For the jury, with the single exception of the compassionate Ira Bickford, found Armand so odious that they were reluctant to accept anything in his favor. But now one by one the jurors succumbed to the cumulative effect of this monotonous parade of young men, all confessing their lewd interest in Ida.

"I would like to recall Armand Rapp," Stephen said when the last boy had left the stand. Armand returned, and Stephen said, "What did you do when you had finished having sexual intercourse with Ida Praul?"

"I . . . I went off a little ways and sat down . . . waitin' for the others to finish."

"And when they had finished?"

"We . . . we left."

"You mean you just left Ida there?"

"Yes. I know we shouldn't . . . but we did. We was all scared."

"Did you say anything to her?"

"No."

"Did you discuss taking her home?"

"Yeah. Johnny wanted to take her, but . . . we was scared she might squeal to her old . . . her mother."

"Why would she do that if she was a willing partner to this act?"

"She was just layin' there afterward . . . making little noises. I figured maybe she was sorry she let us do it . . . and would squeal."

"So you got into your car and went home?"

"Yes."

"Armand, prior to this incident had you ever had sexual intercourse?"

"No."

"Have you ever had what could be considered any kind of education on the subject of sex?"

"No."

"Have you ever had any conversations of that nature with your father?"

"No. Well, I guess he might say somethin' about it now and again. After I got to be about eighteen, he just sort of took it for granted that I knew about it."

"No more questions," Stephen said, turning away. When he reached the table he whispered to Jim Beyers, "That's that. Now we'll see what Cardamone can do. If Armand holds up . . ."

"Mr. Rapp," the district attorney began, "At what point did you decide to drive to that dirt road?"

"After we got off the bridge, I guess."

"And at what point did you decide to go over the bridge?"

"I don't know. We was just drivin' around . . . and we came to Main Street and I . . . I just turned toward the bridge."

"Isn't it a fact, Mr. Rapp, that when you invited Ida into your car you knew you would drive over the bridge and to the dirt road?"

"No."

"Mr. Rapp, when you got to the end of the dirt road and stopped the car did you not force your attentions on Ida Praul?"

"Force 'em?"

"Force 'em."

"No."

"Did you pin her arm to the back of the seat with your body?"

"No she . . . she maybe had her arm around me . . . and it seemed that way."

"Did you not paw her and maul her against her objections? Against her physical resistance?"

"No."

The district attorney stared at Armand with open contempt. After a moment he went on with a new intensity in his voice. "Did you, being approximately twice the size of Ida Praul, grab her viciously by the neck until she was in such pain that she could not resist you and drag her from the car to the hillside?" His voice had risen in volume until he was shouting. "Did you?"

"N—no," Armand whined.

"And while those two young 'boys' held her to the ground, did you force yourself into the body of this innocent child?"

"No . . . no, she wanted to," Armand said with a strange desperation.

Still shouting, Mr. Cardamone said, "Did she not struggle with all her poor strength to prevent you from raping her?"

"No. No."

This district attorney turned to Stephen, his face projecting the same contempt he had shown Armand. Then he turned back to Armand and said, "Just about perfectly rehearsed, aren't you?"

Stephen was on his feet before the question was finished. "Your Honor, that is just about the grossest violation of legal ethics I have ever heard in a courtroom!"

"*You* are speaking of ethics?" Mr. Cardamone asked quietly.

"The district attorney should be cited for contempt, your Honor! He is using the tactics of—"

"Order, gentlemen, order!" Judge Forsythe called. "Mr. Cardamone, in many ways I am inclined to agree with Mr. Hertzog. Your obvious attempt to influence the jury with an unfounded accusation against counsel for the defense is an example of the worst back-alley tactics. You do the People no credit by so behaving. Members of the jury, it is practically a legal cliché that striking remarks from the record does not strike them from the minds of the jury. Every attorney knows that this is true, and it is a matter of honor among them not to resort to making inadmissable remarks which will remain in the jury's mind even though stricken from the official record. That is what the district attorney has just done, and you must find some way to erase his accusation from your memories. Mr. Cardamone, we will have no more of that, please. You may go on."

No doubt the district attorney realized that he had done himself no good with this strategic impropriety. As a matter of fact, several members of the jury, including Janet McNaughton and Ira Bickford, had been struggling with the problem of banishing from their memories testimony they had been told to disregard but had already heard. Success in this endeavor seemed to be taken for granted by the court, and they felt an individual guilt at being unable to achieve it. They did not forget the district attorney's remark, of course, but now they understood, now they felt justified in their previous failures, and their resentment at this attempt to take advantage of their human frailty turned against the district attorney and his cause. Only Mr. Dickinson was unmoved by the judge's plea. He could excuse any tactics used to expose the sins of Armand Rapp.

When he turned again to Armand, the contempt in Mr. Cardamone's expression was still there, but he sought to conceal it. "Mr. Rapp, when you had finished with Ida Praul, you testified that you waited while the others had sexual intercourse with her. Is that correct?"

"Yes."

"Did you not hear her moans—her mutterings of resistance?"

"No," Armand said quietly.

"What exactly *did* you do?"

"I . . . I guess I had a cigarette."

"You had a cigarette. How far away from Artie Schlier and Miss Praul were you?"

"I . . . I don't know. It was dark."

"But you could see them?"

"Yeah . . . sort of."

"Would you say you were twenty feet away?"

"More."

"Thirty?"

"About."

"Were you sitting or standing?"

"Sittin'."

"You were 'sittin' ' thirty feet away, calmly smoking a cigarette while Artie Schlier violated this poor—"

"I object, your Honor."

"—while Artie Schlier had sexual intercourse with Ida Praul?"

"Yes."

"You didn't find your own presence in any way . . . disgusting?"

"No . . . no. . . . What do you mean 'disgusting'?"

"I doubt that you would understand." Mr. Dickinson stared coldly at Armand Rapp. "When all three of you had finished with Miss Praul what did you do?"

"Your Honor," Stephen said, "the witness has already testified as to his behavior at that point. There is no—"

"I see no reason," the judge said, "why he should not be asked to repeat the testimony. Go on, Mr. Cardamone."

"What did you do?" Mr. Cardamone asked.

"We got in the car an' went home."

"And left Ida Praul lying unconscious on the hill?"

"I didn't know if she was unconscious."

"Oh, you didn't know if she was unconscious? Then she might have been?"

"She was makin' noises. I thought she was awake."

"If you didn't know whether she was unconscious, you didn't know whether she was awake. Now, which is it, Mr. Rapp, did you know or didn't you?"

"I . . . she seemed to be . . . awake."

"But you don't really know?"

"No."

"And you would have us believe that after having sexual intercourse with a young girl who you say was ultimately willing, you got up from the scene of this disgusting act and went home, leaving her lying possibly unconscious on a hillside?"

"It wasn't . . . like that."

"What was it like, Mr. Rapp?"

"I told you . . . we . . . we was scared . . . she was sorry an' would squeal."

"And even though one member of your distinguished party suggested that you take her home, you ignored his suggestion and left her—just because this allegedly willing girl might inform on you?"

"Y—yes."

"And you would also have us believe that you were afraid a girl who you try to picture as promiscuous would inform on you and in so doing would confess to her mother her own obscene behavior?"

"I . . . don't know what you mean."

"I mean that you are saying you were afraid that Ida Praul would go home and tell her mother she had just willingly gone out to a lonely hillside and willingly had sexual intercourse with three different boys. You expect us to believe that you were afraid that Ida would do that, Ida, who 'dotes on her mama'?"

"We . . . we was scared."

"And you were not afraid because you knew that she would go home and tell her mother that she had been raped?"

"No . . . no."

Mr. Cardamone looked at Armand for a long moment and said, "No more questions."

Judge Forsythe called the two attorneys to the side of the room, and after a few moments returned to the bench. "The Court will adjourn until one-thirty this afternoon."

When they had finished lunch, Stephen said, "I have to talk to

Cardamone—if he'll talk to me. I'll see you later." The others did not see him again until the afternoon session was about to begin.

"The defense calls John Taylor, Jr.," Stephen said.

Johnny went to the witness stand shyly, but without apparent emotion, and was sworn in.

"Would you tell us your name, please?" Stephen said.

"John Taylor."

"And your age?"

"Seventeen."

"You were with Armand Rapp and Arthur Schlier on the night of August twenty-third?"

"Yes."

"You've heard Armand Rapp's testimony, Johnny. Is there anything you want to add to it?"

"No, sir."

"His testimony as to the events of that night was correct?"

"Yes."

"You did have sexual intercourse with Ida Praul that night?"

"Yes."

"And did she resist you in this act?"

"No."

"You did not force her or take her when she could not resist?"

"N—no, sir."

"She was conscious and aware during the act?"

"Yes."

"Armand Rapp testified that you suggested taking Ida Praul home when you were ready to leave. Is that correct?"

"Yes."

"Why didn't you take her home, Johnny?"

"We were scared . . . like Armand said."

"But if you suggested it, you must have known that you should have taken her home. Why didn't you do it, regardless of the others?"

"I had so much . . . whiskey . . . I was sick . . . and still pretty drunk. I don't think I could have done it alone."

"Johnny, had you ever had sexual intercourse before that night?"

"No."

"Had you ever had any instruction in matters of sex?"

"No."

"Not at school?"

"No, sir."

"Not at home?"

"No."

"Johnny, has neither your father nor your mother ever spoken to you about sex?"

"No."

"Have they spoken about it in your presence?"

"No . . . never."

"That's all," Stephen said. "I have no further questions."

"Mr. Cardamone," the judge said, "do you wish to question this witness?"

"Yes, Judge Forsythe, I do," Mr. Cardamone answered. He walked to the witness stand and said, "Mr. Taylor, you testified that Ida Praul was conscious and aware during your sexual intercourse. Would you tell the court what evidence there was of her consciousness and awareness?"

"Well, she . . . she made a sound during it."

"Oh, she made a sound? Have you ever heard anyone moan in agony, Mr. Taylor?"

"N—no, sir."

"That's an unfair and prejudicial question, your Honor," Stephen said.

"I don't think so," Judge Forsythe replied.

"Do you think it's possible that the sound you heard during the act was Ida Praul's moan of agony?"

"I object, your Honor," Stephen said firmly. "The district attorney is asking the witness's opinion."

"Sustained. Strike the question."

"What sound did you hear Ida Praul make?"

"Well . . . it *was* a kind of a moan . . . but . . ."

"But what?"

"It sounded . . . like she was happy."

The district attorney stared at Johnny, struggling against showing his surprise, and for a dangerous instant he seemed tempted to believe what he had heard. Then: "Did she tell you she was happy?"

"No."

"Did she kiss you or embrace you?"

"No."

"She simply moaned—so you decided she was happy?"

"I . . . yes."

"And that moan was the only evidence of her consciousness—her awareness?"

"No. I spoke to her before . . ."

"Before you had intercourse with her?" A definite note of surprise had crept into Mr. Cardamone's voice.

"Yes."

"What did you say?"

"I just said . . . 'Ida.' "

"And what did Ida do or say?"

"She just moved."

"Moved?"

"She moved her head."

"What you asking us to believe is that you bent over the silent, still figure of a seventeen-year-old virgin who had just been taken by two other men and called her name. She moved her head. You then proceeded to have sexual intercourse with her. During this act she moaned. And you would have us believe that from these signs you decided that she was conscious, aware and happy. Is that what you want the jury to believe?"

"It wasn't like—"

"Is that what you are testifying to?"

"I . . . I guess so. Yes."

Mr. Cardamone stared at Johnny. Then almost with a laugh of a single syllable he said, "Ha. No further questions."

"That's all, young man," Judge Forsythe said to Johnny as the district attorney resumed his seat.

Johnny left the witness stand, and when he had taken his seat, Stephen called Arthur Schlier.

Artie went to the witness stand nervously. He was sworn in and gave his name and age.

"Artie," Stephen said, "do you wish to add anything to the testimony given by Johnny Taylor and Armand Rapp in regard to the night of August twenty-third?"

"No," Artie answered. "What they said was right."

"You saw in Ida Praul only the same meager signs of resistance that they saw?"

"Yes."

"And you felt, too, that they were feigned, put on?"

"Yes."

"And while you were having sexual intercourse with Ida, did she resist you in any way?"

"No, she didn't."

"Artie, had you before this experience ever had sexual intercourse?"

"No."

"Have you ever been instructed in matters of sex, at home or at school?"

"No."

"Your parents have never talked to you about it, or instructed you in any way?"

"No."

"No more questions, your Honor."

As Stephen returned to his chair he saw a new expression on Mr. Cardamone's face as he turned to his assistant. It was almost as if he had been waiting for this new witness.

The district attorney rose and walked slowly toward the witness stand. "Mr. Schlier," he began, "you did hear Ida Praul protest as the car you all were in started across the bridge?"

Artie looked nervously toward Stephen and said, "Yes."

"I truly don't understand," Mr. Cardamone said, "and I would like you to explain to me. Was it beyond your intelligence to understand when Ida said, 'Take me home,' that she meant, 'Take me home'?"

"Your Honor, that's an improper question," Stephen said irritably. "The district attorney is asking the witness for an evaluation of his own intelligence. I cannot see what such an evaluation, even if made, could contribute to this trial."

"Sustained. Strike the question."

"What did you think Ida meant when she said, 'Take me home'?" Mr. Cardamone said with a sudden intensity.

"I . . . I thought she was . . . was foolin'."

"You thought she was fooling?" the district attorney said incredulously.

"Well, like Armand said . . . like it was a game that—"

"Never mind what Armand said. Let's just hear what you have to say. You were in a car with a girl who had accepted an invitation for a ride around town. When you started to leave town, she protested. She said, 'Take me home.' What could you possibly have thought she meant except that she wanted to go home?"

"I . . . I . . ."

"What did you think she meant?" Mr. Cardamone said slowly and loudly.

"I object, your Honor," Stephen said. "The district attorney is browbeating the witness."

"I don't think he is, Mr. Hertzog," the judge answered. "The witness will answer the question."

"What did you think she meant?" Mr. Cardamone said again.

"I . . . I don't know."

"Hmph," was Mr. Cardamone's loud and immediate comment. "You know exactly what she meant, Mr. Schlier. She wanted to be taken home and you knew it."

"No . . . I thought . . . I thought she wanted to go on," Artie said, suddenly and unexpectedly rallying. "She even was laughin' and jokin' after that."

"But continuing to say that she wanted to go home. Isn't that right?"

"Yeah, but we didn't believe her."

"You seem to have taken her at her word about everything else," Mr. Cardamone said disgustedly. "You said that Miss Praul did not resist you during sexual intercourse. Would you describe to the court, please, what she did do?"

"Your Honor," Stephen said, "there is certainly no need for another description of the sexual intimacies which took place."

"This is a prosecution for rape, Mr. Hertzog," Judge Forsythe said, "not for playing truant. The witness will answer the question."

"I don't . . . know . . . how to . . ."

"You said she did not resist you. What did she do?"

"She was . . . quiet."

"Did she put her arms around you?"

"No."

"Did she kiss you?"

"No."

"Did she move in rhythm with your body?"

"N—no."

"Did she do anything at all?"

"She made . . . made sounds."

"Oh, she was making sounds again. Were they sounds of pain?"

"I don't . . . don't remember."

"You remember the sounds, but you don't remember if they were sounds of pain?"

"I mean . . . I don't know . . . what kinds of sounds they were."

"In fact, was Ida Praul not unconscious from the abuse which Armand Rapp had heaped on her?"

"I object, your Honor," Stephen cried.

"Overruled."

"Was she not unconscious from her previous sexual experience with Armand Rapp?"

"I don't . . . know. . . . She made . . . sounds."

"People have been known to make sounds while unconscious. Was that the only indication she gave of being conscious?"

"No . . . no . . . she moved."

"You have testified that she was quiet, that she did not put her arms around you, did not kiss you, and did not move in rhythm with your body. In answer to the question, 'Did she do anything at all?' you said that she made sounds. Now you say that she moved. How did she move, Mr. Schlier? In what way? In what direction?"

"I don't . . . remember."

"You don't remember," Cardamone mocked. "Well, you're going to remember, Mr. Schlier, if we have to go over your sexual experience with Ida Praul minute by minute!" The district attorney unbuttoned his jacket and tugged upward at each of his sleeves. "Now, what was the first thing you did?"

"The first—"

"What was the first thing you did when you approached Ida Praul lying on the ground?"

"I . . . I guess . . . I touched her."

"Where did you touch her?" Cardamone's questions were immediate and very loud and delivered in an almost guttural voice.

"I don't re—"

"That won't do. Where did you touch her?"

"On . . . on the arm, I guess."

"You touched her on the arm. Now, that doesn't make a great deal of sense, does it, Mr. Schlier?"

"On the t—the chest."

"Oh, on the chest. And did she move, did she respond?"

"No."

"Then what did you do?" Artie looked at Stephen helplessly, his eyes pleading for assistance. "Just pay attention to me and the questions, Mr. Schlier. What did you do after you touched her on the chest?"

"I got . . . on . . ."

"Come on, Mr. Schlier, what did you do?"

"I object, your Honor. The district attorney is browbeating the witness. He is—"

"Overruled."

"What . . . did . . . you . . . do?" Cardamone repeated loudly.

"I got on . . . on . . . top of . . . her."

"With your trousers on, Mr. Schlier?"

"Y—yes."

"And closed, Mr. Schlier?"

"Your Honor—" Stephen began.

"Mr. Hertzog, the court must hear this testimony. It may be relevant. You might just as well take your seat," Judge Forsythe said.

"Were your trousers closed?" Mr. Cardamone said.

"Were they . . . ?"

"Were they closed, Mr. Schlier?"

"N—no."

"Then they must have been open. When did you open them? You neglected to tell us about that. I want accurate testimony, Mr. Schlier. Accurate! When did you open them?"

Artie looked as if his trembling might become uncontrollable, rendering him inarticulate. "After . . . after I touched her."

"You opened your trousers for some purpose. Then what did you do?"

Suddenly Artie could hear his mother sobbing. He looked out into the courtroom, and for the first time seemed to see his mother and father. His mother was crying into her hands as they covered her face. His father sat, implacably staring at him. "I got . . . got . . . down on top . . . on top of her."

The district attorney could see the tears in the boy's eyes now, although they were not yet visible to the spectators. "Did you find it necessary to arrange Ida Praul's clothing?"

"What?" Artie said, startled by the question.

"Her dress and underthings, did you have to arrange them?"

"No . . . no."

"Did Ida arrange them for you?"

"No. They . . . were . . ."

"They were what, Mr. Schlier?"

"They were all fixed."

"They were fixed? I think you mean that Armand Rapp had simply left her dress pulled up and her panties pulled down? Is that right?"

Artie's eyes narrowed in an effort to hold back the tears. "Yes."

"Then what did you do?"

Artie Schlier could not believe that he had heard the question, the dread question he had been fearing. To him it was unanswerable here, before his mother and father, before these adults, before these women, before this stern-looking judge. He merely stared dumbly at the district attorney.

"Then what did you do?" Mr. Cardamone said again.

"You mean . . ."

"I mean that I want you to describe for us your next action."

"I . . . I can't."

"Do you remember your entry into the girl's body?"

"I object, your Honor!"

"Overruled."

"Do you remember your entry into the girl's body?"

Artie's mouth was open slightly, his face had become the color of putty and his eyes were wide with terror. It was obvious that for the moment he could not speak.

"Answer the question," Judge Forsythe said.

"Y—yes," Artie said inaudibly.

"Speak up, please," Cardamone commanded.

"Yes."

"Was there at the moment even the faintest response from Ida Praul?"

"N—no."

"Was there the slightest movement?"

"No."

"Was there the slightest indication of passion or desire?"

"No."

"Did she cry out or resist you?"

"No."

"Did she strike you or try to push you away?"

"No."

"In other words, she did *absolutely nothing?*"

"Y—yes."

"Was she not, in fact, completely unconscious? Was she not, in fact, completely unconscious?" the district attorney shouted.

Into the utter silence, Artie said loudly, "Yes! Yes!"

Over the spectators' loud murmur and the judge's gaveled protests, the district attorney said, "And had she not passed into that unconsciousness while you and Johnny Taylor held her to the ground and Armand Rapp had sexual intercourse with her?"

Quietly Artie said, "Yes."

"And did the three of you force your attentions upon Ida Praul in the automobile, then drag her from the automobile and *rape her on that hillside?*"

Artie closed his eyes and said, "Yes."

"No more questions, your Honor," Mr. Cardamone said and returned to his chair.

"Your Honor," Stephen said as the murmuring in the courtroom subsided, "this testimony on the part of my client comes as a total surprise and, needless to say, a great shock to me. I request a recess until tomorrow morning so that I may . . . may determine the validity of the information on which I have based this defense."

Judge Forsythe looked at Stephen for a moment and said, "This court will recess until ten o'clock tomorrow morning."

By the time Jim and Stephen left the defense table, the courtroom had been cleared except for two court officials and the solemnly waiting parents of the defendants. Stephen stood before them for a moment looking very somber.

"What, exactly, does this . . . mean, Stephen?" John asked.

Stephen looked at each of them and said, "Unless something fairly miraculous happens, it means first-degree rape. I won't attempt to predict the sentence. Their ages are in their favor, but their perjury is not. I suppose you can blame me for their perjury, just as we can blame Artie for cracking up—if we care to. I'd suggest that you all stay around. I haven't any idea how long I'll be. I have to see the boys and I have to see Cardamone, but I'd like you to be here when I finish. I don't think there's any deal to be made now with the district attorney, but I'll tell you frankly I'm going to try—and I'll take whatever I can get. I'll meet you out there in the hall as soon as I can get back." He left them without saying more.

Stephen went directly to the visiting room in the county jail where he had asked the guard to take the defendants. They were waiting for him. Armand sat in a corner, his legs stretched out before him. Johnny stood looking out the barred window. Artie sat at the table, his head buried in his folded arms. Stephen asked to see his clients alone, and the guard went outside.

Stephen put his briefcase and his hand on the table and said, "I guess you know what this means."

"Are we . . . gonna get it . . . the worst punishment?" Armand asked.

"I don't know, Armand," Stephen answered. "In the eyes of the court you're guilty of first-degree rape. I don't know how the judge will sentence you."

"Oh, Christ!" Armand said.

"There's nothing we can do now, is there?" Johnny asked.

"Can't we go back in court an' say that Artie was just . . . just scared or something . . . of the D.A. maybe or . . ."

"I'm afraid we can't, Armand," Stephen said. "An attorney can break down a witness who's lying, get him to tell the truth. But you can hardly expect the court to believe that the district attorney could make a witness who's telling the truth commit perjury. Nobody would believe that."

Suddenly Armand lunged across the room and grabbed Artie by the hair pulling his head up from its bowed position. "Why the hell'd you have to do it?" he shouted.

"Stop it, Armand!" Stephen said, pushing Armand back against the wall. "That's not going to do anybody any good. And there's no sense in blaming Artie. The district attorney just picked him out. It could have been you, you know. You were just lucky."

"I couldn't help it," Artie said weakly.

"Forget it," Stephen said. "Well, this is what we have to do. I'm going to see the district attorney now, but I know what he's going to want. When we go back into court tomorrow, I'm going to have to say that all three of you told me the story that you told in court initially."

"You wouldn't just be tryin' to get yourself off the hook, would you, Hertzog?" Armand said.

"I don't give a damn what you think, Armand, but I'm telling you for your own good, and mine, that the best thing to do is to let me maintain that you committed perjury out of your instinct for self-preservation, which is believable and even understandable. We may have to change our plea to guilty and throw ourselves on the mercy of the court. None of you will be put on the stand again, and you won't have to do or say a thing. Then it's up to the judge."

"What do you think . . . we'll get?" Johnny asked.

Stephen looked into his eyes. "I don't think you can expect less than . . . ten years, perhaps twenty." There was for a moment no audible reaction to this information. Then Artie put his head down again, Armand covered his eyes with his hand, and Johnny sat down quietly at the table. "I don't think there'll be any point in my coming back after I've talked to Mr. Cardamone. I'll see you in court tomorrow morning."

He left them still only half believing what had occurred.

Mr. Cardamone was in his office and saw Stephen immediately. Stephen went in and dropped into the chair where he had sat before.

"You didn't want a deal, huh?" Cardamone said.

"All right, all right. I didn't know then my clients were perjuring themselves."

"Aw, come on, *Mr.* Hertzog. You're talking to me, not Judge Forsythe."

"What do you want me to do?"

"What do *I* want you to do? I didn't know you had a choice. I can't do a damned thing for you now. I mean it. I would if I could, but it's too late. Just plead 'em and take your chances."

"That's what I thought," Stephen said, getting up.

"I'd . . . I'd like to say one thing to you, though. Congratulations." Stephen stared down at him. "You did all right until I got to the Schlier kid. You had the dirty end all along, and you did a better job than anybody I know could've done—that includes me." Joseph F. Cardamone stood up, then, and extended his hand.

"Thanks," Stephen said without expression. They shook hands. "See you in court."

Stephen found the three families and Jim Beyers sitting on the benches outside the courtroom. He told them as simply and plainly as he could what he intended to do in court the following day. "I still can't predict the sentence," he added. "All we can do is wait and see."

There was only silence then until George Rapp got up and said, "You got anything else to say?"

"Not a thing," Stephen answered.

George looked at him disgustedly and sauntered down the hall.

"I . . . I am sorry it was my son," Mr. Schlier said.

"There's no need to say that, Mr. Schlier," Stephen said. "The district attorney singled him out and deliberately broke him down. He told the truth. It could have been any one of them."

"Thank you," he said and led his wife away.

"Would you like to come home and have supper with us, Stephen?" John asked.

"I'd like that, if it's no trouble," Stephen said quietly.

"Of course it's no trouble," Mary said, and they left the courthouse silently.

The cell in the county jail, on which Johnny Taylor lay on his cot, staring at the ceiling, was somewhat cleaner than the cell in the Borough Hall. Aside from this, it was nearly identical, and produced the same effect on Johnny. This was the first time, however, in the days that Johnny had been in this cell that he was able to forget his physical circumstances almost completely. His thoughts, his inner struggle, was so intense that he was only peripherally aware of the cement floor and the bars and the loneliness. He had hurt Ida Praul, he knew, both through having taken her that night so long ago and through the painful moments she had spent in court, some of which he understood and some of which he did not. Had he the right to cause her further pain? He asked himself over and over. He felt sure that telling Stephen Hertzog he had met Ida since the rape, and what she had said, would have an effect on the trial. He was not really sure just what that effect would be or how it would come about, but he was virtually certain that it would be helpful to him and Artie and Armand. But he did not want to hurt Ida any more. He tried to visualize himself at the age of twenty-seven, then at the age of thirty-seven, but he could not. He tried to imagine the gradual process of aging, tried to picture the day by day process of growing older inside the walls of a prison—day by day for perhaps twenty years. Then he went to the front of his cell and called the guard at the end of the corridor.

"Could I . . . get in touch with my lawyer?" Johnny said.

"Your lawyer? Now, at night?" the guard said.

"It's important. I mean, it's about our trial. I . . . it's very important."

"Well, I'll have to ask the chief, but . . . well, come on. We'll ask him," the guard said, unlocking the cell door.

The Taylors and Stephen Hertzog were in the midst of a strained dinner when the telephone rang. John answered it, and from the dining room Stephen heard John saying, "Johnny! What is it?" By the time Johnny had explained that he wanted to get in touch with Stephen, Stephen was standing beside John. "Why, he's here, Johnny. What do . . . just a minute."

He handed the telephone to Stephen and stood listening anxiously as Stephen said, "Yes, Johnny, what is it? . . . Can you tell me on the telephone? Is there someone there? . . . Are you sure they can't hear? . . . All right. . . . When? . . . She what? . . . Johnny. . . . Johnny, this *is* the truth, isn't it? . . . Tell them to take you to the visitor's room. I'll be there in fifteen minutes. And for God's sake don't speak to anyone about anything until I get there."

The courtroom was crowded the next morning. Strangers who had not been there before looked at other strangers who had not been there before and wondered about their connection with the trial. By the time the session was ready to begin the families of the participants had been nearly universally identified and the strangers whispered to strangers in an odd camaraderie of curiosity.

Stephen Hertzog arrived two minutes before the warning bell rang and went directly to the prosecution table and to Joseph Cardamone.

"Good morning," Stephen said.

"Hello," Cardamone answered, smiling up at him.

"I've changed my mind. I'm not going to plead them. So if . . ."

"You what?" Cardamone said, dropping a pencil and turning in his chair to face Stephen.

"If you'll just go ahead with the prosecution . . ."

"What are you trying to pull?"

"I'm not trying to pull anything, but I'm not going to plead them."

The bell rang then, and Stephen went to his chair. The jury watched as the defendants were brought into court. Beneath their quite different moods, Mrs. McNaughton, Mr. Dickinson and Mr. Bickford were in complete legal accord. Janet McNaughton sadly resigned herself to the fact that that good-looking Johnny Taylor and shy little Artie Schlier were, indeed, capable of rape and would have to pay the penalty. She was certain that Armand Rapp must have led them into it and felt no remorse over his fate. Robert R. Dickinson was wrathful and knew now for certain the direction his wrath must take, though he was a trifle disappointed that his righteous ire should have been diverted by a mere confession. It was an outrage, too, he felt, that Mrs. Praul should escape judgment. Ira Bickford felt mostly a sense of relief that these clouded issues had resolved themselves and that there was no possibility of a grievous error on the part of the jury.

Judge Forsythe came into court and went through the formalities of opening the session. Then he said, "Would counsel step up to the bench for a moment?"

The judge looked down, then tilted his head and examined Stephen over the tops of his spectacles, and said in low voice, "I was under the impression that in view of yesterday's testimony you might want to change your client's plea."

"No, your Honor, I do not."

The judge looked quickly at Mr. Cardamone, who scowled, then back at Mr. Hertzog and said, "You do not?"

"No, sir," Stephen said.

After a moment of genuine consternation, Judge Forsythe said, "Then will you resume the case, gentlemen."

Joseph F. Cardamone recalled Armand Rapp and John Taylor, Jr., to the witness stand. They answered his questions as Stephen had instructed them to two hours earlier. They told the absolute truth, admitted all of the particulars of the rape of Ida Praul. They said they had lied to their attorney as they had lied to the court. Neither forgot to express his remorse and his realization of wrong-doing. After his final question to Johnny Taylor, Joseph Cardamone turned to the judge and said, "The People rests, your Honor."

"Now, Mr. Hertzog," Judge Forsythe said.

"Yes, your Honor," Stephen said. "The defense calls John Taylor, Jr."

Joseph Cardamone's head fairly snapped toward the sound of Stephen's voice and in an instant his face became a mask of astonishment.

He stared steadily as Johnny approached the witness stand. There was a nervous reluctance about Johnny which had not been there before.

"Johnny," Stephen began softly, "would you tell the court what you did on the night of August twenty-seventh, at approximately eight o'clock P.M.?"

"I'd like to know if this testimony is going to be relevant, your Honor," Mr. Cardamone said.

"So would I, Mr. Cardamone," Judge Forsythe said. "Suppose we wait and find out."

"Go on, Johnny," Stephen said.

"I went down to Third Avenue and stood outside Ida's house," Johnny said, looking at Stephen.

"Why did you do this?"

"I wanted to . . . to tell Ida I was sorry."

"Judge, this testimony is clearly designed to prejudice the jury," Mr. Cardamone said. "I can see—"

"Your Honor, if the district attorney would stop interrupting, he would soon see that this testimony is entirely relevant and in no way intended to be merely prejudicial."

"Mr. Cardamone," the judge said, "there really seems to me to be no reason for you to interrupt at this point. Let's hear the rest of this. Go on, Mr. Hertzog."

"You went to Third Avenue and stood outside Ida Praul's house because you wanted to tell her you were sorry. Why didn't you telephone her or go directly to the house to see her?"

"I didn't think she'd see me if I did that. So I stood across the street and waited."

"And did Ida come out of the house?"

"Yes. She was going to the drugstore for her mother."

"And then what happened?"

"I caught up with her and asked her if she'd let me talk to her."

"And did she?"

"Yes. She was kind of scared at first, I guess, but then she let me walk along with her and talk to her."

"What did you say to Ida?"

375

"I told her . . . I was sorry."

"And what did she answer?"

"She asked me what I meant."

"And you told her?"

"I told her I was sorry . . . I . . . did what I did. . . ."

"Yes?"

"Well . . . when she didn't want me to."

"And then?"

"We talked about whether people liked her or not. She asked me if I liked her, and I said I did."

"And did she ask you how you felt about what happened, meaning about your sexual intercourse with her?"

"Yes."

"What did she ask you about that?"

There was a pause which Stephen most decidedly did not want. "What did she ask you about it, Johnny?"

"She asked me if I liked it."

"And when you did not answer immediately, did she repeat the question?"

"Yes."

"And did she ask you if you thought a girl should allow a boy to have sexual intercourse with her if she, 'likes him special'? I believe those were her words?"

"Yes . . . she did."

"And did she then ask you, in illustration, if you would want her to allow you this privilege if you and she were the girl and boy in question?"

"Yes," Johnny answered, still looking at Stephen so as not to look at Ida, whose head was now bowed.

"And even though your answer to that question was, 'I don't know,' did she then tell you—without encouragement of any kind from you, without any indication that you were agreeable to such an idea—did she tell you that she guessed she would let you if you were 'going steady'?"

"Y—yes," Johnny said and looked down at his hands lying on the railing of the witness stand.

"Did she then suggest that she would like to go steady, go to parties and dances together?"

"Yes."

"And even though you indicated dissatisfaction with such an arrangement did she say, quote, 'And there'd be the other thing. The thing I'd let you do. Whenever you wanted, Johnny'?"

"Yes... she said that."

"And even though you again indicated that you didn't want to go steady with her or do anything with her, did she twice again offer herself to you in return for this proposed social arrangement?"

"Yes. Twice," Johnny said quietly.

"In other words, it would be entirely accurate to say that when you went to Ida Praul to tell her you were sorry for what you had done, she repeatedly offered herself to you sexually in return for your agreeing to date her regularly, even though you discouraged her over and over from such an offer?"

"Yes."

In the silence Stephen looked at Ida, then at the jury. "I have no more questions," he said, going to his chair.

Mr. Cardamone was already approaching Johnny before Stephen had sat down. "Are you asking this court to believe that you went to see Ida Praul, furtively, in the dark of night, for no other reason than to tell her you were sorry?"

"I didn't go to see her. I just thought I might meet her, and be able to say I was sorry," Johnny answered.

"And at no time did you make an immoral suggestion to Ida Praul that night?"

"No, sir, I didn't."

"And you claim that she made immoral suggestions to you, which, in your innocence, you refused?"

"Y—yes."

"Come on, Mr. Taylor, do you think we're all morons? Do you ex—"

"I object, your Honor," Stephen shouted. "If the district attorney thinks there is a more accurate version of this incident, let him put the other party, the complainant, on the stand and question her instead of trying to intimidate my client!"

"I have every intention of so doing! But I'm not going to let—"

"All right, call her!"

"Order! We'll have order in this court, gentlemen!" Judge Forsythe said. "Mr. Cardamone has every right to question this witness and to call the complainant later if he wishes," he said to Stephen. "Mr. Cardamone, you will refrain from browbeating this witness if you wish to go on with your examination. And we'll have no more histrionics from either of you."

"I have no more questions for this witness," the district attorney said.

"You may step down, young man," the judge said to Johnny.

Before Johnny had reached his chair Mr. Cardamone had concluded a brief conversation with Ida. He turned and beckoned to Stephen, who rose and met him in the area between the two tables. They stood very close and talked with quiet intensity.

"If I call her you'll cross-examine, of course," Mr. Cardamone said.

"Now, what do you think?" Stephen said. "I knew nothing about it till last night. What did you expect me to do, not put him up there? Forget about it?"

"Christ!" the district attorney said breathily. "If I get her up there she'll only agree with him anyway. All right. That's it, then."

When they had returned to their tables, Judge Forsythe said, "Mr. Hertzog?"

"The defense rests, your Honor," Stephen said.

"Mr. Cardamone, is the complainant to be called or not?" the judge asked.

"No, your Honor," Mr. Cardamone said sullenly.

The judge looked at the great clock over the doors of the court and said, "There have been so many changes of direction, so many irregularities, in this trial that I think it only fair to allow both the defense and the prosecution ample time to prepare their summations. My charge to the jury, gentlemen, will require about two hours, I should think. If we adjourn until tomorrow morning at nine o'clock, will that give us time for the charge, and the summations?"

"Plenty of time, I think, judge," Mr. Cardamone said.

"I'm sure it will, your Honor," Stephen agreed.

"Then this court is adjourned until nine o'clock tomorrow morning."

As Jim and Stephen were preparing to leave the defense table, Jim said, "Well, it worked."

"Yes," Stephen said glumly.

"You do think it worked, don't you?" Jim asked.

"We won't know until the jury gives us a verdict."

"But we're better off than we were before."

"I guess there's not much doubt of that."

"Well . . . what's wrong, Stephen?"

"I never really enjoy that kind of reprimand, but . . . oh, the hell with it! Come on, let's go give the families a little encouragement. I think we're safe enough for that."

"Okay," Jim said, smiling. "And Stephen."

"Yes?"

"That job offer you made me. Is it still open?"

"You bet your life."

"I'll take it," Jim said.

"Well! Well, that's great. I plan to get started on it as soon as this is over. I couldn't be more pleased, Jim."

"Thanks."

When Jim Beyers left the county courthouse, he went to his office and stayed until late afternoon. Then he went home, and as he entered the living room saw that Kay was at the telephone table with all of her telephoning equipment: cigarettes, ash tray, lighter, crumpled handkerchief and a tall Scotch and water. She was in the middle of what seemed to be an exciting story, and she nodded to Jim as he came in.

"Excuse me, Kay," he said and stood waiting for her to pause.

She frowned for an instant and said into the telephone, "Hold on just a minute, darling." She put her hand on the mouthpiece. "What is it, Jim?"

"I'd like you to come upstairs; I want to talk to you," he said.

"This minute?" she said.

"As soon as you can."

He turned away without waiting for her answer and went upstairs to their bedroom.

When she came into the bedroom, Jim was transferring shirts from a bureau drawer to a suitcase which lay open on the bed.

"Jim," she said, standing just inside the door. "Jim, what . . . what are you doing? You're not going on some kind of trip?"

He turned to her, holding a stack of shirts between his hands. "No, Kay, I'm not going on a trip."

"I shouldn't think so . . . in the middle of the trial and . . ."

"I'm leaving, Kay." She stared at him with the expressionless blankness of utter disbelief. "I'll give you a divorce on whatever grounds you like, although I think it's best for everyone—particularly David and Seth—if we arrange the whole thing as amicably as possible. You can—"

"Jim," she said, taking a step toward him.

"You can go to Reno if you like—or Alabama. There won't—"

"What . . . what are you talking about?"

"I'm sorry, Kay. I don't know any other way to tell you. I'm just going to say what I have to say—and leave."

"Leave . . . ?"

"Kay, it won't make any difference to you. You can have the house. I'll see that your income remains just as it is—unless you remarry, of course. Then I'd continue to take care of the kids until they're out of college. Nothing will change for you except . . . well, except that I won't be around. I don't think that will disturb you particularly."

"Have you lost your mind?" she said. She crossed to the dressing table and sat on the bench, facing him. "We . . . we've been married for almost twenty . . . twenty years. You can't just suddenly come . . . come home one day and announce that you're—"

"Yes, I can, Kay. And it isn't sudden. Our whole marriage has been a kind of prelude to it. I guess it's usually that way."

"Jim, if you're doing this to frighten me—"

"I'm not trying to frighten you. If you'll just try to be calm and listen to—"

"Calm? When you're talking like a maniac?"

"Will you listen, please? We have no marriage any more. You and David and Seth are all so far away from me that I haven't the faintest idea how to reach you. Believe me, I'd hang on for their sake if I thought it would do any good. But our relationship, the lack of love . . . no. Let's be honest about it. The love that never was, that was just . . . emptiness, filled now with our contempt for each other, has poisoned the kids enough. David especially, but soon it'll be Seth too. David has seen us for so long, distant, unloving, cold, trying not to argue in front of him, that he's become like that himself. I think if I leave the atmosphere will change. I'll be able to see him, of course, and when I see him it'll be as I really am—or really was and want to be again. That's not going to happen as long as we're together."

"Jim, stop it! You're my husband. We have children and a home. You can't just—"

"No, I'm not your husband—haven't been for a long time. And you have the children and a home. I truly don't believe I have either. Not in a sense that makes any difference."

"I won't give you a divorce! I'll—"

"Then I'll just leave, Kay. It's over now. I know the only way I can convince you of that is to leave. And that's what I'm doing."

"If you don't care about me . . ."

"I care about you, Kay. I don't love you—don't even like you very much, in fact. But I surely care what happens to you—if you're happy. I'm not sure I understand that, but it's true."

"Don't you care about the children?" she said, and she was nearly screaming in her growing hysteria.

"I care about them more than I think you know."

"Then how can you do this to them?"

"I wish you could believe that I'm doing it *for* them. I'm going to go to a hotel tonight. I'll phone you and let you know where I am. Then after the trial, I may go away for a couple of weeks—give you a chance to think things over when I'm not around."

"I don't believe that you can be serious about this!"

"When I'm gone, you'll realize that I am. You'll have to consider it more rationally, and I hope you'll see that it's best. I'm going downstairs now," Jim said, closing his suitcase, "to talk to David and Seth."

"What can you possibly tell them except that you're deserting them?" Kay cried wildly.

"I'm not quite sure what I'll tell them; something close to the truth, I think. I'm sorry, Kay, but I have to do this." He took the suitcase and left the room.

"Jim!" Kay called after him as the door closed, and her voice was at once angry and pleading. She turned to the mirror then and watched the tears coursing down her cheeks. After a moment she picked up a hair brush and began brushing her hair vigorously, muttering to herself in pieces of sentences that it wasn't true, that he'd be right back, that he wouldn't, couldn't do this—and at that moment firmly believing what she said.

"Hello, David, Seth," Jim said, entering the family room downstairs. "I want to talk to you for a moment."

"Sure, Dad," Seth, said settling into a plastic and aluminum beach chair.

"Would you turn off the phonograph, please, Seth," Jim said.

"Oh sure," Seth answered, squinting at his father curiously.

"Boys, I'm going to try to make you understand something that will be very difficult for you to understand."

"Is it about the trial, Dad?" David asked.

"No. No, it's not about the trial, David. It's . . . I . . . I'm going away."

"Going away?" Seth said as always cheerfully, but with suspicion in his voice. And in that moment Jim was not sure he could go on.

"Yes," Jim said. "It's not something I want to do; it's something I must do. You see, just because people are grown up it doesn't mean they can't make mistakes. Sometimes a man and a woman get together, and . . . and it's just that: a mistake. They get married and they find after they live together for a long while that they just aren't the kind of people who should be together. And then the only thing for them to do is to separate."

"You don't mean you and Mother?" Seth said, his joviality waning, but still present. "You're . . . you're our mother and father."

"I'm afraid I do, Seth," Jim said. "Believe me it has nothing to do with either of you. We both love you just as we always have—and always will. And don't think that your mother and I dislike each other. It's just that we don't belong together."

"Took you a long time to find out, didn't it, Dad?" David said, quietly and with the merest hint of challenge, of accusation.

Jim looked at David for so long a moment that David became truly uncomfortable. "No, David," Jim said, "it didn't. I guess we've both known it for a long time. We've tried to keep things together because we thought it would be best for you. We were wrong, I think. I think we may have done you harm. Now I realize that it's best for all of us if I leave. I hope you believe that. I hope you understand it."

"I don't understand it, Dad," Seth said, eager and frightened. "I don't understand it at all."

"Seth I . . . I know that you're going to miss me, and I'm certainly going to miss you—both of you. Please try to remember that I'm doing this because it's best for you—for all of us. I'm doing it because it's necessary. Try to remember that, and someday you'll understand. Oh, I'll be coming to see you. It's not as if I were going away forever."

"You mean you're coming back?" Seth asked.

"Well, no, not to stay. But I'll be visiting, and we can go places together—to ball games in the city and maybe even on weekend trips if you'd like that."

"What does Mother say about this?" David asked.

"I think you'd better ask her that, David."

"I don't see why . . . why it has to be this way," David said sullenly.

"David, we'll talk about it when we see each other again. We may even be able to talk better after a while. Will you wait till then and see if you can come to understand it in time? Both of you?"

"If that's . . . how it has to be," David answered, looking at the floor.

"I don't want to wait," Seth said, fighting his tears. "Don't go, Dad!"

"I have to, Seth," Jim answered quietly. "I have to. Now, say goodbye to me and . . . don't . . . don't cry, Seth."

Jim left the room and the house quickly. He threw his suitcase into the back seat of the car and wiped away his own tears, knowing as they continued to blur his vision, that they were tears of regret not for what he was leaving, but for what had never been his to leave.

XXVI.

John Taylor stood on the sunporch of his home, wearing a topcoat and holding his hat as he looked out at the physically bright aspects of this crisp fall day. He turned when he heard the footsteps of his daughter and his wife and saw them coming toward him.

"Now stay out of Frances' way," Mary was saying to Lois as she had every morning of the trial.

"I have, Mother," Lois said defensively.

"Yes, I know. Frances tells me you've been very helpful and not a bit of trouble."

"Then why do you tell me to be good every day?"

"Just to remind you. Now, you go on."

"Yes, Mother. 'Bye. 'Bye, Daddy," Lois said and ran across the lawn to the McGovern house. Lois waited until her parents had driven away from the curb, then she knocked on the door and went into the house.

"It's just me, Frances," Lois called, going to the kitchen. She knew Frances would be there, washing the dishes her children had used before going to school. The parochial school, St. Mark's, started half an hour earlier than the public school, and Frances' husband, a foreman at the steel mill, had as always left the house at seven.

"Morning, Lo," Frances said as Lois came into the kitchen.

"Mother and Daddy just left," Lois said, taking a dish towel from the rack above the sink.

"Guess they'll make it on time," Frances said, looking at the large clock above the refrigerator.

"They're giving the summations today," Lois told her, reaching for a plate.

"Summations? What in Christ's name are summations?"

"Oh, that's when the lawyers sum up for the jury all the things that were said during the trial."

"Jesus, Lo, you'll end up bein' a lady lawyer!"

"Oh, I only know all those things because Daddy and I talk about the trial every night after supper. Of course, I follow it in the paper, too, but Daddy fills in the details for me—and answers my questions."

"Well, that's very nice of him, I'm sure."

"Yes."

"You . . . you don't seem to be very upset about it, Lo. The trial, I mean."

"I'm trying to be cheerful, Frances—as much for your sake as anybody's."

Frances looked at the little girl standing next to her. "Of course you are. I'm sorry, Lo. I shoulda realized."

"That's all right, Frances. I cry sometimes when I'm alone. I try not to, but when I think of Johnny . . ."

"I understand, Lo."

"But I can't walk around crying all the time, can I?" Lois said, and now her cheerfulness was transparent.

"Why . . . why don't you get a bottle of beer out of the ice chest?" Frances said.

"Oh, Frances, you aren't going to make me drink beer, are you?"

"Now, don't you get smart with me, Miss. The beer's for me and you know it. I'm spittin' feathers with me hands in this hot dishwater." They both laughed then.

Frances sat at the table and poured the beer which Lois had opened for her. As Lois sat she said, "You know, I really don't see why I couldn't have been going to school these last few days."

"Jesus, Lo! Did you want to?"

"Sure. I'm going to have to go back anyway when . . . when the trial's over."

"Well, that's true. But your mother knows best."

"That's the end of that subject. There's never any answer to that." After a moment she said, "Why do you suppose Mother wanted me to come over here every day?"

"Well . . ." Frances said, but she stopped there.

"I guess she wanted you to guard me."

"Guard you? In the name of God, guard you against what?"

"Oh . . . just things."

"Well, I certainly ain't your guard," Frances said.

384

"What are you then?"

"Your mother just wanted you . . . to have . . . somebody to talk to."

"All right, Frances," Lois said rather absently. After a short time she said, "Frances, may I ask you a question without insulting you?"

"You can try," Frances answered good-naturedly.

"Okay," Lois said. "Why are grownups such terrible liars?"

Frances sputtered like an imperfect firecracker while searching for an answer.

"You aren't insulted, are you?" Lois asked. "I really didn't mean to be insulting."

"No," Frances answered. "No, I'm not insulted. I guess I ought to be, but I'm not. Why . . . why do *you* think adults are all such liars?"

"Because they are."

"A damn good reason, but it don't answer the question."

"Well, take you, for instance," Lois said, "why do you have to lie to me about why I'm here? I'm not stupid enough to believe you, so I work on the principle that I can't believe anything you say. Then when you *are* telling the truth, I don't believe you anyway, and I get even more confused. It seems to me that adults are deliberately trying to confuse children."

"Does . . . does it seem that way, Lois?"

"Sure."

"Did it ever occur to you that maybe the adults don't know the truth themselves?"

"Well, then they shouldn't pretend to." Lois had a second thought. "You mean you don't know why I'm here?"

"Christ, Lois! You're so quick you confuse me more'n I confuse you."

"Well, is that what you meant?"

"In a way," Frances said, uncertainly. "I'm not really sure just why you're here."

"Well, Mother asked me if I'd like somebody to stay with me while they were at the courthouse, and I said no. Then she said, 'Wouldn't you be more comfortable with somebody here?' And I said, 'If you mean wouldn't I rather have somebody to talk to than just sit here alone, sure.' And so she said I was to come over to you."

"That's just what the hell I said, Lois: I'm here to give you somebody to talk to."

"Oh, Frances," Lois said exasperatedly, "that's just the way Mother put it, but it's not what she really meant. If it makes her feel better I'm willing to go along with it."

"You mean you think your mother lied to you?"

"Oh, no. Mother and Daddy don't lie to me any more. At least, they try not to. I guess it's hard for them sometimes."

"Well, I'm sure your mother's just trying to do the right thing," Frances said.

"I'm sure she is," Lois answered, "but if I'm going to have to go back to school anyway, I don't see why I couldn't just stay there."

"I guess you're entitled to your opinion, Lo, but you have to be a good little girl and do like your mother says."

"Yes, but it's hard to do when you think you're right and they're wrong."

Frances looked at Lois with a smile and said, "Yeah, Lo, it sure is. Well, I've got to get me upstairs done."

"Can I help you, Frances?"

"No, thanks, dear. You just go on in the front room and read a magazine. I won't be long."

Lois went into the living room and took a magazine from the coffee table. She sat in a large easy chair and began to leaf through the pages of the magazine. But she did not read or even look at the pictures. Instead she stared out the window at the familiar street, made odd for her by the slightly more eastward position of the McGovern house. She wondered now if Frances *was* supposed to guard her—to keep her from another experience like the one with Brandon. That didn't seem entirely logical. She wondered, too, if Frances knew about her and Brandon. No, her mother wouldn't have told her about that. Her mother thought it was so awful. Her mother thought *she* was so awful. Marked, that's what she said. She did feel different, though. It was hard to say just how. Older? No, not exactly. Kind of as if she had something that nobody else—at least, nobody else her age—had. As if she was—what? More of a person than they were? Knew more? No, not knew more, just *was* more. Except Brandon. He had it, too, of course. When they looked at each other at school, they always smiled, even if they just passed in the hall between classes. And the smile was warm and knowing and excluded everyone else. And she knew from the smile that Brandon felt it, too. Maybe Brandon would ask her to go out with him, to a dance or a party or . . . no. She didn't suppose she'd be allowed to go out with Brandon any more than Brandon would be allowed by the Davises to take her.

Of course, it wasn't bad; her father had told her that. Yet she mustn't do it again until she was much older and married. That was hard enough to understand, but what her mother had said . . . there was that feeling again, that strange, scared feeling. It came every now and then when she remembered what her mother had said. Usually it was just when she was thinking about Brandon, then she'd remember and she'd feel scared and—and awful. But it *was* a good thing—her father had told her that—at the right time and for the right reasons. If you were in love and married. Maybe she was in love with Brandon and that's why they felt so good about each other. Of course, if she was and Brandon was in love with her, they could get married when they were older. And then everything would be all right. But the awful feeling was still there. Oh, she wished her mother hadn't said those things! She hoped nobody had said them to Brandon. She hoped nobody would ever say them to Brandon!

Shortly before eight, the first county employees had climbed the steps of the courthouse. Half an hour later the straggling had become a steady streaming, and by eight forty-five the families and friends and spectators had begun to arrive for the last day of the trial of Johnny Taylor, Artie Schlier and Armand Rapp. Five minutes later John and Mary were seated in the courtroom.

During the first half hour of the session Judge Forsythe and the attorneys conferred. The jurors sat very still at first, then became restless and shifted about in their chairs, but kept their conversation to a minimum. The thoughts which drifted through the minds of those twelve people might have surprised the populace of Audubon County. For it was generally conceded by those who had followed the trial as spectators or in the press (and that was just about everyone) that all that remained to be done in view of the reversal of the boys' story was for the jury to bring in a verdict of first-degree rape and for Judge Forsythe to decide whether or not to be lenient. But the populace at large had failed to consider a tenuous yet remarkable difference between themselves and the jury. They failed to consider the single factor which colored and shaded the jurors' images into vivid pictures, not seen by the populace. That difference, that factor, was responsibility. Now as Janet Somers McNaughton sat heavily burdened by her responsibility, she heard clear, deliberate testimony of the boys telling her that they forced themselves sexually upon poor little Ida Praul. But she saw them, too, alone in their beds in the exquisite agony of ignorance, torturously wondering, doubting, searching. She saw them exposed to the crippling crudities of sexual misinformation of the kind that had so repelled her in the cloying, unnatural atmosphere of girls' schools. And she saw them finally as nearly middle-aged men who had had no youth. But, weighted as she was with responsibility, these considerations were not enough to free her to make the decision she wanted so desperately to make.

Even Robert R. Dickinson, smiling faintly and vacuously at all who beheld him, was uneasy behind his smile. The boys were to be damned surely, but what of Ida Praul, tutored in wickedness by her mother, secretly enjoying (he was certain from his own experience) the masochistic thrill of sexual assault, and becoming finally a profligate temptress? Was she not to be punished? There was her attempted seduction of that boy. Was she not to be punished? he asked himself again. Yes, indeed, she must be. But the law allowed no way to punish her—except to deprive her of her rightful vengeance upon her attackers. But was that fulfilling his responsibility, to lighten their punishment to punish Ida Praul? He wished he could punish them all.

Ira Bickford, sitting seemingly placid, his hands folded in his lap, regretted the whole deplorable chain of events. These were children who had played at a game which confused even adults, and he would have liked to send them all home with their parents and go home himself to his sister and his cello. But the game, played wrong as they had played it, was also a crime, and it was now his responsibility to determine which rules had been broken and by whom. No, that determination had been made when the boys had admitted the crime. What more was there? He had wanted proof and he had it. There was no more. He wished there had been no crime, no violence, no pain, but he wished that always and for the world. There was crime, there was violence, there was pain, and he had accepted the responsibility of dealing with them as a man who never would inflict them upon another human being—except now as he must inflict pain upon those boys for the sake of justice.

Suddenly and strangely all the movements and the subdued noises of the courtroom ceased. There was an important quiet.

"If you're ready, Mr. Cardamone," Judge Forsythe said.

"Yes, your Honor, I'm ready," Mr. Cardamone said. He rose and walked slowly toward the jury. "Ladies and gentlemen of the jury, there are both criminal and civil prosecutions in which a jury is required to remember and consider the names and characters of many participants, to remember and consider the whole series of dates and times, intricacies of many points of the law. These are complicated matters. Today, however, you are faced with no such complications. Three boys took a seventeen-year-old virgin out to a lonely spot on a hill and, by their own admission, raped her. There's no more to it that that.

"There is only one element which might prove confusing, ladies and gentlemen, and that is that in spite of their confession the defendants are still pleading 'not guilty.' That is no more than a legal technicality. The law generously, in my opinion in this case too generously, allows them to introduce into this proceeding any extenuating circumstances, any factors that might affect the nature of this crime. Have you heard any, ladies and gentlemen? Learned counsel for the defense tells us that these boys were sexually ignorant. I think he is confusing sexual ignorance with moral depravity. They were sufficiently informed"—Cardamone shouted now—"to complete a sexual assault on this poor little girl! They were informed enough and depraved enough to pin her to the seat of an automobile and molest her. They were informed enough and depraved enough to drag her to that hillside and hold her to the ground with the weight of their bodies and one by one, each in his turn, calmly, calculatedly to assault her sexually! They were informed enough and again depraved enough to leave her there after using her, in the dark of night more than a mile from her home and from help, leave her there without concern for the injury they might have done her, without the remotest concern for her well-being! No, ladies and gentlemen, this is not the work of three sexually ignorant boys. It is the work of three morally degenerate criminals! In all my years in the law I have never encountered a crime more devoid of morality, more empty of human decency, more cold-blooded and depraved!

"Counsel for the defense has also introduced evidence of the poor reputation of Ida Praul's mother. Alexander Hamilton was a bastard, ladies and gentlemen. So were many other famous men and women. Did their mothers' wantonness make them less great? Does the reputation of Ida Praul's mother have anything, *anything* at all to do with the fact that these boys raped Ida Praul? Does it excuse the rape? Does it justify the rape? Does it even explain the rape? It is a piece of incidental information.

"And learned counsel tells us that this evidence was introduced to support the poor reputation of Ida Praul. Ida Praul was a virgin, ladies and gentlemen. What more need we say of her reputation? Her virginity is full proof of her purity, her chastity, her innocence. The defense has pretty well proved that the atmosphere of Ida Praul's home is far from ideal. Is it not to her credit, then, that the only effect of that atmosphere upon Ida herself has been in her manner of speech? All right. She told dirty jokes with these boys. Does that give them license to rape her? No, because there is no license for rape, ladies and gentlemen.

"We come now to another issue. You have heard that subsequent to the crime Ida Praul made an attempt to seduce John Taylor, Jr. I feel that I must deal with it. We did not examine the details of that alleged seduction, but I'm sure if we had, it would be a horse of a different color. What other conclusion can we draw from these facts: Ida Praul was a virgin until she was seventeen. She was then raped by three boys. Shortly after this rape she gets involved in a situation where she seems to have tried to seduce—or at least offered herself—to one of the boys. Doesn't it seem to you that that attempted seduction was a result of the rape? Doesn't it seem to you that shock of the rape must have had a damaging effect on this girl's morals? Doesn't it seem to you that that attempted seduction is only one more good reason for punishing these boys to the fullest extent of the law? We'll never know, ladies and gentlemen, the far-reaching effects of this crime on this innocent little girl. We know what it has done to her body, but we'll never know what it has done to her mind, to her spirit. Her whole life may well be deeply affected by that damage. It is a horrible thing to contemplate.

"Let me admonish you, ladies and gentlemen, not to be influenced by the ages of these defendants, or by the good reputation and standing of their families in the community. They are old enough in the eyes of the law to be judged by the law or they wouldn't be tried in this court. Don't be influenced by the severity of the punishment for first-degree rape. Think of the penalty this poor little girl has paid and will probably go on paying for the rest of her life. There has been a terrible crime committed, and there must be a terrible punishment.

"The only thing that must influence your verdict, ladies and gentlemen, is that three boys have admitted that they molested and raped a seventeen-year-old virgin. They have admitted that they left her on a hillside late at night, alone, and more than a mile from her home and from any assistance. That's all, ladies and gentlemen—there is nothing else to think about. This is the crime of fiends without morality, without decency. This is the crime of criminally depraved minds, who do not belong free in a civilized society, who must be imprisoned for as long as the law allows. It is rape in the first degree, ladies and gentlemen, and that is the verdict which, as responsible, thinking human beings, you must return in this court!"

In the utter quiet which followed Mr. Cardamone's words only the sound of his rubber heels against the marble floor could be heard as he returned to his chair. After a moment Judge Forsythe said, "Mr. Hertzog, do you wish to proceed now?"

"Yes, your Honor," Stephen said. There was something almost jaunty in his walk as he approached the jury. His face bore a pleasant, nonchalant expression. He seemed particularly, conspicuously unmoved by Mr. Cardamone's oratory. He walked the length of the jury box twice, and as he did so, the nonchalance dissolved into a seriousness which was clearly not related to Mr. Cardamone's words, but to the words he himself was about to speak.

"Ladies and gentlemen, you see before you the four people who are involved in this trial. You know them only as the complainant and the defendants in a very unpleasant legal proceeding. Three months ago you did not know they existed. Now they exist for you, I'm afraid, only as they relate to this trial. But let us suppose that you had met them three months ago. What kind of human beings—and we must not forget that they are human beings—what kind of human beings would you have found? You would have met Johnny Taylor, a pleasant, intelligent boy about to enter his last year of high school. Johnny has a job delivering groceries. When he is going to school he does this part time, but in the summer it's a full-time job. He turns over one-third of his earnings to his mother. At school he is in the upper half of his class. He is on the basketball team. He's invited into the homes of his friends and has his friends into his home. There is not a man or woman among you who would not have liked to have Johnny Taylor as a son.

"Armand Rapp is older than Johnny Taylor, and he has missed many of Johnny's advantages. Armand's mother died when he was quite young and he has come through adolescence without a mother. Immediately after graduating from high school he went to work in the factory where his father is employed. There is about Armand a certain roughness, which I'm sure you have noticed and which I am sure is directly traceable to the lack of a mother in his life. But he is no idler or wastrel. He has supported himself since he left school, and he has never been in any kind of trouble before.

"Artie Schlier is the son of good parents from Germany. His father is a watchmaker and jeweler, and after school and in the summers Artie helps his father by making deliveries. Although he doesn't plan to make it his life's work, he has learned a great deal about watch repair from his father. Artie is Johnny Taylor's closest friend, frequently goes to the same parties and dances that Johnny goes to. His grades at school are average. Artie is an average boy.

"Do you believe, ladies and gentlemen, that these three boys are fiends? Do you believe that they are morally depraved? Do you believe that they are without decency? I don't think you do. But there is a hidden link between them, ladies and gentlemen, and any consideration of their guilt or innocence of this crime must take it into account.

Otherwise it would constitute a miscarriage of justice. And this is that link: they have each grown up in a sexual climate which has nurtured ignorance, fear, suspicion, guilt and confusion. There are differences in these families, ladies and gentlemen. Differences of intelligence, social standing, income, religion, age. Yet there is one grotesque common denominator among them: they have allowed their sons to grow very nearly to manhood without counseling, without instruction, without guidance in the most complex aspect of human development. You have heard each of them testify to this fact. And is it not reasonable to assume that in a home where a boy can grow to late adolescence without hearing one intelligent word in regard to sex there must be some maladjustment among the parents, some Victorian taboo, some stigma which, through the very silence it inflicts, labels sex forbidden and sinful? I hope you and your parents, and you and your children, have been more fortunate, but I cannot help wondering what would have happened to those of us who like these boys were unprepared, confused, misguided sexually, if in that state *we* had suddenly been thrust into as volatile a situation as these boys were. How many of us—how many of our children—merely through a fortunate arrangement of circumstances have escaped the kind of crisis in which these boys failed? And how many of us can say that we would have come through such a crisis wisely, judiciously and with our honor intact? If you ask yourselves those questions, ladies and gentlemen, and answer them honestly, you will realize that the district attorney's crying, 'Fiends! Monsters!' is merely empty, prejudicial oratory.

"And what of the fourth principal in this trial? What would you have found if you had met Ida Praul three months ago? A virgin, to be sure, but tragic as it may be that was the full extent of Ida Praul's purity. She is a girl who has been subjected all her life to the evil and immoral influence of her mother. If there is depravity, if there is lack of decency involved in this proceeding, it is on the part of Mrs. Praul. How could this young, impressionable girl witness the orgiastic, animal behavior of her mother during all of her formative years and have any normal sexual outlook? How could she be cast off, disregarded like a troublesome, worthless inanimate possession by her mother without being deeply scarred emotionally? Gentlemen of the jury, consider your wives, your daughters, your sisters. Ladies of the jury, consider yourselves: what decent girl indulges in vile conversation with three boys, then voluntarily gets into an automobile with them? What were Ida Praul's motives, what were her intentions when she accepted their invitation? Could they have been anything but indecent? If Ida Praul had, like

Virginia Lukens, turned away from these boys, none of them would be in this courtroom today! Can we believe that she wanted to convince them that she could show them what a man and a woman do together, yet did not want to be invited to complete the demonstration? Can we relieve Ida Praul of all responsibility for this happening, when throughout its beginnings she behaved like a competent, experienced whore? Can we truly expect these boys to have believed that Ida Praul did not want to have sexual intercourse with them? Can we, ourselves, believe that she did not want to? Why did she get into the car, ladies and gentlemen? Why did she brag of her sexual prowess and superiority? Why did she exchange dirty stories with them? Because she *wanted* the intimacies which finally took place. When, if at any point, did Ida Praul change her mind? How much responsibility are we to place on these boys because of that alleged change of mind? This was not rape, ladies and gentlemen: it was seduction!"

The interested and the disinterested, the naive and the blasé, the dull and the perceptive were all caught up now in Stephen's oratory. The few people in the courtroom who had thought that they knew Stephen Hertzog were more aghast than those who were strangers to him. For he had somehow assumed the quality of the fanatic, the zealot. His whole being, the total of his existence, was so entirely devoted to his task that, hypnotically, he drew into the range of his influence even the most disoriented of his listeners.

"Let's be honest, ladies and gentlemen. This is not a matter of law. It is not a matter of objections and inadmissable testimony and *ex post facto* evidence. It is a matter of four young human beings having had sex together in a dark and desolate place. It is far more important that we understand and fix the responsibility for the aberrant nature of those four young people than that we avenge ourselves on these boys for the loss of the nonexistent purity of this girl! These are our children, ladies and gentlemen. What they know we taught them, and what they don't know we have kept from them.

"Let us be even more honest. Are we to cut ten or fifteen or twenty years out of the lives of these boys for having had sexual intercourse with a girl who deliberately put herself in a position which made that sexual intercourse possible? Has Ida Praul's life been ruined? Ida Praul, whose chance for a decent, normal life had long before been reduced to a frightening minimum by her own mother! Are we going to punish these boys for the random encounter of their ignorance, their fear, their confusion with the ignorance and fear and confusion of Ida Praul?

"These children are the product of your . . . of *our* community. And before we pass judgment on them, let each of us ask himself what share of the responsibility is his. There has been no act of violence here; there has been an act of abject ignorance, an ignorance with which we have infected these young people as we might infect them with a disease. If you choose, in the name of the blind, eyeless law, to avenge Ida Praul's mythical purity by sending these boys to prison, I, for one, will not envy you your consciences during those years of incarceration—nor during the futile, hopeless years that follow. Acquit them, ladies and gentlemen, for although their sin is our sin, their guilt, our guilt, their punishment would be theirs alone. Acquit them."

Judge Forsythe watched Stephen return to his chair. He stared down at him for a moment after he was seated, his face impassive.

Then he looked at the clock over the doors of the room and said to the jury, "I feel that we should proceed with my charge. It will require some time and will run past the normal time for adjournment for lunch, but it is the last step in the presentation of this case, and I feel that it is expedient to bring this trial to a close. So if you will bear with me for a time, we can see this difficult task through to its just conclusion."

For more than two hours the judge charged the jury, explaining the intricacies of the law. He explained the difference between the first and second degrees of the crime with heavy emphasis on the fact that sufficient provocation and consent on the part of the complainant could reduce the verdict from first-degree to second-degree rape. He told them that a verdict of either of the two degrees was permissable, and he told them, too, that they might return a verdict of acquittal. He warned them against sentimentality because of the nature of the crime or because of the ages of either the complainant or the defendants. "Guilt is guilt," he told them, "and it is your province to decide upon guilt or innocence. Leniency is the province of the court." It was well past two o'clock when Judge Forsythe said, "Ladies and gentlemen, you have before you a series of difficult decisions. You have heard the events which took place on the night August twenty-third. You have heard witnesses testify as to the nature and reputation of various participants in this trial. You have heard the attorney's summations. All of this has been undertaken in an effort to illumine the truth. You must now decide upon the reliability of the witnesses, upon the likelihood of the testimony you have heard, of the credibility of the conflicting accounts offered by the district attorney and counsel for the defense. You must with the utmost sincerity believe what you find believable and reject what you find unbelievable. And finally you must be convinced beyond that reasonable doubt, the nature of which I have explained to you at such length, that the defendants are guilty if you are to reach such a verdict. If that reasonable doubt is in any way present, you are compelled by law to find in favor of the defendants. If you are convinced beyond that doubt of their guilt, you are compelled by the same law to find in favor of the People. I commend you now to the hands of God and to your own consciences."

And with those words the responsibility which, without exception, the jurors had been dreading became officially theirs. Janet McNaughton knew with a new terror that she was not sure how she would vote. She had thought that surely she would know by this time, that at some magic moment the truth and the concurrent knowledge of decision would appear to her. This had not happened, and in this sudden silence of the courtroom she felt tiny beads of cold perspiration on her body and a sick, hollow feeling at her stomach. Robert R. Dickinson was still grateful for the opportunity to punish, but his delusion that that opportunity was furnished with such rightful license that no guilt attached to the act had in this last moment vanished. He felt a confusion which was rare for him, and he stared at Judge Forsythe as if he could not really have finished his instructions without removing the threat of guilt which nearly any decision would bring. Ira Bickford wished that he were not with the other jurors. He wished that he could retire separately to a different room alone with his cello, where he could play until somehow through the music he would know what to do. And if the music did not tell him soon, he would simply go on playing until it did, or if it did not, he would simply go on playing.

When the members of the jury left the courtroom to deliberate, their faces reflected the seriousness of their task. They had from time to time during the trial looked out over the courtroom, examined the faces of the defendants, of the complainant, of the attorneys, of Peg Praul, of the witnesses. But now all twelve successfully avoided looking at anyone except the police officer who escorted them from the room. It was as if they feared the possible contamination of a sympathetic glance.

When Stephen came into the spectators' section of the courtroom, he found John and Mary and the Schliers and George Rapp standing much as they had stood that day at the Borough Hall, which now seemed to them all so very long ago.

"I'm afraid," Stephen said, "there's nothing to do now but wait."

"You did a wonderful job, Stephen," John told him. "I guess we're all grateful."

"Thank you, Mr. Hertzog," Otto Schlier said. "I know it was not easy for you to say some of the things you said. It was not easy to listen to some of them. But what you did was good for our children. We thank you."

"There's absolutely no way of knowing what the jury will do," Stephen said. "There's never any way. Nor is there any way of knowing when they'll do it. I would suggest that you all stay nearby. Let someone know if you're going to a restaurant or anything like that, so that we can get you quickly. If it should go longer than one day, we'll be told when the jury has given up for the night. Then you can go home and, of course, come back the next day. I have a feeling—and I can't say that it's worth much—that it won't be a quick decision. You'd better be prepared to wait it out."

"I think we will just wait in the hall on those benches," Mr. Schlier said. "Thank you," he added as he escorted his wife out of the room.

"I'll be around," George Rapp said and walked away.

"I think I'd like a drink and some lunch," Stephen said. "Why don't you go on over to the hotel. I'll leave word here where I am and make arrangements for them to contact me immediately."

"All right," John said. "We'll meet you there." As they walked down the corridor of the courthouse, John said, "How do you think it looks, Jim?"

"As Stephen said, it's impossible to tell. It looks to me better than I ever thought it could. Stephen Hertzog is one hell of a lawyer."

"I hope it doesn't take too long," Mary said without looking at either of them. "I . . . I'm not sure I could stand it for too long."

But it took longer than even Mary had feared, yet everyone was able to bear it. Peg Praul had not, of course, the same degree of interest as the parents of the defendants. Though she was somewhat anxious for a verdict of guilty, she could not help feeling that the mechanics of her revenge had finished. After all, she had been a figure of some importance in the trial, and she quite secretly enjoyed the negative celebrity. She was, consciously at least, thoroughly accustomed to living with her reputation, and the exposure in court had not particularly bothered her. She was in the taxi with Ida on the way home and settled back cozily in the corner of the taxi, savoring nostalgically her recent and delicious portion of attention.

Ida broke the silence which had prevailed throughout the trip from the courthouse to home. As they walked around the house to the back door, she said, "Mama, it wasn't true was it, what that lawyer said about how you feel about me?"

"What?" Peg said. "What are you talkin' about, Ida?"

"What that lawyer—Mr. Hertzog said."

"Well, what the hell did he say?" Peg asked impatiently, digging in her bulging purse for the key to the back door.

"He said you were . . . indifferent to me. He said you didn't feel no concern for my welfare. That's not true, is it?"

"Now, would I have seen to it that them boys was punished for what they done to you if I was indifferent to your welfare?"

They were entering the kitchen as Ida said, "No, you wouldn't, Mama." Ida took off her coat and went to the back porch and hung it up. As she came back into the kitchen she said to her mother, "Mama, that lawyer said some awful things about me. I wouldn't want you to think they were true."

"What things?" Peg asked, and Ida was puzzled that her mother did not remember the awful things.

"Don't you remember, Mama? Didn't you hear him?"

"I heard him," Peg said irritably. "What things do you mean?"

"He said I was . . . I was immoral," Ida said, looking at the worn linoleum on the floor.

"Oh, that," Peg said pouring a glass of beer. "Don't you worry about that. All that was just lawyers' tricks."

"But everybody heard him. What if everybody believed him?"

"Ida, you got to learn not to care what anybody thinks of you. Just don't pay 'em no mind."

"But, Mama, what about all the kids at school? What will they think?"

"Looks like they thought it a long time ago anyway. That's what I mean. You been a good little girl and didn't get mixed up with no boys, but that didn't stop 'em from thinkin' you was no good—from sayin' to each other that you was no good. So just don't pay 'em no mind."

"You mean people are goin' to say things like that about me no matter what I do?"

"That's what I mean."

"But why, Mama? Because you . . ."

Peg waited for the rest of the question, her eyes flashing angrily. "Because I what?"

"Well . . . you know," Ida said.

"Look, Ida, I got a awful headache. I don't feel like talkin'."

"I don't want people sayin' things like that about me, Mama."

"Well, you did talk dirty with all them boys, Ida," Peg said. "And you did let that Kenny Rimbaud fool around with your tits. What do you expect people to say?"

"Yes," Ida said quietly. "Yes, I did. I think I'll go lay down, Mama. I feel awful tired."

Ida went to the back porch and turned on the electric heater. She took off all her clothes and lay on the bed naked. She did not sleep, but lay thinking of the trial and of what Stephen Hertzog had said about her—and about her mother. It was a full hour later when Ida heard the telephone ring in her mother's bedroom. She could not, however, hear what her mother said.

"Hello," Peg said rather roughly into the telephone.

"Peg?" the voice said. "Is that you?"

"Yeah, it's me. Who is this?"

"It's Charlie. Don't you remember?"

Peg's free hand went to her head where the little pink hat so recently perched and she said, "Charlie! Sure I remember. How could I forget you? I was just wearin' the hat today."

"Oh, the hat. Yes. What are you doing, Peg?"

"I'm not doin' nothin'. Why?"

"Well, I just happen to be in town. Thought maybe if you weren't busy, we could get together."

"Oh, sure, Charlie, that'd be great. Where are you, at Frank's?"

"Yes, but . . . well, things are pretty dull over here. Why don't I just come on over there? I could pick up a fifth of Seagram's on the way. We could have a swell time."

"I'll be right here waitin', lover-boy," Peg said.

"See you in fifteen minutes. So long."

"So long, lover-boy." Peg hung up and went to her mirror to begin primping. After a moment she stopped suddenly, her eyes leaving the mirror and staring unfocused toward the wall. She turned and went to the back porch. She opened the door and leaned into the porch where Ida still lay on the bed. Peg did not say at first what she had intended. "What are you doin' layin' there without any clothes on?" she asked.

"I'm just layin' here," Ida answered.

Peg looked for a moment longer, then she shrugged and said, "I'm havin' a visitor in a few minutes. It's business . . . about rentin' the apartment upstairs if Mrs. Ludlow moves out. It'll probably take a long time, and it'd be better if I didn't get interrupted. There's some franks and beans in the ice box from last night. All you have to do is stick 'em in the oven if you get hungry. An' put some clothes on, for Christ's sake."

Peg went back into her bedroom and changed into what she considered a prettier dress. By the time she had finished, Charlie was at the door. After a few preliminary caresses, Peg got a bowl of ice, two glasses and a bottle of ginger ale from the kitchen, drawing the curtain completely closed as she returned. They had barely finished their fifth highball when they were in bed, Peg's clothes flung about the room in her eagerness, Charlie's placed tidily on and about a chair in spite of his eagerness.

On this day the wind had not gone down with the sun, as people observed it so frequently did. It howled now in the darkness outside. Both Peg and Charlie had fallen asleep, and after half an hour the noise of the wind awoke Peg.

"Charlie," she said softly. "Charlie, you awake?"

"Huh?" Charlie grunted. "What? What is it?"

"You awake?" Peg repeated.

"Huh? Oh. Yes, now I am," Charlie said.

"Oh, I'm sorry, honey. I didn't mean to wake you. Want a drink?"

"Uh . . . yes, I guess so. What time is it?"

"It's just ten o'clock."

"Well, I got time yet. Let's have a drink."

"In a jiffy," Peg said.

"Gee," Charlie said, "I feel kind of funny."

"What's the matter?"

"I don't know . . . I . . . say! I haven't had any supper! That's what's wrong with me. I'm just hungry. I guess I was just so anxious to see you I forgot all about eating."

"Aw, you," Peg said girlishly. "You know, I could eat somethin' myself. Hey, I know what! I'll fix you a drink then I'll run around the corner to the 'deli' and get us some of them pastrami sandwiches just like last time. Huh?"

"You are a jewel of a woman, Peggy," Charlie said suavely.

Peg sprang out of bed and in a very short time had filled a glass with partially melted ice cubes, whiskey and ginger ale. In almost as short a time she had dressed, not very neatly, and was at the door. She went back to the bed and kissed Charlie rather elaborately. "You just stay there and relax. I'll be back in a jiffy."

Peg departed so enthusiastically that Ida heard the slamming of the door. In her musings as she lay on the bed, the upper part of her body uncomfortably warm from the electric heater and the lower part cold from the lack of it, Ida had decided that her mother had not for the last four hours been engaged in business. She had also decided that when her mother's visitor had left, she would go and tell her so, hoping that her accusation might be met with an invitation to sleep in her mother's bed as she had so often when she was a very little girl. Ida got up from the bed, still quite naked, and went into her mother's room.

"Oh!" Ida cried, utterly startled by the lingering presence of her mother's visitor.

Charlie, too, said, "Oh!" and pulled the covers closer to his chin as if by so doing he might cover Ida's nakedness.

Ida felt the muscles of her body tighten in response to her immediate intention of leaving the room. Quite deliberately then she relaxed those muscles and stood, staring at the man in her mother's bed. "Where's my mama?" she asked.

"She went . . . she went to get us some sandwiches. You . . . you're Ida."

"Yes."

"You're . . . you're awful pretty, Ida." Ida still stared at him, seeing now the beginning of the evidence of his sincerity. "You're even prettier than your mother. Did you know that, Ida? Well, you are," Charlie added when Ida did not answer. "You're just about the prettiest thing I've seen in . . . well, in a long time. Do you want to come over here and sit by me?"

Ida did not know—was, in fact, never to know—the answer to that question. She knew only that she would go and sit by Charlie, and that was what Ida thought as she walked across the room, watching him pull back the pure white sheet.

The tension in the Taylor home had become so great that John and Mary and Lois spoke to each other only out of necessity. One would ask another for the salt during a meal. One would thank another for some small favor. But conversation had ceased. After the first full day of waiting at the courthouse, John and Mary and Stephen had decided that it would be best if they, John and Mary, waited at home that evening and during the next day if necessary until the jury came in. It seemed now as if it might be necessary, for it was mid-morning of the second day. They moved about the house much as they would have if Johnny's embalmed body had lain on a bier in the living room. The ringing of the telephone was the most shocking sound that Mary could ever remember hearing.

"Hello," John said and added simply, "Yes. Right away."

Twenty minutes later they made the now familiar trip up the stairs of the courthouse and through the dark marble corridors to the courtroom. The Schliers and George Rapp arrived a few minutes later. John was surprised at the number of spectators who had somehow managed to be on hand. Everyone behaved with a deliberate quietude which made their behavior seem awkward. The footsteps of the jury as they filed into the courtroom and the necessary moving of chairs seemed exaggeratedly loud in the respectful silence, a silence which reached an almost unbearable peak when the jury was seated.

"Will the foreman of the jury please rise?" Judge Forsythe said. And when the foreman had risen he added, "Will the defendants rise and face the jury? Has the jury reached a verdict?"

"We have, your Honor."

"What is your verdict?"

"We find the defendants guilty of rape in the second degree."

The sound of Mary's sharp, sudden weeping and Mrs. Schlier's high, sustained wail could be heard under Judge Forsythe's words. "The prisoners have been found guilty of rape in the second degree. They will be remanded to the county jail to await sentencing. Ladies and gentlemen of the jury, this was a difficult case. I know that it was not easy for you to come to your verdict, but it is, I feel, a just verdict. You have performed a difficult civic duty in a manner of which you may be very proud. This court is now adjourned."

Mary successfully resisted her violent urge to run to Johnny as she watched his tear-blurred figure moving out of the courtroom into what seemed to her now to be permanent confinement. Mrs. Schlier was less successful in her resistance and had to be restrained by her husband. Once again those five adults with nothing in common but the crime of their children found themselves grouped together in a lugubrious tableau as Stephen Hertzog approached them.

"I'm sorry," he said. "I know you can't be pleased with that verdict, but it really is the best we could honestly have hoped for."

"Stephen," Jim Beyers said, "I think that they all understand that their sons did commit first-degree rape. You got that degree reduced and saved those boys years of prison. I'm sure they feel nothing but gratitude."

"Jim's right, Stephen," John said in a voice which struggled against the abject sadness he felt. "We . . . we are grateful. I'd like to take Mary home now."

"You understand, of course," Stephen said, "that I will move to set the verdict aside. I'm virtually certain that it's hopeless. The boys won't be sentenced until the motion is granted or denied."

"What . . . what will the sentence be?" Otto Schlier asked with his attention fixed primarily on his weeping wife.

"I don't know," Stephen said.

"What's the longest?" John asked.

Stephen turned to John and looked directly into his eyes. "Ten years," he said.

Countless times during the month which it took for the processes of justice to consider the motion, John attempted to imbue in Mary a fortifying sense of living in the immediate future for Lois. But what had been since Lois' experience with Brandon Davis Mary's tentative attitude toward her seemed now to turn to contempt. John knew that his last attempt had been made when Mary told him that she despised what Lois had done, and he knew fully that she meant that she despised Lois. He tried still to bring them together, but he knew, too, that he must protect Lois and in protecting her he drove them further apart. He took her to his used car lot as she had so often requested. They went on short excursions together whenever he could spare the time. He helped her with her school homework. He remained constantly alert to her problems and on those few occasions when he was able to sense their existence, he discussed them with her. Mary moved around this new relationship with a frigid and total indifference. She seemed entirely submerged in her suffering for Johnny. She was morose and spoke little. When they returned from their Wednesday visits to the Audubon County Jail, she did not speak at all—sometimes for a day or two. Jim Beyers told John that this behavior was almost to be expected, that it would pass. And John said, "Of course. Of course it will." But he knew that it would not.

It was the Tuesday before Thanksgiving Day when the telephone at John's office rang and Stephen Hertzog said, "I'm afraid I have bad news, John."

"The motion has been denied?" John said.

"Yes."

"I suppose I knew it would be."

"I'm sorry, John," Stephen said.

"It's not your fault, Stephen. Please remember that I believe that."

"Thank you. They'll . . . they'll be sentenced tomorrow morning. Ten o'clock. Would you like me to pick you up on the way to Harrisville?"

"No. No, thanks. We'll drive up. Will we be able to see him afterward?"

"Yes. I'm sure that can be arranged. Cardamone tells me that they'll undoubtedly move them to the state prison right away, so I'm sure we can arrange for a special visit immediately."

"Thank you. I'll see you tomorrow then."

John decided almost without thought that Lois should be allowed to accompany them to the courthouse. Mary looked at him blankly when he announced this and said, "Whatever you say." Then she went upstairs and locked herself in the bedroom.

They sat in the courtroom the next morning for what John gratefully acknowledged would be the last time. The prisoners were led in and Mary resisted John's light and tender touch to her arm. Judge Forsythe entered and spoke briefly to both Stephen and the district attorney. He returned to the bench and in a manner of sad dignity said, "The prisoners will rise." When they had done so, he looked at them with an expression which quite visibly melted from impartiality to controlled compassion. "Armand Rapp, Arthur Schlier and John Taylor, Jr., having been found by a jury of your peers in due process of law to be guilty of the crime of rape in the second degree, you are hereby sentenced to be taken to the state prison where you will remain in custody for a period of not less than five and not more than ten years."

The families of the boys with their two attorneys and a sergeant from the Harrisville Police Force looked like a group of unhappy tourists being conducted from the courthouse to the county jail across the street. No one spoke, no one wept, but their silence was like a giant who walked with them.

The room into which John and Mary and Lois were taken to wait for Johnny was small and dimly brown. There was a table and four chairs at one end, and when they sat there, the police sergeant left them. It was fifteen minutes before the door opened again and Johnny, accompanied by a guard, came into the room. He stood for a moment just inside the door until the guard nudged him gently, and it seemed to Mary that the guard had clubbed her son.

"Hello," Johnny said, and they could see as he approached that his eyes were reddened by what they knew must have been restrained and secret weeping.

"Oh, Johnny!" Mary said in quiet agony.

"Johnny," John said, "I . . . I wish there was something we could do."

"Don't cry, Lo," Johnny said, seeing his sister's eyes wide, unblinking, dropping their tears noiselessly upon her pale cheeks.

"If everything goes right, Johnny—and it will, you'll see—it'll just be a little more than three and a half years. With good behavior . . . and . . ." John was unable to finish.

"I guess we're lucky, at that," Johnny said with a miserable cheerfulness. "It could have been a lot longer than just three and a half years."

"Oh, sure," John said. "Why, we should be grateful . . . you know, to Mr. Hertzog and . . ."

"Yes," Johnny said in hasty agreement. "He did a swell job."

"We were lucky to have him," John said. "We have Jim Beyers to thank for that, I guess." John felt now that he was chattering moronically and that the chattering mocked the seriousness, the sadness, of the moment. But he could not stop. "He's a good friend, Jim Beyers. I guess that's what good friends are for—to help you out in times of trouble."

"Sure," Johnny said.

"You can't have too many good friends," John went on. "You take Frances McGovern. She's been a good friend of your mother's for . . . now, let's see. How long has it been, Mary?"

They all three looked at Mary Taylor then. Her eyes glistened and her lips were drawn in tightly, making two thin, pale lines across her face, which in spite of the tension was curiously blank. John was afraid as he looked at her. "Must be more than thirty years," he said quickly.

"Dad . . . I . . . will you take good care of Lois?" Johnny said. "You know, talk to her, and all."

"Oh, Johnny," John said, looking into his son's eyes. "Yes. Yes. Your mother and I . . ." Again they turned to Mary and the blankness of her face persisted. "I'll take care of her, Johnny. I promise," John said.

"You'll help Lo, won't you, Mom?" Johnny said, leaning slightly toward his mother. For an instant Mary's face clearly showed her pain. Then she turned to John with an almost questioning look and her eyes closed slowly.

"Don't worry, Johnny," John said. "We'll all . . . we'll help each other."

"I'll come to see you, Johnny," Lois said and her voice was remarkably controlled. "Every time I can."

"No, Lois. I don't want you to see—"

"Yes, Johnny. She'll come to see you. That'll be part of it. The staying together. Just try not to change. I mean . . ."

"I know," Johnny said. "I'll try, but it's . . . I don't know what it'll be like. I'm scared, Dad."

"Yes. So am I. We'll write to you, Johnny, every day if we're allowed. Lois and me too. And we'll see you every day we can. Maybe if we stay together, maybe that way we can give you enough company so you won't have to . . ."

"I *will* try, Dad."

"That's about all we can do—any of us," John said. "Johnny, I . . . I want to say this to you now—in front of your sister. All those things that Mr. Hertzog said in court, about our responsibility for this—"

"Dad, it was me, not anybody—"

"No, Johnny, listen to me. What he said was right. I should be going to prison with you, not instead of you maybe, but with you. And in a way I will. But when you get out, I'll make it up to you. Maybe we can go away—live someplace else. Or maybe that wouldn't be right. But we'll figure out what is right. We'll figure it out together, and we'll do it. I promise you, Johnny, that from this day on, you'll have a father every day of the rest of my life. You haven't had that so far, but you'll have it from now on."

"Dad, it'll be all right," Johnny said. "I know it'll be all right."

Then the son, the brother, was embraced and in the uniformed presence of the policeman they all wept with a new lack of shame and a strange joy which they knew somehow to be like life itself, unbidden, temporary, fragile. Then Johnny was gone.